Chronicles of Osmaron

I am Shadite

The strange quadruped called by the name 'spotty' followed its master's every command and trotted off towards the more sheltered rocks.

'Do you think it's an infidel?' a male voice shouted impatiently.

'How should I know?' came the brief reply from his fearless female companion.

'Check the local hills and I will check the banks... be careful!' she reciprocated, as if in full command of the situation.

It was not long before the nozzle of a strange primitive weapon nervously pointed towards Lumak's head, to be followed by a less hesitant command from the dark figure holding the weapon.

'Stand still or I'll fire!' Lumak knew little of the meaning of those words, but realized from the man's expression that he meant serious business. He remained completely still while the human came closer to search his person for weapons. When Ben found his captive was unarmed and observed the strange attire he wore, he nudged him somewhat impatiently towards the house.

The Osmaron Series

Chronicles of Galaxy Osmaron - I Am Shadite

Chronicles of Galaxy Osmaron - The Power of One

Chronicles of Galaxy Osmaron - Escape from Andromeda

Chronicles of Galaxy Osmaron - The Solarian Empire

Chronicles of Galaxy Osmaron - Fertilates

Chronicles of Galaxy Osmaron - Infilates

Chronicles of Galaxy Osmaron - Son of Destiny

Chronicles of Galaxy Osmaron - Jull, The Supreme Patriarch

Chronicles of Galaxy Osmaron - Battle for Andromeda

Chronicles of Galaxy Osmaron - Battle for Osmaron

First Edition

CHRONICLES OF GALAXY OSMARON
I AM SHADITE

My human destiny - Lumak's travels

by

Adrian Graye

NUTRALIAN PUBLISHING
http://nutralianpublishing.com

nutralian
An imprint of Nutralian Publishing
5 Brayford Square, London E1 0SG
http://nutralianpublishing.com

This paperback edition 2005
B00005555

First published in Great Britain by
Amazon KDP 2024

ISBN 978-1-0687902-0-1

Printed and bound in Great Britain by Amazon KDP Publishing.

A CIP catalogue record for this title
is available from the British Library.

This book is dedicated to my good friend Sharon
Sumar.

&

To all those who believe in universal existence and
appreciate the lowliest of life, for like babes, they are
the beginning.

TABLE OF CONTENTS

UNTOLD MOMENTS

Against the Sands of Time the Causal Sea must beat,
Unimpeded in its progress, yet resistant in retreat.
For waves will beat until the Sea runs dry;
Till every causal thing is unified.
As if a wheel, its speed reducing to defy,
constraint and yet a whirling sea within a tide.

Then, all its losses will be entirely covered,
A form of compensation for services rendered.
As when the old gives birth to die, the Mother of All must try,
And give her best before all things run dry.

And yet! Those losses themselves will form,
A sea? No! An Ocean within a storm.
A New Beginning! .. a Plenum! .. a Universe unfold!
A beauty as yet unimagined; Magnificence untold.

Victor E. Roche

PROLOGUE

Since the beginning of human civilizations we had always believed in the existence of gods with their many attributes and forms. In all this time never had we taken into consideration the uniqueness and age of our universe, nor the natural abilities of life to evolve to ever increasing complexities, powers and technologies. The impetus of all those changes being due mainly to the powers of evolution.

If we continued to advance at our present rate it is conceivable that the powers of humanity could become truly awesome in say; another million years. By that time we could be like gods compared to our present-day forms - with lesser intelligence and abilities. Even while using such basic criteria for measuring advancement, it should be apparent that numerous advanced life-forms may exist in our universe at this time. Because of their powers and attributes such supreme beings could appear to us like gods.

Since many stars form Stellar Systems, with similar worlds to ours, it is doubtless that there are many millions of evolving worlds within our galaxy alone and billions upon billions within our almost endless universe. Therefore in this jungle of evolution one should expect to find many supreme beings within this almost infinite Cosmos of multi-verses. Each galaxy giving rise to numerous advanced civilizations, each at different levels of evolution and technological advancement or indeed, all the stars we observe in the night sky could be considered a complete waste of space.

Over the past decades numerous new Solar type systems have been discovered with orbiting planets of their own. With present technologies only the more massive Gas Giants can be detected. However it's just a matter of time before Earth type planets are scanned and analysed. They are still too small and emit too little radiation for close observation by our present technologies.

In our particular plane of universes called our multi-verse, this universe is like a living factory, specifically designed to spawn life in all its numerous variations. This type of life being an extension of matter. Given the right conditions such life will spread its tendrils and proliferate throughout its nooks and crannies for the establishment of a better order throughout the Cosmos.

That order of predation is self-sustaining and infinitely better than just dead lumps of rock floating through the Cosmos to eternity. Our magnificent Cosmos is one of perpetual change due to evolution which gets its impetus from Chaos. Everything, even atoms may evolve to higher and more stable states while discarding the older and weaker versions on route to ultimate Order.

Although the most advanced evolving life-forms in our universe may be supreme beings, we could never expect any of them to be the true God of the Cosmos. Some believe that position could only be assigned to the Cosmos itself, which includes all forms, actions, events and changes. With few reserves, She permits All to exist within her many Planes of Universes. She embodies within herself The Greater Mind which engenders the Greater Purpose for the positive side of our ordered existence.

Since the Cosmos encompasses All, it may be viewed as both negative and positive, good and evil, prey and predator, order and chaos; for one cannot exist without the other, anymore than we can have hot without cold. That is also the reason why we have deadly virus and disease that can decimate our bodies, while others of a more malevolent nature may decimate complete galaxies.

In such a manner that galaxies taking tens of billions of years to nurture primal life could be wiped out within a relatively short period of time, to be measured in just a few millennia.

Life

The most powerful Grand Lords or Gohran supreme beings had evolved from Primordial clouds since the beginning of our universe. Being non- biological they were always fascinated by the processes of living systems within the naturally evolving machinery. Since the beginning they were the guiding force in maintaining the natural order throughout their many planes of universes. All forms of natural evolving life they called Primal, as opposed to others that had been created by technological means. Those they called Synthetic or Artificial.

To them all naturally evolving life were just the natural extension of matter through a type of order that had been set in stone since the beginning of those universes. They had been initiated by the She to bring change and variety to a dead universe.

As atoms combined into molecules, one would expect molecules to combine into more complex systems. However because of growing complexities, somewhere along the line a method had to be discovered to select those types of complexities more suited to long term survival. Finally in order for those better forms to continue surviving they had to reproduce similar templates of themselves. That was when DNA came into the picture. It was then realized that all suitable worlds with an abundance of water and the necessary chemicals would spawn life within 3 billion years of cooling. In other words, the odds of life appearing on such worlds within 1 Cyclon (1.6 years) could be taken as 3 billion to 1. Therefore it became a certainty in 3 billion cyclons of cooling.

Nevertheless the story did not end there with basic life. The process continued to even greater complexities; to create organisms, where each colony of cells became specialized for a single purpose. That single purpose intended for the extension of life, so that the organism could experience its environment in different ways and procreate in order to sustain its own kind. Then the Identity, a part of The She and Godhead, took over that Primal

Form to begin a different process of change throughout the Cosmos.

In a not too dissimilar manner we may view a living universe as we do a complex tree, with galaxies on branches like leaves, some young and old, and even capable of creating new sibling universes. Even then, such complex bodies would follow similar templates to those of Primal Life, where a unique type of order could be followed for a Greater Purpose of survival as The She had decreed.

Our Cosmos contains all things including all planes of universes or multi-verses, all space-times, and plenums. It also contains the Sea of Chaos and of All Possibilities. Call that level of existence the Quantum World if you wish. For that is where the real struggle begins.

Nevertheless even before chaos brandished swords with order there were the Supreme Identities that formed the Godhead. It was they who formed the She and are responsible for everything that have ever existed. These Identities are within each of us, making us part of the Godhead and therefore a part of God. No two Identities can ever be the same, since they are part of a complex matrix that form the Godhead.

Presently the unrelenting process of existence resides within many layers of ever increasing complexity. All such complexities will progress even to infinity and eternity; for such are the ways of The She and of her Greater Purpose that embodies The All.

Sut Lumak, Shadite, 2041 CE

BOOK 1

A new beginning

CHAPTER 1

Om-Chopter
(Several Lyran cycles (months) before the Grand Lord's arrival to their world)

Earth time ... 446 CE

Place ...   Planet Kanaefon in the Globular Cluster of Kalboron within the Osmaron galaxy, known to Earth's humans as the Milky Way.

At that time the Petan dragons were more desperate for food than ever before. Extreme seasonal changes had caused a reduction of fish and other marine life in the great lake. They were not used to farming and not known to wander far from their territories on the rim of the Crethian Bowl. Their only option was to invade the Kanei and steal their supplies of nectar and berry juices as they had done on numerous occasions before.

The large clumsy dragons flew across the lake en masse and dived into the ancient city of Lud, causing much damage to lives and property in the process. They systematically looted the nectar stores destroying most of the enclosures with their occupants, including inner nesting chambers. During the turmoil that ensued many young Semonite hatchlings died.

Chief Duty Queen Magdala was furious. Never before had she experience such blatant destruction and unwarranted disruption to their daily lives. She called her council of elders together to discuss a permanent solution to the Petans. They gathered noisily in her Synhadrin. It was their place for discussing important matters for the benefit of their tribes.

'How dare these monsters destroy our homes, take our food and assault our young like this! We must take drastic measures now or be forever their target at such times. Get me Samos immediately!' she yelled. Subsequently her decisions were put to the vote.

Although a peaceful race, they had enough of rampaging Petans so her council voted unanimously for war against the invaders.

The young Chief Worker Samos soon arrived and knelt nervously before his impetuous queen. She was in no mood for him to show her the usual graces, so she waved him up.

'You are to find Tesien, the ship builder, tell him once again his special services are required for his queen and homeland. Go now and get him here!' she commanded, in pheromones. Whenever Queens were face with dangers they always communicated by pheromones. Such communication had two effects, it passed a powerful message on and also controlled the bearer of that message until it was delivered to its recipient.

'Yes, my Queen,' a nervous Samos bowed and left directly to find Tesien. Never before had he seen his queen so distraught and was worried should she become more furious. Then heads would roll.

The strong pheromones began to alter his mental state, giving him a strong desire to follow her will. They had found their way through his nervous system and were now targeting the relevant centres of his brain. He tried to resist on impulse but it was already too late. Such pheromones only targeted the sexless workers and soldiers. Drones and Queens were immune. Nevertheless Samos knew those effects would dissipate the moment he was in sight of Tesien.

Tesien was an inventor of noble blood, but like those of his kind always a little eccentric in his ways. He was from the same clutch as his queen, making him her brother. He lived in an area near the docks and presently involved in designing a new type of travelling machine. It was one that could move in air like a giant bird and on water like a swift sailing boat. If it worked, it would be the first of its kind ever built.

At that time he was high up on one of its masks. As Samos approached he dived towards the deck, only to be stopped by a lengthy mallo rope tied to something that resembled a thick elastic band. The band took the shock of his sudden stop just before he hit the solid deck. Then he held on firmly to one of the deck hooks and released the harness from about his waist.

'Sorry about that Samos. I saw you approaching from the distance and could sense you were on important business in my direction. I thought our queen would be laying a few untimely young since Petans last attack and would want some revenge for the death of some of our innocent children. Am I right?' Samos climbed the short ladder unto the deck.

'As always, you are quite right, My Siend. She wants to see you immediately.' Samos briefly surveyed the rigging and observed the strange contraption that carried Tesien about the ship unwind. Below deck were a few lamphis workers tightening ropes while outside were others hanging from harnesses. Samos slowly viewed the miracle of a strange design on whose deck he now stood.

'Ah! You want to know what it does? It's a device I use to take me up and down the different parts of this ship. Saves me climbing. I hate climbing, it aches my arms and legs. With this little lever here I can move the crane and rig to cover any part within the ship and be lifted and dropped anywhere. However I must be careful when landing and miss those nasty projections and deck hooks.' Samos realized Tesien had chosen a most risky existence.

'This is ingenious. Truly ingenious!' Samos congratulated him.
'Thank you!'
'Don't be late, her majesty eagerly awaits your presence.' Samos passed on some of his queen's pheromones and was back to normal to resume his other duties.

'Your majesty, Tesien is here,' one of the palace guards announced and she signalled to send him in.

'Tesien, you have kept me waiting. Try not to make it a habit.' She always treated him, her clutch brother, with measured respect.

'Yes, your majesty!' he bowed.

'We require a large vessel that will take several of our best trained soldiers and their weapons into Petan lands. This time we must take immediate revenge for their recent savagery. The destruction of our unborn and store houses. Have you something in mind?'

'Such a journey is ill advised, your majesty, and fraught with many dangers. It will be the riskiest adventure ever undertaken by our kind. We can visit the Petan lands, but in order to surprise them we must take the longest route and follow from along the other side of the Crethian Bourle. There is a special ship I have in mind, but it will require several Lyran cycles in its completion.'

'Complete it urgently! You know our world well and what we need. If anyone can do it, you can. It is imperative that you complete this ship as soon as possible, use as many apprentices as you need. Samos will carry the purse on this one, so ask him for whatever you require. This is war!' He left with a strong desire to do his best, but there was little room for improvement. Anyway, he always liked a challenge.

Several Lyran cycles later the ship was completed and Lucien proud in his handiwork. She had been thoroughly tested, but not even Lucien could know how she would stand against those natural forces during the dangerous voyage ahead, when faced with so many unknowns.

It was her first sea voyage and maiden flight to an unknown part of their world, and that journey would be most testing on every resource, survival skill and sinew of her crew. That loyal crew was well chosen by their brave commander Obe. He was under orders from his Empress Queen to complete that mission at all costs and knew he would never be free until he had completed that most important of all duties.

'Take good care of her for me,' Tesien said, but the Warrior Obe nodded, while carefully observing the ship's prowess with Tesien at it's helm.

Obe was utterly bemused by the intricacies of the technological wonder that stood before him. She was the first mobile warring machine that had ever been built. She looked majestic in the bright sunlight, with ribbed sails out and protective spines that extended like sharp metallic stings throughout her length and breath. He couldn't help wondering whether Om-Chopter would ever sail the violent and unpredictable seas, and least of all, fly in air, with all the devices and war machinery she encompassed.

'Are you sure... she will... float and fly?' A bewildered Obe inquired.

'She may appear slight and weighty, but her alloys are the strongest and lightest. My mechanic, Longe, knows her like the claws on his very hands. She is compartmentalized and her deck sealed. So her chances of sinking is virtually nill.' Tesien, the great inventor and ship-builder expressed himself with such positiveness that Obe believed his every word and gesture.

'I hope you are right! Many lives are involved,' Obe stressed and walked away.

Tesien was a free Hive Worker and one of their most brilliant scientists. His royal status gave him such freedom by law, so he took advantage and attempted such challenging work as a hobby for his queen. But this new project of his was a unique experiment in warfare. If anything, she was probably the only craft that would make it through the treacherous places to the lands of the dreaded Petans.

Om-Chopter was soon launched ceremoniously amidst a crowd of royal subjects including Drones and Queens of the realm. Queen Magdala said a few important words in pheromones and gestures. Then the keen oaring Lamphis and warriors got onboard at the order of their Chief Captain to take their positions for the dangerous voyage ahead.

Longe, Tesien's apprentice, was the only Hive Worker on a ship of Warrior Soldiers and felt out of place. In his Semonite culture Workers were above Soldiers, but here he was under the instruction of his master Tesien, to take orders from Soldiers. He realized it was his duty to follow orders from his queen and was therefore prepared for any eventuality on this mission. He also knew he was the only one among the crew that could fly his Chopter, Om-Chopter.

Longe moved a few levers and Om-Chopter's sails activated and rotated in the vertical position, then they gracefully expanded from the two central masks towards the sides of the mallo boat. Mallo was a type of tough weed harvested from the softlands close to the shore by a few brave Lamphis.

Those hemp-like shoots grew wildly in those areas and could be used for weaving and matting into almost any shape. It was also used for hessian like clothes, ropes, baskets, and information scrolls. Their sea-faring craft contained two giant baskets suitably woven and separated by a thick layer of bitumen that was sandwiched in-between. That method formed a lightweight seaworthy boat that was flexible enough to resist even the most violent storms. The boat itself was reenforced with ribs of titanium alloy.

The chopter was extremely seaworthy, with Tricien wooden masks of extreme strength and moderate flexibility. They had been chopped from the Grey Forest at great risks to both Kanei and Lamphis. Her weaker areas were strengthened with more titanium alloys. Such ships were extremely lightweight and tough, while quite flexible.

The Kanei had always been knowledgeable in the ways of chemistry and metallurgy. It was the way the Semonites were, with extreme senses that could detect the strength, weakness and purity of all substances in nature through smell.

She left port and was on her way under sail power while assisted by those on land with rope, through the narrow Chuz Canal and towards the Sea of Jessel. That path was too narrow for her oars while extended and she needed careful attention to her rudders that guided her on her way. The Lamphis on the banks were coordinated in their efforts while the ropes pulled her at a steady pace.

'Steady! Steady! Steady as she goes!' came the shouts from Aurlsba, their second in command, making sure both sides of the banks pulled with equal tension. Lamphis were sometimes known to lapse in their duties.

At the end of Chuz they would turn left into the Sea of Jessel and follow the near vertical cliffs of the show-line until they arrived at wild Morier, the reversing rapids. Then the Devil's Whirlpool and finally through the Straights of Magellar. From that point Om-Chopter would fly up the near vertical wall of the giant crater of the Crethian Bourle.

Morier was a natural obstacle that drained excesses from the sea of Jessel towards the ocean of Gibro and vice-versa. Since both masses of water were at virtually the same heights, their levels would constantly change with the waxing and waning of the two moons, giving rise to the strangest flows, torrents and rapids.

That place was the most unpredictable of waters and infested by every type of predatory marine life. Many in that stretch had evolved wings to seek more varied prey above the torrents and rapids. Scavengers and predators would constantly skim the waters for whatever they could find, including their own kind. Obe had to time their voyage precisely to coincide with natural moon cycles.

'Release guide ropes! Aurlsba commanded. Ropes were unlatched from their clamps and withdrawn by the Lamphis on the walled banks.

'We must pass Morier, Magellar and lake Chobra Cann before Lyran wanes, or all will be lost!' Obe stressed.

'Yes, My Siend,' Aurlsba replied.

'Seth, activate the main masks and rudders for sea travel. We must conserve power for the climb. If everything goes well, we should pass the Straights of Magellar and enter Petan lands in one Lyran cycle. They have done much damage to our people over past cyclons and will pay dearly this time!'

'On it, My Siend,' Seth shouted above the random noises.

'Get the Lampris on the oars and pass a sweet nectar cube to each!' Obe ordered above the windward noise.

He slid open a draw and observed a large map. Then he viewed the local charts. It was his first sea voyage through that part of his world and wondered whether his charts were accurate in angle and distance. Those charts were compiled with data received from a few insane explorers and drone flyers of past and could not be fully relied upon. Yet he hoped a closer observation would give him an idea of the scales involved. Then he replaced them and closed the water-tight draw.

He realized the extreme dangers faced, but had taken an oath to bring their enemies to justice, and with Om-Chopter the time had come to even the score.

'But.. My Siend... the Softlands in the distance moves for us!' A worried Seth shouted above the strokes of the ores. Then he turned his head around in near panic to shout an order.

'Get the oars moving faster!' he yelled.

Aurlsba couldn't be more surprised. As second in command it was his job to give such orders and not Seth the second navigator. Yet he could read Seth's pheromones and knew he was fully stressed. Nevertheless he would be reprimanded at an appropriate time when sea business was less challenging.

'Napta, get the range locator and check yonder lands. I need to know how fast softlands approaches and when it will collide with the shows on this stretch!' Obe commanded.

His voyage was timed precisely to miss the advancing softlands or floating forests while they followed the shoreline. Then the ship would enter the violent rapids during full flow.

There was a massive splash in the waters ahead and spinelike tentacles held unto a large creature many times the size of their flimsy chopter. The body of the monstrous predator was well hidden from view within the stirring surf while its catch slowly slid beneath the waves in ripples of red. The panicking soldiers glanced in the direction of the disturbance, dismayed by its ferocity, while the under-deck Lamphis remained unconcerned and continued rowing their twenty oars, ten on each side.

'Itan! Itan! Itan! My Siend,' shouted Napta, as he turned his gaze to the stirring waters, not quite knowing what steps to take against such an enormous monster.

'Keep on course! Laviatan stays hidden beneath the waves and will strike at anything that moves within his grasp!' Obe barked, equally concerned.

'30 mecrons to softlands, My Siend!' Napta advised, shouting above the constant noise while placing the range locator back into its neat mallo case.

'Longe, get depth-charge projectiles ready and set spike shielding on both sides. We must continue on our present heading.'

'On it, My Siend!'

'No one, not even Laviatan will eat a painful dish!' Obe shouted and Longe walked towards the first mask and moved a long lever. Then he went to the rear mask and did the same.

Two large spiky nets expanded on either side of the chopter. The spikes were long and sharp and linked to pressurized stores of deadly venom. They were constructed from the lightest titanium alloy, one of the strongest metals ever cast. The deadly net cocooned the ship and prevented anything from getting in or out.

Om-Chopter was perfectly symmetrical and well balanced for both air and sea travel. She was gently led into the breeze with her massive wing-like sails, now disposed vertically, gyrating in symmetry as they took the backward pressure of the westerly gale. They moved eastward and appreciated the assistance of nature.

'Row! Row! Row!' came the constant nag from Aurlsba and the Lamphis put everything into each stroke. Unlike Semonites, Lamphis were more beatle-like, with tough muscles on each of their six massive limbs. They were well suited to such manual tasks. However those lamphis were even tougher then normal, being specially chosen for that voyage.

The handles on the oars were designed specifically for use by them. Small cubicles held them in a fixed position while engaging each stroke. The only things they could hear or see were the handles of large oars and the orders of Aurlsba.

They were intelligent enough to understand the cries and scents of their masters; for they had evolve together almost as a single race since the beginning. During that time they had become the muscles of the Semonites. Nevertheless they faced the same dangers as their masters and whatever they sacrificed was for the good of their mutual families and tribes.

'Our lookout drone, Calebos, flies high over Mytal Rock this day,' Aurlsba commented, watching the distant dot hovering over the citadel on the high rock.

'Me thinks he is misplaced to deliver a message,' chief mechanic Longe replies.

'Bolte rock's ahead. We must slow and wait at its neck to take on coal, ballast and rations for the crossing. Take a middle course towards the centre, Aurlsba,' Obe advised.

'On it, My Siend,' Aurlsba replied.

Mirrors flashed from above the greenish citadel at the top of the high cliff.

'Our Duty Queen wishes you, Obe, a successful voyage,' Longe decoded.

'Send a message back. Say, "I dearly thank her royal highness for her timely concerns, and will bring home many of the heads of our enemies in time for her winter celebrations,' Obe said, and a mirror was directed towards the citadel.

Large baskets lowered from the high rock towards the ship and their contents unloaded and securely stored. They used uncontaminated drinking water for ballast. Nevertheless each soldier carried their own rations.

Ballast was needed on their journey through the rapids. It would keep Om-Chopter low in the waters and enable her rudders to guide her more accurately. It also aided her balance and stability. This time Aurlsba altered his command to the Lamphis.

'Gently right! Stop! Retrieve oars!'

That control moved the chopter to the right, more away from the shows towards the deeper waters. That new course was necessary to engage the turbulent channel head on, but was a lot more dangerous than straddling the show line.

When she had gathered enough speed, the oars were lifted into the ship by another mechanism and stood vertically to further protect the crew.

Suddenly and without warning 6 long spiky tentacles shot out of the waters and wrapped themselves around the chopter, lifting her many metres into the air. Luckily they had their nets on or the thirty soldiers and other crew members would have been emptied into the turbulent waters. The poisonous spikes activated and the unpalatable chopter was flung away as if a piece of cast-off wood.

Om-Chopter soon righted herself as the almost salt free spray drained off her sails and masks to drench all beneath. Water spilled across her curved deck and emptied through drains and portholes. The Lamphis were confused.

'Hold your stations!' Aurlsba shouted and they were satisfied that he was still with them.

A drenched Obe recovered himself from the furthest corner, untangled himself from a pile of mallo rope and dusted his attire with disgust. He extended his long sensory whiskers, then re-curled them. His large green segmented eyes resembling the most beautiful emerald gems, were uncovered from the thick leathery membrane that subconsciously reacted to shield them from such dangers. Nevertheless he was dripping wet and not amused.

Once again the orders were given to man the oars. Their recent encounter with the sea monster had lost them their speed and momentum, which was required to face the next part of their journey.

Obe expected many dangers on this journey, but this one was unexpected. His brave and ruffled crew quickly checked themselves and were immediately back at their stations. Obe soon realized that his recent encounter was most likely a taste of worse to come.

'Quickly take positions and harness yourselves to the guide lines and mask rings. We approach Bolte rocks and must be prepared for the forward rapids.' Obe was sterner.

'Aurlsba, get ready to retrieve oars and man the rudders for close trimming. Longe, get ready to retrieve nets! Aurlsba, keep well away from approaching rocks so take a central course. Morier will now be in full flow therefore attempt to keep her keel away from the smaller rocks beneath.' Obe grew impatient as they got closer.

They could hear the thunder in the distance and were in sight of the stirring currents as they crashed and diverted from large rocks and uneven banks. They entered the place between two high rocks and the torrents were extreme. Om-Chopter creaked as she wandered from side to side with the strong eddies. Suddenly she hit a fast flowing stream and was away like a bullet. The oars were once again pulled upright.

'My Siend, we move at 40 knots. This is much too fast for Chopter,' the first navigator Napta commented.

'I know, but without oars we have less control and can only go as fast as the waters will carry. Keep a lookout for Speelshark and Spyne! Soon we enter Gibro, then we climb the plateau to the crater's sea and softlands! Then we take our revenge on Petans. Be patient!' Aurlsba replied.

'She steers well, even in this great turbulence!' Aurlsba commented above the noises of the swirling torrents and the occasional drenching surf. Napta followed his complement with more eagerness at the wheel.

'She will hold well with ballast. But we must take out half before the Straights of Magellar. After that we dump the lot before our flight,' Longe said.

Obe opened the draw to retrieve the charts and was surprised the mallo sheets were still dry. He thoroughly checked them before placing them back within the watertight draw.

'Keep a straight course! We must pass between yonder rocks! Just ahead will be the end of this stretch. Then we enter Devils Whirlpool. You must take a course towards the right of the spiralling vertex at its centre. Get your oarsbars ready to row hard just before the whirlpool, or we shall be sucked into his hellish depths!' Obe hoped the directions and positions shown on the map were correct.

A large Speelshark shot out of the stirring waters just behind them, extended its fin-like wings and glided towards the chopter. Its array of shark-like teeth showed a formidable white. As it appeared just above the main deck, Longe ducked in the nick of time. It dived unexpectedly towards a soldier, cut him in two from the shoulders and couldn't escape the near vertical side of the boat. There it remained frantically beating its enormous wings and fins against the deck. A quick thinking Aurlsba grabbed a local crossbow and fired three poisonous bolts into the creature. Its struggles were silenced.

'Good job! Get the winch and lift it out!' Obe barked. He nodded his head while glancing at the remains of his dead soldier. Any extra weights will be dumped on this voyage.

They intended to carefully guide Om-Chopter to enter the whirlpool at the furthest side to the right, but not too close to the channel's wall.

The Lamphis rested their oars, took another suck of nectar cube and waited patiently for Aurlsba's orders.

From the turmoils of the past they knew they were in grave danger but could do little in present circumstances. Therefore they decided to take their best short at each of Aurlsba's commands.

'Right! Right! Right! Enough!' Obe shouted.

'Steady... Stea...dy!' Aurlsba shouted while Longe trimmed the sails and rudder as best he could, glancing through a periscope device that gave him a relatively clearer view of their forward path.

CHAPTER 2

The second stretch

Om-Chopter soon approached the spiralling Devil's Whirlpool. Once again the Lamphis were ready at the oars. She had enough speed to plunge to the right and take a path close to the treacherous rocks before being swallowed up by the whirlpool.

The stretch of water ahead was as treacherous as the ones before, but they had to keep their nets down during that operation and oars could not be used until they faced the whirlpool.

The limited fuel they carried could only give them about 50 kilometres of air travel and there was no chance of refilling while in enemy territories.

In all probability the fuel would only be needed for their flight across the dangerous plateau's wall to the Crethian Sea above and for dropping bombs on their enemies. That wall was about 7 kilometres high and could not be climbed in the normal way.

Their present route was the most difficult way to the lands of the Petans, but the only one to surprise their enemies before they had time to plan a coordinated attack. That way their enemies would be caught unguarded.

The waters between the whirlpool and the ocean of Gibro were tamer and less dangerous than their previous encounters. Nevertheless Obe knew he would lose more of his warriors before he reached the enemy lands.

The Lamphy was still under deck and little concerned about the dangers faced. When they were not at the owes, they rested and sucked their cubes of nectar for energy.

'Row! Row! Row!' Aurlsba shouted and they gave it their all. As much as they did it was not enough and Chopter started sliding backwards into the centre of the swirl. The spiralling currents soon spun them around the vertex.

Hard! Hard! Hard!' came the timely order from Aurlsba and the momentum gained pushed chopter away from the whirlpool, just missing the rocks by a hair's breath.

Aurlsba was too exhausted to comment, but his expressions and pheromones told everything. It was their closest shave so far and thanks to her brilliant maker, Tesien, Om-Chopter was still in one piece.

The lamphis rowed their oars to save their lives and Om-Chopter held her course, determined to take it all in her stride.

'Wooooo! That was close!' shouted Aurlsba and Obe nodded his head in agreement. The Lamphis were soaking wet with sweat that fell off their powerful limbs while their narrow tongues were out and dripping. Their hovering tanks of fresh water were almost exhausted.

'Get ready for the waters of Magellar! She is filled with many dangers. Despite her calmness she can be the most unforgiving. We shall require all our reserves and good timing for that crossing.' Obe advised while observing his map. Then he placed them back into the draw.

'Aurlsba get ready to give the order to man oars on my command.'

'Yes, My Siend.'

'Warriors, take up positions near the mask with blades and tie yourselves to the guide-lines. We must be ready to face all dangers!' Obe commanded.

During high-waters, part of that stretch overflowed its banks into the Chobra Cann lake several hundred metres below so they had to guide the chopter close to the high wall to avoid the currents that took everything towards that thunderous waterfall.

Once again they took position to avoid the rapids and the Lamphis gave it their all. However that part was not as tight as the whirlpool and they left unscathed. The Straights of Magellar was calmer, wider and much deeper. Obe realizing unexpected dangers gave his orders.

'Keep a keen eye, Soldiers!'

After the experiences of the past, everything had suddenly become too quiet for his ears.

'Release nets and seal the decks! Give the Oarsbars another cube each and let them rest!'

Longe unleashed his safety line and went to the main masks to move the Levers. Once more the metallic nets with titanium spikes sprung out on either side of the boat while two spineless ones expanded from its sides to seal them in on deck.

It was not long before Om-Chopter was investigated by several predators, but they soon retracted when they observed her sharp spines. Many took to the air to observe her decks, but when faced with difficulties soon went elsewhere to hunt.

Having missed the dreaded waterfalls, Om-Chopter followed the route of the Straights of Magellar towards the ocean of Gibro. They were taken around a bend and found themselves at the neck of the great ocean. Its waters very much as normal as the Sea of Jessel. Softlands had receded far enough away from its shores. Those waters were new to them and Obe realized that monstrous Laviatans could be patiently waiting in such depths. Even so, those ferocious monsters never fished close to show.

'We should move close to the beach in yonder distance. We can make repairs there and fire up for our in-land flight.'

'Yes, My Siend!' Aurlsba replied.

The massive Crethian Crater loomed large before them. It was over 7 kilometres high with a snowy rim and just over 300 kilometres in diameter. Right at the centre of the great plateau or Crethian Bourle was the Crethian Sea, almost at a level of 7 kilometres above the Ocean of Gibro. That place was cold but only part of the sea was frozen.

'This is Petan lands, therefore we cannot remain in this place too long,' Obe suggested, with the chopter getting close to shore.

'Fire up the burners!' Aurlsba commanded. Longe went towards the main mask and pulled a small lever several times, but could observe no flames within the chamber. He released a latch and opened the door of the sealed chamber. Then retrieved a single block of coal and inspected it, sniffing hard in the process.

'Wet! Soaked through and through! They are all wet, My Siend!' he shouted in disappointment. He was so used to shouting that he hadn't realized they were now in calm waters.

'Remove the coal from the chamber and spread it out on deck. Then check our stores. We might have to dry the lot before we can travel!' Aurlsba shouted back.

'Take her closer to the beach. We can anchor there and wait a while. A little delay now will not matter. It will only postpone the death of a few Petans,' Obe commanded.

'We now have more than one half Lyran cycles to do our work and make the trip back,' Obe advised. Nevertheless he and his crew were happier and more relaxed, having foregone so many dangers on route.

Om-Chopter was placed on her extendible telescopic stilts and anchored to that place close to the shore. Well into the distance they could observe several Petan dragons frolicking wildly in the waters. Above the ship on the near vertical walls of the crater they could observe numerous caves. Their territories and homes encompassed the perimeter wall of the massive crater. Petans had always lived that way. Thus they could take advantage of the rising air currents close to the cliffs to assist their flight. However the tribes on that side, close to the ocean of Gibro, were not the ones they were after. The ocean contained fish in abundance therefore they always had enough to eat. So never would they invade others for food and other valuables.

'The coal in storage is dry, My Siend,' Longe said and Aurlsba nodded with pleasure.

'Then we shall use it instead.'

Longe shovelled the coal into the hopper and placed a dry cube of starter fuel in the metallic cinder box within the chamber. He engaged the lever a few times, there was a snap, then many sparks and the flame ignited. Obe could sense the happy pheromones coming from that direction and showed a smile, as if Semonites could really show such facial expressions. Longe had to burn coal for several minutes before enough steam could be created to move the sails.

'Now, we can dump all ballast and release nets!' Aurlsba shouted and it was done.

As the great crater's wall loomed large above them, Obe grew more unsure of Om-Chopter's capabilities for flight. He just hoped Tesien was correct in her designs, or everything would be lost.

There was a local splash and just beyond the rocks a large dragon lifted its blue-green head above the water. It was curious enough and came forward to investigate. That one had a large fanlike crest around its long head. The crest was coloured orange and appeared part of its scaly body. Its arms and legs were powerful and muscular. There it stood for a moment like a large raptor from prehistory observing the new arrival.

That one walked on two powerful legs, with sharp claws on feet, webbed for swimming. The two front arms were smaller. They could be used for holding objects. The six digits on each hand were also webbed for swimming with claws sharp and formidable like the spikes on Om-Chopter.

Their tails were sharp-edged and scaly for guiding them through air and water, but also used for balance. Those powerful tails could have been their main weapon of defence.

Suddenly it stood upright on its hind legs and moved its slitted golden eyes to observe the crew, but did not make a noise to invite others. It only wanted to observe the miracle of a ship from close range by itself; for never before had it seen such a beautiful thing.

Obe had encountered dragons on many occasions before, particularly when they invaded Kanei territories, but those here were different. He admired the creature with awe. They were so different from his kind, who had evolved from a type of insect and had grown to enormous size when they had lost their ability to fly. Kanei were just 1.3 metres tall on average. Drones like Calebos were even smaller, more thinly built and could fly at great heights to warn his people of invading dragons from across the lake. However those Petans here were over 3 metres long, highly intelligent, powerful in strength and very curious.

In any event Obe was taking no chances.

'Man the crossbow!' he yelled to one of his soldiers closest to the dragon. Yet he did not load a bolt, but kept them well at hand and the dragon in his sights.

Aurlsba couldn't wait any longer for more coal to dry, so decided to assist in bagging the still damp fragments from the deck. Nevertheless they were dry enough for a hot furnace.

Obe stood majestically on deck in his fine woven mallo tunic with contrasting purple cape. His face almost human-like while staring at the beautiful, and yet powerful creature that stood only a few metres away. He feared how he and his warriors would fend in battle against such formidable foe. Even with their Om-chopter, its pivoting crossbows, catapults and bombs. Those dragons were tough and built to survive whatever nature would throw at them. They were carnivores that took their energies from other life. Such energies were built into every fibre of their bodies. That type of creature was a fearless warring machine with much energy reserves in their powerful limbs and muscles.

They were so unlike his own kind that only lived on nectar and berry juice. His were not muscular and could remain without food for several months. Food and water was only necessary when engaging in any form of activity.

'Set sails for flight!' Aurlsba ordered and levers were moved on the side of each mask.

Longe inspected the linkages by pulling them gently. Then he scanned her sails for any tears or weakness. The thin fibres and titanium ribs of her sails (or were they wings) had held during all her previous trials and she had remained in tact. Not even a Spyne fish had punctured a single sail.

'Engage Clutch!' Aurlsba shouted.

Longe went towards a large panel with four sets of controls, one for each wing and trimmed the wings for vertical ascension. Clutches were engaged and the titanium shafts on either side of both masks began to move and gyrate. The massive sails buckled like those of an eagle's wings. In an instant her stilts were released and the craft miraculously shot into the air. She moved close enough to the high wall to take advantage of the upward currents and was soaring high.

Longe tweaked a few levers in a manner akin to playing a

musical instrument and Om-Chopter moved forward. Then he made another adjustment and she spun around over the high wall.

Obe continued to glanced at the dragons homes along the high cliff, fascinated and intrigued by their methods of survival. Then he changed his gaze to the towering high cliff above them. By now he was more fascinated by Om-Chopter's abilities in the air.

'Tesien! Oh Tesien! You are the best! You are the greatest,' Obe shouted to the wind.

'She handles well in flight. Even great Calebos will give her praise!'

'That's so, My Siend, and she uses less fuel for our trip than predicted. Master Lucien will be pleased,' Longe replied.

The large dragon was bemused by it all, but decided not to follow. Those dragons were quite capable of travelling to virtually anywhere throughout the crater.

Nevertheless they tended not to invade the territories of others of their kind for fear of territorial disputes and challenges. Although the thinner air at that level slowed their progress, Om-Chopter made good time and was soon at the Crethian Sea. Once again they set sail with protective nets drawn to avoid more flying predators. They had to travel the full extent of the sea while navigating their way through the many floating weed-banks, icebergs and softlands. The final part of their journey would land them within enemy territory, but at a much lower level on the high cliff.

Upon arrival they rested for a while close to the shore and ingested some rations. Once again Longe checked his ship. This time he concentrated more on the weapons. The burners were topped with more fuel and they were ready for battle.

'Shall we announce our presence?' The warrior, Obe, shouted with confidence.

A catapult was loaded and a bomb dispatched towards the edge of the cliff. There was a mighty explosion. A large section of that area broke away and fell into the distant lake below. Several dragons were caught in the slide but managed to escape.

'That should wake the sleeping giants. Now let's see how well these monsters fare against the might of Om-Chopter!' Obe was determined to make his mark.

CHAPTER 3

The survival plan

Although the war between Semonites and Petans had begun, there was a much greater universal crisis. It was one that would in time engulf all those on that world, then our galaxy and in time the whole universe. It would threaten the very existence of all primal life.

For many millennia the Seventh Universe had been at peace from evil predator species. Many were those that travelled throughout stellar systems looting and plundering all inhabited worlds. Of those the Hexolytes were the most advanced in technology and in the art of ensnaring all those innocent civilizations. They in turn were vanquished by the Patriarchs several billion years ago. Others like the Mesotrene were assisted on their way out of our universe by very powerful beings. They were sent to a universe more suited to their type of existence. Nevertheless, peace was always a temporary dream. One that was always as fragile as thin glass. Sooner or later a new aggressive species would arise to shatter that peace.

That new species were not flesh and blood like us, but composed of nano-bots, sometimes called nanites. They were virtually indestructible and needed the chemicals in our bodies for their sustenance.

Their main desire however was to rule the universe, placing all other species under their control. Those that opposed their rule would be eliminated. They had ruined the whole of the Andromedan galaxy and were presently on their way to our own galaxy, Osmaron. Their billions of swarms would begin to arrive well within one millennium. That was, providing they had their own way in all things, but they hadn't.

They didn't realize that several Supreme Beings existed throughout our universe. Therefore minds were afoot to oppose the Javols' move at every step.

Our Grand Lord had set certain survival plans in motion. Within his grand project our galaxy had been chosen to become the hub of operations. Therefore he was to find a few well chosen individuals to assist him in his endeavours. Those in turn would find suitable intelligent worlds for conversion to a more advanced technology. Then at the appropriate time we would fight the aggressor until their kind was no more.

Lord Vektron had previously scanned the Kalboron Cluster and found many evolving species. From all those he had chosen the Semonites on Kanaefon as the first for development and conversion.

Grand Lord Gerra, Supreme Lord of the Seventh Universe, was also interested in that species. His curiosity was so aroused that he decided to pay a passing visit to observe their culture from afar. He never liked meddling in the affairs of others, particularly those that were lower than Class 3 on his technological scale.

At that time Semonites had no knowledge of the atom, advanced mathematics, nuclear physics or indeed any subject relevant to the creation of advanced technologies. They were then classified well under Class 1. Yet, they had great minds and the potential to accomplish his goals.

The Grand Lord was also looking for a new home of residence. It was now the end of one millennium on his present world and he had to move to a new civilization to advance his cause.

As he travelled, he viewed the voyage of Om-chopter and the bravery of her crew, particularly Obe. He had seldom seen such bravery and purpose in any single individual. He also knew the reasons why, but wanted peace among all races on that world. Peace was imperative if he was to use them to fulfill his important purpose. Therefore he decided to interfere if the situation got out of hand, but never in a trivial way.

CHAPTER 4

An incredulous victory

Om-Chopter landed on what was considered a strategic location on the southern side of the cliffs. She remained mounted on her four tall under-stilts. Then Longe fired grabbling hooks to hold her more firmly in place. Her protective nets were lowered to safeguard her crew. There she stood glittering in the bright sunlight while showing her sharp shiny spines to all her enemies. They had previously identified the offending tribe by their yellow crests and a few discarded Kanei items and were ready to teach them a memorable lesson.

The first explosion and rock slide had brought all the main dragons together, both female and male. They had been caught unprepared and were steaming and furious at the stealthy invasion by Kanei into their territories. Territories they thought were beyond the reach of any of the low-landers. Realizing they now had a fight on their hands they bunched together. Then decided to make the first move to destroy the ship before it could reck more damage on their homes and families.

The mighty dragons stood in rank and file ready for battle. They hissed and growled while showing their formidable canines and rasping tongues, hissing and snarling as if wanting to tear the invaders to bits. But with the intention to scare and drive them away. When it came to a choice between war and peace, Petans realized the consequences and would always choose the latter.

They were indeed a fearful sight to watch and could instill fear in the most seasoned warrior. Nevertheless Obe and his group stood their ground in defiance. He and his warriors had travelled far and sacrificed too much to back down and retreat without a fight. After all, he represented his queen on this mission and had taken the oath to serve and obey her commands.

Petans never had use of weapons but were excellent fighters. After all, they were tough scaly monsters and almost top of the food chain on land. They could inflict damage in many ways and were fearless.

Despite their wandering nature they never did violence for its own sake. If only Kanei knew the language of the Petans, then they could communicate and perhaps come to some type of compromise.

'Battle stations everyone. Man the bows and exploding catapults. I want every Petan in this place to pay for their transgressions of past against us!' Obe commanded.

A ladder was extended from the side of Om-Chopter and several warriors accompanied Obe to an area where he could be visible to all. The others, including Longe and Aurlsba remained on-board. Some of the warriors manned the large crossbows and catapults on deck and marked their targets.

Obe removed a scroll from a sealed container. He broke the royal seal and began to read its words.

'A proclamation from her majesty, Duty Queen Magdala.

Because of your ravaging of our homes and cities of past, we have decided to take your own violence to you and your people in these lands. What we are about to do, will be just a taste of what shall befall you and your people in the future, if you do not hid my words and stop the ravaging of our stocks and supplies....'

The scroll was read in Kanei which was a language of hisses, a few gestures and pheromones. It was a language unknown to Petans. They were reptilian and knew not the meanings of those sounds. Neither could they detect the subtler blends of gestures and pheromones. Yet, their leaders realized whatever they said meant war and grouped in rows ready for violence.

Obe lifted his hand and more large crossbows spun on their pivots on the side of the ship to mark their targets. The three main catapults were charged with metallic balls for missiles, but the order was not given to initiate hostilities and engage the enemy.

Petans were fearless giants by comparison and could kill many Kanei with a single swipe of their massive scaly tails. The Kanei were more advanced and had many weapons, including poisonous bolts and explosives that they could release with catapults from a great distance.

They could also fly their strange ship in the air and drop deadly exploding devices, so the Petans were dismayed and desired a more peaceful solution. They also realised the strange ship was protected by sharp shiny spikes that could impale them.

They had already experienced the powers of the ship with the rock slide and was worried that other bombs would be dropped making more rock slides, destroying even more of their people and their homes. They stood in the wake of devastating technologies and there could be more of those machines to follow.

The Kanei were intelligent, industrious and now possessed weapons of mass destruction of which Petans had no knowledge. Neither had they knowledge of such technologies other than the very basics. How could they defend themselves against technology? Nevertheless they had to show a strong face and stand up for the good name of their tribe.

Their largest dragon, Melan, bravely came forward. He was their leader and yellow breasted.

'We are not afraid of you, Kanei, even of your fancy flying machines and its powerful killing weapons. What we do not like is your petulant attitude in destroying our homes and family members. We invaded your lands because our people were hungry and needed more to feed our families. As you may have observed, during this harsh season the fish in the lake had grown small and few, while there are many of us to feed. How can we exist without food?

'When we invaded your lands, we never went out of our way to destroy your kind or kill your people. Neither did we willfully damage your homes as you have done here today. We were only after your food stores and just took a few drums of nectar and juice. We could not ask and most probably would have been told to get lost. You are the industrious ones and can always make more,' Melan, their chief said, but the Kanei did not understand the apologetic words of Melan.

The sun began to set along the western wall so Obe realized they had to take action before it darkened. It seemed that the Petans felt the same way, if only to end hostilities.

The first group of Petans approached Obe's position to do their worst. The first volley of arrows and explosives were unleashed. Several Petans were impaled, but many simply removed the bolts and continued towards Obe's group and the Chopter. They were going to take their revenge irrespective of the consequences.

One of the young dragons threw a small rock which by chance hit Obe on his forehead between his eyes and he fell. Many of his warriors went to protect him while Aurlsba rushed to his aid and leant over him to administer first-aid. He didn't realize that Obe was fatally wounded and dying from his wounds.

For some reason Obe knew his time had come, but was worried his mission was unfulfilled.

'My friends and brave warriors, including Longe our great mechanic, I am proud to have been your commander on this last voyage. Please complete this important mission for our Queen. You must pay them back for what they have done to us! Pay them back....one thousand fold.... pay them back... I must leave you now...Fare..well!' Obe said while gasping for breath. He uttered the word Farewell with his last dying breath.

Suddenly the setting sun dimmed as it became eclipsed by their largest moon. Just beyond their horizon another bright star rose. It appeared as a glowing ball and shone so brightly that the effects of the eclipse were abated. The glowing ball moved in their direction, stunning the soldiers in its wake. Then it stopped above them. There was a blinding flash and stood before them was a most beautiful glowing angel of light. It was neither Semonite nor Petan and moved its head around as if to observe every individual.

The being glowed radiantly and white while everyone within that area went down and humbled themselves before it.

A voice thundered in every language and penetrated deeply within minds.

'Great Obe, your tasks on this world is now at an end. You will be reborn again to face even greater challenges.' Then in front of

their very eyes Obe's body floated in the air and faded into the mist, even while among his warriors, leaving them fearful of their turn.

'My glorious lord, I beg you! Please do not harm us this way!' they cried in their different ways and tongues.'

'*To you others, you will desist from your warring activities, forthwith!*

'*I have a task for each of you!*

'*Henceforth, you will commit only towards assisting your tribes, clans and people. If you follow your lord's commands, one day you will become great and travel even to the furthest reaches of this galaxy and beyond even the farthest stars in the heavens!*

'*I am Lumak, the grandest lord of all and the only one to fulfill your innermost desires. However, mark truly my words this day. Another will come by the same name to assist you in your times of peril. He will assist you in all your endeavours and quests for the common good. Therefore you must return to your homelands and go your own way this day to celebrate this new period of change in the history of your world.*'

Then the being faded into the mist and the ball of light changed direction towards the west from whence it came.

Before Obe's demise brave Aurlsba was second in command, now he was their new commander. After recovering from the shock of the angel of light, he was not sure what had happened to his senior Obe. He had disappeared in front of their eyes and they could have done nothing to save their commander. Neither was a confused Aurlsba sure that he should take command of the ship in Obe's absence. They waited for a while until the Petans left the field of battle. They had left peacefully as if retreating from defeat. Without having had a proper chance in battle Om-Chopter must now take to the air.

Aurlsba was on board Om-Chopter when Obe was hit by the object and could not have observed the incident. Although administering first-aid, he was not sure of the seriousness of Obe's wounds nor his chances of survival. Even in the wake of the Being of Greatness, he could not just leave things the way they were and depart without the body of their great commander. Neither were their battle with the dragons concluded in the honour of their queen. It would now be impossible to locate the enemy and give them their fair desserts. Destroying their homes with bombs appeared cowardly and did not seem fair recompense.

From recent occurrences Aurlsba had no desire to continue the fight, despite the prompting from Obe before he vanished.

'Let's check yonder vale and within the area of the high wall for our leader. We must do it quickly before our fuel wanes!' he yelled.

They scanned the immediate area, but Obe was nowhere to be found. Om-Chopter had just enough fuel left to make the jump across the furthest crater's wall. Therefore he made the unwilling decision to return home via the Ocean of Gibro.

'This must be the two great losses of my entire existence. In one day a lost commander and a lost battle,' Aurlsba admitted despondently to Longe.

'My Siend, it was not our fault things went the way they did,' Longe replied, trying to calm Aurlsba's fury.

On arrival at the high cliff overlooking Gibro, they had to wait at the high wall for the moons to position themselves and the waters change in the homeward direction.

They could have taken the closer route to home over the lake and across the Great Forest, but that area was virtually unknown and their reserves of fuel were not enough to carry them all the way, so they decided to take that path homeward.

Despite Aurlsba's disappointment with the way things went. He was even more worried for himself and his crew for not having fulfilled his queen's wishes and Obe's promise to her.

After the appearance of the Grand Lord on their world, word soon got around the many Petan tribes. They now considered Om-Chopter to be one most revered by the gods.

When Om-Chopter landed on a distant cliff overlooking the Ocean of Gibro, many Petans came out to watch the glittering marvel that could take so gracefully to air and sea. The dragons showed their prowess in the air by their strange aerobatics while trying to be friendly. They could precisely time air currents and manipulate their wings to gain virtually any angle and speed in flight. Even Aurlsba and his crew marvelled at their dexterity, power and control. They became friends and began to share food and rations of nectar and berry juices. Then the Petans were allowed to view the great ship and marvelled at its designs.

It took half a Lyran period before the canal would change direction and take them back towards the sea of Jessel.

They were still concerned, but saddened by the untimely disappearance of Obe, not knowing the true nature of his demise. If indeed he was dead.

They soon came to the conclusion that Obe had been taken away by the supreme being to some other distant place to fulfill another great mission. After all, Obe was probably the greatest warrior known to the clan of Kanei and would always be honoured as such.

Two more warriors were lost on their return trip, but Aurlsba was as fearless as was Obe. He knew Om-Chopter well and had taken all necessary precautions. Longe the mechanic Worker was hardened by his experiences while his appreciation for warriors and crew had grown to one of admiration. By journey's end he had learnt every one of Om-Chopter's more subtler traits.

When they arrived at the mouth of Morier and into the Sea of Jessel, more mirrors flashed. This time Calebos, the Drone, was soaring even higher on the wind above the cliff.

'You have completed your duties most admirably for our Duty Queen. Come home quickly so we can celebrate a great victory in your honour,' the message said.

Aurlsba was surprised by those words. He realized a battle was neither lost nor won. No one had gained that satisfaction because of the untimely interruption by the Angel of Light. And dear Obe was lost forever because of it. He was utterly saddened by the whole affair and thought they should be seriously reprimanded because of it. The loss of such a great warrior out of battle should have reflected badly on his rank and warriors. Yet they wanted him and his crew to celebrate a great victory.

When they arrived in the Sea of Jessel, the softlands were receding from the rocky shows and they sailed close to the coast to avoid further encounters with Laviatan, the most dreaded sea monster. There were many such Laviatans within their territories that stretched far and wide throughout the seas and oceans of their world. They shifted their territories with the movement of the floating forests.

Om-Chopter was still with fuel so brave Aurlsba decided to flag all convention and fly her straight into the City of Lud. They landed in the main square amidst a large reception committee. As Aurlsba and his brave warriors disembarked they were cheered by many.

Aurlsba waved like a conqueror to the crowds and they waved back. During the welcoming celebrations they were treated like real victors for a battle they had not won and Aurlsba grew suspicious of such proceedings.

Once again the bright star appeared overhead and they were awed by its brilliance. With one bright flash the star changed into the image of their commander, Obe, and they were utterly astonished. Everyone, even the crowds knelt before him. In the minds of Aurlsba and the crew, Obe had transformed from their plane of existence and had been promoted to be among the gods and yet, here he was, still among them in the flesh and in powerful glory. Then the angel of light, now in Obe's image, began to speak.

'My dearest people, this marks a glorious period in our history. With keen endeavour we shall gain power on this world and in time win against all our enemies. From this day on, no more will our territories be invaded by the Petans from beyond the lake. For those of you that still worry about such invasions, we shall build a great wall to separate us from the great Bourle.

'Henceforth you will all be educated in the new ways of the kingdom. Great Queen Magdala has been chosen as Empress Duty Queen and henceforth shall be in charge of all Semonite lands throughout our world. However, all Duty Queens

representing their fiefs shall always have a democratic say in running their own territories.

'I bring a greater order to our people. In time even the Petans will gain from our successes. For they are also part of our world and share our history...,' The Grand Lord presently in the image of Obe spoke with greatest sincerity and they believed his every word. Everyone listened to the godlike figure, still glowing radiantly.

After that encounter the Semonites had never been the same. Although Obe was lost, to Aurlsba and his warriors he had been found in even greater glory.

With greatest dignity the new empress queen bowed to her crowds while accompanied by her partner drone, Tilkien. She was over twice his size and they looked a strange couple, but the crowds of Workers and Soldiers cheered all the same.

Om-Chopter was taken to an area and placed on a specially prepared pedestal. There she would remain as a monument and constant reminder to the Kanei of their first great voyage to the lands of the Petans. She would also symbolise their first victory against the dragons. For although a battle was neither fought nor won, that day symbolized a turning point in the relations between Kanei and Petans.

Magnificent Om-Chopter would also remain a constant reminder of the day when the Grand Lord arrived on their world.

From that moment on, life on Kanaefon would never be the same. They were soon thought the ways of the atom and would advance their sciences in many fields. The knowledge of which would one day make them one of the most advanced species in the Osmaron Galaxy.

Presently they had expanded throughout their own globular cluster of Kalboron and were another important species within the Greater Purpose for the benefit of all life within our universe.

BOOK 2

In human form

CHAPTER 5

A Saint is born

(Just over one thousand years after Obe's death.)

Earth time... 1650 CE (about 1204 years after Obe's death)

Place... Beautiful Kanaefon

It was said that both moons aligned themselves to form the most spectacular eclipse at the time of Sut Lumak's birth. At that eventful moment the Great Chasms overflowed and the waters roared over the high walls.

Only the Grand Lord knew that the real Obe had returned; He had kept his original body and identity stored within the Greater Mind until the time was right. And at last that time had come; for he had planned it that way. During this period Obe would not be a soldier, but more a gentle Hive Worker and peace maker. As promised, his name would change from Obe to Lumak.

Not even Lumak would remember his past life as the Great commander Obe; for all those memories had been erased, if he was to make a clean start during his new corporeal existence. Nevertheless, records of his previous existence had been recorded in the Greater Mind and would become accessible to him at a later date.

As was foretold by the Grand Lord, the great adventurer was back and would not be stilled in his purpose. As a young Semonite he had to learn the ways of his people all over again and overcome his own challenges towards maturity. In all this he hadn't lost his most endearing attitude... to go where none of his people had ever ventured before.

The ageing Empress Queen, Magdala, soon gave up the reigns of Kanei power to her daughter. She was Lumak's mother and Ushaia by name. She was now under the guidance of the Grand

Lord and the paths of their lives changed irreversibly for ever.

His mother was brought up in an age of change and wanted well for all the tribes on her world, including the Petan dragons. She soon realized there was not enough for the Petans and arranged a system of barter and commerce between both races. Then the western Petans were able to survive without stealing the products of others. Both races were too dissimilar to live together and had to continue their survival paths independently.

As a young hatchling, Lumak was always aware of the problems faced and saw their solutions a challenge. During that period of his life he was possessed by unlimited enthusiasm and found many solutions for both Kanei and Petans.

One day while wandering within the city of Lud, young Lumak came face to face with the great monument of Om-Chopter. She was enclosed in a large structure for protection. As he approached, for some unknown reason sadness filled his eyes. A sense of déjà vu had overcome him as he viewed the massive ship.

Of all her ancient loyal crew only Longe and Aurlsba still remained alive and they were old and feeble. As he passed the worshippers kneeling near the monument, he brushed gently against them, not even realizing their past adventures together in a previous existence. Aurlsba had never recovered from the loss of his captain, Commander Obe, on that faithful day. Yet, both turned about and greeted the stranger as they would Obe himself, despite his reduced age.

'She was indeed a remarkable one and carried well on sea and air. Our Tesien was truly a great inventor.'

'Indeed, My Siend.' Aurlsba humbled himself before Lumak, realizing he was princely.

'She handles well in flight. Even Calebos will give her praise,' Lumak said, not realizing the impact of his last words or why he said them. Suddenly they realized that Great Obe had really returned and was now truly among them in the flesh. They clearly remembered those same words uttered by him years before when crossing the high cliffs on the way to Petan lands. They were uttered in exactly the same manner.

'Good day, Gentlemen,' he said while the old soldiers bowed in his honour as young Lumak passed them to view the inside of the ship.

'Good day to you, Great Obe,' they replied, while acknowledging the strange moment of universal truth.

Lumak did not immediately realize the significance of that moment or what had transpired because of his chosen phrase. It flowed out so naturally from his mind as if he was under the control of another.

From that moment on he would always visit Om-Chopter to meditate and say a prayer before he left on each of his missions. Longe and Aurlsba became two of his best friends and counselled him in the ways of strategy and warfare, while Lumak counselled them in the ways of peace.

THE WARRIOR LORD

Lumak pondered the stories told to him about the time of the Grand Lords arrival to their world, which coincided with Obe's death and realized the strangeness of those events. He meditated on the past:

'My ancestors recalled a small but very bright star that circled the planet three times, as if analysing our world for some specific purpose.

'In those days there were constant intrusions into our territories and cities by the Petan Dragons. Food was scarce, causing them to prey on most life. However, in our case they were only interested in our nectar stores. The agile flying reptiles would be carried by the strong air currents from the Great Chasm and skilfully use them to glide into our city.

'It was during one of those struggles that the Grand Lord arrived. Then it was Obe and Om-Chopter that saved the day. The fearsome dragons seeing the sight of such a glorious spectacle were awed and scattered into the four winds. Since that time they

thought the Kanei were the specially chosen and never vandalized our city again. That time was over a generation (1500 Earth years) ago. It was well before we knew about splitting the atom and modern day technologies. Presently Petans move freely through our cities and frequently visit Om-Chopter's monument on pilgrimage.

'At that time the Grand Lord appeared as if out of the brightest light like one of my great warrior ancestors, Obe. There he remained in full view of everyone and in full radiance like a god, which he was. His appearance shook the high priest and holy men of that time. Our culture has never been the same since. Yet, before his arrival we were a stagnant species, with very basic technologies and contented in a simple living off the land on a daily basis.

'If anything, the Grand Lord revived my people and gave them a real purpose with a more positive reason to exist for the common good of all life within Osmaron. And that was not all, he realized the needs of the Petans and placed them securely within his plans. After the conversion of my mother and her subsequent promotion as the most royal Empress Duty Queen, changes began to occur throughout my world for the good of all and not just the Kanei, my race.

'To make our people feel more secure, the Great Wall was built soon afterwards and constructed to a great height. It was just high enough to prevent hungry Petans from gliding over using the air currents into our territories. Since then, all Petans have been kept well at bay and even now, the weapons of my people have become too powerful for any local intruders to circumvent.

'After those changes, even the worst of the Petans realized peace was always to be preferred over war. They could always receive nectar and other essential requirements through trade. Presently, both species are almost as one. There is always trade between us with mutual respect on either side. Gone are the days when we feared each other. All that was due to the intervention of our Grand Lord. In but a short time he significantly changed the direction and course of all life on my world.

'*Presently the great metropolitan city of Lud straddles the southern plains like a crystal gem. With its tall sharp crystal spires still remaining on its oldest buildings as a constant reminder of our distant past. Since that time its varying modes of transport and communication had expanded even to our local moons. All needed to handle our ever expanding civilizations within Kalboron. With future programs and enterprises for other globular clusters and more within inner Osmaron.*

'*Since that time we have grown from little babes and are now one of the most powerful within the whole galaxy. All that was due to Obe and his unselfish sacrifices for us all.*

'*And beautiful Om-Chopter remains a constant memorial to that incredible period of change throughout our world and elsewhere.*

'*Soon after our Grand Lord's arrival, the Royal Palace was built towards the west of the Great Wall and included the Great University of Goh. It was sometimes called the University of Lud. That was where special scientists and engineers were rigorously trained. It was here that the first Shadites came and went, finally to face the dreaded Labyrinth of multiple values and concepts in the face of extreme dangers. It was indeed the final test that could sometimes take one even beyond the boundaries of death itself; the final baptism before immortality could be attained.*' Lumak pondered those incredible thoughts while calibrating some of his most sensitive equipment in order to squeeze the last drop of efficiency and amplification from them. He was presently the commander of a Black Ship in space, trying to find new civilizations for conversion to fight our mutual enemy the Javols.

CHAPTER 6

The Grand Council convenes
(In the wake of the Javols invasion of Osmaron)

Universal Time.... Ten point five ex nine cyclons, universal.

Period.... Secondary Serenic.

Place.... The Sixth Plane within the Plenum of Goh.

Within the galaxy of Andromeda an advanced human civilization called The Ancients had created a new Nano-bot life-form. Although initially intended as an almost indestructible warrior, with the unique ability to exist within virtually any hostile environment, something went wrong during their experiments for the perfect soldier. They caused the existence of the most dangerous Nano-bot creatures called Javols. Those Javols were almost indestructible and soon took control to quickly destroy the world they called Silo along with all its over 10 million human population.

Being Nano-bot and metallic in design made them resistant to most weapons and very difficult to kill. Further, they were able to change their forms at will, to the point of becoming invisible or take on a different form. That way they could camouflage themselves from their enemies. Then they could link themselves together and become a single giant monster to create more havoc. Afterwards they would separate into individual Javols to feed. They enjoyed feeding on biological creatures like us. Such were the powers and desires of the great monster they had created.

The rapacious Javols' organism required certain chemicals in the form of iron, phosphorus and others. Those could readily be found in the bodies of most primal life. Therefore they found all life with blood flowing through their veins an easy and convenient source for food.

Once they realized their powers, they considered all naturally evolving life, known as Primal, to be unnecessary in their plans of domination and would use all such life solely as food. To secure our survival, it became imperative that immediate action was taken to stop their unrelenting progress leading to the extinction of all primal life within the universe.

SERIOUS DANGERS AHEAD

Presently they had destroyed almost all animal life within the galaxy of Andromeda and were on their way to the local galaxies. They were expected to arrive within Osmaron (our Milky-Way Galaxy) and Earth in the near future. Therefore we were to prepare well in advance of their arrival.

Presently Earth's humans and other Primal civilizations within the local galaxies had no knowledge of their existence nor relentless progress to devour us all.

Grand Lord Gerra, one of the Gohran supreme beings of the seven universes were normally restrained from direct involvement with lower life-forms. However he must now intervene to assist all primal life within our sector of local galaxies. His direct actions would be imperative if Primal civilizations were to survive the Javols' onslaught. Therefore a meeting was called to discuss those important matters. That urgent meeting between the seven Gohran supreme lords was held within the Greater Mind.

'*Lord Gerra,*' Grand Lord Rahmann commenced. '*For several millennia we have been aware of the dangerous situation fermenting within your seventh part of the seventh universe. Although within your home region, we all face perceived consequences should this Javols' blight become endemic... Thus leading to the inevitable disruption of all life, not only within your home and third galaxy, but also within the neighbouring first and sixth parts of our primal universes... From what I see, the consequences to civilization could be dire.. should this disease continue to spread uncontrollably.*

'*Judging from your previous reports it is inevitable that many young and promising civilizations will follow the same course as the Andromedans... to ultimate extinction within but a few generations.*

'We further appreciate your inability to engineer any significant causal change by way of force or agreement, in order to impede their progress within that galaxy. They are not of the primal type and will not communicate or compromise in any agreement for mutual benefit.

'Because of those and other less prominent factors of which you are doubtlessly aware, we are of the opinion that you are unable to alter future events significantly within that galaxy.

'In light of those observations we are not pleased, but nevertheless welcome your present report on current developments and perhaps any new plans and suggestions you may offer to this council. Hopefully, by way of a solution for the eradication of this rapacious and impetuous blight from the seventh part of our universe once and for all time...'

Grand Lord Rahmann was always forceful in his utterances and never known to mince his words. His other six brothers respected him for those qualities. Nevertheless all seven supreme beings of the seven universes had existed since the beginning of that plane of seven universes, and were each unique in their own attitudes and aspirations.

Being super-intelligent, they soon realized that power for its own sake was a flawed way of reasoning. It took many to make a whole, each with their own unique attributes and abilities. They also realized that all life should be free to evolve and set their own bounds within the Cosmos and not be impeded by any forms, least of all by evil Javols; for such were the ways of The She.

After Lord Rahmann had finished his speech and resumed a lower stature within the ring of power, another Grand Lord stood up. Sarius, now Chairlord of the then presiding council of the rotating Heptarchal Nexus turned his gaze to Lord Gerra:

'Lord Gerra, we now require your visualisations on this most unpleasant matter...' He uttered those words in a calm but sharp

telepathic thought.

Within the large plasmic swirling chamber were the seven rulers of the known universe, each portraying a different type of visual representation. Their forms depicted the most predominant life on their respective adopted worlds within the more disordered, lower dimensional and temporal planes of their dual existence.

They would transform themselves into the most intelligent life-form and take up residence on any one of the suitable chosen worlds within their dominions for a period of one thousand cyclons (1600 years). That way they could always remain in touch with their evolving children and in the process guide them along a more positive direction in line with the Greater Purpose.

Although not of matter nor of any substance known to our present material universe, the great Gohran beings appeared almost transparent in that misty and boiling plenum of the Greater Mind, within the innermost sphere of Gohenna or Goh. But there were many small balls of light that formed above and beneath them in groups of seven. Those were the messenger entities they called Luminites. Ever so often a group of seven would descend. Then they would spiral away from a ring of light into the darkness of the great void.

That unbounded void of the Greater Mind extended to infinity in all directions, if indeed concepts of direction were relevant in such a plenum. The Luminites obviously carried some form of causal information from their meetings to other dimensions or levels of power within the seven universes.

Grand Lord Gerra was now a beautifully coloured Semonite. He resembled the giant bee-like warrior called Obe, when viewed materially. He extended his height above the other seemingly seated forms in order to address the Grand Council.

'Grand Lords and others of the Heptarchal Council of Universes, may I address the primary questions posed and others indicated by Lord Rahmann's opening speech?' His thoughts were clear and precise.

'There is indeed little doubt that the Javols pose a great threat to all primal life and ecological systems within our universes... although not immediate. They have not yet acquired the necessary technologies to cross intergalactic distances within periods less than two thousand cyclons (about 3200 years). That technology will not be available to them during the next millennium.

'This inability on their part allows us enough time to plan our strategies and prepare Osmaron and other local galaxies, by unifying all main civilizations within them. Those found useful will be suitably trained and introduced to higher levels of technologies in anticipation of an invasion.

'I must further emphasize, that neither we Gohrans, nor our Ploran colleagues can in any way intervene by way of direct participation in any wars or destructive measures which in themselves will lead to loss of life and the disruption of the natural order. We have taken an oath to preserve life at all cost and cannot be seen to partake in such ventures. I have therefore appealed to the Greater Purpose for the reawakening of Jull, the Patriarch Warrior and family members. They will be reincarnated at the appropriate time. He is to be assisted by several younger civilizations more suited to the task ahead.

'As you may remember, he and his father Aron successfully assisted us in neutralizing the Mesotrenes and Hexolytes during the upheavals of the Juvine Period.

'We have observed several of the Javols and know well their resourcefulness and insatiable rapacious nature, not to mention their mental capabilities. However, they are not a creative species and tend to individually specialise within narrow fields. This tendency to copy and rely on others for science and technology has always made them week and mentally inflexible, although the opposite is true of their physical nature. I am sure this aspect of their mentality was an in-built part of their original programming. They acquire their information from those they enslave and learn new technologies by taking things apart and copying their designs.

'From data received, we can accurately calculate incursion times for all local galaxies and prepare well in advance of their arrival, while taking into consideration gradual improvements in their own technologies. Further, we should realise that most of the advanced life within their own galaxy would have disappeared into insignificance well within the period of one millennium. In light of those visualizations, I have decided to have the galaxy Andromeda seeded with many screened observation probes. They will observe their progress on all counts and inform us of any change in their modus operandi.

'At an appropriate time, the few Andromedan survivors will be evacuated to Osmaron, assisted by my Shadites. Lord Vektron and others have supplied the necessary technologies for the construction of an Omegron Portal of incredible range that will link both galaxies together. I shall assign one of my best Shadites to the task of finding suitable worlds within Osmaron for the purpose of conversion to Class 5 technological status. That level is just ahead of the Javols'.

'In the interim period, many black ships and maulars will be dispatched from Osmaron. They will arrive in Andromeda just after one thousand cyclons. Their main function will be dual: to plant new and fully screened replacement observation probes within the system and to deceive these Nano-bot Javols into believing our technologies to be of an inferior nature. Thus giving them little reason to pursue a course in creating very advanced technologies. Hopefully it will induce a false sense of power and superiority in the minds of an arrogant species set on universal domination.

'By so doing, most of the primal technologies within their home galaxy, Andromeda, will be lost well before they are able to harness them constructively.

'Grand Lords, you can appreciate the enormous task we have ahead of us in unifying those local galaxies, with numerous life-forms, each differing in their technologies, perceptions and languages. Because of the urgency of this matter, I have decided to take direct causal action in all stages of the unification program and will appreciate any encouraging efforts on your behalf.

'*As you all know, direct causal action has not been initiated for several billion cyclons; not since the meeting of two parallel universes at a critical stage in the development of our home universe. That was when the more ancient Mesotrene Universe met our relatively newly habitable and rather energetic one. Then due to a rift in the space-time between the universes, forming several connecting corridors and giving passage to their kind we were invaded.*

'*It was then necessary to use force to chase those unwanted Mesotrene settlers back to their own dying universe, but not without first having imparted to them the necessary technologies to rejuvenate their own universe. At that time we learnt that it was sometimes expedient to take direct action if any part of the whole was severely threatened by infectious viral invasions that was detrimental to the whole. It was then essential for us to assist the antibodies of the host universe in whatever ways necessary against those attacking from the outside.*

'*The situation now is somewhat different; for although the whole universe could be infected eventually, there is the much longer time scale of perhaps several million cyclons, given their possible acquisition of class seven type technologies. However, even without attaining those levels, the Javols will eventually seriously alter the natural order. Our present survival matrix will change in favour of one with little adventure, creativity, love and other more humane aspects of being, which is essential to a normal primal existence... Thus threatening all civilizations to a type of slavery within a dormant survival culture as observed within Andromeda. This change in the status-quo or natural order of primal evolution implies a form of black death to all advanced primal intelligence throughout the universe.*

'*Many species will become enslaved or absorbed as mere food supplies and those that pose a threat, made extinct in the process. By all accounts, the disruptive mess is much too great to contemplate. Therefore, direct causal action is necessary at the highest level, but in such a manner as not to detrimentally affect civilizations that involve primal species below Class 1 levels of technologies.*

'This new criterion interferes only slightly with the natural evolution of those life-forms and hence, does not preempt prime directive two... "In order not to detrimentally confuse and retard, by allowing young evolving primal systems and civilizations to adopt technologies not of their own making..." unless prime directive one was enforced, ... "Natural evolution, advancement and continuity must be maintained at all cost for the benefit of all primal structures and evolving systems and their species,..." The Javols are not primal structures, neither are they evolving in the truest sense of the word,... and are therefore excluded from this equation.' Grand Lord Gerra addressed, emotively.

Grand Lord Gerra had the right to invoke direct causal action if it was essential for the survival of all primal life within the universe. He knew that he could not have been outvoted by this council currently in session, knowing that it was soon to be his turn as Chair Lord. During his time of office he would be able to sway their votes in his favour. However, the implementation of direct causal actions meant he could partake and intervene directly with his many evolving worlds within the seventh parts of all seven universes, and the Plorans, who were directly under his command could also be involved more directly.

Each of the seven grand lords rotated positions every thousand cyclons. They rotated their office just after the general stock taking of their respective universes, and after they had completed their future plans in line with their directives. It was after that time that they would find a new adopted world on which to settle.

'Lords, we have currently registered numerous civilizations within the other two local galaxies, ranging from point nine upwards, but so far have not contacted a leading culture with the attributes necessary to take the lead within any one of those galaxies.

We are now searching some remote civilizations within Osmaron and elsewhere. I am presently awaiting reports from my Shadites within those systems.

'I am therefore unable to lend any further relevant information

at this session, but will inform all members of this council as and when more relevant data becomes available...'

Chairlord Sarius now focussed telepathically on all members.

'May we put the Direct Causal Intervention matter to the vote? I should however stipulate that such intervention will only be undertaken by Grand Lord Gerra. All such action should be relevant to his dominions only.' He paused as they lifted their wands of status.

'The vote is carried. I must therefore thank my lords for a unanimous vote in favour of Grand Lord Gerra's intricate plans and now, may we continue with the next topic on the agenda.'

Grand Lord Gerra, Supreme Lord of the seventh part of all seven universes was very pleased with the voting outcome. He was now free to indulge in new forms of technologies and most of all, meet many diverse life-forms within the galaxies at risk from invasion. Not in many aeons had he the opportunity to visit so many worlds. However, most of the important tasks would be left to his loyal Shadites and Plorans. They would be the ones to clear the way and teach those life-forms new types of culture and technologies.

Nevertheless he realized that the almost indestructible and rapacious Javols would soon overrun the whole of the Andromedan galaxy, destroying and absorbing all its numerous life-forms in the process.

He also knew numerous Javols were on their way to Osmaron and the Triangulum Galaxy. The task ahead was truly enormous.

The Ploran Lord Vektron and his people were pleased with the outcome. They always wanted a home world of their own but could not. They were an ancient race of beings and not allowed direct action in the lives of others within the present universe.

The small colliding Galaxy called Hydra, the harbinger of change, once the Plorans own home galaxy, was presently cutting into and colliding with the remotest parts of Osmaron, and would soon be absorbed in its progress. She was yet unseen by Earth's humans but could now be considered a permanent part of

Osmaron.

This event gave the Plorans full access to our galaxy as their birthright. That aspect alone would make them more protective towards us. In time Hydra would come under Osmaron's own internal controls. Therefore, the Plorans were now equal Osmaronites and would take a firmer stand to defend their new adopted home galaxy against the invaders.

Yet, all those populations will be safe for now... to develop their new brand of technologies aided by his loyal Shadites, and hopefully prepare themselves well for when the numerous swarms of Javols' begin to arrive within those doomed galaxies.

Hopefully, with the aid of the more advanced minds within the three galaxies, many civilizations will be brought together and solutions found to neutralize the rapacious foe before they are able to multiply and take root; for after that, the galaxies and their Primal civilizations could be forever lost.

CHAPTER 7

Young Lumak

1 Cyclon.... 1.6 Earth years.

Lumak remembered the first time he met Grand Lord Gerra. That experience in itself was a dream fulfilled and perhaps the most exciting moment of his life. He resembled one of his ancient warrior uncles in great detail. That was the one who's giant statue was positioned centrally in the main square. His painted images was everywhere on walls and in the homes of many.

The only difference between the Grand Lord and Obe was the winged multicolour insignia. It included a central blue circle and was always positioned immediately below his left shoulder.

He had been told numerous times about the great adventures of Obe and his crew with Om-Chopter. Obe's image had always been displayed on a Gaina tapestry that hung majestically in the main hall of his mother's palace. Gaina was one of their greatest artists who only dealt with royalty. He had painted Obe on the mallo tapestry just before he left for Petan lands.

The great Kanei warrior, Obe, was honoured for his many efforts in stopping the Dragon Monsters from invading their cities. The great spikes on the many buildings were another of his brilliant ideas that deterred them from landing. Even with all those selfless efforts he pursued to save his people during perilous times, he had become their greatest warrior and strategist in battle.

Now even in death he was represented by the Grand Lord, almost in person and so real. It was as if he was still alive among family and friends to assist them as he had always done. Now even aged Aurlsba and Longe had accepted the Grand Lord as such. Even though for some unknown reason they knew he wasn't the real Obe. It was just the way the Grand Lord honoured Obe, by keeping his image always alive in the minds of the people.

The Grand Lord was then wearing a beautiful purple tunic with a small cape.

'So... how did it go?' Satcha, his friend inquired.

'It was brilliant! I could almost touch the tunic he was wearing. The scents were all new and incredible.'

'Please, tell me more!'

'I went into his inner sanctum on the words, *"enter!... enter!"*, and stood firmly at attention while he scanned my form. Then he smiled.'

'You come well recommended by several of your peers, Toka, Rodia, Satcha, to mention but a few, and of course your illustrious mother, our empress queen, Ushaia.

'I understand that you are interested in many subjects...biology, chemistry, physics, microidology, planetology, electronics, logics, communications, mathematics... with a slight bent towards the social sciences?

'Do you think you are capable of such an enormous workload?' the Grand Lord inquired.

'Yes, My Siend. I will endeavour to use several types of physical and psychological aids to assist in achieving my goal,' Lumak replied, in a most positive manner.

'Before you can be thought more complex matters, may I seriously recommend a brain implant? It is completely painless, but will expand your mental potentials more than ten fold and can be removed or upgraded as and when better models become available. In your case, this is a most necessary addition; for as your mind grows and your consciousness expands you will gain the ability to perceive in greater depth, and so also will be the requirement for much larger memory storage. You can also link your implants directly with the Greater Mind, further aiding in the analysis of complex problems. Problems requiring several generations of your time to solve on your own, but barely seconds with those enormous resources at your command.

'All that is required by you, once connected with the Mind, is to locate the relevant directories and shelves, so to speak. Its virtual environments can accurately model or simulate any form or condition by a simple thought command. Your conscious mind

may then be utilized purely for conceptual thought, thus eliminating most of the irrelevant day to day psychological noise that distract from a single purpose.

'However, this is your decision to make and will involve a matter of faith in your Lord. Please think about this matter carefully and arrange another appointment with the desk computer on your way out.

'Now I must bid you good day, young one,' the Grand Lord said.
As I left the desk computer interrupted my progress.

'Please select an appointment card. It is valid for one Lyran period.'

I took the card and memorized the date and time of my next appointment.'

'A Brain Implant? That is truly incredible. I do believe one day you will become a great Shadite like your mother and travel the way of the stars,' Satcha said.

'It's my dream and only ambition, dear friend.'

'You look worried. Is it about the implant?'

'Yes... I can't imagine what it involves. He said it was a safe and painless procedure.'

'You worry too much, Sut. Most of his people must have them. That's why they can communicate with us so easily'.

Several years later while on another mission, the Shadite Lumak reflected on that period in his life and the operations involved during his brain implants.

Although he was petrified at the time about such changes to his mind, he had little choice in the matter if he was to take advantage of his ambitions and learn of more advanced technologies. Therefore he decided to have the implant fitted during his next visit. As the Grand Lord had previously advised, the process was completely painless and involved a trained robot inserting the tiny nano-bot device into the relevant part of his brain. Then there was the use of a large helmet which was specifically designed for his type of head. It was used for linking his mind to the implants and initial training.

After the small device had been fitted he was again asked to inhale a small amount of the bluish microid dust and given large amounts of information from the Greater Mind to aid in his learning program. All that was before beginning his ten cyclons long university career and a few hundred cyclons ago.

The whole process of the operation took several detons (tens of minutes). It was carried out in one of the bio-laboratories by a strange looking alien they called the Human Plato, who was also Shadite. At that time Lumak thought the strange creature was a god because of his much larger size and powers. It was he who thought him the more subtler menus within his brain implants and the proper use of those Virtual Worlds within the Greater Mind.

'And now, here I am in outer space and in one of the large black ships searching for interstellar life. Even perhaps for strange types like the human Plato, with his overall pinkish complexion and soft fleshy body covering that he called skin. The human creature also chewed his specially prepared solid foods with calcareous deposits he called teeth. He was of the predatory type and always full of emotion, which showed in his soft facial muscles. How strange these human types were, with vocals similar to Petans and no sense of pheromones whatsoever.

'That Human was so different from my kind, which didn't have flexible jaws and lived only on rich nectar and certain juices that were crushed from cultivated fruit berries. Those fluids were sucked into mouth cavities with a retractable proboscis like a tubular tongue.

'So many varied and different life-forms exist within our universe. Yet, many followed a similar path and purpose during their evolution. Those were usually guided by the loving arms of the Greater Purpose, despite the enormous cultural differences between them and the great distances separating their relevant worlds and systems.' He thought such matters out for a while, reflecting on the enormity and purpose of it all.

'If only we had the powers to transfer minds from one life-form to another, then we would be able to sense the emotions and

feelings of others. Then we could see the universe through the eyes of others and in the process feel their problems and fears as we do our own. By so doing we would be able to understand and empathise more with others, thereby reducing misunderstandings and wars. Then we could judge all cosmic life to be equally important, despite their relative levels of intelligence and advancement.

'It is quite sad that we are always so selfish towards all outsiders and assist in the survival of our own species at the exclusion of all others. Nevertheless although different, most intelligent species must aspire to the same basic needs and goals at relevant stages of their evolution.' Lumak pondered, then sadly reflected on the death of his close friends Aurlsba and Longe.

'What a great honour... The Grand lord went to their funerals. He said he would take them into his glorious arms and keep their spirits in a safer place, out of harms way, until their next corporeal existence.' Lumak pondered over those thoughts with reverence and sadness.

Somehow, Lumak knew the Grand Lord had the powers even to bring the dead back to life. But Aurlsba and Longe were now too old for that and would be reborn into a brand new existence at a later date.

CHAPTER 8

The probing of Osmaron

In the wake of the Javols invasion of the local galaxies, the Shadite Lumak was given the responsibility to scan the two local galaxies, Osmaron and Triangulum, for intelligent life. That new mission was truly enormous but urgent. He realized that once suitable life was found they would have to be educated and trained in more advanced technologies. There was only about 200 cyclons (320 years) left before the Javols arrival in Osmaron and not enough time or Shadites available to probe the two local galaxies. Therefore many probes were dispatched randomly to listen for signs of any intelligence.

Presently Lumak's main task was to locate all unknown intelligent civilizations within Osmaron, but he was keen on finding just one unique civilization suitable for conversion to a higher technological level. Then they in turn could assist him in probing for others.

Given the urgency of his current mission, Lumak began his new task with great enthusiasm and much planning. His crew were well chosen from known Kanei families and always competed. Nevertheless it was a task more akin to finding a needle in a haystack than a systematic and orderly search based on experience in the field.

Initially he tried to gain as much information as possible by linking his mind directly with the Greater Mind.

He continuously scanned its many libraries for information on intelligent life. All information received that way was either too ancient or their type already included in the Greater Purpose. In past the recording process relied on its own methods of stock-taking and tended to ignore those civilizations with lesser classification than three. Those below level 3 were assumed too young for any direct involvement in the Greater Purpose.

Not being too successful with his initial searches, he dispatched more powerful eavesdropping probes to specific locations within the galaxy. He was then aided by the ancient Plorans, who had previously supplied his people with very advanced technologies. Then he patiently waited for a response.

A FINE AND LOVING CREW

Lumak's crew was suitably chosen so he knew well their capabilities. He realized that in time one of his many methods would find an easier way to locate his quarry, so his course was one of trial until he found acceptable solutions during an enormous task.

He had tuned his receivers to many frequencies and analysed numerous planetary systems of varying technologies. He was only interested in the range from one to three on the technological classification scale. Below Class 1 was considered too young.

He had set his sensitive automated probes to detect non repetitive sequences of electromagnetic radiation within specific frequency bands. At present he refrained from using H-wave technology. He considered that form of inter-dimensional communication too advanced for species below Class 4.

Each sensitive probe received and analysed data while scanning their specific regions of space in order to ascertain the precise location of the source of those signals.

As usual there was always much competition among his on-board departments and his few over-enthusiastic soldiers always tried to gain more favour in his eyes. However knowing the consequences of dishonesty and underhanded behaviour, meant such healthy competition always followed rules of fair play. Even so, Lumak's own personal team usually won the day among a ship of most efficient operators.

His present crew was close to home and chosen from well known families on his world. They were direct relatives of Aurlsba, Longe, Napta, Seth and others. However Jamkai represented his own family. Each were head of their own groups and constantly fought for recognition and promotion.

'Oommm... This is going to be an almost impossible task,' Lumak thought aloud, not finding even the smallest thread of creative thought to follow or guide his enthusiastic efforts during his current search.

'Jamkai, I've had enough of that galactic arm for now. Let's target the third and most unpopulated one in the system. I have a hunch we might find something out there,' he said, while pointing a claw to a part of the large 3D galactic image of Osmaron. Lumak usually followed his haunches and for some unknown reason that one was strong.

'But My Siend, that arm is the least populated and contains many dead and dying worlds close to the rim,' Jamkai replied.

'Yes, I know about that. They were obviously destroyed by predatory species in times gone by. But those monsters have since left those unfortunate systems. Anyway, send a few probes just beyond that volume of space. It is possible that the predators didn't go very far beyond that region. Anyway, I must know what's out there. Even when it's uncharted.' Lumak moved closer to the 3D holographic projection and pointed to a small region within the galactic image of Osmaron. Then he left their operations room for some well deserved rest.

Lumak and most of his crew had spent the best part of two sleepless days and nights in his quest for new civilizations so their bodies needed rest. In just three hours he was back on his feet, took some nutritious juice from a local dispenser and went directly to the ship's main communicator. Lumak realized he needed a new approach and new ideas seldom came from a tired crew.

'My most beloved crew and its many competing family teams. May I take this rear opportunity in thanking you for your many sleepless sacrifices. But those of you who are too tired to open your eyes may now take some well deserved rest. Take as long as you need... But not more than six hours!' There was a sudden mad rush for their different cabins. Then he glanced at Jamkai and he also disappeared, leaving Lumak all on his own in that part of the great black ship.

The Kanei language comprised of pheromones, gestures and

guttural hissing sounds. On-board communicators were designed to relay just the pheromones and sounds through special molecular detectors and transceivers. That method was usually quite adequate for remote communication. Gestures and sounds were considered more respectful and personal. They would sometimes travel many kilometres to communicate that way with each other.

After having recorded large amounts of data that were superimposed on background noise, the computers filtered yet another sequence in the low energy spectrum. That information appeared to be of no significant importance, and he continued his analysis in his usual methodical manner. Obviously such transmissions could only be propagated by a very young civilization. One with very little, if indeed any knowledge of H-Wave technology. Then surreptitiously he noted the source of the communication. It had come from the new area probed by Jamkai. It was within the region previously considered unpopulated by any important civilizations.

'This is unreal... almost an impossible chance.' Lumak double checked the source, but could not believe his senses.

Three Ploran probes were precisely aligned and targeted in the direction of the source, just within that spiral arm of the Osmaron galaxy. That part of the galaxy was inconspicuously situated and well beyond any commercial pathways.

Nevertheless analysis of the received data over the next few ryons - slightly longer than one Earth-day period - would confirm the existence of advanced life in that region. At least those in that stellar system were able to communicate with electromagnetic radiation and that was good enough.

His present task was to translate and collect data from the information received for analysis. Then he would be able to chart their type, cultural norms and bio-profiles. It would then be necessary to establish certain parameters, like surface temperature, planet size and mass, atmospheric constituents and other equally important factors to aid in the formulation of a more extensive planetary profile. In any event, high levels of free oxygen would signal the abundance of primal life, given the use of visual probes within the vicinity of the system in question. During such surveillance a more detailed picture could only be gradually enhanced over a long listening period.

'Wooo... That is fantastic news! I shall send three of my best Ploran probes ahead of the others. The other three can be slowed and used as H-wave relays.' Lumak muttered those words to himself in the absence of his chief engineer, Jamkai.

An excited Lumak immediately dispatched three advanced Ploran probes towards the source, then relaxed and waited.

Ploran probes used a form of inter-dimensional drive and could travel across our galaxy within a single day without time dilation. It was a technology that was currently beyond the knowledge of his Kanei people. They had been made by the Octans and were almost massless.

All sensitive Ploran probes and most of the main computers on board ship were directly linked to the Greater Mind. It would analyse and translate the bulk of input data using primal evolving concepts, while linked to billions of conceptual equations. The Greater Mind almost knew all and its incredible powers were made available to Lumak because of the urgency of his new mission. It was only a matter of time before he received communication from the Mind as intelligible data flowed in a continuous stream from those distant probes. The received data was full of ordered sequences with little distortion and breaks. Nevertheless the three recent probes were still on their way to the system in question. All data would be significantly improved as they approached their target system.

CHAPTER 9

The Greater Mind

It is well known that the Greater Mind functioned at all levels and had existed since the beginning of our universe. It held knowledge of all advanced civilizations since then and contained previous sciences and technologies within its many Virtual Worlds.

Since the Greater Universal Mind was cosmic in scope it encompassed all planes, dimensions and universes. It was inextricably linked to all Shadites and advanced civilizations that were within The Greater Purpose.

Presently the great sphere resided within Kalboron. It was known to always follow the Grand Lord to his new residence. It was like a large bluish planetary globe that permeated the whole system with a strange bluish glow while following a similar orbit about the parent star. The massive globe was not composed of normally vectored matter, but was an extension of Grand Lord Gerra's own body in space and time.

That part of his being was itself the mass of a stellar system, but engineered in such a manner as to show virtually zero mass within our space-time. Being at a higher dimension it was impervious to all normally vectored matter in space and time. That way it did not occupy normal space to hinder motion and life within the regions it permeated.

It constantly absorbed radiation from the parent star for some physical operations within that plane and by so doing emitted a slightly bluish haze. Some considered the Mind to be Gohenna itself; a type of heaven chosen ones went to after corporeal existence. It was sometimes called by the shorter name of Goh, but it was thought that each of the seven Grand Lords or Supreme Beings of the Seven Universes had similar Mind Globes and Gohenna represented their mutual points of intersection in all planes, universes and relevant dimensions.

Within the Greater Mind virtually all things were possible. The Mind was a conscious living entity in its own right and could on its own accord act without the presence of the Grand Lord. Yet, it contained part of the Grand Lord's psyche. Therefore to all intents and purpose he and the Mind were one.

It was also linked inter-dimensionally to other minds, including every Shadite and Ploran within the known universe.

TECHNOLOGICAL CLASSIFICATION

The Mind utilized technologies learnt during tens of billions of Earth years. The most advanced of those could be classed technologically as ex nine or Class 9 on their classification scale. That form of classification represented a linear knowledge and expansion in intelligence over a period of ten to the power of nine (1000,000,000) years of continuous advancement. Zero time on this scale referred to the time of their first successful nuclear test ±1 year. This method followed a simple equation, where for $x \leq 0$, Years $(Y) = -(1/10^{\wedge}(x)$ and for $x > 0$, Years $(Y) = 10^{\wedge}x$. Where x is the Class.

This in human terms represented a period of about one billion years of advancement since the invention of the atom bomb. Since many species evolved socially and technologically at different rates, this was just an average value and measured well with human development. After all, most predatory and warlike species like humans tended to evolve similarly, with periods of aggressive turmoil and peaceful coexistence.

There were also periods of pestilence, pandemic disease and natural disasters. However the negative aspects of survival speeded technological advancements, while peace tended to make people more complacent. Therefore the two extremes tended to cancel to give a near constant rate of advancement.

By so doing, all species that had split the atom were considered to be at Class 0, technologically. However such a classification also went the other way and Class Class -1 represent 10 years before Class 0 By a similar method of comparison Class -9 represented a period of -1000,000,000 (-1 billion years) before

Class 0. This classification from -9 to +9 represented technological advancement over a period between -1000,000,000 and +1000,000,000 years. That way, all advanced species could be compared on a technological basis and assisted as and when required.

Obviously, for longer time scales Class 10 and Class -10 could be used to represent +10 billion years and -10 billion years.

Such a high classification of the Greater Mind almost represented the beginning and end of all knowledge. But it was thought that those limits could never be reached, since any new knowledge gained further shifted the boundaries. Nevertheless the Greater Mind contained information since the beginning of our universe, and that knowledge was about every major event in history.

Even so not every important event in history had been recorded and the process of recording such information was always biassed in favour of the most well known civilizations above Class 3. The lower and less advanced were simply ignored and allowed to grow and advance in their own chosen ways.

Within the Greater Mind contained Virtual Worlds of all possibilities, wherein any experience could be sensed or felt, or any material object created for virtually any purpose. Further, all such creations could be transferred into our physical universe (the real world) by a simple process called substitution. This was done by the simple replacement of the Virtual Object by an equivalent mass of water or a simple chemical, mass for mass.

RE-SITING THE GREATER MIND

After the Grand Lord had fulfilled a thousand cyclons (1600 years) on a chosen world, he and the Greater Mind would move to a new and more relevant one within his dominion in the seventh universe. That world was usually above Class 3, but his choices also depended on his future plans. Then he would take the form of one of its primary life-forms and continue his long-term plans. Mostly it was to lend assistance to his primal children and save them from themselves or from other unseen threats against which they were unable to survive.

His methods would in time align all universal life within the Greater Purpose for the benefit of all evolving primal life throughout those universes. That form of newer order benefited life much more than the random prey versus predator survival game played out throughout the Cosmos, known to many as the Natural Order. To us Earth humans, that method was more akin to an oasis of democracy within the most brutal and savage desert of random coexistence. However with the blessings of the Grand Lord and his long-suffering Shadites, that oasis was constantly expanding to encompass our universe and beyond.

All Shadites had been given the unique ability to assess all of the Mind's libraries for information relevant to their missions. Since the Mind transposed through all planes and dimensions, they could utilize its numerous powers from anywhere within the known universe for technology and travel. In most cases the large buckles on their broad metallic belts could be used to gain entry to its innermost corridors. Grade 1 Shadites like Lumak could access all its facilities directly through their brain implants.

CHAPTER 10

A new civilization

Lumak's special probes soon entered the stellar system within that unknown part of Osmaron and began to relay information via H-wave while orbiting.

The Greater Mind connected and a thought suddenly entered Lumak's mind through his brain implants. It was accompanied by a flood of visual and other relevant information. From the data stream The Mind had constructed different models of the primary life-forms and other diverse cultures within that strange world. The most intelligent types existed in two basic independent forms, male and female. They mated randomly and gave birth to mostly singular young dependent offspring. This method of procreation led to virtually no population control. They were so unlike his own kind whose queens mated seasonally and only when there was a need for new offspring. Within his culture the individual's survival was based on functions within the hive hierarchy that was composed mainly of sexless individuals. Those life-forms were more like Petans.

'Wow! A complete human world... and so different to our own,' he thought aloud as he contemplated the differences using the Shadite Plato as a reference. Plato was the only human type he knew.

He wondered how well he and his kind would cope in a world of predatory humans. As he surveyed the strange world, he could observe no great softland forests floating on its oceans, or indeed any visible craters like the Crethian Bourle. There was no evidence of elevated oceans and seas.

'Surely, this world is much older than mine. Most of its continents have already been worn down by natural erosion over many aeons,' he thought.

The Mind was now computing behavioural norms and attributes

for the species concerned, with probable characteristics due to predicted evolutionary changes over several million generations. That process worked backwards in time, locating relevant nodes and roots on a genetic tree.

Although a once basic predatory species, they had since become very complex with a rich culture. There were thousands of cities throughout that water-filled world. This was so unlike his single main planetary city, Lud, which had been brought into planetary significance during the last millennium by Grand Lord Gerra. The relatively new university city of Goh, named after Gohenna, was currently being expanded and would be even more extensive than his own city, Lud.

The information flooded into his mind in many colours, shapes and sizes, showing the millions of manufactured products and foodstuffs. It was all truly overwhelming. No one, not even The Greater Mind had any idea that such a class one technological life-form had existed in that hitherto uncharted and presumed uninhabited part of the galaxy.

'How could such an important species have existed within the known universe without ever having been recorded by the Greater Mind?' he thought.

Many important questions popped into his crowded mind. One was whether the products and foodstuffs were compatible with those on his own world. If that was so, there could be an exchange in trade.

A human form was presently quite visible, although out of focus. It appeared very similar to the Human Plato, but with much paler features and ten fleshy claws at the ends of its arms to Plato's eight. Other features were quite similar. Yet, their life cycles were so short, barely fifty cyclons (80 years) for each individual. How could such a short-lived species have become so technologically advanced? This factor alone would have played a major part in retarding technological growth at the higher levels... not enough time to pursue a truly difficult project and witness its completion. Yet, they tended to learn quickly from each other and were highly creative and imaginative.

Population growth would also be a considerable problem with such a heterosexual society, without specific population targets and a natural mating period during each year. This in turn would lead to a critical culture with high death rates due to new strains of disease, as nature tried to compensate. Nature always optimised a species for its own survival causation and would take the bugs out of the cupboard when they went contrary to her long term survival goals. Population growth limitation was one of her easier strings to pull when a population became too large for its environment. If nature failed that problem could always be further assisted by bio-engineered viruses. However a clever species could always find ways around nature. They would quickly find antidotes to her pandemic diseases and make machines to compensate. Such civilizations seldom survived extinction because of such blind methods.

He now had a relatively clear picture of the life-form and their sociological profiles. There were several similar species of choice within the Mind's libraries and the human Plato's type was the most obvious, having met and communicated with him over a period of several cyclons through their special implants. They had also become good friends, even in their different incompatible forms.

He decided to scan through the Mind's libraries to gain a thorough knowledge of such predatory species. During that time he observed several bipedal forms, ranging from reptiles to cat-people and after some serious thought decided to classify the new life-form within the same category as Plato's type.

Having woken from several hours of well-deserved sleep, Lumak found himself transposed to one of Grand Lord Gerra's private sanctums. Perhaps it was all in his own mind; for the technologies of the Mind were awe inspiring where virtually any environment or form of reality could be simulated or created within its domain.

The Grand Lord came towards him, casually.

'Ah... Sut. It's inspiring to see you in such a perceptive mood having acquired your first roving success. Have you completed an analysis of the current situation, in light of our mission's

objectives?'

'Yes, my Siend,' Lumak replied with certainty.

'Then what is it to be?' the Grand Lord asked with keen interest and anticipation.

'I must visit the strange world and establish relations with its people. Obviously, not in my present form.

'I am to initially absorb their cultures and over a relatively short period of time, learn of their intimate likes and dislikes, assisting whenever I can under the cover of some benevolent organization. When the time is right my real duty will be to explain certain facts and advance their technologies'

'Yes! My son. You are correct in every detail, but you must never expose your true identity to such juvenile species. They are still quite young and immature by our standards. Any premature exposure to our ways could seriously jeopardise our plans and the future survival of our galaxies.

'You will be given all the necessary information and assistance through the Mind. Use the simplex portal and have it programmed for convergence within an unpopulated area of that world. The three probes that are now in the vicinity can assist in the alignment process. That mode of travel is more practical in this case.

'When you arrive, mingle with the local people for a while until you become fluent in their language and in the use of your newly adopted human form.

'Never forsake them, for it is through their love and affection that you will gain your new human identity. Then from there you may travel to the more populated regions of their world, still helping their kind, until you form important contacts and become known. After that initial part of your mission have been accomplished, it will be just the simple matter of acquiring your new identity papers.

'When you have achieved those goals, you may visit the more advanced natives of that world to establish a more permanent foundation.

'A special white gown has been prepared for your initial landing. You may also use it for your official duties on that world. You can

always use your Shadites' Cloak if you find yourself in serious danger. Several other items have been prepared and will be with you shortly.

'I bid you success and good speed on your intricate mission. I shall require a preliminary report after your immediate arrival to that world.

'And now, may I bid you a temporary farewell?' The Grand Lord uttered the final words while the whole room about Lumak faded into his original cabin. He soon realised he was still on board his black ship and in his bunk resting.

Lumak considered his transformation into a male human type like Plato and dreaded the thought of eating and swallowing solid foods. He also didn't like the idea of becoming a predator that would kill and eat other intelligent living creatures. To him, killing innocent life for any purpose was a universal crime. He wondered whether vegetarians existed on the human world they called Pleron.

From what he had recently learnt, unlike his own life-form with an outer skeleton, their bodies contained an inner skeleton with many organs to process complex nutrients. There was also a single heart that pumped oxygen and other nutrients throughout the more complex body.

In stack contrast, his own body contained many simple glands throughout, that processed all the nutrients absorbed. Unlike the humans with so much to go wrong, all his organs could be substituted and would regrow when they became too old or inefficient in their operation. That was one of the reasons why his people lived well beyond a thousand cyclons (over 1600 years)

Lumak pondered over those ideas, not quite knowing how well that next mission of his would turn out. Despite the very advanced technologies of the Mind, there was always great dangers to overcome on a strange new world with no one to assist. Nevertheless he had always rose to the occasion on previous missions.

Jamkai returned to his desk and continued from where he left, not knowing of Lumak's most fortuitous discovery. It was several hours since he went to his bunk and was not yet updated on the latest findings. When he arrived, the area of their post was filled with supervisors.

'Oh.... Jamkai, please join us if you are up to it!' Lumak shouted, hardly able to hear his own voice above the chatter and excitement.

'Silence! People, I know we have all worked exceedingly hard during this operation, but our team found a suitable first civilization within sector 357. However, you must not be dismayed by our fortuitous successes, there are many more civilizations to discover. Nevertheless, at this time I would like each of you to concentrate on analysis. We need to know everything, and I mean every single thing about the life-forms in question. I shall give a prise for the one with the most thorough analysis.'

'My Siend!' they shouted, ecstatically.

'People, since our main search program is presently on hold, I think we should return to normality and get our sleep as and when required,' Lumak said and many bowed with disappointment and left. They wanted to continue their focus on the search.

'You are telling me you found a new civilization?' Jamkai whispered with excitement.

'Yes... and in the very place you didn't want to search. Good thing my whiskers were twitching at the time,' Lumak replied and Jamkai went forward to check the galactic map. He could now observe six new points within that area, three green and three blue.

'You have dispatched our best stellar probes to investigate, My Siend?' he inquired.

'They will be in close orbit within five centrons (about 3 hours). Then we can make a more thorough analysis of the system. This time we shall take it easy, and give the trophy to another team,' Lumak said and Jamkai knew the score.

Nevertheless his team was the first to locate the target world so the other teams would always consider Lumak's team as number one in their present search. As always, gaining respect and acknowledgement was endemic among Kanei.

CHAPTER 11

Lumak's 13th mission

Within the southern hemisphere on Kanaefon all political conferences and decisions concerning tribal matters would be taken at the first week of the second Lyran period. That was just before the beginning of the dance banquets, when her royal highness was out of chambers. During that time all other queens would pay homage to their Empress and Duty Queens by bringing them gifts. They selected their drone partners during those spectacular court dances.

Workers and Soldiers were not allowed to partake during those most spectacular ceremonies and entertaining sessions. They only supplied the necessary facilities and sustenance.

This was also a special occasion for Lumak while preparing for his new mission. Being Shadite, he had the freedom to do as he pleased, even as a most senior worker. He now had to say a special farewell to his mother and father before setting off to places unknown and could not wait for the awakening of spring. His new mission was going to be a long and dangerous one and he knew not when he would return to his home world.

Dressed in his black Shadite's Cloak he disregarded all social conventions and to the utter surprise of everyone in attendance, walked directly through the winter palace towards his mother's throne. Then he bowed.

'I am to go on a long journey almost immediately and have come to bid a personal farewell,' he said in their strange language with a combination of noises, gestures and scents. She then bowed her head to him and smiled in her own way.

'Be careful my beloved child and take whatever you need for your journey. Give this seal of authority to Chief Worker, Somas,' she replied, showing concern as she handed him the square metallic coin token. Since he couldn't refuse such gifts, he moved closer to collect the item and bowed his head at the same time in a manner of utmost respect, to both his mother and father. On that occasion everyone within that large room remained perfectly still and at attention at the presence of a Shadite.

He bowed to his mother a second time, from the waist, then turned to his father and finally to the group in attendance before walking out with dignity in his stride and wearing that awe-inspiring long black cloak and cape.

From there he went directly to Om-Chopter's memorial to meditate and say a prayer for his lost friends, Longe and Aurlsba, knowing they were safe in the bosom of the Grand Lord.

Then he went directly to the local space port. While ignoring his mother's coin and its benefits, he pocketed the item as a keepsake and boarded one of the shuttles that would take him to the black ship that was assigned to his special mission.

That Black Ship was run by his own chosen family members and the children of seniors of tribes. It contained its own brand of strange alien technology. Nevertheless, they had no authority to leave the Kalboron sphere. They were only allowed to get close to the periphery of Osmaron where the intergalactic noise and radiation from Kalboron were at a significantly reduced level. Here they would set up their sensitive listening devices again and release their much faster interstellar probes. Those large black ships were not capable of intergalactic travel and would have traversed Osmaron just under a century, which was too long a period for that most urgent mission.

Finally he called his senior crew members together, while dressed in the Shadites Cloak.

'So my dearest relatives and friends, the time has finally arrived for yet another of my special missions to a distant world... and regrettably, I must leave you to your own devices however unfortunate they may be.'

'You are leaving us?' a sad Jamkai enquired.

'Yes! This time I shall be visiting a strange human world within Osmaron. The one that you have spent your recent efforts analysing. So you may wish me a little luck on this most dangerous mission; for this time I think I am going to need it.'

'Ahhhh!' they flared with surprise, desiring the great adventure themselves, but Jamkai remained reserved.

'Ahhhh! To those of you with a notion of such adventures, they are fraught with too many dangers. Anyway, I can guarantee that very soon many of you will visit that world and even other unknown parts of Osmaron. But you must wait for Shadites like myself to pave the way. I shall leave Captain Jamkai in charge during my absence. It was his team that discovered the new world, so that's his reward.'

'Ooooooh!' They nodded disappointingly.

'Yet, you have all done equally well with the analysis and I think the gains of my team was mainly due to luck, so this time we are all equal winners and will each deserve a prize. Nevertheless, you may continue your systematic search of every part of our Osmaron galaxy for intelligent life. You must leave no stones unturned. As usual, all such data must be entered within The Greater Mind for a thorough analysis.

'You know us, My Siend. We never leave a challenge!' Jamkai stressed, and the others cheered.

'I shall always be able to check your entries, and at the same time keep an eye on you. I shall always be watching over you from afar. You may remain in touch with me by that method but with short messages, and don't make a habit of it,' he said and they were awed and intrigued by his powers and freedom. They always looked up to Lumak and worshipped the very path he trod.'

'My Siend. Do you know when you will be back,' a concerned soldier called, Miand, inquired. Miand was from Obe's queen's tribe. For that reason Lumak had always treated him with kids gloves; for he was in the image of the real young Obe as he was in the tapestry on the wall.

He was always egging for promotion and was now more worried for his chances than ever with Lumak's absence.

'I am not sure, Siend. I have a strange suspicion that this one might become the most prolonged mission of my life. But I am sure I will see you all again soon if only through The Mind. So don't worry on my behalf. You know, the same thing happens to

Mother from time to time, and she always returns. Anyway, for your many services in past I have decided to promote everyone on this station to seniority. And you, Lieutenant Miand, is now promoted to the rank of Captain,' Lumak replied with sadness in his manner.

That day all his seniors were promoted to captains and they were astonished, for it was two positions ahead of their present rank. As was customary, they offered him their personal keepsakes and jewellery, which they placed around his neck, but he soon removed them and handed them back.

'Come on Guys. You know how I feel about all this sentiment. Anyway, I can't take any of this where I am going.'

'Please take something to remind you of us,' Jamkai begged. Then he took a small silver trinket.

'You just do your jobs to the best of your abilities in my absence, and follow a good and clean path,' he said, sadly.

Then he left his faithful and efficient workers and soldiers to run the great Black Ship as he had done on other occasions. He knew they would follow his every command in the process. Even so, he was slightly fearful of this new assignment as a predator and in human form. He never had those particular feelings and sentiments before any of his previous missions and took it as an omen of some dreadful disaster that was to befall him.

Although Lumak had used the Mind on many occasions for intergalactic transposition, he wondered whether the Grand Lord would insist on him using that mode of travel. Then he realized it was quite possible the Mind did not contain that type of human within its scanning process. Also there were no Black Ships in that part of Osmaron. He knew from previous experience that landing on the surface of a remote uncharted world in such a manner was always a hit and miss affair. It was not always possible to get precise positioning data from the visiting probes.

He would have preferred to make the trip by a specially adapted probe or screened frigate. Then he could choose the area and control his landing. Then he realized a ship or probe would be too large for his landing and could initiate further problems on a populated Class 1 world. Being absolutely alone on that journey, there were many aspects regarding the urgency and preparation of his future mission that concerned him. In particular his day to day survival after landing on that populated world.

Once again he visited his cabin to meditate on those topics and to get a clearer picture, but the worries about his future mission did not abate.

CHAPTER 12

Within the Greater Mind

He walked directly to his bunk to get some sleep before commencing the lengthy project ahead and was soon awakened by a strange figure dressed in white.

'You are to be transposed from here to the innermost part of the Mind. Then your body will be transformed into the human type,' the figure said and Lumak followed.

They entered into a large room with many human operators. Alien equipment was strewn about everywhere. The human operator guided him to a special room with many transparent cubicles. Each containing many probes and other systems unknown to him. He lifted a transparent cover and beckoned.

'Please enter. Your body must be transformed and trained before your arrival on Pleron.' Lumak did not reply.

Lumak knew that on previous missions his body was always transformed during transit and realized this new human type was unknown to the Mind. It was not a standard type and the information would not be updated until he arrived and informed the Mind. The probe sent to Pleron(Earth) could not land to take the relevant DNA samples so they had approximated the human type from observation.

As he lay in the perceived crypt, utter brightness overwhelmed him. It tended to last for an eternity. The top lifted and he was assisted into another area of the room by a semitransparent being in human form.

'As you see, I am also a part of the fabric of this unique space-time continuum that permeates all things. To us a body is but a container used to store an identity and by so doing will anchor us to a given realm or plenum. So do not be afraid of anything,' the figure said. He thought he was dreaming, but was overwhelmed by it all. For a moment he wondered where he was. Nothing in that place was recognizable. He remained silent and followed instructions. Then that place faded into another more solid one and the being became real.

'Your material body has been transformed into a close approximation to the human type, with Shadite Plato as its main template. However, fingers and toes have been suitably altered to mirror the Pleron type. This is only a close approximation. It will be necessary to complete finer adjustments after your arrival on your destination world.

'You must now take a short time to practice and play, in order to learn the strengths and weaknesses of your new form. At the same time you will learn of your new senses and modes of communication. For that purpose special androids and trainers have been assigned. Follow closely their instructions for speedy results.

'Since you have such little time remaining, you must try your utmost to learn the ways of your predatory human type,' he stressed. Then the being communicated with others telepathically and they entered the room.

'Your body matrix must also be altered in transit. This is necessary if you are to survive a physical ordeal on route. You may even survive the unlikely event of your body entering a stellar environment. Therefore you must reinstate your mass to normality by revectoring after your arrival. This is done by adjusting and pressing the large button on your belt buckle. Make sure you have safely arrived on solid ground before full revectoring. After that operation your body will be as fragile as the natives of that world.'

Then he was eagerly escorted to another room for training. Once more he was left on his own without any assistance. This time he was made to stand in front of a body scanner close to a wall. Then another operator came forward to assist.

Lumak suddenly tried to move his feelers, but there was no response. He tried to feel them, but his face was soft and his body completely changed, with different conflicting senses and urges. Even his vision had suffered. It was less sharper, more tunnelled and limited. He soon realized his inadequate perceptions was real and due mainly to comparisons made by his brain implants.

'You are now a male type of the human species. Your implants have been programmed with some habitual data. You are expected to update and modify that information after your arrival on Pleron,' the operator said. Then he took him to another room where he could exercise. Then he left.

Lumak remained perfectly silent as if in a daze. By now he had become disoriented and felt his many urges and senses completely jumbled and intermixed. To him it was like finding one's basic mind in a brand new body and having to relearn simple functions like breathing, feeling and walking all over again. Not to mention the strangest sense of smell. Then there was liquid pouring from his eyes and many other emotional responses he knew nothing about, giving him the most peculiar urges, likes and dislikes. He realized the human type was optimized for a certain environment on the surface of a planet where chemicals and other dangers were prevalent.

With disorientation came slight nausea and giddiness. Those were feelings he never knew existed. Suddenly his legs crumbled beneath him and he fell unto the solid floor surface in an effortless pile.

He may have been asleep for quite a while, because when he awoke the giddiness and nausea had vanished. His muscle control and senses were still not fully under his control. Nevertheless his new human brain was learning quickly, even without his conscious knowledge, the survival ways of that new life-form. The simulated laboratory conditions were engineered purely for that purpose.

Being now a predator, with eyes focussed forward he was able to see within a much narrower field of view and objects appeared more distant. His special feelers with their sensitive pheromonic sensors had been replaced by a most inefficient nasal membrane. His overall perception and visibility in darkness had become extremely limited. To top it all, he now had aggressive feelings and tendencies, with uncontrollable swings of moods and tempers which was in the basic nature of all such predators. Then he began to view his dilemma with a new perspective while making comparisons with his original form.

'Such a body would have great difficulty living in the dark within the lower chambers of a hive, with tens of individuals moving hither and thither. They must be pure surface dwellers, gathering and hunting during daylight hours and retiring at dusk,' he muttered those words to himself in a strange new implanted language, but his lips were not moving.

He suddenly became conscious of long threadlike hairs on his head and shorter ones on other parts of his body and thought, 'here is a similarity'. But in this case he was not sure of their uses other than for protection against the environment.

Although his imagination ran freely, it was only a matter of time before the Mind would further enlighten him on their true nature and purpose. He was expected to transcend those experiences himself as part of the learning process. The Mind would only assist when he was wide off the mark in his analysis, and really required that new knowledge. Most of it would have been too confusing and may have been modified or seldom required after his arrival on the new world.

He then realised that his new human senses, all things considered, were a lot simpler than his original. His present vew of the world was mainly visual, without the added colours, interleaving of pheromones and subtler scents. He could no more sense the substance in any given material by smell alone and was only limited to light reflected off surfaces.

However the internal organs within the body were quite another matter.

'Little wonder those organisms lived a mere fifty cyclons (80 years). So many things could go wrong on the inside... and outside with such soft fleshy tissue.' Then he sighed with tiredness and once again fell asleep.

Lumak had to take another two days to learn the use of his strange new body. During that time he had not attempted swallowing solids. He was placed on a very stringent program of exercise for developing his strength in relevant areas. In all that time and despite his welling hunger, he was only given nutritious liquids to drink. Somehow the idea of eating solid foods was way beyond his imagination and the effort appeared not worthwhile when one was able to take fluids as an alternative.

Once again he found himself in front of the senior figure.

'Your training has been completed. Your time here is finally at an end. You should therefore prepare yourself for your journey.' Then he took Lumak to another cubicle.

'To where are you taking me now?' Lumak inquired aggressively, with rebellious tendencies. He had constantly been moved from pillar to post and had enough. But the figure ignored his disagreements through his implants.

'You must answer my questions if you want me to cooperate with your ridiculous plans!' he again begged. The predatory instincts were beginning to surface and he needed reassurance. He was not yet able to form fluent words to speak aloud and that aspect worried him.

'Your trip is in the morning, so please have some more rest, and prepare yourself well,' the operator said and locked the door behind him. The place was so white and brilliant that Lumak had no idea that he had been taken to a larger cubicle for confinement.

'Get me out of here, now!' he yelled over and over with his newly found voice until his speech was almost normal. Yet he continued punching the door with his fist to get their attention, but no one came to his assistance. He felt utterly lost, betrayed and ignored. Tears began to flow down his cheeks where he stood. Then he knelt before the door and his tired figure fell into deep and certain sleep.

CHAPTER 13

Humble beginnings

Lumak eventually awoke fully refreshed from his long sleep. After coming to terms with his new situation was finally ready to depart. As he left his bunk he became aware of a presence within the large cubicle. He realised the figure was that of Grand Lord Gerra, but it was difficult to know with certainty. Those images and perceptions could equally have been generated by the Greater Mind.

Having had his long rest, he was much calmer than before. His rebellious streak had dissipated. Nevertheless he was no Semonite that blindly followed instructions. Like a rebellious adolescent he always wanted to know more about his activities and safety implications. Yet he had faith in his Lord and knew he always meant well.

His environment faded into another. The Grand Lord now stood close to a large casket. He withdrew three items and placed each on top of the flat surface that separated them.

'Do you feel better?'

'Yes, My Siend! The long rest appears to have done the trick,' Lumak replied through his brain implants.

'Don't worry, it will soon be second nature.'

'Please come forward,' he suggested, in a mild voice.

'You are expected to wear these three items at all times. They can be made invisible through your implants. Only you may wear and use them. They are tuned to your psyche.

'This winged insignia and medallion with the blue inner circle represents The Greater Purpose and what we stand for, including your Shadites' Clan. You are required to carry them on your person at all times.

'The wrist watch contains a timepiece, compass and a micro computer. You may use its many modes through your implants. It resembles a type currently used by many on your destination

world so even if it is misplaced no one will appreciate its more subtler functions.

'You must keep the utility belt hidden under your outer gown at all times. Its functions are well known to you. Being a Grade 1 Shadite, you may control most of these items directly through your brain implants. The hooded Shadite's Cloak of Goh should always be held at close range. It is now an important part of your being.

'The White Gown will give good protection from the environment and can be used to conceal those items. Its pockets are able to shrink whatever they contain. The White Gown should be worn until you are able to attain the local native's attire. It can be adjusted through your implants to more suit the native's mode of dress.

'You may, when ready, enter the third cubicle in order to be revectored and transposed to your new destination.

'I shall await your immediate report and god's speed.' When the Grand Lord finished saying those words he faded into nothing, but Lumak's strange surroundings still remained, as if waiting for him to change his clothes and follow his Lord's instructions. Those bizarre occurrences once again reminded him that he was within the Greater Mind of all possibilities.

He clipped the belt across his waist and struggled until his body was contained within the White Gown. Then he moved forward to collect the smallest items which he placed in an inner pocket. To his utter amazement they simply disappeared. He pretended wanting them through his implants and they reappeared at about quarter their size in the pocket. They returned to normal size when they were fully retrieved. He played for a while with the strange behaviour of the White Gown learning its different modes of operation.

'This is incredible!' he said with amazement and smiled for the first time as a human.

After some slight readjustment for comfort's sake, he fixed the insignia unto his gown just under his left shoulder. Then he folded the Black Cloak into a neat bundle and placed it in a concealed inner pocket.

He fitted the small disposable oxygen mask over his face and walked into the third cubicle. For a brief moment he observed the six striped walls of the transposing unit. They looked bizarre and remained perfectly still. They were covered in equidistantly spaced bands of silver and black. The furthest walls appeared white and seemed to recede to infinity. The silence in that area was cutting and the anticipation nerve racking for any human.

There he stood and waited. When least expecting the cubicle came alive. Then the bands began to pulsate and alternate. The strange motion sent his body into a spin. His feelings of nausea returned with more tears flowing down his cheeks. He wanted to get out but all entrances were sealed. All those unexplained feelings soon changed to one of overwhelming fear. For the first time in his human existence he screamed at the top of his voice in an attempt to overcome those human weaknesses, while the portal device took his body away to a place unknown.

Suddenly he was completely overwhelmed by a very bright light which seemed to penetrate everything including his very soul. Then he felt himself swimming in a sea of liquid energy and yet he was moving towards somewhere.

He was now travelling through what seemed to be a long tunnel of the strange substance. After what appeared to his senses to be a period of one deton, approximately ten minutes in Earth time, the tunnel walls began to acquire a darker shade as the moving black bands expanded at the expense of the silvery ones, until he could only see complete blackness.

'Ooooooooooooooh!' he screamed. That long breath continued almost until his arrival on the surface of the world they called Pleron, known to its humans as Earth.

As if through his brain implants his screaming stopped and he felt his feet rest on an uneven surface. To make sure he rotated the knob on his belt buckle by about 15 degrees. With a quick snap both ends of the tunnel vanished. He remained stationary in that position with slight disorientation, while observing the single moon shining through the partially clouded sky. It was then that he realized he was not on his home world or indeed anywhere that he had been before. 'Made it!' he yelled with a happy smile.

Everywhere around him was almost in complete darkness, but for the erratic shadows cast by the bright moon. Many shadows were from what he considered to be unknown vegetation and local hills. He checked his posture and body orientation while stamping his feet several times to sense the density of matter underfoot through his implants. He was to ensure that his almost massless body was on terra firma. When he was absolutely certain, he pressed the buckle on his belt to vectorize his body into the normal matrix of that strange world. Then he removed his oxygen mask.

'I can breathe! Everything appears normal and I'm all in one piece,' he murmured, while touching several parts of his body to ensure nothing was missing.

He was presently on his own on Pleron, the name given to his new world by The Mind for reference purposes. The same was called Earth by its many human inhabitants. The reality of his ordeal suddenly became apparent when he felt the cool night breeze against his face, to be accompanied by a myriad smells and sounds. Most of those he thought his human brain would grow accustomed to in time. After all, he was on a human world with human senses. Others he would ignore, while sifting out only those sounds and smells required for his own survival and safety. He knew that the special drugs in his body would temporarily protect him from all contaminants including viruses until his immune system kicked in.

He must now find a comfortable place to rest for the night and consider future plans before his frail body became much colder. He buried the disposable oxygen face-mask which would dissolve in days, leaving behind no visible trace of his arrival to that world.

His sudden presence must have caused a major disturbance in that quiet area of the hills. The local dog began barking and would not stop. It soon ceased its barking when the occupants decided to take firearms and search the area for any would-be trespassers and thieves.

'Father! Do you think it's more refugees from the border!' Sarah exclaimed in Turkish.

'Could be! But I'm not sure! We always have to be prepared for the worst! Ben replied. He only knew the Turkish language.

'Come on Spotty! You sniff them out and I'll do the rest!' Ben shouted and the search was on. The dog Spotty was a quiet and methodical hunter and would not give up easily.

Spotty followed his nose to the place of the disturbance, but could not pinpoint the exact position of his quarry.

It was not long before Lumak heard a sound and saw what appeared to be a little predatory monster moving in his direction. From what he could observe in the limited light, the animal was much smaller than a human and ran on all-fours. He thought for a moment about his safety, but decided not to use the Black Shadite's Cloak unless absolutely necessary. Anyway it was important to make first contact which was difficult in his present situation.

The dog passed a few metres from his temporary enclave, but doubled back in a confused manner in his direction. Its very sharp calcareous canines showed a formidable white in the now brighter moonlight, even reminding Lumak of those dreaded reptilian flying Petan Dragons of his own world. Although he could have pressed the buckle on his belt and re-vectorized, he was not the type to be easily frightened by those close encounters and such technologies may have caused further problems. Using mild sounds which he strained to vocalize, he began to whisper to the animal, trying to calm its emotions by friendly persuasion. But the creature became even more agitated and continued back towards the direction where he lay hidden.

The quadruped was again called by name, which sounded like "Spotty" and the animal trotted off towards the more sheltered rocks. He didn't realize the animal had already discovered his location and had gone to fetch its master.

In those remote parts of Turkey, trespassers were always unwelcomed guests and many would fire their weapons first and ask questions later. Over the years there had been much unrest in the southern areas close to the Iraq border and country folk were always weary of strangers.

'Is it an infidel or a refugee, I wonder?' shouted Ben.

'How should I know?' replied Sarah, nervously, gun in hand but fearless.

'Check the local woods and I will check the banks... be careful!' he yelled, as if in full command of the situation.

He new Spotty had located its quarry and wanted his daughter Sarah to be well away while he made the arrest.'

It was not long before the nozzle of a strange primitive weapon pointed directly at Lumak's head, to be followed by a nervous command coming from the male figure holding the gun. The dog Spotty came close while sniffing at his reflective attire. That strange robe of Lumak reflected light in rainbow colours because of an active force-field.

'Stand still or I'll fire!' Ben shouted in Turkish, while pointing the torch directly in Lumak's face, temporarily blinding him. The light was too much for him so he closed his eyes and placed his hands above his head. He didn't know why he had adopted that particular posture of submission. It just seemed the right thing to do at the time. Lumak knew little of the meaning of the words uttered, but realized from the man's expression that he meant serious business. He remained completely still while the human came closer to quickly search his person for a weapon. When he found he was unarmed and observed his strange attire, he nudged him along somewhat impatiently towards the house. The wind was gaining pace from the south and carried with it dark clouds, which meant the beginnings of a prolonged and heavy downpour.

Lumak was surprised and confused by the events of those few moments. Nevertheless he decided to act his present innocent stance. It seemed to reap the most benefit during his present dilemma. He was also unable to communicate with his captors. The language they spoke was beyond any form of interpretation by his brain implants. He also realised, in those few brief moments, that his pinkish complexion was completely different to the local natives. He would have to find speedy solutions to those personal problems if he was to be accepted within their tribe. That was assuming he survived his present ordeal

'By Allah, what do we have here?' Ben exclaimed, sarcastically.

'Over here, Sarah! See what I have found!' Although sometimes annoyed by refugees steeling their crops they always assisted with food before sending them on their way.

She immediately appeared on the scene, again followed by the faithful canine. The dog was almost jet black with spots and stripes throughout, hence the name Spotty. He continued sniffing the alien for a while, not quite knowing what to make of his strange scents, then gave up and left for the comfort of the house.

'Do you think he is a spy or... What is a person like him doing in these parts... way up in these hills?' Ben asked, expecting an intelligible comment from his daughter.

'No father, he can't be a spy. Just look at his clothes, and he doesn't appear to have weapons of any kind. But he could be one of those foreigners on a pilgrimage or religious quest... perhaps even a doctor. He could have got lost and took the wrong path,' she replied, eyeing the strange figure and pulling at his white gown as if to test the strange fabric. It seemed to reflect the low light in different colours. Sarah was highly intuitive and soon realized the strange character did not pose a threat to anyone. Then she searched him for a hidden weapon.

'Dad! Dad!' she beckoned. While pulling her father away for a few quiet words.

'Dad, no wonder he is freezing. He has no underwear, whatsoever. And that cloak of his acts like its alive.

'Yes daughter, I know! He is a very unusual character altogether. And that cloak of his is quite strange. Almost like its alive.'

'He could be almost frozen. He has no weapons so lets offer him a room for the night. We could let him have mum's room.' she said.

'How do you know he is not a ninja warrior or someone with a knowledge of the Martial arts. He could kill us in our sleep?' Ben inquired of his daughter.

'You search him again then and I shall go to bed,' she replied, as if intolerant of her father's nervous disposition in a situation that warranted less. Ben then signalled the stranger to come forward again for another search and this time found the strange belt. It appeared to be made of a flexible metal, but there were no weapons on his person. Bengizara Khan realised some merchants and tradesmen sometimes hid their money in large belts in case of bandits and thieves, and soon handed the items back to Lumak. Then he shouted to Sarah.

'He is clean! One hundred percent clean, my daughter!'

'Then please bring him in out of the cold and I shall prepare the little room for him.'

'My daughter, what if he is still an infidel or criminal, with a knowledge of the martial arts. I shall have to take him to the village even at this late hour and hand him over to the police. They can sort him out. I will not risk our lives by having such a person in my house and under my own roof!' he insisted.

'Is he dressed like an infidel, soldier or bandit, Dad? He is more like...' she paused for a while, looking him over again in the bright lamplight. She then realize he was wearing flexible golden sandals that went up to his knees, which to her was indeed strange.

'Anyway, it's getting late and cold, with bad weather on the way. We cannot visit the village now for the police. We can figure him out in the morning,' she added, with a yawn.

Although Ben was not in full agreement with his daughter, he always preferred to keep the peace. In any case he could not subject a stranger to the cold winds and frost of that gloomy night. Not anyone in such a state and with such inadequate clothing. Neither was he going to endure a drenching or the freezing cold journey to the village police. Without further argument he held Lumak's hand and pulled him into the living room.

Sarah made a few noises of displeasure while preparing the little room and soon came out holding a few unwanted small items. The house contained four large rooms, a courtyard with sheep pen to one side of the house. That property was well isolated from other local plots. Their family had lived there for many generations.

'Dad, I have cleared a few things from the small room and made the bed with two clean blankets and a pillow. Perhaps the stranger might like a hot drink before retiring?' she inquired, again with another yawn.

'I don't know,' replied Ben.

'He doesn't appear to understand or speak a word of our tongue. He is so different. I just can't place his kind.' Ben then pointed to a cup on the table.

'Drink! drink!...' He shouted at the stranger, while moving his hand to his mouth in gesture. Lumak, realising what he meant from Plato's strange eating habits, shook his head and opened his eyes in a positive manner.

'Dad!' yelled Sarah, from the kitchen.

'Why don't I make us all a chocolate drink? His pink features could be due to prolonged exposure to the cold weather we have been having recently. Perhaps due to poor blood circulation.'

'Perhaps?' Ben replied, still not convinced.

'It's our responsibility to take good care of our guests, you know and he doesn't appear to be well.'

'Whatever!' Ben was tired and getting impatient.

'The field doctor once explained those symptoms to me when I was working with the refugees over the border. He called it hypothermia,' she said, as she lit another oil lamp and departed to the small kitchen to prepare the drinks.

A now worried Ben took the stranger and placed him close to the warm fire. It was always in his nature to be hospitable, but the stranger was unknown and those factors worried him. After all, they were just poor shepherds and had to obey a strict regime in order to survive.

Lumak took the drink with him, while being ushered into the small bedroom. The door was suddenly shut and bolted from behind him as he entered.

The room was quite bare, with a small paraffin lamp on a little bedside table, but there was no electricity or signs of any moderate Class 1 technologies. Although still cold, he felt restful and decided to drink the observably hot but bizarre concoction of almost boiling liquid before retiring. Despite his recent tribulations he was enthusiastic about his safe arrival and wanted to communicate those recent experiences to the Mind for a full analysis. He also thought that perhaps the Mind could analyse the strange language and update his implants with a full cultural profile of that tribe while he slept. He could then slowly change his physical appearance more in line with the natives or perhaps another distant tribe. Since his arrival, most of his original fears had dissipated, but he still had to gain the confidence of his new adopted family.

He removed his outer gown and fitted the Shadite's cloak with the broad belt. After he was relaxed and realised everyone was asleep, he pressed the small button and the buckle together and concentrated his thoughts. Then he downloaded all his experiences since his visit to Earth.

It was not long before The Mind responded and just before dawn a full language profile was downloaded with the necessary instructions for changing his present appearance. He became excited by those possibilities and suddenly realized he could never be alone on Earth while the Greater Mind was always there to assist.

Achieving the necessary physical changes were quite straight forward and could be accomplished with the use of bluish microids (nanites). The capsules containing the strange powder was found in one of his belt pouches. That process would take barely a few seconds each night while wearing the black Shadite's Cloak.

Although he was able to make changes to his biological system, he was careful not to move outside of what he considered acceptable bounds.

CHAPTER 14

A new family

Earth time... 2041 CE

Planet... Pleron (Earth)

Just after dawn he was awakened by Sarah. She knocked three times on his bedroom door before noisily releasing the latch.

'Are you decent!' she inquired in rough English, with the intention of getting a response from the stranger.

Although a little apprehensive at first, Sarah had plucked enough courage to take him a hot cup of her own brand of green tea. She did not know how to address the situation of his presence, but was usually a brave individual. Being a keen hillbilly, she was not used to having guests and was quite shy of strangers, particularly young men from foreign countries. Lumak carefully took the cup from her and closely observed the creamy substance for a moment before placing it on the nearby table.

'It's hot tea, with milk and sugar. I hope it's to your liking?'

'Oooh,' he bowed.

'Breakfast will be ready in an hour or so,' she said in Turkish, while making a few relevant gestures. Then she carefully observed his pallid features for any positive signs of recovery from his supposed hypothermia.

'Than..k you!' he replied in English, forcing the words out of his brain implants. Since his arrival it was the main language in his implants, and he realize she knew a few words.

'So you speak English? I am afraid my English is not perfect.'

'Ye..s!' he replied.

'You look much better today.'

'Ye..s!'

'I was right. Your complexion was mainly due to the cold and you could have been in shock from over exposure when we found you. My father was also a bit unkind to you. He used to be a military captain, you know, and sees infidels and traitors everywhere. Please forgive us. We are poor shepherds and have to be so careful these days.'

'Ye..s!'

'Anyway, do you feel better now?' she inquired, sympathetically and in reasonable English.

'Much ... bet ... ter ..., thank ... you. Ta...mam' He replied monotonously with a few well chosen words in her language. He had included more details of that language among others since his recent update but had never communicated that way before.

'So you do speak a little of our language as well? You can remain here for a while to recover, if you wish. This place is isolated and no one will ask any questions. Although Dad gets aroused at times, his bark is much worse than his bite, so ignore him for now.'

'I would like...' Lumak replied, still monotonously.

'In that case, would you like to help me with the sheep?

'From the weather reports, it's going to be a nice sunny day today and a little exercise might help your circulation. The fresh air will also do you some good.'

'O..k!'

'Dad has gone to the village to collect some groceries for me and will be back quite late, so he won't be around to argue the matter.,

'O..k!'

'It is Saturday, you know? And there is much work to do. Anyway, if he follows his normal stops he should be back before noon. That is, if he doesn't decide to have a few games of dominos with his village friends and spend more of the grocery money on unnecessary items. It will give us enough time to take the sheep to the hills and come back before he returns.' She was quite excited by the idea of a newly found friend.

'Do you have many ... sheep?' Lumak inquired.

'Just one small herd of twenty-six. Sometimes it gets larger. But I can't handle much more than that number, even with Spotty's assistance, so we sell off any surplus to the village butcher after the lambing season. It so happens that you just missed the birth of our last lamb.'

'Oh...!'

'We also have a horse called Saracen. Dad saddles him during the daytime, when he is not harnessed to the cart.'

'I un...der...stand! Do you also eat ... these creatures?' Lumak asked with curiosity.

'I don't personally, because I am a vegetarian. But my father has on occasion.'

'Oh...!'

'Do you also eat meat?' she inquired.

'No! I am also vege... tarian.'

'In that case, I am very pleased to meet a fellow vegetarian and kindly join me for a vegetarian breakfast.' Then she placed her hand out and he shook it firmly with a broad smile of approval. She had always been a good judge of human nature and somehow knew her present company was of little danger to anyone. During that time of the year shepherds and vets were busier than usual with the ewes and lambs and hers were no easier task.

Sarah left, but soon returned with a pair of brown corduroyed trousers, a white shirt, a light blue jumper, thick socks and leather sandals. She dumped the items on his bed.

'Put these on. They will keep you warm and are more comfortable to wear.' She said, staring at his strange attire with golden sandals.

'Thank you, Sarah!'

Although very much like a fish out of water, Lumak felt a lot more settled within his human self. His predatory feelings, although still within him, did not surface and he soon realized that most of those emotional responses were due to hormones and uncertainty. Those emotions were necessary when faced with certain dangers and the mammalian form reacted quite differently to Semonites in that regard. It seemed that what hormones did for humans, pheromones did for his Semonite people. The only main difference was that pheromones were airborne and came from others, while hormones came from within the human body.

He followed her into the dining room and after making many

mistakes due to his clumsiness, assisted her with breakfast. Then they sat down and began to eat, drink and chat. Sarah was fond of oats porridge with cinnamon, toast and coffee, and introduced Lumak to the same. Since he was not yet used to chewing solid foods, he spent a long time masticating the contents before swallowing in uncomfortable gulps. That was until the swallowing process became less self-conscious. Occasionally he would cough and splutter but coffee served as a good lubricant during those episodes.

'This area is not suitable for sheep farming, you know. Not enough grass for proper grazing. So I take them up to the hills each day. Up there the vegetation is much greener but the winds are colder. I enjoy the view from the hills, it makes me want to go places and see the world.'

'Sou..nds like a very ni..ce nice place to be.'

'Where are you from and have you been in this area long?' she inquired, choosing her words carefully and not wanting to offend her companion.

'I am sorry... Sarah, but I am unable to re... re... member my name. Neither am I able to... to... fill you in on my past. I am sorry for my lapse in mem... ory,' he replied robot-like but apologetically, while translating the data through his brain implants.

'You mean to say, you have forgotten all of your past, including your own name and family?' she replied with a sarcastic demeanor.

'Everything beyond you ... finding me in the bush is... is still very hazy to me. You might have to wait a little ... little longer for answers,' he said, still looking ill and pinkish, although not as much as when found on the previous evening.

'You speak a few words of English with, I think... an American accent, so that must make you an American with a little knowledge of Turkish. You could be a doctor or someone with a high education,' she conjectured, while probing his features for any signs of origin, but could find none.'

'Perhaps, but I am still not ... not sure,' he again stuttered, trying to form those delicate sentences.

'Don't you carry any papers?'

'I could find none. Could have lost them in the hills.'

'You must not let dad know of your present situation. He tends to see red in everything and might think you are a foreign spy. So I shall give you a temporary name and you must keep well away from the local police and militia. Since the southern problems a few years ago, we have had more than our share of murdering vandals and refugees. Now, everyone in these parts are over sensitive to unknown visitors, including tourists.'

'I under...stand!'

'I once knew an English doctor... by the name of George Peterson. Yes, he was called Doctor George Peterson. The poor man got killed just before he was due to return to his home in England. He and several of his colleagues were blown to bits by one of those large missiles when his building took a direct hit. That was a long time ago, so dad and the local people will not know of that fact.'

'I see!'

'You can use his name for now and must attempt to relearn your English language by listening to the radio. I shall get you some English books when I next visit the village library ... Remind me also to get new batteries for the radio. You must play along with Dad and don't give too much of your weaknesses away. Anyway, he only understands a few words of English, so pretend to speak to me in English and only a little in our language,' she advised forcibly, further observing carefully his pallid features.

'I under...understand!' he again stuttered.

'You are a very strange one, you know. Perhaps you are one of our ancient prophets, returned from the grave to accomplish some great purpose.'

'I don't think so!'

'Do you also pray? Never mind! You will learn soon enough. Since my mother's death, bless her soul, I decided to pray twice daily. You may join me after supper if you wish?'

'I don't mind!'

'Come now and help me clear the yard and take the sheep to the hills.' She encouraged insistently.

While observing her every move, he clumsily assisted in clearing and sweeping the wet yard. Then he followed her to the large old pen where the sheep and other animals were kept overnight. She called the dog and unlatched the lower half-door.

The sheep soon began to walk out of the stable in pairs and retraced their instinctive route towards the hills. Spotty followed from behind while keeping the stragglers in line. The lambs were many and playful and spotty had his work cut out.

'Spotty!' she yelled and the dog came running towards her while wagging his tail. Then she grabbed his jewelled collar and took him over to Lumak.

'He is my best friend, you know, and a hard worker at that.'

Lumak hesitantly followed her every move and fondled the dog's head, sometimes gently pulling his ears.

'Hello Spot..ty!'

Spotty accepted him as a new member of the family and soon darted off towards the herd, while wagging his tail and resumed regrouping the few persistent strays.

'These dog creatures... they are so unlike the sheep, they...' he paused for a while.

'Dogs are carnivores. They can also be predators and scavengers, while sheep are mild-tempered herbivores. Because of the sheep's mild nature, they are natural prey for most predators.'

'Oh?'

'Untrained dogs can be a great danger to sheep. They enjoy killing them, you know. I was once told that all dogs were originally taken from the wolf family, which happens to be a natural enemy of sheep and most other animals. Wolves can kill and eat almost anything including humans. But they are not a threat now and do not live in these parts anymore.'

'I see!'

She suddenly went forward to assist Spotty with the herd.

'In ancient times life in this place might have been similar to living beyond the Great Wall. This is indeed a harsh world in some areas. There must be a constant struggle, not just against the elements, but also to save oneself from being eaten alive.' He mumbled those words to himself realizing the great differences between both worlds.

The track up the hill was just wide enough to take four sheep abreast and that was with no room for any traffic coming from the other direction. They could only move that way in single-file during an emergency and then one would have to act quickly because of the almost vertical drop down the precipitous hillside.

Spotty followed closely behind with Lumak while Sarah led. For some reason the flock preferred her in the lead and raced along with little interference from Spotty and Lumak, who now followed at a quick pace. It took them close to forty minutes before they arrived at the plateau. It was lushly covered by very green grass, intermingled with the occasional daffodil and white lily.

It was now early spring with large amounts of moisture on the ground and in the air. This was mainly due to the early morning frost soon to be melted by the morning's sunlight. The ensuing mist at that altitude might have aided the plant growth. In the distance they could observe a high waterfall which reminded Lumak of the Great Chasm's wall. But the waterfall on his world was over 70 kilometres long and 7 kilometres high.

'We have arrived!' she exclaimed, stretching both arms aside to embrace the air, while panting from the brisk walk.

'Do you feel better?'

'Yes, I feel just ..great.'

'Let's take them over to the other side. They prefer the new grass over there and we can return home and see what Dad has been up to.'

He went over to a cluster of lilies and plucked several with their stems still in tact. Then he handed them to Sarah.

'These are for you!' he said, romantically.

'Well... thank you!' she replied, surprised by the unexpected gift.

'I have never been given flowers before by anyone!' Then she went up to him and kissed him on his cheek.

'That is because you are a very nice person!'

On their way back to the house and while close to home they

were surprised to observe Ben's figure in the distance walking briskly towards them.

'Sarah, are you all right!'

'I was worried, leaving you here all alone with this stranger. I know you can take care of yourself but I couldn't help being worried, so I came back as soon as I could.'

'Oh dad! You are now being quite silly. He is a good man and a lot better than some of your companions in the village.'

'Oh!'

'He is an English doctor by profession!'

'An English doctor, eh? Good heavens!'

'Well, he is!'

'What is he doing up here. I mean in these remote parts?'

'He said he was on a mission and got lost in the hills. Then during his wanderings had suffered from over exposure from the cold.'

'I see?'

'He was lucky to have found us when he did and you know the rest.' She replied convincingly, while showing sympathy for Lumak.

'Is he ok, now?'

'Yes, Dad. The long walk and rich mountain air have revived him a little. But he'll need a few more days to fully recover.'

'Good!'

'I hope you didn't mind me giving him some of your unused clothes?'

'No, my daughter, I am very pleased to have any English doctor under my humble roof, and I am happy for him to remain here as long as he wishes.'

'Thanks, Dad!'

'Does he understand our language?'

'Not very much yet. He has only recently come to our country and only knows a few commonly used words and phrases. I think he could have learnt them from a phrase book recently. But he seems to be a quick learner, so you must be patient with him and use gestures when you can. Anyway, I understand a little English, which should be enough for both of us,' she replied, making her father feel more at ease with the stranger. Then Ben changed the topic of conversation.

'Ok, Sarah, enough said on that topic.'

'What's the matter. Dad!'

'It's about Simon?'

'Do you mean Marion's Simon. Our friend who lived near the Mosque?'

'Yes, Dear, the same. You were just about thirteen when they left the lower valley. We grew up and went to school together. Well, he says he is going to move to West Germany. His two eldest sons have lived there for more than two years now. He reckons his sons have become very rich in their restaurant business. Anyway, they have sent for him and his wife, Marion,' Ben said, sadly.

'Why is he really leaving his home and friends, Dad? He can't be doing it just for being close to his sons and their money?' a noble and perceptive Sarah replied.

'No, my dear, his wife has cancer and he thinks she will receive better medical treatment over there. You know, they are very advanced in that country, as your doctor friend and Emil will tell you.

'Gracious Allah! I never knew Marion was so ill! I haven't visited her in such a long time! Oh greatest Allah! I must visit her tomorrow!' Her eyes were tearful.

'The poor woman... I sometimes think we should sell out and also go to one of the more advanced countries in Europe. This is no place for you, my daughter, with so many bad memories and we are forever scratching for a living. Why don't you marry this doctor? He seems to like you. He can always embrace our Moslem faith afterwards, you know. I am sure he wouldn't mind having such a beautiful and hard working wife like you. Then he can take you with him to England and you can be both very happy together.' Ben was quite upset by the impending loss of yet another of his closest friends.

'No, Dad! Are you mad!'

'Have you been drinking Raki?' she exclaimed in disbelief.

'No, my daughter!'

'Anyway, I don't know him very well. He could be already

married for all we know and anyway, I am still a young woman.' Sarah felt very embarrassed in front of the stranger and looked quite apologetic towards Lumak for her father's untimely remarks.

'Well, I am very worried for you, my dear. I can't see a great future for us in this place. Not as poor shepherds in this part of the country, endlessly scratching for a living.' Ben expressed those words with sadness in his voice.

Ben realized that Sarah was now a young woman and as customary in that part of the world, would soon be married, but in the present climate he could not see how to find a way out of their present hardship.

CHAPTER 15

Doctor at large

Lumak was keen on acquiring more detailed knowledge of Earth and its many species, including its local flora and fauna. Earth's plants and flowers were less than half the size of those on his home world and appeared more toxic. He had collected a pocket full of shrubs and flowers from the hillside. Those he laid out on the little table in his room for study and analysis by observation. Unlike his previous Semonite form, with its acute senses strong enough to analyse most items by smell alone, his human senses were limited. His sight was only in a relatively small part of the visual spectrum, and smell was almost non existent. All those deficiencies hampered his investigation.

Even with those problems he was finally getting used to the hormonal imbalance and other emotional turmoils within his system, as his brain adjusted to its new parameters. A sense of normality was at last being felt, but only in the human way. Therefore he decided to begin work towards his final goal and gain a more thorough understanding of Earth and all her life-forms, including his present family.

A happy Sarah had completed most of her daily duties earlier than usual with Lumak's more efficient assistance, and was in the kitchen humming a rock-n-roll tune while preparing dinner. The tune was an old Elvis Presley number called "Jail-house Rock".

Her father had gone to the local temple for prayer and Spotty was quietly sleeping in the dining room close to the fireplace. Ben only visited the temple when he had serious problems and wanted that level of privacy and reverence. He received an army pension and with the odd vegetables and other produce from his land, could just survive. However the cost of living due to inflation was always on an upward spiral and those financial problems were a constant worry.

Lumak had decided it was time for another conference with the Mind, so having latched the door from the inside, unbuttoned his shirt to gain greater access to his communicating belt, which he always wore about his waist below the shirt. The moment he pressed his buckle Spotty stood up and began to bark. The commotion soon brought Sarah out of the kitchen to investigate. Although she could find no one about, she became worried and decided to call Lumak for assistance.

'I am sorry... Doctor... George... for disturbing you!' she yelled, while frantically knocking on his bedroom door. During this time Lumak quickly buttoned his shirt, opened the door and pretended to be observing some flowers while sitting on the side of the bed. However it took a little while to break contact with the Mind and a blueish haze was still present in his room and quite visible to Sarah.

'I think there may be someone lurking about outside.' He quickly followed her while pretending to check the area at the back of the house. The moment he left, the dog stopped barking and returned to its place of rest near the fireplace. They completed their search of the area but could find no one.

'I wonder what caused Spotty to become so irritated and aggressive. He is usually so good and mild-tempered in the house. Anyway, he is very peaceful now and whatever it was must have gone.'

'I am to study some of the rear plants I brought back with me from the hills. I was just about to prepare them for further analysis and had dissected a few. Do you think it could have been because of their strange smell?' he inquired, again pretending.

'I don't know, but dogs are very sensitive creatures and are easily aroused,' she replied and smiled romantically at him and he returned her smile.

'Would you like to come with me to the temple for prayer after dinner?'

'Yes! if you like!' he replied in much better pronunciation and she went back to the kitchen in an even happier mood than before. This time she changed the tune to "Until the 12th of never."

Apparently she was given an Elvis Presley album on her 13th birthday by her mother and had repeatedly played it until most of the tunes had been memorized. The old player and headphones had since passed their sell-by date and currently part of a rubbish pile in one of the corners of Lumak's room.

Dinner time commenced at dusk, just after Ben's arrival. Lumak, coughed, sneezed and spluttered through the spicy meal. Baring the light morning breakfast, it was his first real human meal and his taste buds and other parts of his body were not yet fully prepared for the bombardment of those new experiences.

He soon settled down, however, drinking lots of orange juice to wash the lumps down, which also tended to alleviate the irritation. Sarah was very apologetic to him for putting too many chilies in the very hot curry and he realized it was a good enough excuse for his inadequate abilities. Ben ignored it all and was only interested in satisfying his ferocious appetite.

After dinner they fed the dog with the same and relaxed together by the fireplace for a while, listening to the local radio.

'Dad, I am taking George with me to our temple for prayer. So see you in one hour's time.' Then she put on her shabby old winter coat and pulled Lumak along.

The small temple was more than two hundred metres away to the south and built close to their family's cemetery. That place had seen better times since several more peaceful and richer generations.

Before entering unto its mosaic floor, they removed their sandals.

The old temple building was built in the eighteenth century and had a central larger dome with two smaller ones on either side. They were both suspended by marble pillars. The interior was immaculately kept. Although within Ben's family lands, it was situated close to one of those favourite mountain passes that had been used extensively in the past by travellers and pilgrims.

Sarah always kept several sweet smelling candles burning at the altar which gave the place a unique aura and atmosphere.

Having removed their sandals, Lumak was intrigued by the rear beauty of its interior, in particular its painted ceiling, and quietly followed all of Sarah's suggestions in prayer.

Soon after entering the building she placed him on her right side. As he knelt, he pondered his plight on this strange world. He realised just how much he had accomplished within the short time of just a single day since his arrival to this strange planet they called Earth.

He had now made new friends, and all things considered, they were not a bad lot. Like most species at their levels, they had more than their fair share of problems, but they believed in The Greater Purpose which they called Allah or God and that couldn't be bad.

Yes, he had achieved greatly and would help wherever and whenever possible to ease their lot. The Grand Lord will also be very pleased with his accomplishments but he must continue to have similar successes. As he pondered those thoughts she came closer and nudged him on his shoulder.

'It's time we left. It's getting late!' she whispered. They got up and walked towards their sandals. Then they left the temple with the candles still burning in their cups.

'This is a very old building. Isn't it?'

'Yes, my family used to be very important in this area many years ago and had it built for passing pilgrims and tradesmen. Border wars and general hardship chased everyone away except us. Many have gone off to the cities or foreign countries like Western Europe or America.'

'Oooh?'

'My father and I only remain because my mother was buried here and he still owns most of the lands in this area, which has become almost impossible to sell. He would like to marry me off to some wealthy person and send me away from this place, but I can't leave him here to fend all by himself. There is too much work for any single person.'

'I see!'

'You know, you are the first real friend I've had since my mother's death, which is now more than two years. I see other people only when I visit the village and I am not allowed to speak to strangers or young men. All my girlfriends since school are mostly married.'

'Oooh!'

'Girls in these parts are very shy to make friends with young men, and the old women are suspicious and gossip constantly. So you are a ray of welcomed sunshine and joy in this poor girl's almost dead life.'

'Sarah. I will always be your best friend and we can always find exciting things to do together,' he replied in near perfect English.

'When will you return to England, Western Europe, or wherever you are from?' she inquired, sadly. Lumak was then completely filled with human emotion and felt like stretching his arms out to embrace her, but held back, just in case it was not the socially acceptable thing to do. He turned to her and looked her straight in the eye.

'Don't worry about my leaving. When I leave, you and your father will be free to follow and you may remain with me as long as you wish. Both of you are now my only true friends in this whole wide world.' he replied. She looked him in the eyes for a moment.

'Are you really a doctor and can you heal people and make them well again? George, are you a special saint? Have you come because of my mother?'

'I don't think so?'

'You know, I prayed a lot since she died,' she said with some misgivings and sadness.

'I am sorry for talking nonsense, but when I visited your room before dinner - that was while the dog was barking - I can swear I saw a bluish haze about you and heard you talking to God. You must not worry, your secret is safe with me.'

'Are you sure it's what you saw!'

Lumak was not sure about what she saw during that very brief encounter, but did not intend to furnish any further corroborative information to reinforce or strengthen those memories.

'I am very sorry for the way you found me when you entered my room, but I was very intense in my studies of the flora I collected from the hills. I was observing some bluish petals against the lamp shade when you entered. I am very sorry if the reflection caused you discomfort,' he said, looking very apologetic while acting out his pretence.

'Yes, that could be it. Anyway, don't worry about me, I am now a big girl and used to fending for myself. At that moment I just didn't know where to turn and you were the only one about.'

They were soon back home and chose the living room for greater comfort close to the large log fire.

After yet another nightcap, Lumak retired to his room and slid the inner door-latch in place to prevent further premature interruptions to his program, then linked with the Greater Mind.

He still had to make slight changes to his facial muscles. His original human form only included basic facial movement which sometimes gave him the incorrect facial expressions or not enough for Earth's human type. He entered the new data, inhaled some more of the bluish dust. His body slowly transformed into an almost perfect Earth type human, but there was still the subtler changes made to nerves and muscles. He carefully observed the three-dimensional image of himself or simulacrum in the Mind, while altering many of its features. Finally he held an extensive conversation with himself, grinned, smiled, just to ensure all his facial muscles were in sync. When he was fully satisfied with his newer self, he walked into the place of the simulacrum and the conversion process was complete.

He now had light brown hair and dark brown eyes with a fair but not pink complexion. His face still slightly resembled the Ancient Shadite called Plato. However, he was quite handsome by Earth's standards, with an equivalent age of someone in their late twenties to early thirties. His present complexion was much closer to the natives.

With all those internal changes, his basic features hadn't altered significantly. Yet, he was very pleased with his newer body. The original of which had been fully accepted by Sarah and her father Ben.

He was now considered a very important member of their family. They tended to ignore or overlook his more subtler changes, which could have been attributed to his returning health and present outdoor activities. Nevertheless he never took those changes too far away from the original type to which they had grown accustomed.

As far as Sarah and Ben were concerned, Lumak had almost fully recovered from his illness and had become a very useful extra pair of hands to have about the place. Ben also realised that his daughter was in love with the handsome stranger and would not stand in the way of her happiness.

Lumak gradually enhanced himself over several days, each time letting Sarah get used to the new changes. If for any reason she could detect new subtleties in his complexion and expressions she didn't like, he would make an excuse and slow or even reverse the process. At other times he would improve certain more masculine features, like muscle tone to enhance his physical stature.

Occasionally he would send messages via his relative Jamkai to his other friends and family and they would send messages back via the Mind. Despite his powers to travel anywhere within the known universe, he could not visit his home world in human form. Also he had taken the Shadite's oath and could never visit his family until his mission was completed and his mission on earth had only just begun.

Although a fish out of water from an alien pool and in one of the most backward regions on Earth, he had always placed his faith in The Greater Purpose.

CHAPTER 16

The miracle of the lamb

Lumak had almost fully adapted to life on Earth. With the assistance of the Greater Mind his body had been improved to near perfection, while he became more skilful with language. As usual, he always assisted Sarah with her daily duties including taking the sheep to the hills. In the process she had grown very close to him and vise versa.

'Do they always have young at the same time of the year and so close together,' Lumak asked, while observing the lambs who appeared to be of the same age.

Being a keen biologist he realized it might not be the most natural course of events. The process had to be planned and instrumented at the right time each year depending on the breed. He never liked the idea of tampering with the natural evolution of other life-forms. He knew such meddling spoiled the species, because of interbreeding and genetic optimization by the most dominant predator species, which in this case was Earth's humans.

'We used to call the village vet to artificially inseminate them. That way we could make them lamb at almost any time of the year, but it became too costly. Also, Dad preferred the more traditional methods.'

'I see!'

'Since the gestation periods in ewes are almost the same, we have to ensure they mate at the right time. This is ensured by certain drugs and diet. Then we de-worm them a month before lambing.'

'It's a convenient method.'

'Bir, get back in line!' she shouted and the lambs stopped their frolicking and were back and following their mothers.

'That one is Bir, she is the first born and eldest of this years young. Over there, is On-iic. He is the 13th and last to be born. He came into the world just two weeks before your arrival here. They say sometimes the first can be the last and the last can be the first, and those two are the strongest in my memory. We had just 13 this year.'

'I see!'

'We could improve our stocks with artificial insemination, but that method is too expensive for us small farmers. Anyway, we are happy the way they are and try our best, even when nature is always so unpredictable,' she said and Lumak smiled at her type of wisdom.

'You know them all by name?'

'Yes, I name them when they are born and mark each with a different ribbon. Their names are also written with indelible ink between their shoulders. But I always remember their names.'

'You are so attached to them. They are like your own family. You must love them very much?'

'I suppose it's because I have to take good care of them if they are to survive. You know, they each have a unique personality as well.'

'The young ones are so beautiful and lively.'

'Yes, they are experiencing life for the very first time and will sometimes take risks beyond their natural abilities. This is why we keep a constant eye on them.'

'The process of life throughout the Cosmos is so unique, incredible and fascinating. It must be so, even to the Grand Lord himself,' he said and realized his slip of the tongue.

'I suppose you mean, Allah! Yes, it must always be so for him as well. Now, you know the reason why I can never eat them.'

'But your father does on occasion?'

'My father is a soldier. He was trained to be fearless in battle and can kill and eat virtually anything to survive, and killing is in his nature.'

'I see!'

'Our family is from a long line of warriors, since the birth of Mohammad.' Lumak could see parallels between his own Semonite clans, with Soldiers and Workers specializing in similar tasks as humans, but the demarcation lines were not well defined.

Lumak could not understand why she went out of her way to take such good care of those creatures when she was going to send them off some day to be slaughtered. He soon realized that human society was too complex to analyse by any presumptions on his part. Survival was a complex issue and even more so within omnivorous societies.

While on their way back from the hills that day, Lumak sensed something was missing, but didn't realize what it was. That was until his sensitive ears heard a familiar cry. Then he moved closer to the precipitous ledge to investigate.

'What is it?' Sarah asked, while Lumak stared towards an area near the bottom of the cliff.

'It's a stranded lamb. May have fallen down the side of the precipice when we were not looking. It's alive but one of its limbs appear to be broken.

'Oh my God! Its Bir! She is my very first born. How can I get to her from here. I must save her you know! I must save her! The poor thing must have been there and suffering since morning and without any feed. How could I not have observed her missing?' Sarah cried, becoming ever more hysterical. Then she burst into unconsolable tears.

'Don't worry, I will get her for you!' Despite the almost vertical descent Lumak carefully climbed down the cliff.

The poor little creature realized he was there to save her and tried to move towards him, but was limp, so he quieted her and she remained where she stood. He removed his jacket and tied it about the animal so that her limbs were free and she was easy to carry. He walked along towards the end of the cliff until he could find a lower gradient to climb.

The mother of the little lamb bleated as she recognised her lost child.

'We must keep her warm. Take her into the house and place her near the fireplace. Dad can go to the village and get the vet, but I don't think we can save her now. I am afraid she will have to be put down. It's the kindest thing we can do. It will save her much suffering,' Sarah said with that compassionate look in her eyes.

Lumak did not know what Sarah meant by the words "put down", but realized it sounded like a very last resort and quite final. Analysing everything, he soon took the situation in hand.

'You must both go to the village now. Then one of you can show the vet the way back, while the other can take the cart with Saracen home. Hurry now before it gets too dark.' They realized he was talking sense, so they both left immediately for the village.

He was soon back in his room and wearing his Shadite's Cloak. Since he had no real technology other than what he could use from the special belt, the only person that could save the lamb was his friend, the human Shadite Plato. But Plato was now in galaxy Andromeda on another of his important missions. Nevertheless Lumak was a Grade 1 Shadite and had powers over all other Shadites of a lesser grade.

He soon entered the mind and connected through Plato's implants.

'Plato, sorry for this interruption, but I have an emergency and think you are the only one that can assist. Can you make it on my beacon through the Mind?'

In an instant, Plato stood in the room beside him. He couldn't believe his eyes, for before him stood another human who could well have been his younger brother. He was used to seeing Lumak as a Semonite, but now he was a human and very much like himself.

'Come! I must show you my problem.'

'Plato observed the animal. She had multiple fractures in one leg, a fracture in another and mild concussion.

'When do you want her back?'

'In about 15 minutes.'

'My Siend, that is no time at all.'

'See what you can do, Pal, and keep me informed, in case I have to take some other action.'

Plato's people had the necessary technologies to repair bodies and limbs so he was soon back with the lamb, fully repaired and like a completely new animal.

'Pal, I owe you a lot for what you have just done for me. You know where I am if you should ever require my assistance.'

'Yes, my Siend. Farewell for now until we meet again,' Plato said and bowed in his usual manner, showing respect for his senior. Then he placed his fist on his heart with a slight bow in Shadite salutation and faded from view as if he was never there.

Sarah and the vet soon arrived. It was growing dark and the headlamps of the Landrover shown brightly in front of the house. She rushed into the house and beckoned him to follow. The lamb was standing on all fours near the fireplace with Lumak looking on. The vet, Azize, lifted the animal to observe its frail body.

'There is nothing wrong with this creature. She is as perfect as the Lamb of Allah.'

'What do you mean?' Sarah probed. He placed the lamb on its back again for further observation.

'Don't you mark your lambs anymore?' It was then that Sarah observed that all its indelible markings had disappeared. It was indeed a miracle that had occurred.

'I don't understand. She looks exactly like Bir,' Sarah said, concerned.

'I am not saying she is not the same animal. It's just one of those miracles that occurs occasionally and I so happen to be one of the lucky ones to have witnessed the great powers of Allah,' Azize said.

Sarah stared at Lumak and knew that it was all his doing, but it was all too far beyond her comprehension.

Suddenly, and without warning the lamb began to bleat and her mother responded from the distant pen. Sarah lifted her favourite lamb and took her to her mother. When she returned she could not contain her happiness and excitement.

'How much do we owe you?' she inquired of Azize.

'Not a thing! I haven't been on such an adventure since I became a vet.' He was also the son of Marion in the village and knew Sarah since school.

'Don't worry, Pal. We shall make it up to you in due course,' Lumak replied. Then Azize left.

'I don't know what you did and I don't want to know. You are indeed a strange and powerful one. Don't tell Dad about this miracle. Just let him know that Bir's leg was not as bad as we thought and she will survive.'

Ben arrived much later with Saracen pulling the large mainly wooden cart. He was cold and bleak and wandered whether it was all worth the sacrifice for a little wounded lamb.

'You are getting George to be just as bad as you. We should have put the poor animal out of its misery from the time you found her below the cliff. I hope it was worth all the effort,' he said, feeling cold and uncomfortable.

'It cost us nothing, Dad, and Azize reckons she will live. So there!' Sarah yelled, showing her disagreement.

In all this, Lumak remained as quiet as a lamb, never wanting to inflame the situation between Sarah and her father and neither would he take sides during any of their disagreements.

CHAPTER 17

Love and money

Lumak thought, as far as humans were concerned Sarah was a prised specimen. In that regard he was quite correct; for her body was very well proportioned, with a beautiful girlish face and penetrating light brown eyes. She was also very strong, responsible, resilient and tough, both physically and mentally. It had been acquired from her p
resent healthy and hard way of life. She was a pride to be with; always asking questions about things she didn't understand and yet, being always protective and caring towards him. Of all her attributes, her senses of justice and intuition excelled.

The Worker part of his Semonite psyche could not fathom those deep-seated feelings but his more powerful human emotions tended always to take over, until all his feelings and desires were completely human in content. The predator side of himself was strongest and always had the upper hand.

With Semonites most things came naturally. One always fitted into their predictable routines, while with humans much planning went into simple activities. Every activity appeared to be random, as and when required.

Everyone within his tribe was selected from birth for a specific purpose. Individuals, most of all workers and soldiers, were not in a position to do as they pleased unless they were of high status. But here, he was in human form, pondering those thoughts exactly like a human would. He thought of the wonders of the science and powers of the Greater Mind and contemplated the outcome of those strange sexual urges and desires that sometimes overwhelmed him. Suddenly he changed the focus of his emotions and turned to Sarah.

'Sarah, I would like to visit the city. I think it's time you and I had a holiday together. Can you speak to your father and perhaps all three of us can leave for a short vacation?' he said, in almost perfect English, but with a few Turkish words thrown in to stress the point.

'You have been listening to those radio adverts again, haven't you? You should never take those adds too seriously. All they do is make money out of poor suckers like us. If we decide to go on holidays it will not be with any of those special offers or packaged tours. We can do it at quarter the price if we lived with family and friends.'

'Ah!' he nodded. But listened carefully to her arguments.

'I am also very interested in a break from this place, but who will take care of the sheep, Spotty, Saracen and our home while we are away?'

'We need only be away for two weeks!'

'Two weeks is a long time to go without food and water.' she advised.

'When last did you visit the city?'

'When I was a little girl of about nine years old. My mother took me along when we visited my younger aunt on her side of the family for their wedding. You know, I also have an uncle in the city. Have you got any money?'

'Money?'

'Yes! Money! We'll need a fair sum of money, even for one week's holiday. First of all, we have to travel several hundred kilometres by coach and bus. Then we have to buy food and when we get there, pay our lodgings to the hotel or at least give aunty or uncle some money for keeping us. That is if they have a spare room. In total it might cost us more than two hundred euros and the coach will take at least eight hours for the journey.'

'Everything in this world is so difficult. So many things hinder progress. Although they give the impression they are free to do as they please, they cannot and need money to do everything, and they can only get money by not being free in the first place. Is this really freedom or a false sense of it? What a very strange notion of survival,' he muttered to himself.

'Ok, we get lots of money!' he said to her in no uncertain terms.

'If I had five hundred of your money, would you then come with me to the city?'

'Of course I would.'

'That's settled, then,' he replied.

'If you can get five hundred, that will be more than enough, and also the biggest miracle of all,' she replied, thinking that perhaps his memory had returned and he had recollections of a bank account somewhere.

He now knew where he stood on the issue of finance and would have to think up some new money making schemes very quickly.

Ben had been quietly reading the Koran and was now fast asleep in his favourite armchair. The log fire was burning brightly and the room extremely comfortable and cosy. Spotty yawned and went back to sleep, snoring.

'I must go to bed now,' she said. 'I have to make an early start tomorrow. You can carry on listening to the radio and give dad a nudge before you retire. Don't let him know you listen to the radio in our language, unless you first give him the impression that you would like to learn it,' she whispered in his ear and then left her room.'

'Ok! I will!' he whispered back.

Lumak took the small radio to his room and nudged Ben on his way out.

He had completely scanned the human body through the Mind and knew almost every part, from the smallest molecular structures to the largest cells, then the organs and finally the organism. He also knew the reasons why their cells aged so quickly and how they could be enhanced and repaired.

With the use of bio-engineering even the brain cells could be repaired or renewed, but to his knowledge such concepts, including the technologies of that form of Micro Robotics(nano-technology), were not yet available on Earth. He could not introduce any out-of-order technologies without the Grand Lord's permission. Nevertheless they were within Class Five and that meant he had a free hand in his experiments.

He thought that perhaps he could become someone like a doctor-prophet. He found particular groups of humans posing as religious leaders could always get away with murder and were believed to almost any levels of incredulity.

He also knew that many diseases, in this very harsh environment of Earth, was due mainly to invasions by micro organisms and viruses. But some genetic types like those due to hereditary and cancer, were caused by irreversible changes within the structure of the cell due to faulty genes. It was in the nature of warm-blooded creatures like mammals to generate and enhance the creation of such changes and diseases over several lifetimes.

To Lumak and his Semonite people, the first 100 years of life were just childhood. Old age came over 1500 years later. To him that should be the normal life expectancy of any normal people. However he was Shadite with an eternal lifespan and the powers to change form and become younger or older as he chose. Even with the powers to change into a completely different form.

He reasoned: *'If there were no large animals and mammals on Earth, there would be a significant reduction in such diseases, for unknown to humans they were one of the main contributors to forming an ideal culture in which those microbes developed. Yet, many diseases could now be cured, with the exception of some severe strains of cancer and those of an hereditary nature.*

'Cancer was mainly due to a sudden change in the cellular blueprint or genome, which quickly transferred the corrupted information by replication to other local parts of the body in a manner that did not assist the greater organism. The process was also enhanced by certain chemicals.

'The hereditary group of cancers could be cured by targeting those cells with suitably modified sub structures that had been cloned from the patient's original cells and aided by blueprint inducing drugs.

'The cancerous group could then be destroyed by bio-engineered target cells and viruses with a short lifetime, which while pretending to be cancerous, could then target cancer cells and replicate their kind. Then grow quickly to isolate areas of the cancerous cells from its neighbours. Others could be used to constrict veins and arteries thus reducing blood supply to the cancerous growths.

'With all those changes, the clones could prevent other required nutrients from getting to the short-lived cancerous cells, while preventing their replication. After a period corresponding to just over the lifetime of the cell, they would then be dissolved away naturally within the system. Leaving all unwanted debris to be absorbed by the bodies own defences. But this method could also be aided by blueprint assisting drugs. Those would target most of the good cells and enhanced their replication at the detriment of others. However, in very severe cases this method would require constant re-introduction of the cloned serum before the patient was completely cured.

'It would be so much easier to introduce a million micro robots within the system and instruct each individual to carry out a specific and systematic reconstructive tasks on specific cells within a given location. They could then rebuild the whole system to a new plan, given normal body resources. Cut away old tissue, rejoin new ones, form neuron cells and branches to basic proteins, while linking them into their correct positions... even severed limbs could be regrown in such a manner. It would be akin to building a house from scratch from a blueprint with its many rooms and utilities.

'Here, large amounts of neuron-data could be stored in temporary data stores while the repairs were under way, even in the individual Operator Microids. The complete personality with all its emotions and memories could be stored in a single external memory module. But such mass storage devices were not yet available on Earth. Neither were the complex transmitting systems.'

As he pondered those thoughts, he realised he was not getting any closer to a solution to his current monetary problems. Perhaps the Mind could show him a simpler approach.

There was a gentle tap on the door and Lumak got up to answer.

'I heard the radio. Why are you not yet in bed?' A concerned Sarah inquired, but continued.

'I am worried. I just heard a noise outside my window and when I drew the curtain I saw a bright light coming from the direction of the temple.'

'You did? This is very strange.'

'Yes, it is! I am very sorry, but could you please come with me to investigate. I am a little jumpy tonight and Dad is fast asleep. We can take along one of the shotguns if you wish. They could be bandits or thieves after our livestock,' she said, with a most worried expression. He gazed at her in her night clothes and thought how angelic she appeared despite her moodiness.

'No, it's much too cold for you. Let me go on my own. It's not very far and I can always shout if I need your assistance. Please keep guard here with the other gun and wait.' Then he took the gun, checked to see if it was loaded. He quietly removed the cartridge while she was not looking and went towards the temple along the narrow gravel path.

As he approached he could observe the bright light. It came from inside the building and pulsated for a brief moment before dimming as he entered. There in the dim candle light stood a radiant human form.

'Ah Lumak, there you are!' the Grand Lord said.

'My Lord. I am indeed surprised to see you here, on Earth!' a startled Lumak replied.

'I can't let you have all the fun, you know. Anyway, I am here on business. Since your last report, I see you have made many good friends. You have accomplished so much since your recent arrival.'

'Yes, My Lord! I have been quite fortuitous!'

'I have analysed this species and now have a clearer picture of their likes, dislikes, weaknesses and strengths.

'As you said in you recent report, they are quite suitable for our purpose so I have made my choices. However, they need a saviour; someone who can save them from themselves. Perhaps a lovable person with superior powers that can represent them in the face of their God.'

'My Lord?'

'Whom do you think would be the ideal candidate for that task? You may however think about this matter carefully before committing yourself.

'I shall remain here on this world for a brief period with Lord

Vektron the Ploran, and make a few more observations throughout this and other local systems before returning to your home-world.'

'Yes, My Lord. I can only do my best in the circumstances. But with the lack of their money currency it is not always easy to move about. Therefore, I think it will take some time before I can seriously attempt such a noble task.'

'Yes, Sut. I realize your immediate problems... You can marry the girl, you know. But only if you need her company on a more permanent basis. You will have my sincerest blessings in that regard.

'Son, despite your present situation, your future path appears to be with Earth's survival. It's relatively clear of problems, so continue in your present vane.

'You should now get back to your friend because she gets quite anxious. I shall await your further daily reports in due course and must bid you farewell... The Mind is constantly updated!' Grand Lord Gerra said as he faded into nothing, but in the process moved a candle holder too close to the edge, so that it fell and rolled towards the entrance. It was all planned to give Lumak a realistic excuse.

For a brief moment he pondered the Grand Lord's arrival on Earth.

'This is most significant. Perhaps it was because of some new development or deduction from the information he received through the Mind. But what could be so important to take our Grand Lord almost half way across the galaxy to this world. After all, he always has such important matters to attend,' Lumak muttered those words to himself, realizing there were incredible changes afoot.

He soon arrived back at the house and found Sarah still waiting at the door.

'You took your time!' she scolded, impatiently. 'What was it, anyway?'

'Just candle light being reflected off the outer wall. One of the candles fell down and rolled close to the entrance while still alight. It must have been due to the wind.

'That was all? I thought I saw a moving light.'

'I spent a little longer having a thorough look around the area with the lantern, just in case, but found nothing,' he replied and bent over to kiss her on the cheek.

'Yes, its quite windy. Sorry for disturbing you!' she said.

'Good night!' he said teasingly, as he put the lantern out and parked it on a local hook. Then he placed the unloaded gun within the locker in the hall-way and returned to his room still pondering events of the previous few minutes.

'A saviour!... a saviour!...' he muttered to himself with a pencil in hand while making a few notes in English on one of Sarah's letter pads.

'If only I could find a cure for one of their worst diseases. I might have to wait for the correct opportunity to arise or somehow become a member of their medical profession...'

For a while Lumak pondered over several ideas in his mind regarding miracle cures. Finally he searched the mind for new ideas on the topic, but nothing of relevance could be found for his human type. The short-lived human body had never been considered a suitable vehicle for longevity and because of those and other reasons had been ignored.

'If only they hadn't so many parts to go wrong on the inside and there was not so much bacteria and germs on this planet, humans could live much longer. They also ate and drank many substances that were never meant for them. Even the fruits they take for granted were meant for certain mobile species with which those trees had grown a symbiotic relationship in the distant past. Although many of those life-forms had since disappeared from the planet the plants still continued bearing those fruits in hope of the species return. I must take note of all dangerous poisons in all those foodstuffs and list the dangers in a book for future reference.' Lumak realized that although such poisons were almost nonexistent, they accumulated and could significantly reduced the natural age of the individual. Many also aided the human organism in getting cancer, allergies and other lingering illness. Not to mention their common use of alcohol, other dangerous beverages and habits.

CHAPTER 18

Confession and proposal

The following morning was glorious and bright. Everywhere birds were singing. There was a tap on his door and Sarah entered. She was radiantly dressed in cotton white and beaming with life. Sarah was changing from the naive hillbilly shepherdess, to a most serious and determined young woman. She was now considering a new future with Lumak and those new attitudes had changed her focus on life.

'Would you like a cup in your room?' she asked, merrily. He admired her feminine charm for a while, coupled with such beauty, then smiled.

'You look so incredibly cool and radiant today. Have you won a prize or something?' Then he went forward to kiss her on her right cheek. Then she moved away in her usually shy manner.

'I am very sorry, but we are out of tea today,' she said apologetically, while placing the mug of hot coffee on the small table. They always tended to have tea that time of day, but coffee was a good substitute when tea was lacking. He always liked his tea hot and white with two spoonfuls of sugar. But coffee was equally acceptable. He generously sipped, while glancing at her beauty.

'You can have a break from all your heavy duties today, because I want you to remain as beautiful as you are now. Anyway, I should be quite familiar with the routine by now,' he said, and she gazed at him in that penetrating manner, when she thought he was ill or out of his head.

'I suppose... you are feeling all right today?' she inquired with quiet skepticism.

'Of course. I am feeling fine... But I have an important matter to discuss. Something that you might not like.' Her happier disposition took a sudden dive as she became worried for him and what he had to say.

Lumak was currently having a struggle with his conscience and looked very worried for what might result once having spoken his mind.. He had said so many lies and exaggerations since his arrival that he now felt little deserving of her affections. Nevertheless how could he have told her the truth about himself and the Grand Lord's visit. He realized he was in a dishonest relationship and knew not how to repair the damage, reverse the process and come clean so they could move on.

He dearly loved her and would even sacrifice his entire cause for that love. Never in all his existence had he felt that way before. Suddenly he plucked the courage to utter some words of importance to her.

'You know, I am extremely fond of you, but before our relationship can blossom, I must come clean with you and tell you the truth about myself and my reasons for being here. I mean, being on this planet, Earth. Then it will be up to you to kick me out or take whatever steps necessary.' She stared at him as if stunned by his utterance of those few ridiculous words and followed his rather pathetic expressions.

'He must be in some serious trouble. Perhaps the military or government is after him and he might have only recently remembered its ramifications. What could it be?' she thought, as she prepared for the worst.

'It would be nice for old times sake if we could keep this conversation between ourselves for now, as it could have very severe repercussions.'

'Of course. I agree. Anything you want!' she replied, looking even more bewildered, but nonetheless playing him along.

'I am not of this world. I am here on a special mission. My mission is to fulfil human aspirations in order that they may become great and powerful within the universe. If you like, I am on a mission from God.'

'Oh. I see?'

'When you and your father assisted me that day, it was my first day on Earth and I was confused, having just arrived as if from nowhere.'

She gazed at him continuously, but this time in total dismay.

'George! Enough said!' She took a few steps towards him and placed her hand at his Adam's Apple as if to check his temperature.

'You know, I think you have a slight temperature. You could have caught malaria or some other bug. From now on you are to remain in bed until you are feeling better. I have some medicine that I would like you to take twice daily,' she insisted and quickly left to collect the tablets and a glass of cold water.

'If you get any worse, I shall have to take you on the cart to the village to see Doctor Emil. Now take the tablets and go to bed! You need more rest!' She ordered, while handing him the items. He knew he had little choice in the matter and quietly took the tablets with some of the water. Then she made sure he went to bed and tucked him in.

'Now everything has backfired. She will end up doing all the work, even without my assistance. This was definitely not my intentions for today, of all days. How stupid have I been.' Lumak muttered those words to himself, realizing that honesty was not always the best policy.

A moment later and Sarah left to attend her daily duties. By now he was completely dumbfounded by her reaction to his truthful explanation, but he would not press the matter further. At least not until she was ready. He decided to play along with the illness game until midday. He still had some planning to do if he was to solve the financial problem and take her to the city on their brief vacation. Therefore his supposed illness would give him some time in private to think over new ideas. Anyway, he was working contrary to his superior's advice in giving her such information regarding his true identity and purpose, so he was pleased in the way things had turned out. Nevertheless he was quite guilty for not assisting her with her duties and also the many lies and excuses that he had said to her and Ben since his arrival to cover up his true purpose. He carried on his exploration through the Mind libraries, but could find no suitable money making enterprises.

Although the Mind may have had the answers, he didn't want to rely too heavily on technological magic while he was on Earth. He could better realise their problems if he faced their difficulties and tried their methods of solution. Unless of course when there was no immediate solution, then he would find a different option, and in view of his urgent mission, take the next step on the technological ladder of advancement. That was providing he didn't progress beyond Class 5, technologically.

Feeling bored and restless, he was out of bed just before midday and went out to look for Sarah. She was never very far away and was found in the yard cutting logs for the fireplace.

'Hi! I am sorry I couldn't help you sooner, but now I feel a lot better. The medicine you gave me worked a treat. Please let me help you, I need the exercise.' He bent forward to take the axe from her.

'Are you sure?' She closely observed him for any signs of illness. They collected what was left and went to the shed with the axe and balance of wood chippings and small logs.

'You look a lot better. It was not malaria, but could have been a waterborne virus or something in the air. It could even have been an aftershock from your ordeal in the hills before we took you in,' she advised. They dumped the wood in the storage shed. Then he gave her some help with the remainder of her daily chores.

That day Ben had taken the sheep to the hills and decided to visit an old friend after the animals had been left grazing. It was therefore no surprise to them when he arrived with the flock a little after five p.m.

Ben appeared very cold and unhappy, but they didn't wish to probe his business further. There was also a very cold wind blowing that was not expected at that time of day.

When they had finished dinner, Lumak again went off to his room to carry out some more studies. It was not long before Sarah knocked on his door and took him one of her favourite nutritious nighttime chocolate drinks.

'I would like to talk with you about something of importance.'

'You look so charming when you appear insistent and you know, I always like to hear what you have to say,' he replied, joyously.

'I just asked dad about our holiday in the city and he said yes! He said yes! Isn't that great? Isn't that marvellous?' she cried, with a burst of happiness and innocently landed in his arms.

'Yes! Yes! Yes! That's fantastic!'

'But he said he'll only agree if we lived with his younger brother in the city. After all, I am a good girl, you know.'

They were both completely overwhelmed by emotion and he grabbed and squeezed her around the waist. Then their lips met and he held on to her tightly, kissing her for as long as he could, while overcoming all her resistance to move away. Then she tore herself away from him, never uttering a single word as she went for the door.

At that time her father Ben was willing to go to almost any lengths to make concessions on her behalf. He had also taken the young man, namely George Peterson, on board and if he was really a doctor that was recommendation enough; for the young man would always be able to take care of his daughter responsibly and financially.

She had taken so well to this young man, almost as if destiny had played a hand in their lives and he seemed to be such a responsible type, always taking the hardest share of her duties. He was even beginning to speak a few sensible words of his language. But he would not like his only daughter disappointed in anyway if things didn't work out. He would therefore have to help and make little sacrifices whenever he could. After all, the young man was another one of those spoilt western foreigners, used to holidays, frivolous adventures and suchlike. Even so, he will need to have a serious chat with him in order to learn of his true intentions towards his daughter, even if he had to use sign language and so Ben reasoned.

At dinner that evening there was a very happy atmosphere at the table. On that rear occasion a small bottle of wine was included. It was no great surprise when Lumak went over and whispered in her ear.

'Will you marry me? Will you marry me?' he asked twice in

English. She turned around and looked at him with that excited expression.

'Of course I will... if you insist!'
He then turned to Ben.

'Ben... I marry... your daughter. You permit me? I have... your permission?' He uttered those words perfectly in Ben's language. Ben smiled with happiness and could not contain his emotions.

'Come on, my son, this calls for a stiffer drink. I have a bottle that I saved for just such a celebration. I'm sure Allah wont mind on such an important occasion,' he said boisterously and opened a small trunk from which he retrieved a bottle of Scottish Malt Whisky.

'This bottle, I have had here for the past three years, awaiting such a time like this to celebrate within my family. And now, let's have a stiff drink.' He collected two small glasses from the sideboard.

'I shall give you my permission only if you promise to take good care of my daughter. After all, she is my only daughter and my only child. Do you promise?'
Then turning to Sarah, Ben smiled.

'My daughter, please explain what I have just said to your future husband in English. I must be sure he understands my every word.'

Then Sarah spoke to Lumak, telling him what her father had said in English as if he didn't fully understand the first time. Nevertheless she always tried to please her father.

'I shall, with all my heart, Ben,' Lumak replied, bowing his head in the process.

'That's good enough for me, my son!' Ben said while pouring the drinks into the two small glasses.

Lumak took a gulp of the strong liquid and almost choked himself to death. He hadn't realised whiskey had to be sipped and not drank like water.

'Are you ok, my son?' Ben handed him a glass of water.
'It went down the wrong way! I didn't realize it was so... strong!'

Lumak soon recovered from his gasping and after a few more

sips of the alcoholic drink, was in the mood for more celebrations.

He soon realized the only people and things missing from his engagement was Sarah's mother, his own family and an engagement ring. He could do little about returning her dead mother to her, or invite his own family, but needed money to get her a suitable ring.

'How can I get money! How! How! How!' He probed within himself. He became quite agitated by the fact that he was hindered in his actions and deeds by such a simple and yet seemingly insurmountable problem.

He realized that his skills as a scientist would get him a job eventually, but all that would take too long and he had to hit while the iron was hot.

CHAPTER 19

A new identity

That evening they retired late. By that time they were a little inebriated by previous celebrations, but not drunk. After the strong Scotch Whisky, Lumak and Ben returned to a sweet and almost alcohol-free wine that Sarah preferred. Sarah had innocently drank more than her fair share of wine, while Lumak was beginning to enjoy the new experience of alcohol in a human body. However they knew better than to exceed their required amounts on religious grounds.

There was much happiness, but it was tainted by a little sadness. Sarah's mother was not there to partake in their engagement celebrations. Also, Lumak could not have invited any of his alien family. Those cultural aspects brought home to him the enormous differences and dissimilarities that existed between both species. In any case he could send them a message through the Mind and hoped one day they would all be together in one big celebration.

After the excitement was over, Sarah briefly visited Lumak in his room for a private chat about future plans.

'George, we are really going to get married! I never thought I would ever be so lucky. I mean, in meeting a suitable partner, and here you are! Do you think we will be happy together?'

'I think we will be very much like we are now, full of happiness and excitement, but never forsaking our responsibilities. All I want, is to be with you from now on. And whether we are rich or poor, it doesn't really matter. Because I love you more than anything,' he replied. Then they embraced and kissed.

Lumak then retired and found he was too unsteady to work and too excited to sleep, so he continued with his planning until he was too exhausted to stay awake. Soon after he was awakened by a seemingly bright light and a rumble from outside his window. He jumped out of bed to find a sealed letter and package on the nearby table.

The envelope had the winged insignia seal and was written in English, *'An important message from your lord.'*

Lumak was utterly surprised but also amused. He lifted the envelope, broke the seal, and began to remove its contents.

'Our Grand Lord must also enjoy the experience of being one of the natives. He sincerely loves and admires new cultures and even enjoys to partake in their ways. What an admirable Lord,' he muttered to himself.

The letter started:

Your stay on this world have now become imperative, as certain very important decisions have been taken at a higher level. I also think you to be best suited to this mission.

I trust you enjoy your new body form and its new senses, and in this regard it may be advantageous for you to take a mate at this juncture for mutual assistance and benefit.

Your travelling papers have been prepared and new identity full-proof, so you may update your implants with all relevant data.

You may now destroy this memo by placing it within the envelope and pressing the royal seal in the usual manner.

Your gracious and loving Lord.

He pressed the central unbroken blue circle and rays were emitted from that area to engulf and disintegrate the complete envelope and the item simply vanished. He stretched forward and took the packet which he immediately opened to find a passport and other important papers within.

The passport was English-European. His place of birth was England. He was born in a small town called Chessington. His new name was Doctor Jeffery Longhurst.

Then he opened another envelope which contained five hundred used US Dollars. That envelope he kissed with overwhelming joy before putting it in his inner breast pocket while continuing to read the other documents. Then suddenly the realization of the money dawned on him and he sprang out from his chair and took an excited leap into the air.

'Yoo hoo! Yoo hoo!' he cried, overwhelmed by happiness. He

was completely overcome by human emotions and over excited with the knowledge that one of his main problems, namely money, had been solved. As he fell unto the floor he hit the side of the chair and there was an almighty clamour. The noise woke the dog who immediately began to bark, getting everyone out of bed in the process.

Although quite embarrassed by the resulting turmoil, he decided to take the initiative and went to explain with passport in hand.

'I found it! I found it!' he yelled, convincingly. 'It was behind the bed all this time. It must have fallen out of my coat pocket on the first day of my arrival and everything has come back to me, as clear as glass.'

'You mean... you found your papers?' Sarah inquired, equally excited.

'Please let me see?' She insisted and he handed her his passport. She quickly glanced through its pages.

'Doctor Jeffery Longhurst. You are Jeff and not a George after all.' She was not disappointed but went up to him and kissed him gently on his lips.

'After all, we really have a doctor in our family. I always knew you were a doctor. You always looked so much like one... just your manner,' Ben said, also overwhelmed by excitement.

Later that evening Sarah knocked and entered his room once again.

'You are still awake, I see? I thought I heard sounds coming from this direction. There is so much excitement in this house these days. I am so restless about everything. I just can't close my eyes anymore,' she said while glancing at the other papers on the table.

'You found some more papers? Can I look?' she asked, excitedly.

'Yes, my love. Of course, help yourself.'

'So you are really a Jeffery?' she asked again, while reading the other certificates.

'And an English man from England. A Longhurst and a doctor? You are also single and not married, I presume?'

She looked directly at him with those piercing eyes and placed the papers back on the table.

'Of course I am single. That is something I could never forget,' he replied and she was satisfied with his answer.

'You see, I was almost one-hundred percent correct. You are a doctor, but unfortunately you are not a George, so I shall have to call you Jeff instead. If you don't mind.' He nodded his head and smiled with approval.

'My love, I now have all my papers. They were found behind the bed just over there. So now, we have no problems travelling after we get married and you must not be worried about anything. I love you dearly and shall marry you. And that's that!'

'And what about dad and the farm? Who will take care of Spotty, Saracen and the sheep after we are gone? We can't take them all with us. Can we?' she said, with her hand on his shoulder and looking into his eyes.

'Don't you worry about that minor problem, my love! Things can stay the way they are for now and we can have a second home in England or even in America. From now on we take things at our leisure and at our own pace, so you must not concern yourself, not even about money.

In the mean time I shall remain here for a while. Then after we get married we can organise things to function in a more efficient and self-reliant manner. This is a very beautiful place and quiet retreat, and we should never give it up, if only for your mother's sake.'

She moved both her hands on each of his shoulders. Then she hugged him. Finally she took the initiative and kissed him as long as she could for having loving thoughts of her dead mother. She then tore herself away from him with as much will power as she could muster.

'Good night, Darling!' she said, and quietly left the room.

He realized that very soon he was going to have a wife with many responsibilities and needed a more fruitful occupation. Preferably one that would follow his long term plans within his current mission.

There were lots of ideas and designs but they were either too alien or of a different technological classification to Earth's present levels.

In utter disgust and frustration Lumak banged the table with his fist and retreated to bed. In any event, he now had enough money for their holidays in the city and who knew what would have transpired after then.

CHAPTER 20

Strangeness in the hills

The following day Lumak escorted Sarah and the animals to the hills. On arrival they placed the sheep to graze and sat on a large rock. From there they gained a broad view of the large v-shaped valley, with the little river noisily manoeuvring its way towards the distant river Tigress. Far into the distance they could once again observe the foaming waterfall coming off a bare vertical cliff. This time it was stronger than usual. That incredible spectacle gave them a sense of cosmic wonderment and a yearning to travel and experience those wonders.

That spot had always inspired Lumak and brought back memories of his home world, family and friends. Although he was able to send short messages to them via the Mind, he hadn't mentioned anything about his human form or his future human wife. There were too many differences, culturally. He would have to wait until Sarah was ready for that incredible experience and that could only happen after she accepted who he really was. Sarah was quiet while considering their future together.

Lumak got up and held her shoulders firmly from behind while glancing into the distance.

'What a beautiful place you have here. Its powers penetrate deep within the soul and absorbs one until they become at one with the Greater Cosmos.' He said those words with a sense of ultimate enlightenment and she felt his innermost senses almost as if they were one person.

'I know exactly what you mean and I feel exactly as you do. Allah is truly remarkable and his universe truly wondrous,' she replied, equally aroused by their similar feelings of oneness.

He almost mentioned the similar beauty and power of Kanaefon his home world, but suddenly realising his over enthusiasm, stopped short of any further free-flowing of those words. Then he change the topic of their conversation to something more down-to-earth.

'When did you leave school to help your parents?'

'At the age of sixteen, just after my mother died. I had little choice in the matter. Dad insisted that I attained a little knowledge of the outside world before I began to assist him here. Perhaps deep down he wanted me to find someone away from this locality to marry. Well, our family, although religious, has always been quite liberal and modern for Moslems, and never followed too strictly its disciplines.'

'I think you and your father are great people,' he replied.

'Anyway, although our families were quite large and well known in these parts, we have since diminished and now not many of us Khans are left remaining. We used to be a military family in the past and lost most of our men in wars of one sort or another. Dad retired early only because he was seriously wounded in the leg. When the war and problems in the south became more serious, I decided to join the Red Cross to assist. So I visited my southern cousins who were also involved during that time. Then I took a short nursing course and assisted the wounded as best I could.'

'Love, you must be very brave,' he commented.

'It was then that I met Doctor George Peterson. I was then very shy and took a little while to settle into my duties. He put me in touch with his European girlfriend, Carol, who took care of my accommodation. It was she who thought me most of the little English I know. I wonder where she is now, and why all the questions?'

'I just like to hear your voice. But I also want to know more about you personally, so that I can sense your worries and know of your likes and dislikes,' he said, in a playful manner.

'Are you looking forward to our city holidays?' she inquired with further curiosity.

'That and perhaps a second job, so that I can support my family much better.'

'Me also! Although I get much job satisfaction from my daily duties, our survival here is getting a lot more difficult. I would like to do some other job, but I can't see how or where,' she said, with a tone of uncertainty in her voice.

'I might have a suitable job for you in the future. As my wife you can also be my assistant. But I have to get started first.

'Would you like to assist me in the future?' he asked, whispering in her ear.

'You know, my knowledge of such medical things are quite limited. But I am willing to learn and assist you as much as I can.'

'Don't be too modest. You have a lot more potential than you realise,' he replied.

Suddenly he felt a shiver along his spine. It was not from the cool mountain breeze. He felt his body sinking into the soil and immediately released his hands from her shoulders. He thought hard and fast, as if wanting desperately to return to his original position and his body returned to that position. He soon regained his composure as he felt terra firma once again beneath his feet. But that was not all, as he sank so did his environment begin to fade into that of his home world with it's two moons. He could clearly observe the interposed patterns of both environments.

'I wonder what must be happening to me. How could I have vectorized in this manner without using the cloak? I was not told of this unpleasant side effect after my human transformation. Apparently, it was triggered by my wanting to travel. My solid body began to fade, allowing me to travel through solid matter, and I am sure if I continued, I would have found myself on my home world. There seems to be two parts to this bizarre anomaly: moving through solid matter and travelling to any point within the known universe. Perhaps I can separate them into their distinct parts, to be used individually. I wonder if the Greater Mind had anything to do with this. I must experiment with this new human attribute and learn how to control it mentally,' he thought, as Sarah turned around to see what caused his long period of silence.

'Are you now feeling ok?'

'Yes, my love. I am fine. I was just thinking about us and the wedding.'

'It's time we started back to the house and left this beautiful spot and the animals to the Greater Cosmos. Do you agree?' she said, while both moved away from the rock still holding hands.

After they arrived home he removed the envelope with the money from his pocket and placed it with the others on the table. Then he called Sarah into his room.

'What is so important! I was just preparing dinner!' she said, showing slight annoyance for his bad timing.

'Darling, can you please explain the significance of the passport and other items that I've received, and whether I need anything else for our trip to the city?' She glance at the pile of documents on the table with surprise.

She leant forward and collected them, including the envelope with the money and began to check them one by one.

'Your passport... birth certificate... about five hundred dollars. Five hundred... American... dollars!' she exclaimed, almost in a state of shock.

'You have... five hundred US dollars here, you know! That is about three thousand liras and over one thousand euros! Do you realise what you have here?' she shouted again in utter excitement she went closer to show him the pile of notes, but he smiled.

'You had it all this time without telling me?' she inquired, in a more sombre mood.

'I found it with the papers yesterday, but wanted to tell you about it when we were alone together,' he replied and kissed her.

'Keep it in a safe place for me, Love. From now on my welfare and finances are your responsibility. So take all my papers away and put them in a safe place until they are required again.'

'I do love you with all my heart,' she replied and left with the items, gently closing the door behind her.

After she departed he tried to regain his thoughts of the strange occurrence in the hills and wondered of its true potential if harnessed in a correct manner.

He knew that he was given a human body and that he was able to exist exactly like a human, but beyond that he could have been capable of almost anything, given Class 9 technologies, with special implants and the cloak. He then realised that although his body was human, its matter could be phased at an angle away from normal causal matter and by controlling the angle through his implants could become indestructible and disappear at will.

However, by focussing on an environment he could also automatically transmit his vectored body to that place, without the use of any energy or his black Shadites Cloak. This was probably because he was massless during that process and there was no energy without mass given those conditions.

But those modes of operation had to be learnt and practised within his implants. Hence, he now had the power, even without the Black Shadite's Cloak or the Greater Mind, to travel through the oceans of matter with all its changes in density. He could visit anywhere that he had been previously almost instantly in time. Yet, like a normal ocean he would require his own oxygen to breathe if he intended to remain in that state for any length of time. He was now unaffected by all matter outside of his physical domain.

'How can I explain my newly found powers to Sarah? How could she understand the basic concepts of Inter-dimensional Transposition?'

'It is so difficult to explain. Like a separate universe within this basic one, even with laws of its own. The Grand Lord could possibly travel anywhere within the known universe by simply folding space and sliding along his own timeless corridors. Not too unlike the one he and I travelled here by. He could even alter the course of history by displacing causal lines of importance; for any slight change in the past could cause an incredibly large one in the distant future, with either fortuitous or disastrous consequences to many life-forms within those future time frames.

'Even so, there were many parallel universes and only the relevant one could be selected within the Quantum World. Therefore such changes could never really occur when carried out from an historical past that was directly linked causally to an existing future. In other words, no material object of the same type could ever visit the past of its own history within a given time-line.

'Despite the Grand Lord's great knowledge and abilities, he had certain principles and the primary one was never to tamper with the natural order unless it was unavoidable. He went out of his way to follow the basic plan which he called The Greater Purpose. Survival of the present natural order was more important than all

others, and the only reason for his presence within this strange world with its equally strange life-forms.'

Lumak also realised that the Grand Lord was quite capable of knowing the outcome of causal situations hundreds, even thousands of years in the future.

'Despite his usual pretence, to be playing along with normality. It was probably his way of having fun, being another player in the cosmic game and knowing that the smallest ripple affected the largest wave. However, his presence always placed a particular stamp on the natural order. By so doing, all life could eventually evolve in a better and more productive manner within The Greater Purpose.

'He enjoyed seeing his children achieve higher levels of existence, even if they had to stumble many times along the way towards attaining those goals and he sometimes had to pick the pieces up himself after each fall. This was the process he had trained his Shadites to engender. But sometimes disasters happened through no fault of their own, or in the case of the evil and rapacious Javols, because their innocent creators wanted to penetrate broader boundaries of science. Sometimes finding knowledge was also groping in the dark until one found a glimmer of light to follow and that guiding light could also lead to death and destruction.

'Yes, that same method of trial and error could also lead to the creation of monsters. For inventions were seldom the children of their inventors and many children were disappointingly disobedient and tended to follow their own unruly attitudes and behaviour. Nature had her own way of revealing her purpose to her creative children and the positive side of that nature including life, was engendered by The Greater Purpose.

'Hence the idea of good and evil. In that way, I suppose, one could consider evil and death as the Lesser or Negative Purpose. Yet, both purposes have always worked side by side in nature, either to the benefit or detriment of all life. We could never get a full appreciation of one without the other; for that was the way of the Cosmos and the She. Yet, although different, like prey and predator, one could not have hot without cold or beautiful weather *without storms. Every number had an inverse which reflected in its Identity. However, the natural order was one thing, but ingenuity and imagination quite another. Intelligence could always break those natural barriers by modelling the real world in ways that were considered outside of the bounds of the so-called natural order.*

'Thus far, higher intelligence and order due to technological advancement have continued and now, almost any structure can be created, even types not of the natural primal order.

'Technological Order is mostly to do with the mind and that type of order is outside of everything; for any thought or idea can in time be created or circumvented using the natural order or some other tool to create its modus operandi.

'Either way, the Grand Lord was probably the best Universal Lord and the most capable in implementing such change for the better,' and so Lumak reasoned until his eyes became tired and he fell into a deep sleep.

Although he had tried on many occasions to find some new money making venture, he realize that such notions of commerce were beyond his way of thinking. His purpose on Earth was for another reason. He also realized he needed more time to learn and mingle with human society.

Perhaps his holidays in the city would guide him along the right lines. During this time he might even meet someone to point him in the right direction and so he thought with hope in every stride.

CHAPTER 21

Lumak's first patient

It was morning and the birds were singing in the nearby trees amidst noises of sheep and fresh scents of spring.

Lumak was awakened by bright sunlight through the thin window curtains. It displayed bizarre shapes from moving branches on the opposite near snow-white wall. He immediately got out of bed, yawned with both hands outstretched. He struggled to put on his borrowed clothes and went outside to the large water tank. He had a good wash in the cold stale spring rainwater before returning indoors. That water came off the roof guttering and was ideal for that purpose. Although cold, it was refreshing and tended to awaken him for his daily duties. Sarah always used the local spring water for cooking and drinking. That water was kept in a large earthen jar in the kitchen. Since that area in the mountains was relatively unpopulated, pollution was virtually nonexistent.

He soon knocked on Sarah's door with a cup of tea. Then he did the same for Ben.

During their breakfast discussions Sarah had mentioned the five hundred US dollars to her father and that single factor was all that was required to make Ben's day.

'Dad, Jeff found 500 US dollars and all his papers behind the bed.'

'That's truly incredible news. You must have lost all your memory from the cold to have not mentioned that sum of money before,' Ben admonished him. Yet Lumak maintained his silence. Ben realized he must have missed them when he searched him. But he didn't look into his broad belt.

Having had an early breakfast, a happier Ben decided to take the sheep to the hills on horseback, while riding in front of the herd with Spotty following to keep the stragglers in line. Perhaps Ben wanted to give the couple more time together in order for them to discuss their personal affairs.

They sat for a lengthy breakfast, both assisting each other while chatting.

'Sorry Love, I don't have much family left in England to speak of, or to visit our wedding. My real parents are dead, you know. They died in a car crash several years ago and I am afraid, that just leaves you, Ben and myself. But my parent's house is still there with a few odd cousins in Scotland,' Lumak said, sticking rigidly to his cover and not in anyway wishing to destabilize their relationship. He was always quite clever and cunning in planting certain information in Sarah's mind.

Nevertheless all that history regarding his family was in the letter he read and had been absorbed into his brain implants. It was essential that he kept his cover, while creating a new identity and plausible life for himself if he was to complete his mission. Anyway, all those facts and relatives did exist. Not having seen the real Jeffery Longhurst for many years, they may even have recognise Lumak as such. Therefore in this regard his new identity was foolproof. Even so he still wanted to move to a more advanced country where he could more effectively fulfill his purpose and begin his many advanced projects to save Earth and the universe.

'Your parents are both dead?'

'Yes!'

'I am so sorry. I forgot to ask you about them. I was so rapped up in my own selfishness,' she said, being overly apologetic.

'That was many years ago, so don't worry about it. Where do you think we should hold the wedding?'

'I don't know. Our family is very poor and we haven't that many friends locally, with only a few relatives left in the city. I suppose Dad has been quite worried about my getting married for sometime because of those reasons. But I would like Dad to be with us for the wedding. It is also very important for him, you know.'

'Ok. We get someone to look after this place and hold the

wedding in the city. Your father mentioned close friends in the village. Perhaps they could remain here for two weeks while we are away?'

'But his wife is dying from cancer and he has to take care of her on an almost full-time basis. They are also very poor and we might have to leave them some money, if they should come here and that is a very big, if,' she replied.

'As a doctor I have certain powers, you know. What if I was able to cure her from her present illness. It's quite likely that I found a remedy for this type of illness during my recent studies. All I require is some special chemicals from a chemist and a couple pieces of equipment. I recently read about them and saw photos in our medical book. If I make a list will you help me find the items?' She glanced at him in a doubtful manner, but didn't wish to ask any questions on a subject of which she had less than a basic knowledge.

'Ok, Darling! Whatever you say!'

Lumak went off to make the list. When he was finished, Ben arrived with Spotty and Saracen. She took the list from Lumak and began to read it in his now quite legible handwriting.

'I understand some of these chemicals like Potassium, Iodine... Phosphorous... anyway I have to visit the village today, to see my friend Marion. Also, we are out of some necessary groceries, and it's time I introduced you to the village and some of its inhabitants.'

They sat on the large wooden cart and followed the old bumpy road towards the village. That dusty road was full of potholes giving quite a chaotic ride. Soon Sarah handed the reins to Lumak who felt quite at home instructing the horse Saracen. Of course the horse Saracen knew the route by heart.

'Keep well away from that large hole over there. The last time she broke our rear axle. I gave her the name Nessy.'

'Why a her, males can be worse,' he replied.

It's because I read once about a monster in a lake in Scotland, England. And the hole can become a small lake when it rains. There is also a small stream across this road further down. It can be a river when it floods, carrying large boulders blocking our path.'

Their first stopping point was at the grocery shop which had been recently refurbished and under new management. It had been transformed into a more expansive self-service.

After they collected the necessary items with a few extras, they went towards the drugstore that was at the other end of the main street. Sarah handed the list to the pharmacist.

'Yes... yes... aha... ah!' he read.

'I am afraid we cannot supply these four items. I am sorry, they are only available from the city. The syringes and other items we have in stock. I know of a suitable medical store that will stock these at a most reasonable price. I can give you their address and phone number, if you wish.' Then he receded to the rear of the shop to collect the other parts of the order he had in stock. He soon returned with the items and a note.

'That will be thirty-four liras please,' he said and Sarah opened her purse to get the money.

'I am sorry I couldn't be of more assistance, Sarah, but if you have any problems in finding the larger items, please let me know and I can order them for you.' Sarah bashfully glanced at the man who she recognized as one of her fellow final year students in the local school.

'Olaf? Is that really you?

'Yes! It's me alright!' he replied in Turkish but he could understand English.

'This is my doctor friend. Doctor Jeffery Longhurst from England and he is my fiancee.'

'I am so pleased for you. Sarah. Anything you or your future husband require... you need only ask. And I also have a phone you can use to call the city, if you wish.'

During this time Lumak was looking through the large catalogue on the counter and was surprised by the enormous list of medical equipment portrayed.

'Can you get most of these items?' Lumak inquired.

'Yes! Most!'

'In that case, could we use your phone to call the city store and arrange an order. We can reimburse you for the call. Just add it to the bill when the order comes in,' Lumak said.

'In that case, please let me order the items for you. I know of a city supplier dealing in used and surplus military gear. They also import equipment from abroad. Those we can purchase at the most reasonable rates. Perhaps I can contact them on your behalf, Doctor,' Olaf said.

'Ok. See what you can do. But they are required urgently,' Lumak stressed and they left.

'I can ask dad to call in to see if the order has been received in two days. We can now visit Simon and his wife, Marion,' Sarah said.

'That's a very good idea. I also have to take a small sample of blood from Marion for some preliminary studies.' Sarah stared at him with tranquil surprise and utter disbelief.

'You will just go up to her and take some blood? People do not just give their blood to anyone, you know. To them it is a very personal and private matter. Anyway, what will her local doctor think of your interference with his patient. It might even be illegal and he will get to know about it you know, and when he does he will not like it a bit!' she said.

'You can talk to her for me then. Tell her that I am a special researcher in cancer and currently carrying out a project in this area that might help her. Don't mention about our future marriage for now unless she asks. There is still time enough.' Lumak tried to keep everything on a more professional basis.

'I shall try, Darling, but I can't promise anything.'

They soon arrived at Simon's house and were greeted by his very pale and frail wife at the door.

'Hi, Sarah. What a pleasant surprise. I haven't seen you in ages. I was talking about you with my husband just this morning. Azize also told me of his recent visit to your place and the miracle of the lamb. That must be a sign for something great in your future. Blessed be Allah! How about you, my girl... and your doctor friend. Your father told me all about your friend, and congratulations on your engagement. Please sit for a while and we can have a little gossip,' Marion said, having one of her better days from pain.

'Thanks! Please meet Doctor Jeffery Longhurst!' Sarah said proudly and Lumak put his hand forward.

'It's a great pleasure, Marion!' Lumak replied.

'You only just missed Simon. He went to the shops to collect a few items for me, but he won't be long. You both, come and sit here while I make you a cold drink.' They could observe she was in serious pain despite her medication. She went over to the large refrigerator to collect a container while they sat down on the settee. She handed them each an orange drink.

'Thank you, Marion. Jeffery is a special doctor from England. He has been doing some research in the mountains with herbs, in conjunction with special drugs. He also think he might have a cure for certain strains of cancer,' Sarah said convincingly. Marion glanced at Lumak in painful dismay, then she turned to Sarah with glaring eyes.

'You say, you think he has a cure for cancer?' Marion replied with utter curiosity.

'Only for certain types at this moment,' Sarah replied, showing little concern.

'How do you know which type people have?' Marion asked with more curiosity.

'He usually takes a small blood sample for analysis, but...' Sarah hesitated.

'But what...' Marion interjected.

'We only paid you a social call and I am afraid we might have to get Doctor Emil's permission first. You know how protective these country doctors can be towards their own patients. Unless of course... you decide not to mention anything to him. After all, it's only a very simple test,' Sarah replied. Marion suddenly sat down in her chair and stretched out both her arms.

'Take as much as you like. I'm going to die soon anyway.'

'Are you sure?' Sarah replied.

'I am very sure! If you have a syringe why don't you take some of my blood now. The loss won't kill me and I will not mention a word to Doctor Emil. You have my word!' she insisted.

'You are in luck. It so happens that we just bought three hypodermic syringes from the pharmacist,' Lumak said. He removed a syringe from the packet he was carrying and handed it to Sarah.

'You are now my nurse and helper, remember,' he whispered and Sarah was surprised, but took the syringe from him all the same. Lumak handed her a piece of cotton wool dipped in alcohol with which she sterilized the area on her arm. She searched for the blood vessel. Having attempted three times then took an almost full syringe of Marion's blood. Finally she placed the cotton wool over the area before bending her arm to stop any further bleeding.

'Keep your hand like this for a couple minutes. I am sorry, but we should have used a larger needle. These are not the right ones. It took a little longer to fill the syringe.' Sarah apologized. She was out of experience and had tried several times to find the vein. Sarah then handed the syringe to Lumak who pushed the needle into a bottle cork to seal its end. Suddenly he realised how deviously his woman's mind worked. She had given Marion the impression that she had made the decision all by herself.

'That's all right. I didn't feel a thing. Sarah, you are still a very good nurse. I hope you let me know about the test as soon as possible.'

'The very moment I know, I shall tell Ben and he can tell you next time he visits,' Lumak replied.

'You guys seem to be much closer than you let on. Come on, tell me some news,' Marion inquired, with a happy grin on her face. Despite her pain and suffering she could still show a happy smile.

'Keep this between us for now. We would also like to take a city holiday but have to leave our farm in capable hands while we are away. That's our main problem at this moment in time,' Sarah replied.

'Wow!... that's incredible news! Congratulations to you both again! Let me see if I can find someone suitable to help?'

'I am sorry, Marion, but we have to leave you now,' Sarah said, as they both got up.

'You both must visit me again soon. And I will very much like to know about the tests, as soon as possible,' Marion said, again stressing the point.

'Don't worry, we'll be back to see you in a few days, so please rest yourself in the mean time,' Lumak said and they left before Simon returned.

'I'm sorry Sarah, but I need a small refrigerator to store the blood before it goes off, and for that we also require a small generator. So I must return to Olaf's place and ask him to help.'

Olaf, I need your help again. I require a small fridge and a 1kw generator. Where can I find those as soon as possible?'

'Don't worry! I have exactly what you need. I have a small refrigerator that I haven't used for a while and a 1kw petrol generator I used when we had more frequent power cuts. You may borrow them.'

'That's great! I only need them for a short time to complete a special project.'

By the time they left the village their cart was almost full of items.

While on their way home that day Sarah was worried about planting false hopes in Marion's mind. She saw the look in Marion's eyes and the insistence in her voice. Therefore she turned her attention to Lumak and his supposed cure for cancer.

'Darling, are you sure you can cure her from that type of cancer? From what Dad said, they have been trying all the latest drugs from Europe with little success? Even Doctor Emil has given up on her. He reckons she only has about a month left in this life at most. I know you can sometimes work miracles, but I wouldn't like to see her disappointed in any way. Even when she is about to die.'

'Darling, you must have faith in The Greater Purpose and Allah. Believe me when I say, she will be fully cured from her illness within a fortnight.' He said those words with absolute certainty in his voice and she believed.

Although Sarah was not sure about the methods used, she had faith in Allah and realized, if he was a prophet that was sent by

Allah to change humankind, Marion would be cured in exactly the way he said. She held on to his arm and snugged close to him during their journey home while pondering those thoughts.

'You know, Darling, you are indeed a very strange one and I dearly love you, including all your strange ways. Lets hope this new miracle of yours works for Marion as well.'

'And I will always love you as I do now!' he replied.

'I only wish this road of ours was less bumpy. Now there are two of us, so I shall have to make a nice thick cushion for this old leather seat,' she said and slowed their horse Saracen to take the narrow bend.

CHAPTER 22

A cure for cancer

When Sarah and Lumak arrived home from the village that day, they found Ben sitting comfortably by the fire sipping a cup of hot coffee. It was a cold afternoon and they were almost frozen to the bone. To Lumak, it was a new experience, being as vulnerable and suffering like the natives. In 2041, Global Warming caused great swings in the planets atmosphere and it led to extremes in climate change, with unpredictable weather and severe storms.

Despite all his protective powers, Lumak could use none of them while in Sarah's presence and had to pretend to be a normal individual, with all its weakness, aches and pains. That way he gained her sympathies and she could fulfill her motherly instincts. Ben poured two more hot cups and handed it to them.

'Did you enjoy your visit to our local village?' Ben inquired.

'Yes, Dad. We visited Marion, but Simon was not about,' Sarah replied, not mentioning a word about injection needles or cures for cancer.

'I think Marion and the other village people are great, but I need to start my research work. Dad, can I use a small room or shed as a temporary laboratory for my experiments?' He said those words in pure Turkish.

'Son, please help yourself to whatever space you need. Even build on the land outside if you wish. I can get some workers from the village or assist you myself if you like.' Sarah collected some items of grocery and went towards the kitchen.

'I know it's a little late for lunch, but I shall cook us something anyway.' Then she placed some logs on the fire and rubbed her near frozen fingers.

'We can discuss these matters afterwards. I am sure we'll come up with something after I have shown Jeff around, and there is also the fourth room,' she said. Then Lumak followed her into the kitchen and began to assist her with the vegetables.

After lunch she took Lumak around the house and barn, showing him every square inch of the place. The fourth smallest bedroom was used for storing and drying clothes and in a complete mess.

Lumak had a thorough, but disappointing check of the place and finally decided on the fourth room.

'Nowhere is really suitable, but perhaps... if I place a small table over there. The clothes line could then be positioned between these two points. What do you think, my love?' She nodded her head in approval and both began to shift items about. Then several previously discarded items were taken away. Finally the whole dusty place was thoroughly swept with a large broom.

'No time like the present,' Lumak said, as he commenced setting up what little equipment he had acquired once the dust had settled. On the small table he fitted the old used microscope he had acquired from the pharmacist, Olaf. It was his original that had recently been replaced by a more advanced model. Olaf, being one of those enthusiastic biologist cum pharmacists had many such bits of equipment lying about. Those he seldom used was lent to Lumak.

Sarah soon decided to have the clothes line fitted outside. After all, the cold winter months were now almost at an end. Ben gave her a hand and placed two nails, one on the house and the other on the closest tree for the line. Then Ben mounted his horse Saracen and decided to visit the hills to collect the sheep. Too many quick changes always made him nervous. But they were for the future of his daughter and son-in-law and that was as good a reason as any.

Spotty was left asleep close to the fireplace. Anyway the flock was usually well behaved on their return journey in the evenings, with a full stomach and wanted to get home and be in the shelter and warmth of the pen as soon as possible.

Although Lumak was still short of several pieces of laboratory equipment, he knew that he could always cheat a little by using the technologies of the Greater Mind to find answers. That simple task could be accomplished by linking with his implants. As a Grade 1 Shadite with special powers he didn't need the belt for that purpose anymore, other than to store the bluish microid dust and a few small cylinders and gadgets. Nevertheless he tended to hang on to his old established methods and always used the local technologies whenever possible.

Time was pressing and he was afraid that the blood sample would soon become unusable, even while stored in the small refrigerator that they had borrowed from their village friend. The small petrol driven electric generator, although noisy, was soon installed in a dugout area within the basement of the house. It was placed in a large padded wooden box for absorbing and reducing the noise and vibration. The exhaust led out to a large plastic pipe. It only ran for a few hours each day and never at nighttime. He use the late hours for his paperwork and analysis with the assistance of the Mind.

Having done most of the preparation, any experiments was to be carried out quickly in order to limit contamination in that highly dusty and unsterilised environment. He realized he was going to receive the other items from the city soon enough and who could have known how he had attained his results and so he reasoned. 0That was providing they were reproducible by present day technologies and equipment used on Earth. He was going to wear the Black Shadites' Cloak for quickest results and was not going to be disturbed by any means while creating and observing those molecular structures within the Mind.

After recording every step of his experiments, he would be able to use his matter conversion process to create and transpose the serum within the Mind. Then the experiment could be realized by the atomic conversion and interchange of a simple glass of water. However all such experiments would have to be conducted late, after Sarah had said good night and was tucked comfortably in bed.

The dog, Spotty, was another problem. The creature tended to bark whenever he communicated with the Mind. It could have been something to do with the ionisation of air molecules, perhaps due to an excess of ozone generation. This factor may have triggered the sensitive smell centres of the animal. Even so, Spotty seemed to have gotten used to that particular smell and no longer associated it with danger.

For once, Lumak realised the less than basic nature of his so-called laboratory environment. Nevertheless it was a start in the right direction and he always favoured a challenge.

During his visit to the village he had observed several highly technological items. One of which she called Television, so there must also be very advanced medical apparatus in the major cities. He must learn more of the advanced technologies of Earth. Perhaps the Grand Lord and Lord Vektron had already entered all such relevant data on those relatively advanced devices within the Mind libraries since their recent visit.

He left the room for a moment and visited Sarah while preparing dinner.

'My love, can I help you with the cooking?'

She glanced at him in utter surprise, realizing he never cooked. Neither did she like too many assistants in her kitchen, which was her sacred ground. As far as she was concerned, too many cooks spoiled the broth. Even so, she didn't mind him peeling the spuds or sifting the rice.

'No, Darling, it's not necessary. Anyway, I have almost finished. Did you like your trip to the village, today?'

'Very much!'

'They are all very poor people, I am afraid. Most of the young ones have left for the large cities, but we are all a tough and resilient lot.'

'I understand what you mean, and I liked the new experience very much. I would love to help every sick and poor person on this world. Perhaps one day we'll be able to help them as well,' he replied, with sincerity. Sarah didn't realize it was the first time he had visited a human village and had spoken to others other than her and Ben.

'Well, in that case, you can go by yourself to the village whenever I need any urgent items of grocery. That is, when dad is not available. Would you?'

'Anything for you, my love. When can we have the other items I want ordered?' he asked.

'I require some more money from you. They cost a total of two hundred liras which is about thirty dollars. Very expensive, you know. If you still want them, Dad can get some postal orders from the village post office tomorrow and we can complete the order forms after dinner tonight. I have some spare envelopes in my room.'

'Thank you for everything!'

'No problem!' she replied.

Then he gave her a little kiss and went back to his makeshift laboratory.

Later that evening, after Sarah and Ben had retired, Lumak decided to connect with the Mind. He latched his bedroom door from inside and using brown masking tape, sealed the air in his room from Spotty's sensitive nose as best he could.

First of all he wanted to finally improve his human body and looks by adding the final trimmings. Like tuning the major organs more precisely and adding more subtler facial expressions. He had fed a lot more information into the Mind about his type of human body and mind. All that data could now be used to substantially upgrade his body and senses of perception, including specific emotions. All those numerous feelings and desires, with their expressions were natural to humans because of their unique evolution and had to be included. There was also the knowledge of the many languages that he had learnt from the radio and books. But his main reason for connecting to the Mind was to find answers to the cancer problem and in so doing create a serum.

After preparing several sterilised utensils, he removed the syringe from the cold packet he had taken from the refrigerator and placed half of its contents within one of the containers. He went over to the White Gown and removed the Black Shadite's Cloak from a concealed pocket. Then he slid into the cloak and placed the hood over his head to seal everything, including noise from his senses. He inhaled the bluish dust, pressed the buckle and its inner red button, and soon found himself within the confines of the Greater Mind.

For a moment he contemplated the new environment of the mind. Although he was still within his room, a part of the mind was superimposed within. It was an incredible universe of Virtual Reality, where almost anything was possible; but one had to tune their mind to the requirement, desire or creative process. For a skilful Shadite like Lumak that process was second nature. Nevertheless there was a great difference between the Greater Mind and Virtual Reality. Whatever was created within the Mind could become real and be made to exist in our universe by a simple transference process and that process worked both ways. Therefore whatever he had in his room he could use within the mind, but with the more advance technologies and equipment within it aided by his imagination.

Since he could synthesize virtually any matter or energy through the mind, he soon filled a small container with water, removed several of the special microids from the small container on his belt and placed a few in his gloved hands. Then he concentrated for a while. Suddenly the water within the container was replaced by the strange microid substance. That way he could always replenish his supplies. That process of fabrication and transference applied to any molecules and compounds.

Once more he began to form a link between his body and the idealized one within the Mind. Very soon his own body began to change to the almost perfect simulacrum of himself.

He went forward to the mirror in his room to observe the changes and was completely satisfied by what he saw. He moved his facial muscles about for a while, smiled, grinned and blinked his eyes, but could find everything in perfect working order.

As usual, he was always worried that Sarah might pick up on certain abnormal changes. He didn't want her to worry any more than usual on his account. Despite those concerns he was pleased with himself and hoped Sarah would also be pleased with what she saw in the newer him.

His next task was to formulate the serum. He placed a single drop of Marion's blood from the syringe into the palm of his gloved hand and it was absorbed as he concentrated. A complex matrix now formed within his mind as he found himself travelling, as if through the single drop of blood, observing each molecule in turn, until he came upon a cancerous chain. Then he would stop to enter and check out its composition until he arrived at the nucleus of the contaminated cell.

The Mind was mapping out the complete cell structure and making direct comparisons with what it considered to be a standard good cell. Showing bad DNA groupings and links while at the same time simulating substitutions that would lead to improvements.

He had to find a way to engineer a suitable anti-cancer serum and its living media from the information received. His present task was to find a natural source of large cells with all the necessary substructures and proteins as a basis for building the more complex serum. However many biological systems were quite similar and the acquisition of such building blocks was not going to be a problem. His idea was to use a suitable virus and engineer it to accurately target Marion's cancer cells. There were numerous bacterial cells that could be re-engineered into such types.

He soon found that a combination of natural foods, plants and a small amount of the patient's own blood would fulfil his immediate requirements. Using Marion's DNA he created a similar human patient within the Mind on which to experiment. From that patient which was the identical simulacrum of Marion, he could extract as much blood and other substances as required. When he completed his first sample it was injected into the patient and the whole process speeded up a thousand times. To his amazement the patient was permanently cured within the specified time.

He carried out several such experiments. Changing the sample strength while adding other chemicals to speed certain operations until he was satisfied. Then he poured the contents within one of the smaller sterilised containers that he had prepared earlier that day. He simply swapped the water in his room for an equivalent amount of the serum in the Mind, mass for mass. Since such substitutions were always of equal mass, both universal systems always remained in perfect balance. Then he revectored his new body into the room with the serum instead of the water.

From what he had learnt, he had several choices in acquiring the complex protein molecules. They could be extracted from normal foods like rice, tomatoes, potatoes, and so on. Finally he decided to use products that were more commonly available in Sarah's kitchen and potatoes tended to carry a rich mix of many substances and heavier starchy molecules.

Once again he checked his human features in the large mirror while talking to himself until he was fully satisfied.

Then he removed the Black Shadites' Cloak and hid it within the large inner pocket of his White Gown. He realized it would disappear until it was needed again. Then he quietly went to the kitchen to collect some more items. He peeled and crushed them with the addition of others and chemicals to make a suitable rich cocktail. Then he filtered the contents through a strainer and several layers of cotton wool.

Finally he located the other ingredients and attempted to separate them with the apparatus he had previously acquired from the city. Although not fully convinced of the results, he realized he almost had the process ready.

He wanted to manufacture the second batch of the special serum himself with indigenous technologies, but if that aspect was not yet possible, he could always have acquired a second batch from the Mind by the simple water replacement method. After all, the solution had been found and that new data would always be available in the Mind for any Shadite to use.

In all this, his main problem was being able to reproduce his samples on Earth with indigenous equipment and products. Therefore he broke the process down into steps and listed the possible, difficult and impossible. He soon found there were no items on his lists that were impossible to create on Earth.

CHAPTER 23

Made on Earth

He was soon to be aroused by Sarah who could not sleep and got up for a glass of water. She tapped gently on his door and he went to open it with his eyelids almost closed shut from tiredness.

'Hello, I am sorry for disturbing you. I saw your light was still on. What are you doing this late?' she inquired with a yawn.

'I was trying to find an easy way to make the anti-serum. I have only just finished my preliminary checks. Sorry about the little mess on the floor and table, I shall clear it up in the morning.' He was sleepy and yawned. She moved closer to him to observe his features.

'It's already morning, you know... Somehow you look different... more handsome and healthier than usual. I think you must now be fully recovered.' She moved closer to more carefully observe his features, not realizing he had only recently undergone a major body upgrade.

'Yes, my love. It's all to do with the clean mountain air we breathe.' He distracted her by showing the pink serum in the test-tube and she yawned again.

'Do you seriously think it will work, Darling?' She stood staring at the pinkish bubbling concoction that appeared to be almost alive.

'If I know anything, is that my serum will work,' he replied with even more certainty in his voice than before. But Sarah didn't wish to labour the point.

'In that case, we must inject her today.'

'Yes, we must! It is important, because its strength will weaken and the mixture won't last for more than a couple of days in this place and at most four in the refrigerator. It almost took me all night to prepare that first batch in this makeshift laboratory, you know, and I don't want to do it all over again with these outmoded facilities!'

'Ok, Darling, we can visit her after we have completed our daily duties. Why don't we start now on the house and after sunrise we can have breakfast and begin on the outside? I will get dad up at six. He can take the sheep to the hills and return with Saracen in time for us to set out for the village. We can also mail that urgent order at the same time. You can have a nap in the afternoon if you are still tired.' Sarah always tried her best to assist him whenever she could.

Despite his lack of sleep, he felt a completely changed person with his newer body, full of exuberant energy and excitement. By tackling his tasks in the right order and multitasking it wasn't long before all the work about the place was completed. The changes to his body had made it a lot more efficient, faster and stronger. Also, all of his human emotions and feelings had been adjusted and were finely tuned to those of a super human in peak Olympian condition.

When Ben returned from the hills he was surprised to find all the work about the place was done. Even the logs had been cut for firewood.

'Someone has been very busy today!' Ben exclaimed, while watching the diminishing pile of larger logs near the house.

'Have you seen him lately. It's like he's possessed by a demon. I saw him tackle three jobs at the same time and he didn't even make a mess,' Sarah replied and Ben was amused.

Saracen was soon harnessed to the cart and by ten they were on their way to the village.

They arrived at Simon's house just before midday. He greeted them and they went in to see Marion.

'I am very pleased to meet you, Doctor,' Simon said.

'She is in bed today. I am afraid it's one of her bad days. Although I have given her stronger medication, she is still in severe pain. I don't want her to become too dependant on the drugs because her body will gradually become more used to them and she will require stronger doses to overcome the same amount of pain. Anyway, why don't you go in and say hello. That will make her happy,' Simon said, as he took them in to see her.

'I've brought you some oranges and eggs. How are you today?' Sarah asked Marion, while placing the basket on the local table.

'Not very well, I am afraid. My husband wants to take me away to Germany, but I think I shall not make it and will not be able to see my sons and grandchildren before I leave this world. My situation is just hopeless. Even the special painkillers appear to have little effect... so much grinding pain.' Marion moved her body slightly to make herself more comfortable and clenched her teeth in the process.

'I have some very good news for you,' Sarah said.

'We had some serum made specially for you. Jeff tells me it will reduce your pain and perhaps the cancer too... but it's still experimental. We shall have to inject it into your arm.'

Marion turned her head to glance at Lumak with distress written all over her pallid features.

'You have made a serum that you think can reduce my pain and even cure my cancer?'

'Yes, I have put a special cure together, but it might not be one-hundred percent effective the first time. That is because of your present medication. You might need several injections over a period of three weeks or so.'

She immediately lifted her right arm for the injection. At that moment Marion would have done anything to reduce her discomfort and nagging pain.

'Please let me have it now. I am going to die anyway. I trust you both and you have a godlike face like the prophet himself. You are a very good man and Sarah should be proud to be with someone like you,' she said, while glancing at Sarah.

It was then that Sarah remembered the wounded lamb, Bir, and the looks in the little creature's eyes when she was near death by the fireplace. They were looks of desperation in the face of an unknown. The poor creature could do nothing about her wounds and was fully dependent on others to assist. Then there was the fear of an inevitable future, which would most likely have led to death as the most probable outcome. Then sadness filled her eyes as she could see parallels between both situations.

'It's time you had a husband, you know. Living all alone with your father in such an isolated place is not safe and you need young company as well, my dear.' Marion said those last words while squeezing Sarah's hand. Lumak removed the small syringe from the holdall and handed it to Sarah who injected its contents into her arm. After about half an hour they decided to leave.

'How do you feel now?' Sarah asked.

'Ok, I suppose, with your pleasant company,' she replied.

'The serum will need a few days to take full effect. During this time you should remain in bed. You must not take any pain killers or other forms of medication during this time. The serum must be allowed to do the job on its own. You might also need another injection to strengthen the dose, but that can be done in a few days time. Your cells will have to work together in order to destroy the disease and too much activity will reduce the effects of the serum,' Lumak stressed.

'Ok, Doctor, I shall tell Simon and remain here in bed until your next visit or until I am otherwise advised by you.' She gradually went limp and Sarah was worried in case the serum reacted with the drugs she was already taking, but Lumak went over to check her pulse and Sarah did likewise.

'It's working, Sarah. She is only asleep, but her temperature will begin to rise before long as the anti-viruses begin to react and reproduce using the cancerous ones. After a short while her temperature will begin to stabilise. Let's go and do some shopping now and return in an hour to give her a final check before we leave for home,' Lumak said, quietly.

They left her bedside and went to find Simon. They met him at the door while returning from his shopping.

'Your wife is now asleep. I think she requires lots of rest at this time, so don't let her get out of bed for at least three days. You must promise me that you won't and here is a special diet sheet that Jeff has prepared for her. Make sure she has those vegetables and fruit on a daily basis, they will help her to recover,' Sarah said with a very determined attitude.

Simon was quite baffled by the news that his wife was asleep. After all, she was lucky to get more than two hours nightly sleep and she seldom slept during the day. But when he looked she was really comfortably asleep and even snoring. What was he to expect next? He didn't wish to understand what had happened, but his wife was already better for seeing them and Sarah would not lie to him. Therefore he decided to fulfil his promise to Sarah if it could in anyway help his wife and reduce her suffering.

'We shall return and look in on her again after we have completed our shopping,' Lumak said and they both left.

They returned after the hour and again checked her pulse and temperature, but she was still fast asleep and with a slight but stable level in temperature.

As they mounted the cart for home, Lumak hugged and kissed Sarah.

'What was that for? And in public!' she exclaimed, while pulling away from him.

'I just felt like being close and owed you something for always standing by my side and trusting me. It was just my way of thanking you and telling you how much I love you.'

'I am sorry, Darling, but these people might start to gossip about us and I wouldn't like them to get the wrong idea before we are married. You can kiss me when we are home and behind closed doors. And I don't want it to be in front of dad either. We must show him some respect, you know,' she said, in her usual positive and to the point manner.

After Sarah had spoken her mind, she changed her attitude and became very happy and talkative. He realised there were subtle cultural rules in the game of love which tended to restrict his advances, but on the other hand, also made him want to get even closer to her.

To them the three days passed very quickly. During that period he had received several laboratory items from the city via Olaf, the chemist. Azize, the vet who was Marion's son, and Olaf knew each other well and Azize would deliver items to Lumak at short notice. Lumak could modify and adapt most of the equipment to his needs.

Ben journeyed to the village twice during that time and visited Simon to give her fruits and vegetables. He was thoroughly questioned after each visit by Sarah under Lumak's guidance. Ben thought it was just because of their concern for Marion and knew nothing about the serum.

On the third day they got up early and completed their domestic work as usual before taking the cart to the village. The suspense was too much so they decided to visit Simon's house before they did any of their own shopping.

When they knocked on Simon's door they were greeted by a very cheerful man who could not contain his happier thoughts. With outstretched arms he welcomed them into the house.

'She is still in bed, but she is so much better. She told me about the special medicine you gave her, Doctor, and I am so grateful for your help. I had no idea that you were doing research in the field of cancer. If only I knew before, perhaps I could have given you some assistance. Whatever you need, Doctor... money, equipment, anything!' Simon said.

When they entered her room she was still in bed, but sitting up and reading the newspaper. She glanced at each of them as they entered, but held her final gaze on Lumak.

'Hell, Doctor. I feel great. My abdomen pains have almost gone without the painkilling drugs. Just a slight ache towards my back, but that could be due to my long stay in bed. The swellings have also reduced. I cannot tell you how good I feel, Doctor Jeffery,' she said, then turning to Sarah.

'That's fantastic news!' Sarah exclaimed.

'Please come and sit over here, my dear.' She held Sarah's hand.

'You must always take good care of my doctor for me. His special miracle medicine is working. I can feel its effects where the major growths were. Like it's eating them all up... with a warming sensation. I am so thankful to you and your future husband for saving my life.' Marion began to shed a few tears of joy and happiness.

Lumak went over to her and placed his hand under her chin to check her temperature, but really with the intention to stop her crying. He was also overtaken by events and felt like bursting with joy.

'Yes, Marion, the serum is working quite well, but I am afraid you will require a second dose. This is because it was degraded by the pain killing drugs in your system at the time it was given. This time, however, there will be no need for you to remain in bed. Providing you do not overexert yourself.' Lumak removed the small syringe and handed it to Sarah. By now she had become his full-time nurse. Sarah then gave her the injection.

'I shall again visit you in three days, just to make sure everything is proceeding to plan,' Lumak said in a most professional manner.

'Yes, Doctor. Can I now get out of bed, please Doctor?'

'Yes, Marion, as soon as you wish, but remember what I said. Simon can take care of cooking for you over the next few days. We must now leave you and do some more shopping before we return home.'

On their way home that day Sarah didn't know how to cope with the incredible news of Marion's sudden recovery. Jeffery had made a cure for cancer from basic herbs and foodstuffs. How could that be possible? Even the Americans hadn't yet a cure for that type of cancer and he hadn't any proper equipment. Not even a proper experimental laboratory. How could he have achieved so much in such a short time?

She remembered the evening of his arrival. He was pink and dazed from the cold and wearing that white reflective gown with strange flexible golden sandals. At that time he looked exactly like an ancient prophet. Was he really who he said he was... a special prophet from God to assist us? After all, many very strange things had occurred since his arrival. Not to mention her lamb's miraculous recovery and the dog barking for no reason. Then there was the strange light from the temple and that other occasion when she entered his room. But now, there was the serum which was equally strange.

Lumak nudged her from her daydreaming.

'A nickel for your thoughts,' he said. She then glanced at him and smiled.

'I don't quite know what to say. I am completely baffled and dumbfounded by what you have done with Marion.

'You know, Darling, you are truly a remarkable person to have done such an incredible thing. Don't mention Marion's recovery to dad yet, just in case the process takes a little longer than expected,' she said quietly, not quite believing in those events herself.

'All right, my love. But I did tell you on several occasions that my methods will work and I always keep my word,' he replied and returned her smile. Sarah didn't wish to pursue the conversation regarding Marion's miraculous cure. The whole episode was too much for her to have accepted immediately. Lumak realizing the situation soon changed the topic of their conversation.

'You know, having observed the speeding vehicles in the village, I think riding like this on a horse-driven cart to be a lot more romantic.'

'I have never been one for cars, trucks or lorries. They create too much pollution that can damage our health and the environment. But we need buses and coaches. I read recently that our fuel reserves are almost gone. All such forms of transport will soon become too expensive to run. Anyway, only the very rich can use automobiles these days. Our mode of transport with Saracen's single horse power will always remain the same, and he doesn't need petrol or gasolene,' she replied and Lumak saw much humour in that argument.

'I love you so much and I think we are perfectly matched, because we get on so well together. I can read your moods and you also recognise mine. Please, only change for the better and be always very tolerant with me, because I always mean well in the long term. Whatever I accomplish is for both of us, you know,' he said.

She moved closer to him on the leather covered padded wooden seat of the cart.

'You must do likewise for me and promise.' He promised.

CHAPTER 24

Doctor Emil's visit

Finally, it was doctor Emil's turn to visit his patient, Marion. He usually went to see her once each week and sometimes more frequently when he received new anti-cancer drugs from companies in America and Germany. Some were free experimental samples that he accepted from well-known pharmaceutical companies. Although they had not undergone all relevant tests for certification, they were of an acceptable standard for field testing on humans. However he would also accept certain prescribed drugs from overseas on behalf of his patients' family, who could afford those expenses. Some drugs could be acquired at a fraction of the price that way. He also received small funding from the larger companies for some field trials, which he would use for running a more efficient medical practice.

Occasionally he used his terminal patients as so called guinea pigs and kept accurate records of past pain relief, drug dependency, other important detrimental factors and the occasional cures. Those could never be fully substantiated without further tests and biopsy. Such information he relayed back to the companies and were used for his own records. His terminal patients had little to lose either way and dangerous side effects were not frequently the case with modern-day technologies. Anyway, all such modern drugs had been rigorously tested on other animals and laboratory cultures before their release into the human population.

Dr. Emil was a true professional and a most conscientious individual that would go out of his way to assist any of his patients. He never took anyone or anything for granted and would always explain the known characteristics of the drugs to his patients and their next of kin. He usually had their permission before such drugs were administered. Anyway, they were never in a position to query his intentions. Even so, he never abused his position of trust.

  This time he had no special drugs from America or Germany and was paying one of his scheduled visits to carry out his usual checks on one of his terminal and dying patients. His visit was on a Friday morning in pleasant weather. Her front door was partly opened, so he knocked three times and entered slowly.

  As he entered the house he heard someone singing. As he proceeded toward the kitchen he was astounded.

  'Is that you Marion? He shouted.

  'Who do you think, Doctor?' A surprised Marion jested.

  'I am seeing you but I can't believe you are up and about, even preparing lunch.'

  He was surprised to find Marion cooking lunch and that was not all; she was full of joy and happiness and singing merrily as if she had exceeded her normal amounts of fruit wine.

  He went towards the kitchen and immediately apologised.

  'I am very sorry, Marion, but the front door was open and I became curious when I heard the singing. Now, I can hardly believe my own eyes. You are standing right in front of me and seem to be the one doing the singing.' He was utterly surprise, but still glancing about the place to see if another person was assisting her. Then he proceeded towards her to take a closer look at her pupils and other relevant body indicators. He knew that cancerous patients sometimes had temporary bouts of seemingly painless periods of remission, but never had he observed any far gone cancerous patients like Marion in such a state of ecstasy before. The whole situation was quite unprecedented. The woman looked so normal, with little signs of any drowsiness caused by the pain relieving drugs and if there were no drugs, there should be lots of pain.

  After all, recent tests showed conclusively that she only had about a month to live and that was with the best present-day drugs. He pondered those thoughts for a while.

  'Marion, I would like to carry out some more checks on you. Please come over here and sit with me for a while...' She stopped the cooking, washed her hands and followed him into the livingroom.

He carried out several checks on her body, felt the lumps, checked her glands and the swelling, where they should have been, with little irritation to herself. Then he took a sample of her blood.

By then he was completely dumfounded by her seemingly full recovery.

'Marion, I think you are recovering from the disease. I don't know how or why, but by Allah you are getting better. This blood sample... I will take personally to the city hospital laboratory tomorrow for analysis. I might also need you there later for a full body scan, but that is not essential at this stage.

'My son is now a senior biologist there, you know, so I shall ask him to take special care with your sample... in case there is something special in your blood. I might as well take a urine sample while I am here,' Emil said, with excitement in his voice.

After he had collected both samples, he departed, still utterly confused by the paradoxical situation.

Doctor Emil left early the following morning for the city by landrover. After meeting his son, Jeremy, had lunch at the hospital canteen. It was at that time that he discussed the drastic changes of his patient Marion. Jeremy was equally intrigued by his father's findings and curious in acquiring authentic results, if only to clarify the matter.

Jeremy knew his father well, a reserved, patient and logical mind. He was never one for taking un-calculated risks or foolish pranks in order to spend time away from his important duties. But in this case the man was quite disturbed. Even to the point of driving those many hours to the city over its bumpy roads. And it was all for no real reason than a simple blood analysis. His impatient father had also made a telephone call to his wife the previous evening, just to ensure that he, Jeremy, would be around to await his arrival. Therefore there must be something in his findings.

In any event, how could he fit these tests in at such short notice without first consulting his boss, Professor Chairmowich. Perhaps he could stay late that evening and complete some basic checks with the Electron Microscope. If finding anything of significance, he could show it to the professor in the morning. The professor would then be obliged to give it priority.

   He entered the large university laboratory and booked his appointment with the electron microscope for six-thirty p.m. which was then a vacant period in its log. Then he decided to quickly prepare his samples and stored them before continuing with his scheduled work.

When he finished, he called his wife, Karen, to tell her he would be home late that evening. Then he took the samples over to the microscope. Introduced the wafer thin slices of the targets he had prepared and began to scan and record them, looking for special features during the process. He continued scanning and photographing until he had all the necessary information. Then he went over to the image processor. That device screened the information in a manner more acceptable to the human observer.

   The AI computer assisted equipment could automatically highlight those unusual areas easily missed by the human observer. Certain search characteristics could also be programmed into its search routines to save time. It could also carry out its own magnification, enhancement or reduction on the stored image by the simple touch of a button. The image could be scanned in Virtual 3D and at almost any angle.

   After having found what he was looking for, he made a few sketches and took several printouts. Then he was ready to complete a report for the professor's eyes only. It was written in such a manner that the professor would consider it a very important read during his spare time. After all, he was a very busy man.

He spent the rest of the evening going over and tidying his work with the aid of the lab computer and when he was fully satisfied, he left for home.

The following morning he checked the professor's appointments for the day and arranged to visit him at ten o'clock. That was just before he left for his first lecture of the day.

   He tapped on the door and entered. The professor, now

completely grey, was dictating a letter with his secretary.

'Hello, Jeremy. How can I be of assistance?' he inquired, breaking from the course of his previous sentence.

'I am very sorry, Sir, for this intrusion, but I have discovered a matter of extreme importance to us.'

The professor stared at him, observing his features and the insistence in his voice.

'Brenda, is there anything else?'

'No, Sir, I think I have everything for now,' his secretary replied and went to the adjacent office.

'Ok, young man. Why the great urgency? What have you got that's so important? I can give you five minutes, so please make it snappy.'

Jeremy handed him the file and showed him some of the images and other printouts which included scenes of cancerous cells being torn apart by some other cell that also digested its contents. Then he briefly mentioned his father's observations of the patient, Marion.

'What you are saying... is that, we may have stumbled on a cure for this persistent strain of cancer? A cancer eating cell?' he shouted, with optimistic enthusiasm.

'It seems to be the case, Sir, but it's early days yet and I shall require your permission to take these tests a step further. We have a patient we can study in Dad's village and I have a strong gut feeling about this, Sir. What if we are on the brink of a real discovery... for finding a general cure for cancer? We could become the most important hospital in the whole of Europe.'

The professor thought hard and deep for a moment, staring at his desk with both hands on his forehead in amazement, while glancing at pages of the report.

'Ok... you are not one for wild gestures and have been with me for a long time, so let me try and arrange something after my lecture. It's a pity we are so busy at this time of year. You can get one of our best post-graduate students to assist in some basic tests for a little extra money. That will free your hands to carry out your own analyses on the sample. But please try and get quick results and don't mention a word of our project to anyone for now. Not even your lab assistants!'

'Ok! I understand!'

'The less people know about this important venture, the better. You must also tell your father to keep it very quiet for now. A cure for cancer is an incredibly important thing and as you said; it could put this whole country of ours on the world map. Not to mention our beloved hospital and its lack of essential funding and modern resources.'

'I agree!'

'Jeremy, if we follow this work through, we could also get a Nobel Prize for the project. It could make you and your family very important, so don't take this discovery too lightly.'

'I wont, Sir!'

Suddenly realising the significance of his recent findings, Jeremy was now more eager than ever to see it through to the very end.

Jeremy did a further analysis on the sample to back his original findings and were astounded by the results. Then he handed the professor a more up-to-date copy of the report.

'This conclusively proves the point. I think we are unto something of importance, here,' Jean-Claude said with even greater enthusiasm.

Professor Jean-Claude Chairmowich, although originally from eastern Europe, had been educated in France. He had a French mother and Polish father. During his appointment in Turkey as a chief medical officer, he had received quick recognition and promotion for his enthusiasm, dedication and hard work. After his marriage to a local nurse, he had adopted the Turkish nationality and way of life. He was presently responsible for one of their university hospitals in one of its main cities.

The following day Professor Jean-Claude Chairmowich called Jeremy to his office.

'Jeremy, we are going on a long trip to your father's village to see his patient. Please make the necessary preparations.'

CHAPTER 25

A visit from the city

Jean-Claude and Jeremy were soon on their way to the almost forgotten village in the mountains. Jean-Claude always used his landrover for such trips. Its four-wheel drive tended to cope much better in and out of the rough and pitted roads of those areas.

On arrival they visited Jeremy's father's house and were just in time for lunch.

'That's quite a surprise! I thought you were going to fax me the report,' Doctor Emil said, showing slight irritation by their untimely arrival, but receiving his guests all the same.

'We couldn't. We found something of great importance,' Jeremy said.

'Yes, I'm afraid, and it was a decision made in a hurry due to previous engagements,' the professor said.

His surgery was at the rear of his large house with its own separate entrance. On this occasion they entered from the front and went into a more private room.

'Dad, this is my boss, Professor Chairmowich,' Jeremy said while introducing Jean-Claude. They had never met before.

'Dad, I also brought along the report on the tests as requested. This is a lot more important than I originally thought. We could have here a permanent cure for cancer, so we must keep it quiet for now. Anyway, I thought we should discuss some areas of the report before visiting your patient,' Jeremy said. Then they decided to hold a meeting to discuss those important matters.

Jeremy explained their current progress to his father, and stressed the reasons for secrecy.

They soon decided to visit Marion. Simon, her husband, greeted Doctor Emil and his two companions at the door and took them in to see Marion. Simon was quite intrigued by the visit of such important people to his humble abode and overreacted in his efforts. They had just finished their lunch so Marion was watching an old television program while knitting.

'Hello, Marion! Please meet my son, Jeremy, and Professor Jean-Claude from the city hospital. You have suddenly become a most distinguished celebrity. These important people have come all the way from the city just to see you. You know, your miraculous recovery could lead to a permanent cure for cancer and we would like you to assist us in finding out why. If you don't mind, that is? Also, we have to make sure your cancer is completely gone.' Emil continued nervously.

She immediately stood up, shook their hands in turn and offered them a seat. While they were together, Doctor Emil took her to a remote chair and began to carry out his usual checks. It was then that Marion made a slip of the tongue. Luckily it was not overheard by the professor or Jeremy.

'I still can't believe in your miraculous cure? We are completely stumped by it all,' Emil said.

'You can always see the English doctor at Ben's place for more information. He gave me the anti-serum...' she said. Suddenly realizing the slip, she put her fingers to her lips, gapingly, as if struck by a lightning bolt, but the cat had already been let out of the bag.

'Who?'

'It's Sarah's young friend. He is experimenting on a permanent cure for cancer,' she whispered.

The doctor suddenly realising the implications kept her silent for a moment until he finished his tests.

'I have not heard what you just said, and don't you utter another word on the topic,' he whispered, in no uncertain terms and she nodded in agreement.

Having received all the information they required, the professor and Jeremy left the following hour, taking with them the freshly acquired samples to the city hospital. However an astute Doctor Emil did not mention another word on the subject to anyone. He had to see this clever doctor for himself and find out whether he had really found a lasting cure for cancer before anyone jumped the gun. Also, if there were any gains to be had, he would have preferred it stayed with his poor country folk.

Lumak was removing weed in the vegetable garden close to the house with Sarah when they heard an engine stop, a door banged and then a man's voice.

'Anyone about!' Doctor Emil shouted.

'Over here!' Sarah shouted back and they turned around to see the doctor walking towards them. Sarah left what she was doing and took Lumak with her to greet him. The doctor was well known and respected in those parts by all.

'Please meet my fiancee, Doctor Jeffery Longhurst,' she said proudly and Lumak went forward to shake his hand.

'So you are the eminent English doctor. No one told me of your presence hereabouts.' He studied Lumak for a while.

'I only arrived here recently. I am afraid... I haven't been able to do very much or meet many locals since my arrival. I am now trying to help Sarah and her father to run things. We will soon be getting married, you know.' Doctor Emil forced a smile and put his hand out.

'Congratulations, Doctor! Congratulations, Sarah! I had no idea of your intentions, but I have not been here since your Mother's... ,' Emil did not wish to restate the circumstances of her mother's death.

'What brings you here, Doctor?' inquired Sarah, innocently. Doctor Emil suddenly became quiet and serious.

'I have been to see Marion.'

'I would like to apologise for interfering with your patient. I just felt I could assist in some small way, and we didn't have the time to get it pass the normal channels, she having such a short time.'

'Some small way indeed. Doctor, please do not play the innocent and modest part with me. All recent tests suggests that Marion has completely recovered from her illness... a complete remission. Do you know what that means, Doctor? You have obviously found a lasting cure for certain deadlier forms of cancer. Do you understand what you have really done, Doctor? You have found a way to save millions of innocent lives and their suffering; that's what you have done!'

Emil was unable to fully contain his emotions, so he went up to Lumak and embraced him as if he was a long lost son; for that was the way he felt and the only way he would gain release from his emotions at that moment.

'I realise that, but I want to carry out more experiments to help others,' Lumak replied.

'Do you like our country, Doctor? We have never had things as easy as you in England. We work very hard and achieve very little. When you marry Sarah, you will then become one of us and just half English. Then again, we are all Europeans together. If you find a cure for all types of cancers in our country with our equipment, that situation will place a completely different light on things. It will place our country and even our little village and your place here on the world map. Do you understand what I am saying to you, my son?' Emil said, with more emotions tinged with patriotism.

'Yes, Doctor Emil. Why don't we go into the house for a cup of tea or a cold drink?' Sarah asked and they went indoors. Then they changed the topic of the conversation.

'Sarah, how is your dad? The last time I saw him was several weeks ago in the village, and at that time he seemed quite worried.'

'He is ok, Doctor. He is just a little dissatisfied with his life at the present time. He went to the hills to collect the sheep just before your arrival. He should return in a few minutes,' she replied.

Doctor Emil and Ben were the best of friends when they were younger. They had grown up together and went to the same primary school.

'Jeffery, I would like you to go to the city and meet my son, Jeremy. He is a biologist in one of the leading university hospitals and his boss Professor Jean-Claude Chaimowich will also want to see you, all expenses paid of course.

'Really!' Lumak replied ecstatically.

'Why don't you take Sarah along. You could then stay with my son and his wife if you so wish.'

Doctor Emil was absorbed by it all. It was as if he had just adopted a new son and daughter.

'I shall make the necessary arrangements with my son today and let you know when it's ready. So please make the necessary preparations in the mean time, and I will not accept "no" for an answer.'

'Sounds fantastic!' A happy Sarah exclaimed. Lumak was also ecstatic with that result.

'I must now leave you before it gets too late.' They escorted him to his car.

'So much for our attempts in finding a place to stay in the city during our holidays!' Sarah said cheerfully. Then they returned to the house after seeing him off.

Lumak left her for a brief moment and when he returned she couldn't believe her eyes, for he was wearing the white gown and golden sandals that he had arrived in on that first day.

'How do I look?'

She was stunned by the image of the man.

'You... are... not... going to wear those clothes in the city. Are you, Darling?' she asked, with that famous stare that could turn any lesser mortal into stone.

'Yes, my love.' He was serene.

'You might look out of place in a modern city,'

'In future, this will be my stately uniform...this will be my dress when I am on official business. At other times I can wear whatever you suggest. You may do likewise if you wish, or wear the most beautiful city clothes. Because from now I want you to twinkle like the brightest star in the heavens.

'Are you feeling ok, Darling?' she inquired.

'Yes! On top of the world! As I said, from this time you will become my most beautiful little star, but don't you ever overdo the colours.'

She listened and smiled with an impression of partial acceptance for his strange attire.

Lumak felt a turning point had come in his program. The very first door had opened in their lives. It was as if suddenly a small mountain had been lifted off his shoulders.

CHAPTER 26

Preliminary journey to the city

Ben soon arrived and was surprised to see Lumak dressed in the strange attire. Sarah soon explained the reasons why they were acting in such an excited manner.

'Dad, guess what? We had a visit from Doctor Emil. You just missed him. Jeff's cure for cancer has worked! It's an incredible miracle! It's worked!'.

'You mean to say his experiments were for curing cancer, and he has found a lasting cure?' an astonished Ben replied.

'Yes, Dad. She is completely cured of her cancer! He saved the poor woman's life!' Ben couldn't help hugging Lumak, even while he was wearing the strange attire. Lumak was speechless and just smiled without any explanations of how his methods worked.

'Who? Which woman?' Ben asked, impatiently.

'Marion! Simon's wife!

'Oh! Greatest Allah!' he yelled, with utter astonishment.

'Doctor Emil wants us to stay with his family in the city. Jeff is going to visit the largest university hospital to see an important professor called Chai..mo...vic. What do you think, Dad?' Sarah just couldn't hold back her happiness.

'I think it's unbelievable. It's bloody marvellous. I don't really know what to say. It's such incredible news. Don't you worry about this place. I am quite capable of looking after things here in your absence,' he replied, still admiring Lumak's strange dress, and remembering the day of his arrival when he almost shot him dead. What a big mistake that would have been.

Ben couldn't make much sense from what Sarah had said but accepted that his future son-in-law was a super genius, although one of those slightly eccentric people that tended to wear odd costumes. To have created a cure for cancer meant that he was a very clever English research doctor, and if he continued with his research and became successful, his daughter Sarah would be very well supported financially.

He wouldn't stand in their way of progress. Not at any cost. So he must assist his daughter and son-in-law to make the necessary preparations for their important journey and so he thought.

'Dad, if everything works out, and when things improve I will like us to build a large and beautiful house on this land for our family. Then I will stock it with all the latest appliances and a few responsible helpers. Then you can be free to do as you wish, even come along with us on special missions. I would also like to interview one or two young sheep farmers on my return,' Lumak said. Sarah was very quiet, feeling excluded, but listened to the men discuss future plans as was customary and went back to the kitchen.

Since their engagement he tended to call Ben Dad instead of Ben, short for Bengizara, which was his first name.

Sarah was weary of the male chauvinistic attitude of her father, which Lumak tended to pick up. Most of it had existed in their society for millennia and despite more modern trends, was not easy to surpass. Anyway, it was a male thing and she would quickly deal with her future husband if things got out of hand. She also realized their attitude was mainly to do with the excitement of the moment and many such plans seldom came to fruition in light of day.

Lumak had returned to his makeshift laboratory and began typing out a report in near perfect English. He had borrowed a small electric typewriter from Olaf, the village pharmacist, while on a previous visit for another purpose. At that time most of his equipment had been borrowed from that same place. Olaf and Lumak had become good friends and both assisted each other. Lumak advised him in his business and very soon his trade expanded to include many useful items.

Although Lumak had learnt the art of writing, he found the process slow and tedious and required too much patience on his part. He had also found a pen much too slow to manipulate while thinking. His thoughts were always kilometres ahead of the print.

He soon found he could tune his implants to the electric typewriters keyboard and after a little practice was able to type at speeds in access of one hundred and fifty words per minute. That speed was the limit set by his fingers and the typewriter's keys and mechanism.

He drew most of the sketches free hand from memory, but here again, his implants simply transferred the almost identical images to the paper with near perfect straight lines when they were needed. Because of his brain implants, his thoughts had almost perfect control over all his muscle groups. When he had finished his report, although compiled by typewriter, pencil and simple crayons, it could well have been considered a highly professional document that had been prepared by a good publisher.

The report took him two days to compile, while giving Sarah a hand with her normal duties. After that time they were ready to visit the city.

When Ben arrived from the village that day he carried a note from Doctor Emil. It simply informed them that arrangements had been completed and they could visit the city when ready during the next few weeks. Further adding that his son Jeremy would see the professor and arrange a special meeting to be held as soon as possible and at their convenience. Sarah joyfully read the note to Lumak and Ben.

'Now, and all of a sudden, everyone of importance wants us.' She held on to the note as if it was the most important message she had ever received.

Being his first time away, Lumak intended to remain in the city for a maximum of two weeks. He didn't like the idea of leaving Ben alone with no telephone in the house in case of emergencies. Perhaps Simon and Marion would remain with him for a while. After all, they had agreed to assist and would not refuse at this crucial time.

The following day they visited the village and asked Simon and Marion if they could assist. They agreed with the change and would find someone to take care of the animals for little wages.

Then the couple visited Emil's house, told him of their plans and asked him to make the necessary arrangements with his son, Jeremy. Then they went to get their travel tickets.

'I didn't realize we had so many places to go before a simple visit to the city. It's a good thing we are not travelling to England, then we would require shots and God knows what else,' Sarah complained.

'I know, my love. It's a very hot day and I'm also sweating like a pig,' Lumak replied and she realized he was taking the mickey.

When they arrived home that day they were laden with groceries and utterly exhausted, but relieved that all preparations had been completed. All they had to do was prepare their clothes and pack their cases.

After the packing was over, Lumak held her in his arms tightly and kissed her several times, showing as much affection as he could, given present circumstances and she reciprocated his affections.

They were now as one on the same roller coaster and he knew that wherever he went she would follow.

They left the following morning for the village. That was after having had a large breakfast with porridge oats, and after saying goodbye to Spotty their dog. They took two suitcases with them, several smaller travelling bags and Ben drove the cart. From Emil's house they went to catch the local bus to the coach station, waving at Ben and Saracen as they departed.

From the station they would take a long-range coach to the city.

CHAPTER 27

Their final journey to the city

Lumak was enthusiastic on his trip to the city as they entered the long distance coach. Both sat quietly towards the rear with intentions of admiring the view.

'I love these seats, they are so comfortable!' He said.

'I see what you mean. Not like those on our favourite cart transport!' She replied and he grinned.

'Never!' He exclaimed.

' I once rode a similar coach when I was nine but it was never as nice as this,' she was now more relaxed after the first rougher part of their trip.

Sarah being a keen observer of people was focussed on two men and a woman entering the coach. As they passed towards the rear they reeked like vagrants not having a bath for months. She realized they carried no baggage or indeed backpacks, which was expected on a long journey.

'Watch those three. They could be up to no good.' she whispered.

'You think they are robbers?' he whispered back.

'I am not sure, but they look the type and smell that way,' she replied.

'Don't worry! You are safe with me,' he jested with little concern.

Lumak always carried his special Shadite's cloak underneath his clothes with the special belt, so was always prepared for any eventuality. In his mind, he would swiftly disarm those vagrants and send them on their way.

However, how could he accomplish that feat with all those passengers on the coach. He would have to create a distraction. When their attentions were distracted he could then work is magic, or so he thought.

Stopping the coach was not a problem. He could interrupt the driver and press the brakes while invisible. Then he could disarm and get the robbers off the coach. During that time he could frieze the coach and its occupants in a time stream. Thus, the passengers, including the driver, would be frozen in time until released at his discretion.

The coach was once again on route with a cheerful and talkative lot of passengers while the supposed robbers remained seated at the rear. The toughest guy suddenly got up and walked towards the driver as if to ask him a question, but pulled out a gun and pointed towards his head. He said mildly in Turkish:
'Don't say a word. Carry on driving and I'll tell you when to stop. Or I'll put a hole through your head!' he was serious and meant business. Soon after, the other two at the rear retrieved their weapons and pointed randomly at the passengers.
'Lets have some money and jewellery, even mobile phones are acceptable. So get moving or I'll start shooting!' the shabby girl commanded.
'We are in a hurry, so hurry up or I'll shoot someone just for entertainment!' the other stressed.
Lumak observing the dangerous situation that could quickly get out of hand, decided to make his move before anyone got hurt. He had to be quick with whatever move he made. Using the buckle on his belt, he simply froze time in the area for a few minutes.
Realizing the state of those desperate vagrants, not having eaten for days. He decided on a less violent plan. Anyway his Shadite's cloak contained one of those shrinking pockets full of golden coins he sometimes used for barter. Coins he could never used for currency but could reproduce while using the powers of the Mind. Although such coins were not acceptable currency he thought perhaps those would-be criminals would find a way to trade them.
During that short but frozen time he disarmed them and while invisible, forced them out of the coach. They were afraid but amazed. They stood in front of the black hooded figure frozen and in shock.
'I know you guys are in a difficult situation but robbing coaches will get you nowhere other than jail.' Here, take these gold coins

and be forever good and kind to others, because I shall be watching!' then like a shadite he faded into nothing and was back in his seat fully dressed as if nothing had happened.

'Did you have anything to do with this!' Sarah exclaimed the moment she realized the coach had returned to normal without the robbers.

'Perhaps?' he replied, fully pleased with his actions.

'How could you? You had simply vanished and was not in your seat. I was frozen and could observe everyone was also frozen.' she probed for a sensible answer.

Yes! It was me! I didn't want to see anyone hurt,' he replied.

'But they disappeared from the coach. How could you do that!'

'How can you know anything when you were frozen at the time? He replied.

Lumak then realized that Sarah was one of the few sensitive people not affected by time in that way. Perhaps she had other hidden powers she was not aware of or so he thought. Anyway, the threat was now over and they could be more relaxed on their remaining journey.

They were still wearing their worst clothes for the dusty coach trip and felt a little worse for ware given the circumstances of their journey. When they arrived it was late afternoon. There were many waiting at the main station to receive their families and friends. It so happened that the main city coach station was quite close to Jeremy's house. They had to fight their way through the multitudes and await their turn for a cab.

Lumak had never seen so many humans in one place before and realized the city was going to be a very different place for any long term survival. Nevertheless Sarah was pleased about their safe arrival. There were so many bad rumours about kidnaps, not to mention their recent experience, that she always dreaded those trips.

In this case however, the coach journey was quite a straightforward trip, with only a moderate amount of violence on route. She was happy with the knowledge that things had become quite peaceful in those parts once again except for the minor incidence.

Despite their exhaustive and bumpy trip, Sarah was awed by everything, most of all the tall skyscrapers. Then there were the many illuminated and animated advertising signs. Suddenly she felt in the mood for the change and looked forward to her city holidays. She had not been to the city for such a long time and there had been so many changes since her last visit. She was also excited by the thought of seeing members of her family and friends after such a long time. She always liked to be around people, which hopefully will be a great change from her isolated existence in the remotest hills and so she thought.

Nevertheless once she settled she would endeavour to become a real woman again, with long and clean fingernails; to wear nice clothes and have soft and beautiful hands like those city girls she had seen in the papers and fashion magazines. How could she ever thank her future husband for making it all possible. After all, it was all due to his brilliance as a doctor.

On arrival at Jeremy's house they were greeted by his wife, Karen.

'Hi! You must be Sarah and the English biologist, Doctor Jeffery. I am pleased to meet you both.

'This is a great place!' Sarah greeted.

'Hope you like it! Jeremy will be home a little later. Please leave your things here and follow me into the dining room. Faizal will take them up to your rooms when he returns from the market.'

They bowed their heads respectfully as they entered and moved their cases inside the doorway.

'Did you have a kindly trip?'

'Yes! It was a little bumpy and we had to divert a few times on route, but there were no guns or fighting,' Sarah replied. Not mentioning anything about the three robbers.

'Thank goodness for that.'

'This is a very modern home. With so many facilities,' Lumak commented.

'We try our best. I've been looking forward to meeting you. Jeremy's father couldn't stop talking and complementing you both,' Karen said.

Sarah quickly glanced around the local rooms and was impressed with the furniture and other items for service and beauty.

'This is really a nice and comfortable home,' she complemented again.

'Let us have some tea together and I can show you both around afterwards.'

When they had finished tea, which comprised mainly of vegetable burgers, orange juice and small cakes, she took them to their rooms and then for a general tour of the house.

Karen was petite, slim and beautiful. She liked her jewellery and makeup, and both women clicked the moment they met.

The couple were both surprised by the many foreign appliances in the kitchen and elsewhere, including a microwave oven, washing machine, spin dryer and electric food mixers. In the lounge were a large almost brand new wide screen television with digital video recorder, camera and cable. Lumak was bemused by it all, but equally impressed. He knew he was where he wanted to be and finally on his way towards achieving his goals.

Sarah soon realized that her existence in the country hills were a million kilometres away and a thousand years in the past from that type of existence.

Jeremy arrived earlier than usual and although he expected his visitors on that day, was not sure at what time they would arrive. Those long and bumpy trips could sometimes take much longer than expected and they never gave out estimated times of arrival at the main coach stations. But they would be much safer travelling by passenger coach than most other means of transport. Yet, he wished they had arrived safely.

Jeremy had since found the whole situation with his father a complete mystery. His dad and other people had obviously kept important information from him. After all, why did he have to put up those country strangers in his home on their holidays to the city. And did they have something to do with the miraculous cure for cancer? All he knew was that the girl Sarah and her future husband; a very important English doctor and biologist, were coming on a holiday break and he had to put them up. What was all the drama and secrecy about?

Jeremy and his wife Karen was still quite young. Both studied in England with a fair knowledge of the English language. She used to be a fully qualified nurse and met Jeremy at one of those hospital dances. He was soon accepted by her family who were from different parts of their country.

Jeremy was in his early thirties and Karen in her late twenties, but with no children.

The domestic helper, Faizal, had arrived later than expected from the market with much groceries and immediately began to assist with preparing dinner, while being questioned by Karen for his late arrival.

Sarah had began to assist Karen in the kitchen, while chatting about her new and old experiences of the city.

On his arrival that day, Jeremy observed the suitcases parked near the door and was even more curious. Karen had just finished cooking dinner and was watching one of her favourite European soap operas on television when he joined her.

'Darling, where are our two visitors?' He kissed her on the cheek and sat next to her.

'They went to unpack and have a bath.'

He got up and went to the kitchen for a cold orange drink, but soon returned.

'Darling, who are they really and what is it all about. Dad was so mysterious on the phone and her fiancee is an English doctor, of all people. You know, very strange things have been happening in that village and I wonder if there is a link between him and those other occurrences?' he whispered.

'I don't know, Darling. Why don't you ask him?'

It was not long before Sarah appeared, followed by Lumak. They were both wearing new clothes and looking radiant. They introduced themselves to Jeremy and shook his hand before going into the dining room for dinner.

'I am pleased to meet you Jeremy. I must say there is a strong resemblance to your father,' Lumak said.

'He has his fathers chin and his mothers nose and eyes,' Karen commented and they laughed.

After dinner both men went over to the small bar and Lumak helped himself to a little vodka with lots of tonic. It also happened to be Jeremy's favourite drink. Lumak was very good at analysing taste through his implants so it was just a matter of time before he knew every molecular part of the substance, even down to its precise age. He could do the same for whiskey and wines.

His main reason for analysing food was to isolate all the trace chemicals that were detrimental to the human body. That was one of the main reasons why so many people had food allergies and lived such short lives. By so doing he could supply a health list to hospitals and relevant organisations in the future. He had realized that most natural foods consumed by Earth's humans had small quantities of poisons that were detrimental to the body. In his original Semonite form that would never have been a problem, since their senses were highly tuned to extract such information from all materials, including the air. Nevertheless Semonites only ingested pure nectar and berry juice.

Jeremy became more relaxed and found in Lumak a library of information on every conceivable topic of discussion. But he also found him a pleasant and fun loving individual.

'You appear to be a very good doctor from what I hear?' Jeremy inquired, while doing a little subtle probing.

'Yes, I suppose... in biology, among other things.'

'Do you know anything about research work in America and England on cancer?'

'Nothing too specific. I have been too busy over the past weeks on my own projects. So please forgive me if I'm not up-to-date.'

'I have recently read the latest papers on certain types of prevalent strains and think we have a long way to go before finding lasting cures for such types?' Jeremy said.

'That is not always the case. Once a cure is found on a particular type it is always easier to find other cures using similar methods.

Since it happens at the genetic level, why not modify it at that level.'

'You are talking about gene-splicers. We are no where close to that type of science yet?'

'Well, Jemmy, I trust you don't mind me calling you Jemmy and you may call me Jeff. All my friends call me Jeff. I have recently isolated a deviant group of chromosomes that can cause cancerous formations and runaway cell growth. With that knowledge, I have been able to formulate serums for curing most, if not every type, and the work was carried out at the genetic level. So there is little need to worry about such types in the future.'

'Yea, but I still think it's not possible!'

'My friend, the job is done! I have recently written a report on the subject. You are free to study it if you wish. It should make exciting reading.'

'I still don't believe you! It sounds much too easy to be true!'

'I can assure you. It's not as difficult as it sounds. Are you also involved in such research?' Lumak asked, innocently. Jeremy assumed he had been found out and was being kidded along in a similar vane.

'Do you know of a woman by the name of Marion in your local village.'

'Yes, Jemmy, she is a friend of ours and was also suffering from cancer. I administered the serum to her. She should be fully recovered by now. The original serum preparation was not too effective, I am afraid. It took six days to complete her treatment and remove all traces of the cancerous tissue from her system. My latest adjustments can reduce that time period to under three days, with a slight increase in temperature on old and chronic patients in similar condition. It can also give an age reduction of approximately ten years, depending on the age and genetics of the patient,' Lumak replied most positively.

Jeremy was by now completely baffled and confused.

'Could he be winding me up? No one has ever gone that far before, not even the Americans in acquiring a lasting cure. After all, I have read most of the medical journals on the subject and never heard of a special serum... a permanent cure for all types of cancer... with an age reduction? Anyway, perhaps I should read his report first before I make any assumptions or jump to any premature conclusions.' Jeremy took a large gulp and emptied the glass. He decided for another refill and nervously poured himself another tall drink with lots of tonic water.

'Doctor... Jeff, you must have been to a great university?' Jeremy inquired almost stuttering.

'Yes Jemmy. The best. The University of Goh. I am also a doctor in Stellar Sciences and Micro Robotics, you know.'

Jeremy was now convinced of a leg-pull on his behalf and decided to change the topic.

They soon joined the women in the lounge. They watched television and chatted for the rest of the evening on a varying range of topics.

When it was almost time to retire Lumak went to get the report and dropped it into Jeremy's lap. Jeremy quickly scanned through its pages, observing the sketches and realised that most of them were identical to the images he had taken with the Electron Microscope. But the report went much deeper into topics that he knew nothing about. Neither had he read them before in any medical journal.

It was genetic engineering on an unprecedented scale, where complex cell structures were represented in a 3D diagram format, giving one a much clearer picture of functionality as well. He quickly realised that even he, with all his years of experience, could only understand the very basic concepts. It was so completely beyond him as to be almost alien in origin. The article was so expressive, so unique, so logical and yet, so beautiful. He was expressionless and dumbfounded. Regretting his inadequacies in comprehending its subtler concepts.

'You prepared this... incredible report, all by yourself?'

'Yes, Jemmy, how many times? It's my job, after all,' Lumak replied, unconcerned. Then Jeremy handed him back the report.

'Will you please accompany me to the university tomorrow. I would like you to meet Professor Jean-Claude and please take that report along. My God, this is truly incredible, and you have not been kidding me along. You have really found a cure for all forms of cancer, by using a sample of the patients own blood!'

'Jemmy, strictly speaking the patient's blood is not necessary. In future a broad range of the serum can be extracted from grown synthetic genetic material. Then just a mouth swab will be required from the patient for type-matching.'

'By Allah, he's done it! He has really done it!' Jeremy shouted at the top of his voice and Karen and Sarah soon entered to see what the problem was.

'What's up with you guys. I can't watch my program with all this noise!' Karen screamed.

'Karen, that man over there has found a lasting cure for all forms of cancer. The bloody man has done what every brilliant mind on this planet have been trying to accomplish for the past century. And we are the lucky ones to be here to witness this miracle of all miracles!' Then he went up to Lumak to firmly shake his hand for having accomplished the greatest breakthrough of all time.

'You sure?' a bewildered Karen replied.

'Yes. I'm afraid so, Karen,' Sarah interjected and she was dumfounded.

Suddenly, Jeremy realized that his hopes and dreams of glory had flown out the window along with his Nobel Prize. The strange English doctor from the hills was none other than the one with a permanent cure for cancer. But how could he have done it with such little resources and in that virtually unknown part of the country?

Many questions began to flow through Jeremy's mind in an attempt to siphon off a little reality from the unbelievable situation. From the few pages of the report he was able to comprehend, the man was really a super genius and all those supposed ridiculous answers he gave; he was not kidding him along. Everything he said was really the truth.

He wondered how Jean-Claude would receive the bad news and disappointment in the morning.

CHAPTER 28

The university hospital

The following morning Sarah got up earlier than everyone and was soon joined by Karen in the kitchen. She was not used to the city noises and had a restless night. Lumak decided to wear his new grey suit which Ben had given him. It was the last suit Ben had bought before the death of his wife and was very fashionable then.

Both men were of a similar build at just under two metres tall, so his clothes fitted Lumak well. He remembered Ben recovering the suit from the large almost watertight trunk before they left. This is where he stored most of the family's special jewellery and clothes used only on the rarest of occasions. It contained several camphor balls which gave a sweet smell and isolated well its contents from insects and damp. The single wardrobe was utilized by Sarah for her more frequently used items of clothes.

'If this fits you, my son, it's yours, and here are these brand new shirts and trousers. I have always felt uncomfortable wearing suits anyway. I had enough of uniforms in the army. It was bought under the insistence of my wife, you know, when we planned a city holiday. Sadly, that was not to be. Perhaps it was meant for you and my daughter instead. History has a strange way of repeating itself in many ways, you know, and now my beloved Alexandra is with Allah.'

'I am very sorry, Dad.'

'Anyway, other similar clothes you will find a lot cheaper in the city stores. Perhaps these will do you for now until you get yourself organised, my son.'

'I thank you very much for these, and I am very sorry for leaving you here all by yourself, but we will make it up to you in due course.'

Now, here he was in the big city with all its smells and noises and wearing that same suit, while Ben was hundreds of kilometres away. How changeable the circumstances of life were; for even recently he thought he would never be able to support his wife and their future family.

It was therefore of great surprise to both women when they saw a well dressed Lumak walking towards the breakfast table with briefcase in hand.

Sarah gazed at him in amazement.

'Good morning, Darling!' Sarah kissed him on the cheek.

'Good morning, Love!'

'I see you are quite prepared for business today, but thankfully not in your favourite gown.' she said with a broad smile.

'Yes, Love. I am accompanying Jemmy to the university hospital today. He would like me to meet his Professor, Jean-Claude, but I should be back before lunch,' he said, as Karen entered and greeted them.

It was not long before Jeremy arrived, also wearing something special and they sat together for breakfast.

Jeremy was the first to finish and turned to his wife for a quick word.

'Darling, I have left the car keys on the side table, so feel free to use it today and show Sarah around while you do your shopping. I know of a short-cut that will only take us twenty minutes. If we leave now we'll be in time to catch the professor before he sits with his secretary. This will also give Jeff a glimpse of this part of our city,' Jeremy said and both got up and left.

Lumak soon began to absorbed the atmosphere of the place. Although somewhat polluted, it was his first leisurely experience of an Earth city, with all its skyscrapers and ancient buildings intermixed as far as the eye could see. The year was 2041 when most cities were overbuilt. In Earth's case a soaring global human population of over 9 billion.

'This is truly an incredible planet of cities,' he thought.

The only thing that disturbed him was the enormous traffic and to his disadvantage, the pedestrian crossings were not as numerous.

He realized how differently Earth's society would have been if portals had been invented. Without the use of roads and such outmoded forms of vehicular transport, the planet would be much cleaner. There would be a lot more land areas available to build on. Such portals could be fitted within the home. From there one could follow virtually any destination. However in such a more disordered society high security would be essential, if one was to avoid criminals gaining entry to the property of others.

'Doesn't the traffic ever cease?' he said to Jeremy in jest.

'Only when the light changes to red and even then you can't guarantee some fool wont break the rules. When crossing this traffic I never take anything for granted, not even the most professional drivers,' Jeremy replied, but Lumak took it all in his stride like an accustomed city dweller.

They arrived earlier than expected and stood in the corridor while waiting patiently for the professor to appear. It was not long before he entered and was greeted promptly by Jeremy.

'Good morning, Sir!' Jean-Claude glanced at him and the stranger while retrieving the door key that he began to insert into the lock.

'Yes. Good morning gentlemen! What's going on Jeremy?'

'I brought a special person with me today. Someone of great importance to us. He is an English biologist by the name of Doctor Jeffery Longhurst. I think we have been barking up the wrong tree, Sir,' Jeremy whispered. 'He has all the answers, Sir.'

'Jeremy, please ask your friend to follow us into my office. We must not discuss such matters out here,' Jean-Claude insisted, still very confused by the situation and even more security conscious than before.

'Now, Jeremy, what is this all about. Is it to do with the special tests you are carrying out for me?'

At that moment Lumak stretched out his hand to the professor.

'I am Doctor Jeffery Longhurst. I am very pleased to have met you, Sir,' Lumak said, while opening his briefcase to retrieve the special file containing the report. Then he handed it to the professor. Jean-Claude flicked through its pages quickly and stopped at an area in mid pages.

'This is brilliant, Jeremy. Never before have I seen anything like it,' he said, turning to Lumak.

'Did you do all this work yourself?'

'Yes, Sir. I began this preliminary report two days ago. I wanted to take along some relevant information, just in case.'

'A preliminary report?' Jean-Claude muttered to himself, slowly scanning the pages a second time.

'It's all there, Sir. I mean, what is relevant to the reduction of cancerous growth by anti-body stimulation and other means by the special serum.'

Jean-Claude was dumbfounded. By this time his secretary had arrived and seeing the silhouette of the three figures through the opaque glass, knocked on the door and entered.

'Brenda, please get us a pot of coffee and some cups, and stop all calls. I shall not be disturbed at this time.' She immediately left. He eyed Lumak for a while.

'Are you married, Son.'

'No, Sir, not yet, but I intend to be, very soon.'

'He is marrying one of our country girls, Sir. From near the village we visited; my father's village. She is an original Khan, you know. One of the descendants of one of our greatest and most ancient and bravest hill clans,' Jeremy interrupted, proudly and at attention.

'Yes Jeremy, I also know my history? In that case, I am very happy for you both. Shall I call you Jeff?' Jean-Claude said and Lumak nodded in approval.

Jean-Claude was not one for mincing his words and realised the significance of the incredible situation in which he now found himself. This was an opportunity of a lifetime and he wouldn't detract one iota from the possibility of such a promising future.

'Will you come and lecture for me at this university? We can supply you with everything you need, within our budget of course and you can be put on a retainer and made a professor; after you have completed your first major work... which is already in my hand. That also includes your own laboratory and if you are successful, we shall get grants and sponsors from all over the world. By then you might have the whole university to assist in your own work. Not to mention a Nobel Prize.'

Lumak could not believe his luck and kept nodding his head, showing little concern in what was offered.

'You can use whatever facilities and manpower you require. All we expect in return is... a mention of this university in your studies. That's all I ask,' Jean-Claude said, in anticipation of some great disappointment but instead Lumak smiled.

'Of course professor, but I shall also need to help the suffering people hereabouts. Which includes the city as well. I will not accept any payment for those services.

'All serum can be supplied by this hospital through me. A form of partnership if you like. This will give you more funds and place your name on the world markets. However, we shall need a small processing plant for manufacturing serum in the desired quantities. I have already put those plans together.'

Jean-Claude felt completely naked and inadequate in Lumak's presence.

'Jeff... I shall make all the necessary arrangements and get an agreement drafted for our mutual benefit relating to what we have discussed.'

'Perhaps I should put together some more serum of the basic type used in the village. They cover the most common blood groups. All I shall need are these items and materials,' he said and handed the list to Jean-Claude.

'That will be great, Jeff. Is there anything else that we should discuss before winding up this meeting?' a busy Jean-Claude asked.

'No, Sir. You know, this city is such a fine place. I am getting to like it and appreciate its people and their needs already... So many beautiful people. I think we are going to do some very great work together in this place,' Lumak replied, with that glint in his eye and with such enthusiasm that everyone in that room felt like taking on the world. For he had that effect on people.

He firmly shook Jean-Claude's hand again and both left his office.

'Are you sure you can make it home on your own?' a worried

Jeremy inquired.

'I can draw you a map if you like!' Lumak replied and Jeremy's worries dissipated.

Lumak left Jeremy in the university and made his own way to the house via another route.

Among other things, he had a perfect sense of direction and was never afraid of getting lost anywhere. He just wanted to see the place for himself and absorb its moods and dangers, and on a more materialistic level, to locate and view its many shops, banks, restaurants, clubs, theatres, cinemas, libraries and holy places.

Lumak was excited by the fact that he had made his first real technological breakthrough and had found suitable contacts on Earth. He realized that he was suddenly on his way to fulfilling his most important mission and Sarah's dreams.

CHAPTER 29

Lumak's first job

It was just afternoon when Lumak arrived home. The ladies had recently returned from the shops and very happy in seeing him. In that short time Sarah had acclimatised well to city life and wanted to partake in its many activities. Although excited with his new appointment, Lumak tended to be reserved about such things, and held his overwhelming emotions.

'Hello, Darling. Did you see the professor?' Sarah greeted, with utter curiosity.

'Yes, Love, the professor wants me to lecture at the university. He has put me on a retainer!' he busted out.

'A retainer? You have got a job?' Sarah exclaimed and they embraced for a while.

'It'll be a senior position and I will be able to make my own decisions, within reason.' He continued to explain what had transpired at their meeting and she went up to him again now happier than ever and kissed him.

'I have been talking with Karen and what she says make lots of sense. Why don't we get married here as soon as we can, and with the money you earn, rent a small apartment or house. She is willing to help us organise things and we can always send for dad when we are ready. He wont mind being away for a month or so, but we'll have to arrange his journey for the wedding,' Sarah said.

'Ok! Ok! But let's not get ahead of ourselves. Wait until things are finalised with the university. I don't want us to depend too heavily on Jemmy and Karen. They have their own responsibilities, you know, and they are already doing us a big favour.'

'Ok, Darling. Whatever you think.'

'Have you paid Karen the money for our board and lodgings?' he whispered in her ear and she immediately left and went to her room. She soon returned and joined Karen in the kitchen. Sarah had been so excited since their arrival that she had completely forgotten about those money matters.

'Karen, this is from Jeff and myself towards our stay here,' She said, while handing her two hundred US Dollars.

'With all the excitement I forgot to give it to you yesterday.'

'No, Sarah. Please don't worry about your stay with us. You are our guests and we are very happy to have you both.'

'I am sorry Karen, but this is only towards food and one hundred is towards a suitable present we were unable to find for you in the village. We shall make the balance up to you later,' Sarah insisted and Karen, knowing that she had little choice in the matter, took the money and placed it in a box. She used that piggy bank mainly for charity.

'If you are sure that it's alright. But I accept under strong protest,' Karen said, smiling.

Sarah and Karen had become the best of friends since their shopping treks and got on together better than most sisters because of their happy dispositions.

Jeremy, on the other hand, felt very respectful of Lumak and treated him more like a senior brother. He was never sure of himself when Lumak was around. The man was so knowledgeable and overwhelming, and always so correct in his assessment of things. In fact, the man Lumak was so clever in his replies that he always thought he was being kidded, even when he was telling him the honest truth.

Jeremy was very tolerant and entertained his guests to the best of his abilities and they became like family to him and his wife, Karen.

So many changes had occurred over the past week, leaving Jeremy quite confused and unsettled. He realized he could never catch up in that particular race. Not with Lumak at the wheel. Neither did he know where it led, but he didn't mind partaking as a passenger if the genius Lumak remained behind the wheel. Nevertheless very soon he would have to regain his composure and follow some new direction of his own ambitions and so he thought while glancing through the evening papers.

'Ah, Jemmy, there you are.'

'Hi.'

'Like a drink?' Lumak asked, as he entered.

'Yes! Please do! Make it a tall one with lots of soda. I think I am going to need it.'

This time he poured two vodkas with lots of tonic and took one over to Jeremy.

'I was just thinking. So many things have happened since your arrival. It's difficult for me to absorb it all,' Jeremy said.

'Yep! I have that way with people. How would you like to work with me in the future. I have great plans with the university's assistance and I need someone to run the production plant for me when it's ready. It will start at double your present salary and you can also have your name close to mine on journals and such like. But you will have to prepare the articles yourself. Jean-Claude can have his name close to mine on work within the university.

'I would like to help, if I can,' Jeremy replied.

'I intend to utilise all the latest equipment from Germany and the States, so it could be a great challenge for you as well. You could even be placed to receive your own Nobel Prizes on some aspects of our future projects, but that's up to you,' Lumak said.

Suddenly Jeremy's eyes lit up. It was due to Lumak's mention of his own Nobel Prize. He realized that there were more than a single way to skin the chicken and when one method failed he could always try again.

'Wow! That's great news!'

'This so-called insignificant city of ours will one day become one of the best for cancer research and longevity on this planet, after I am done with it,' Lumak said with that glint in his eye and Jeremy realized it would happen exactly that way.

Once again Jeremy felt like a kid on his first visit to kindergarten and yet, he believed Lumak's every word and knew he could pull it off in exactly the same way he had convinced Jean-Claude.

'Jeff, I am very interested in your offer. Perhaps I can have a look at the plans after dinner.'

The first batch of the serum had been prepared within the

university and tests were being carried out on selected patients within the nearby hospital building. For thoroughness, similar tests were being conducted in several city hospices and on those terminal patients that had been sent home to die in the presence of their families.

Jean-Claude was by then completely satisfied with Lumak's knowledge and approach, and after a few worst-case patients had promptly recovered, he decided it was time to publish a paper to the scientific community worldwide. It would be backed by articles in prominent medical journals and such like. After all, they had now accumulated records on over fifty patients, most of whom had been declared terminal. Those same patients had recovered within a week with a single dose of the pink serum. Yes, among other things, including a knowledge of his own existence and sanity, they now had an almost total cure for cancer. So without further ado he summoned Lumak to his office.

'How are you, Jeff. I am sorry I couldn't have seen you sooner. I had a full timetable which also included our own special project. So many important people to contact in France, England, Germany and the USA, but I intend to make it up to you. You wouldn't believe how excited I am about our project together and it's gaining considerable momentum. In all my life I've only dreamt of such a situation!'

'That's fantastic news!'

'My wife and I are having a social evening on Monday next. We would both like you and Sarah to be our main guests. Jeremy and his wife Karen are also invited.' Jean-Claude turned his attention towards the pile of documents on his desk.

'I'm afraid we have to complete them for legal reasons. I had our solicitors draft these agreements in triplicate, so please come and read them before you add your signature to the areas crossed. If there are any points that are not clear, please underline them in pencil and he can make the necessary changes. Let me call Brenda.' Jean-Claude buzzed his secretary.

Lumak read the first, which was to do with his appointment as lecturer to the university at a retainer of twelve thousand liras a month. This sum was equivalent to about two thousand US dollars. He was surprised with the amount and only expected a few hundred dollars. He signed each document in turn with Brenda standing by to witness the proceedings.

The final large document related to the proposed chemical plant and included twenty percent prophet to the university after all repayments and overheads had been deducted. It was a straight forward partnership agreement with Lumak holding the major part of the investment.

'I also have a few good friends in high finance. I had words with our largest bank today and they are willing to back your project to the hilt, with the recommendation of our university hospital, of course.' Lumak signed that copy and handed it to Brenda who scribbled her signature close to the "witnessed by" part.

Finally was the single internal copy that gave him full permission to use or borrow all available equipment or personnel in the course of his experiments. He signed that sheet as well. Then Jean-Claude handed him a prospectus.

'I need to have your formal approval in order to publish your paper to the scientific community. They are now very interested and these here are for our patent lawyers. I thought, perhaps, that we could print it on the university letter headed paper, and on the front cover could mention, "by Doctor Jeffery Longhurst, Professor of cancer research, The University Hospital", et cetera,' Jean-Claude further added.

'Yes, John, you have my full agreement,' Lumak said. He preferred to called Jean-Claude, John.

After he had finished the lengthy and delicate procedure, he underlined two areas in the prospectus.

'Perhaps we could modify these lectures to include some aspects on cloning and I shall have to talk to you on a brand new subject called Micro Robotics. It is a branch of what you call Nano-Technology. That is when we both have some time and it can wait for now.

'That sounds to me to be an interesting new subject,' Jean-Claude replied not knowing anything about Nano-Tec.

'John, I can't thank you enough for your assistance with

everything and would like your name mentioned on all our documents with the university, if you don't mind. And please convey our thanks to your lovely wife and tell her to expect us at your evening party,' Lumak said.

Before he left the university that day he had another request to asked of Jean-Claude.

'Can you arrange a large room for my lectures. I require a special screen and some projection equipment. I seldom use chalkboards and such like. I prefer to show images in 3D or virtualized. Students absorb information with those types of images much more readily. We could use 3D head sets, but they are too cumbersome in the class room.'.

'Yes, Jeff. Let me arrange something. There are several such empty rooms on the second floor.' He picked up the internal phone and dialled four digits.

'Farouk, can you come to my office immediately, I have an urgent job for you.'

The man soon arrived almost out of breath.

'Farouk, please show Doctor Longhurst the empty lecture rooms on the second floor,' Jean-Claude said and they both left together to locate his new rooms.

CHAPTER 30

Jean-Claude's party

Farouk took Lumak towards the larger complex which was in a separate building that was used more for meetings, lectures and entertainment. It also housed the main auditorium. They entered the nearest elevator and Lumak was intrigued by the technologies used in its design. Elevators or lifts were not as instantaneous as portals and could only move along vertical routes formed by simple guides and cables. The whole process reminded him that he was on a world with basic Class 1 technologies. They soon arrived on the second floor and he was taken to view the three vacant rooms.

One contained many empty benches fitted with old Bunsen burners and the second used as a deposit for old or broken chairs and desks.

Finally they visited the third room which had a long green board on the front wall and four chairs and desks. That room was much larger than the others.

'This room will do just fine and I can use one of the others for my personal secretary. In this one we could probably seat over sixty students, and with specially designed desks, about eighty or so.' Farouk listened patiently and nodded in agreement each time.

'Whatever you say, Sir,' Farouk replied. He was the university's general odd-bods man and could put his hands to most things, but did not appear to be the strongest figure of Olympian health. Lumak couldn't help observing the man's pale and slim features.

'Farouk, please prepare this room and the one next door. I want this place to look very modern, so let's get these rooms decorated and try to find us some suitable desks from your catalogues or elsewhere. And please keep me informed on progress.'

'Yes, Sir!'

'You appear frail and exhausted. Are you ill?'

'I am ok, Sir. I have only recently recovered from a bout of TB, but I am getting stronger.'

'In that case I shall get you some special medicine. And from now on you will work just half day on your current salary, with free canteen meals. Normally I would send you home on leave, but I need this job done urgently. Anyway, you can choose a few good workers and supervise them for a change.'

'Ok, Sir!'

'I am going to have some strong words with Jean-Claude about my decision in this matter. However you must swear to me that you will relax while on duty in this hospital and revitalize your body during your rest periods. You must under no circumstances exert yourself while you are doing this job for me,' Lumak insisted, in no uncertain terms. The only thing Farouk could think about at that time was his financial security.

'But Sir, no one in this university will agree to your terms. And my irregular attendance might get me the sack,' Farouk argued, with a worried frown on his pallid face.

'Farouk, I am not called Doctor Longhurst for nothing. I have just taken you on as my patient and have certified you as such, so please accept my decision in this matter!' Lumak said, impatiently.

'Maybe Sir,' Farouk said, still worried for his future.

'And now my friend, we are going to the canteen for a big meal, anyway,' Lumak ordered and a worried Farouk followed without any further complaints. No one could ever refuse Lumak anything, least of all Farouk.

He insisted on taking Farouk to the canteen for refreshments and a friendly chat. He always liked to know the people he dealt with on a more personal basis. But on that occasion he also wanted to ensure Farouk had enough nutrients in his system so he could complete the task for him without fainting on the job.

Farouk was quite undernourished and his condition worried a caring Lumak, who considered human life a lot more important and precious than anything else; least of all, money. Later on that day he visited Jean-Claude's office to discuss many matters and brought up the subject of Farouk.

'John, I hope you don't mind, but your man Farouk is now my patient. He is currently still recovering, so I've taken it upon myself to allow him to do light duties for half time. That is until his health improves. If his salary poses a problem, I don't mind contributing towards his pay packet myself. But the man still needs lots of rests. I'm afraid if he continues in his present vein he will not be of use to anyone, least of all himself,' An unhappy Lumak said in no uncertain terms.

'Yes, I know about Farouk. He is a very stubborn man that insists on working when he should be recuperating at home. He's supposed to be convalescing on paid leave at home but insists on coming to work. I have had words on that score with him on several occasions, but he ignores my concerns. I think he is a loner and needs us a lot more than we need him. Some people are like that, you know. Anyway, I shall have more words with him again if it will help.'

Lumak suddenly realized that he had jump the gun with Farouk. Nevertheless, despite his disposition in all this, he was a good man that needed care, and he would assist even if he had to use a completely different approach.

'What a very sad world it would be if we were all the same,' Lumak replied and Jean-Claude understood his meaning.

When Lumak arrived home that day he reminded Sarah and Karen about Jean-Claude's party on Monday evening and gave Sarah some money for new clothes and shopping. Then he went to discuss business with Jeremy.

'I have made several lists of reactors, valves, pumps, containers and ancillary equipment that we can acquire from a large German company at subsidy prices, less import duties of course. We are exempt on medical equipment, so I shall include it all as medical, with the university's logo and name stamped on all transactions. I would like you to look them over and tell me what you think,' Jeremy said and handed the equipment lists to Lumak. Lumak took less than one second per page as he flicked through the pages like a money counter and handed the long lists of items back to Jeremy. Since it was all done subconsciously, Lumak didn't realize he was closely observed by Jeremy,

'Jemmy, change item forty five to ten cubic metres and add an extra pressure release valve to item one five three. Everything else seems to be correct.' Jeremy was absolutely stunned and gasping with surprise at Lumak's incredible reading abilities and retention skills, not to mention his super-human speed.

'How could you read and absorb information that quickly? I don't believe it's humanly possible! No one can ever read and understand that much information so quickly!' Jeremy was completely baffled by the situation. Then he checked the items and found Lumak was correct in his decision and knew he wasn't being kidded along. Lumak realizing his error and Jeremy's curiosity soon decided to turn the conversation around.

'Yes, I know Jemmy all about not being a normal human. I have been told that I am a genius. You know, there have always been very superior memory men from time immemorial. I just happens to be one of the best. But I am equally good at most other things, so that makes me an abnormal freak and that's something I shall have to live with all my life,' Lumak replied, seemingly with utter disappointment in himself.

'You are no freak! You may be bloody clever and brilliant, but you are no freak! It just takes a little time getting used to, because you are like God among simple mortals and knowing I could never win with you makes me feel like an ace jerk.' Jeremy replied, sympathetically.

'Don't be so silly, Jemmy. You keep underestimating your true potentials. We all have different spiritual gifts, you know. Even some that we may never realise. It could just mean that I am doing the jobs to which I am naturally suited while you have not yet found your forte and may never find it, simply because you cant imagine yourself as a sculptor or painter. But if you stick with me I can guarantee you much greater mental potentials.'

When they were finished with the chemical plant lists, Lumak asked him for a list of best suppliers in the fields of optics, lasers, holographic displays, and virtual imaging equipment and he gave him the names and phone numbers of more German, French and English companies. Jeremy was an incredible source of such information, since he ordered many diverse pieces of equipment for the university from most European companies.

Lumak made some more inquiries from the university during the following days and located all the special equipment he required. Although purely experimental, he was sure he could modify them to suit his purpose. So he ordered three of each type.

Later on that day Lumak and Jean-Claude visited the bank for a loan, using his present salary, the partnership of the hospital and a feasibility study of the project backed by the university's recommendation. He was allowed twenty million liras for start-up purposes, with a more substantial loan when production and sales became on-stream.

His most immediate requirement was a reasonable amount of land for future expansion and a ready-made building.

He intended to take the project in two scales of production that were to be phased in over a period of two years, subject to supply and demand. Even so, he had grossly underestimated the demand. Jean-Claude and Jeremy now had a lot more extra work and workloads were constantly increasing.

Lumak began to prepare his first lecture for the advanced students and didn't want this first and most important of all lectures to be too involved in technical jargon. Neither did he want it to be monotonously serious. Nevertheless he intended to use some Micro Robots in some basic experiments to gain the students interests. Those he could retrieve from the Mind by the usual substitution process.

He realized he couldn't realistically involve his untrained students directly in the more complex and virtualized types of mind experiments. For that purpose they required very powerful Macron computers that would place them within a Virtual World. During that time the special microids had the ability to enter the minds of any person, causing telepathic communication between him and all members of the class. That type of complex operation could only be carried out on trained minds and preferably on those wearing brain implants.

He also realized he could only use those more advanced methods on more advanced life-forms with specific Brain Implants. Nevertheless by limiting their numbers he could use a suitable untrained person as a guinea pig without any risks.

Despite those limitations, he could always improvise and would soon receive the screen controllers and holographic projectors which were quite adequate for his present exercise. Perhaps by then he might even have had the Virtual Image Projectors up and running.

He considered the use of 3D glasses and headgear, but it was not as flexible. Although not the most ideal, his chosen method was the only one he could use given present levels of technology.

He was told that the equipment would arrive within a couple of days and could not at that time enter a firm date in the prospectus for his first lecture.

Monday was another one of those hectic days that Lumak spent chasing orders and builders to get both rooms completed on time.

When Lumak got home that evening he was exhausted and quickly had a bath. He got dressed in another of Ben's suits and joined Sarah and the others for their trip to Jean-Claude's party. They took Jeremy's small car and arrived in the early evening to be greeted at the door by Jean-Claude and his wife.

'Jeff, meet my wife, Alex, short for Alexandra,' Jean-Claude said, and Lumak realized it was also the name of Sarah's mother.

'I am truly pleased to meet you!' Lumak said with a firm handshake.

'Jeff, I would like you and Sarah to meet a few important people.' Jean-Claude took them away from Jeremy and Karen, who were presently in conversation with his wife.

'Please meet our current American Ambassador, Gerald Fraser and this is an old American friend of mine, Michael Cockburn. He happens to be Science Editor for The Times. He made this a stop-off call after he received knowledge of our article while in Japan and is very interested in your project,' Jean-Claude said and they shook hands.

'I hear you have made a breakthrough in a cure for most types of cancer, by cloning predator type cells from the original. Man, that is really something if it works,' Michael said, with a strong Southern American accent. Can you tailor this thing to any individual blood group?'

'Yes, Michael, we can do it for any human and most animals. Once we know the DNA structure of the recipient. Actually, there are no limits to my system.

'That is something, Man, if you can accomplish what you say you can. I shall need some more information from you, though. Something I can take back with me for a small pilot article. And I might also require a list of your cured patients, if you don't mind, that is,' he said, enthusiastically.

'I shall be only too pleased to furnish you with such information through the university before you leave. Why don't you visit one of my lectures on the subject early next week. Let us have your hotel number and perhaps I could ring you and arrange something in the mean time. You could also visit us for supper one evening this week.'

'I suppose I could hold on here for up to a week or so. After all, this is breaking news, but I shall have to call the office and clear it with them first.' Michael soon got on his mobile to head office. In the mean time Gerald Fraser, the USA ambassador, came forward.

'So you are the brilliant scientist I've heard so much about from Jean-Claude. If you have done as he says, one day you will be the richest man in the world. However, I sincerely hope all that happens after I become president of the USA. Then you can come over to my country and do some great work for us as well,' he said and Lumak was intrigued and smiled.

'Anything you desire, mister future president of the USA,' Lumak replied in jest. If only he could read the future then he would have realized that Gerald Fraser was correct in his predictions.

That evening they met several very important people, many of whom were close friends of Jean-Claude. They were people that he had met on his international lectures and conferences around the world.

CHAPTER 31

The University of Lud

The carpenters under Farouk's guidance and engineers were now quite busy preparing the lecture room. Many of the special items had arrived, with the exception of the large screens which were to be delivered by special transport from a distant supplier. It was expected to arrive the following day. Lumak and Jeremy did as much as they could in the circumstances. Farouk had taken Lumak's advice and refrained from hard work while on special medication. However he had a new spark in his steps and accepted his new job for Lumak with vigour.

Jeremy was an expert in reading German blueprints and decided to acquaint Lumak with the translation of some technical words. He was surprised when Lumak took him through the drawings and even explained areas of which he was not knowledgeable. Although German was one of those languages Lumak hadn't got around to learning, to Jeremy's surprise, he caught up within minutes. He never forgot anything and soon had an adequate knowledge of that language and most of its technical jargon.

'Jeremy, a call for you. It's someone called Manfred, from Berlin,' he said and passed the handset on.

'Yes Manfred! That's good news!' Then he turned to Lumak to advise on what Manfred said.

'He says some of the urgent equipment is on the way. The main ones couldn't be tested in time!' Then to the utter surprise of everyone in that room Lumak took the phone from Jeremy and began to communicate with Manfred in near perfect German.

'That's ok! We can do the testing here. We shall call you if we need assistance!

'It's on its way, guys, and should be here first thing in the morning, so we might have to work a little overtime to get this place ready on time. Any volunteers?' They realized they wouldn't be going home early that day.

Lumak got home quite late, but stopped at a large temple on route to meditate and say a prayer. Since his prayers with Sarah at their country temple, he had found the process appeasing to his spirit and had taken it up to reflect and contemplate on his past life and more serious cosmic matters. That process also reduced the nostalgia felt while away from home and friends in distant stellar systems and galaxies. Despite his new human form, the memories of his past missions and friends were still vivid in his mind and constant in his thoughts. He also contemplated the Javols approach to Earth and the near extinction of humanity along with so many other life-forms throughout the galaxy.

Most of all, he missed his sessions at the main square in his home city of Lud, with his long departed friends, Aurlsba and Longe at the monument of Om-Chopter. Those were the best days on his home-world. It was during that period of his life that he had taken up prayers and meditation.

He also had a hard time coming to terms with his dual existence and most of all his new predatory type. As a shadite he had a long past with family and friends and could hardly continue that past existence while on Earth in human form. There was also the trauma felt by all those experiences and changes since his arrival. Although putting on a brave face, the kickbacks were many. Nevertheless he soon found a suitable method of release through meditation and prayer in Sarah's family temple. During that time he could replay events of the past through his implants and by so doing gain release to feel more at one with those he had left behind.

Lumak was now convinced that he had full control of his human self, to do almost anything he desired with little assistance from the Greater Mind. He had at last mastered all the thought planes in his brain implants that were required to retrieve, digest and exchange information within the Mind's immense continuum. It was now an almost complete extension of his own mind in every sense, and so he thought.

The resonance of his being was so immense that he felt a complete oneness with the Cosmos and what he called the She. It was the part of the Cosmos that maintained continuity in the natural order. In his mind, The She was the more feminine side of cosmic nature or Mother Nature. She supplied the laws of existence perpetrated by a side of the more self-aware or living part of the Cosmos. She was required for the evolution of life and all modes of existence that followed a specific plan. That plan also included universes and multi-verses, which he considered to be types of living organisms in their own right.

The Greater Purpose, on the other hand, was the renaissance of a newer order, where the wild predators would see the light and become more tolerant and respective of their prey. However the Greater Purpose required intelligence and technology in its enactment. Nevertheless once that order began to permeate all things, the Universe would change for the betterment of all. That Greater Order could only have been initiated after high intelligence and conscience had been ubiquitous throughout the Cosmos.

Even with all those powers he felt lacking within himself. What was the use of all that power without love and all the other more nobler human attributes. There was also the games of pretense he had to sometimes play with his fiancee and close friends. He had many doubt's about the suitability of his type for Earth's mission. After all, he could never be completely honest if he was to retain his cover and complete his Earthly mission. Many galaxies with their numerous life-forms depended on the success of his present mission.

His conversion into the human form was the most difficult he had ever experienced. It was probably because it was his first transformation as a class one mammalian predator. Further, although they used Shadite Plato as the main template for conversion, Plato's type of human was quite different from Earth's.

'Perhaps Plato would have made a better candidate for this mission. After all, he is already human and would have fitted in a lot easier,' he thought.

Yes, this 13th escapade of his to Earth had turned out to be the most difficult of all his past missions. Even so, he considered the process of self-improvement a real challenge and a project on its own. Therefore he decided to face those weaknesses for the benefit of everyone, most of all, himself.

As he knelt within the great temple for prayer that day, nostalgia caught up and his mind began to return to his earlier life in another form on his home-world...

Lumak thought for a while and found himself back on Kanaefon, remembering the first day he arrived at the University of Lud, known to many of its later students as the University of Goh. That name was short for Gohenna, the final resting place, also known to Earth's humans as Heaven. The Grand Lord had introduced those mysteries to his world over a thousand years before and the university followed the principles and religious beliefs embodied in those Gohran philosophies.

As a young Semonite sibling, he had left his family residence in the valley of Knom with some personal belongings and was sat comfortably in the fast moving shuttle craft. Those were the small craft used for transporting just eighty passengers with little freight to different parts of their world. They were so called because of their dual role and sometimes used to shuttle passengers to and from the large freight liners and cruisers that sometimes hovered several hundred kilometres above the planet. The larger ships were mostly on route to local and distant worlds within the Kalboron globular cluster. There were many established manufacturing settlements and mining colonies within those local systems and such off-world transport was essential for mutual survival. Portals were not yet used for long distance travel for security and other reasons.

Lumak was then just ten, fully grown, very shy of strangers and completely naive. He was different from his peers, having led a more sheltered life in his family fief; well away from city ways and technologies. Many had considered him very unusual as a Worker, but his mother, presently the Empress Queen, was patient. She allowed him to develop in his own way. It was a great sacrifice on her part, but the Grand Lord had always played a hand in his life.

He remembered watching a Vide-play for the first time. It was a projected 3D image augmented by sensations and pheromones. The play was so realistic that he thought he had become part of the scenery, even moving and talking to himself in like manner. He soon became frightened by a certain scarey course of action, while being chased by a dragon monster and had to frantically remove the visor from his head. That action was much to his disappointment, embarrassing smiles and chit-chat of many of his peers. He had never forgotten the vivid realism of that humiliating experience.

'Ten croples please for your travel ticket,' shouted the robotic assistant and he disappointingly handed him one of the many square coins chief worker, Somas, had given him for the trip. It was really a token that excluded him from all such payments. That nudge shook him back into reality, as he found himself listening to a metallic voice just in front of his seat.

'We are now on final descent to the Goh Complex within the City of Lud. Please be prepared!' The voice snapped off.

It was not long before the doors slid open vertically and he found himself being pushed along the large moving corridor of a tramcar. He could view the ginormous observation tower in the misty distance. The other enormous structure was composed of three massive pillars that supported a large floating sphere perhaps a kilometre above the planet's surface. Part of that sphere was presently immersed in several bands of clouds. It was about ten kilometres away to the left of the tower.

Near the sphere the sky was much hazier than elsewhere, with the occasional electric discharge of enormous power. He was subsequently told it compensated for ion losses and ozone depletion, and maintained a healthy electrical balance within that part of the planet. There were several such devices throughout Kanaefon that maintained its atmosphere in an almost perfect condition. Since the arrival of the Grand Lord to Lumak's home world, everyone began to consider a living world as a real person, with real needs and those needs had to be supplied in order to maintain that type of life-form in perfect health. In such cases, planetologist were considered to be planetary doctors.

There were also several large orbiting stations used as look-out posts and scientific experiments that could only be carried out in space, well away from the planet's atmosphere and gravitation. The largest of those were the communications relay station for Kalboron. That one used the relatively new H-Wave technology. That form of technology worked faster than light speed and could traverse the whole galaxy in less than a second. It utilized a form of symmetry embedded in the Quantum Sea.

Many of the numerous satellites were barely visible in the dull sunlight, being over fifty kilometres above the planet.

By noon the distant sun was shining in full radiant flow and the large trees showed shades of orange and blue-green astride the massive blocks of the university complex that fleeted past as he travelled.

He could have been transported another two kilometres when his section of the conveyor broke away from the main drag and found himself diverted towards a siding. It was then that the platform abruptly stopped, with the voice saying:

'You have arrived at your programmed destination. Please enter a cubicle?'

He got off and entered one of the small hexagonal terminals of which there were many. There was a bright light and as if by magic, he immediately found himself in another building several kilometres away. He was ushered by another robot towards a desk.

'Your identity card, Please!' demanded a worker assistant. He took the card and inserted it into a small machine that made a burring sound. He was then given back his small case with another and was subsequently escorted to his tiny room.

He had little rest that night, having been completely overwhelmed by the absorbing power of the place, its unusual noises, scents and the panoramic sceneries. With buildings that extended kilometres into the sky and numerous Lamphis with their automated robots and equipment that could be observed everywhere during his walk-about.

The Lamphis controlled all such machines and were responsible for all manual work. They were not a lower class, slaves or even inferior. It was just their jobs and they did their duties with efficiency and enthusiasm for the greater good. They were not Semonites, but a large beatle-like creature that had evolved with them since the beginning.

He was up earlier than usual and decided to walk to his college block which was just a stone's throw away. As he followed along the small path that straddled the moving walkway, he admired the great Safona leaf trees that intermingled with vine growth, giving the look of a large closed conical orange leaf rapped by several spiralling circles of blue-green.

The Safona were not trees in the truest sense, but more like a single giant growing leaf that folded about itself with its stem in the soil, thus having the shape of a giant cone. It collected all its nutrients by osmosis from the air and soil and could survive in the harshest of environments.

This was one of the most fertile areas of the planet, and they grew like giants several metres tall. The resultant plant was an orange or violet looking pod, with a hollowed inside where all forms of smaller insects would dwell. On the outside were large arrays of small flowers for nectar and suckers that occasionally released themselves from the parent to be blown away to begin their own survival.

Each flower would be shed almost immediately after fertilization, leaving behind a small bud that would grow into yet another sucker. The parasitic Spile Vine assisted the Safona by trapping water and other nutrients within its vertical cup-like leaves which turned over and emptied their contents over the plant when a specific level of the liquid had been reached. That was a great inducement by the vine for having a suitable plant on which to climb, out of the way of the lower predators and poorer levels of light. But here again, the vine flowers could only be fertilized by the smaller flying insects at a higher level on the plant. Those insects seldom ever landed on the ground because of small reptilian type predators.

There were many avenues of Safona and giant ferns, all planted in precise rows and giving the place its own unique beauty and overwhelming power of expression. The many pheromones and other natural smells made young Lumak feel alive and thirsty for knowledge.

He found it very difficult to express the enormity of it all and remembered entering the large building with the inscription "Stellar Sciences" above the main doorway in Kanei script. He had to visit to sign-on and get acquainted with the different areas of his part of the expansive university.

Lumak's course began the following day and he was advised by the desk computer to visit the library building for more equipment and at the same time collect his computer book which contained the bulk of his course material. He was then directed to a small room with several students in attendance and specially adapted seats and desks.

He remembered his first rotating portal. There were several students waiting in front of what appeared to be a transparent doorway. After entering their destination codes on the local panel, they would simply stand on a rotating platform and vanish from view, to be observed much smaller within the portal's corridor. The corridor colours would suddenly change to that of their destination's.

'It's like bringing the mountain to the traveller,' he thought.

'What an incredible device... To be able to curve or replicate different volumes of space that were separated by incredible distances, as if they were overlapping.'

When the student entered that portal his distant figure could clearly be seen within the portal walking along the new corridor, despite the fact he was several kilometres away. Light was obviously curved or shifted in the strange manner of the portal. When another student pressed a different destination code, he and his corridor with its different colours would simply be replaced by the new one.

On Kanaefon there were no chemically driven automobiles or production plants with their resultant pollution. Moving pavements, elevators, escalators and portals were sited within city limits and LPD shuttle craft used for longer distances. The power sources for all those devices were based on nuclear fusion which was one of the cleanest forms of energy. Many of the more powerful generators were sunk deep within the planets surface and well away from its communities.

Suddenly he heard a distant voice.

'Jeff... Jeff,' Sarah shouted, and he realised he was day-dreaming.

'Yes, my love!

'What are you doing here?' he said in surprise as both women walked towards him in the mosque. Sarah and Karen were returning from the shops when they decided to visit that particular building, knowing that it was one of Lumak's favourite haunts for his meditation and prayer. They had obviously visited the university to collect him on their way home.

He accompanied them to the local streets for more shopping and in the process bought a large bag of sweets which he gave to local children as he walked by.

'Thank you, Mister,' they said, as they took the gift and ran away.

He admired Karen's nerves for driving the motor vehicle with such little effort in and out of the dense traffic. However when they arrived home he had the keenest desire to run a warm shower and wash those pollutants from his body. As he journeyed he could observe the rubbish that had been carelessly thrown about and realized the problems involved in maintaining a city with such a large human population.

Such rubbish were viable candidates for spreading all forms of disease through rodents. Within the cities on his world all such tasks were carried out by reliable robots controlled by Lamphis, who's main purpose of existence was to keep all such surface areas spotlessly clean and that they did with pride and relish.

Lumak realized that Earth's humans had a knack for creating rubbish and pollution, with little thought for the greater environment or the survival of their future generations. He hoped that there was still time to repair the planet's atmosphere and ecosystems before the onset of greater undesirable changes that could spiral out of control and cause even greater destruction, leading to mass extinctions. He also realized it was already too late for many of the coastal cities, currently being submerged by rising seas and oceans.

Lumak knew that Mother Nature, although tolerant to her children's silly ways, could become a formidable fore if her place was threatened. Then she would begin her process of elimination and that process was one of mind as well as body. Sexes would become blurred and distorted, moods change for no reason. People would begin to riot for no great purpose. By so doing all the infra-structures built over several generations could be torn down in a short period, leaving humankind where they started several millennia before; for such were the powers of Gaia and The She.

'Think of human survival without its utilities, fuel, supermarkets and all its diverse forms of transport. All those facilities we take for granted could be eroded within a short time,' he thought.

CHAPTER 32

The lecture room

The carpenters and electricians were actively preparing the lecture room. Several pieces of equipment had arrived and temporarily stored in an adjacent room. The large screen and projectors were still on their way and that aspect delayed the installation. Farouk had grown to respect and admire Lumak. He made sure that he and his crew did their very best job and the rooms made ready on time.

With several blueprints spread out on the floor, Lumak and Jeremy began assembling some of the smaller units within a local spare room, while a responsible Sarah eagerly took and relayed messages between them and the workers. Once the sub units had been tested ok, that part of the work was done. Then it was just the simple matter of connecting all those units together. During this time Lumak had involved the more advanced student engineers in some of his own designs and many of them had little sleep during that period.

By the following day the large screens and projectors had arrived by lorry. It was now a simple matter of completing the programming and fitting the complete system within the lecture room. Despite the many problems faced, that task was completed within another two days. That was after the workers had finished their hammering and the room had been thoroughly cleared of all obstacles. They completed the work on the screens and tested the programs while the new chairs were being positioned and fitted. The desks were an integral part of the chairs and fitted inconspicuously between the arms of the chairs. When required, they could be retracted and lifted in front of the participant. That type of seat was a new design and took less space, further increasing the sitting capacity.

'What do you think, Darling?' Sarah inquired. She sat comfortably in one of the chairs and began to manipulate the desk in front of the seat, but was having problems.

'Simply pull the handle forward and flip the lid over,' he said and she was successful.

'Now how do I get free?'

'Do the reverse to your initial actions.' Lumak said, but went forward and lifted it for her, then he lifted her out, held and kissed her.

'Not all our customers will have a manual for these seats, you know,' she complained, but it was the only way he could seat so many in the space available and provide a small desk. Anyway the desk was not always required.

After setting up and testing some equipment, Lumak, now Doctor Jeffery Longhurst to all concerned, was very pleased with his handiwork and Sarah thought how neat the place looked with its several rows of red upholstered chairs on a greyish setting.

'Darling, it's all so fantastic. It's... like a little cinema,' she said.

'I just hope everything works properly on the day.'

There had been so many changes and upgrades to the equipment that even Lumak had his doubts. The room itself was painted white and the carpet red to match the chairs, but his desk was light grey to match the chair panels.

The main door held a bronze name plate that read: "BIO-ENGINEERING by Dr J. Longhurst".

After a sequence of test on the equipment, the place was finally declared ready for his first lecture. He was pleased with himself for having accomplished so much in such a short time. Now it was his turn to entertain his friends and colleagues. It was to thank them for their assistance and Professor Jean-Claude was at the very top of his list.

Finally, he was able to select a date for the lecture. He called the professor's secretary to arrange a meeting and she gave him priority for later that afternoon.

Jean-Claude was very pleased with progress, but as usual was inundated with masses of paperwork. At that time his main concern was in getting ready the first serum samples that were prepared within the university. They were to be used on another fifty worst case terminal patients. Those patients had been specially selected from different parts of the country and had been thoroughly checked by many independent specialists from around the world. Their cure would be the first major proof of the serum's effectiveness.

Lumak had received much correspondence from abroad since the first article was published and momentum was building as more organisations became aware of the break-through.

Many were interested in meeting Doctor Longhurst to discuss the contents of his paper, and the previously adequate switchboard was now overwhelmed with calls from everywhere. All particulars were recorded and they were simply told that several lectures were planned for the following weeks.

Lumak knocked and entered Jean-Claude's office.

'The equipment has been tested and I am now ready for my lectures. The room has a sitting capacity of seventy eight, so it should be enough for now,' Lumak said, expecting mainly students.

'That's fantastic news! Can we send out invitations?' the enthusiastic professor inquired.

'After I have completed the first lecture with our students here. Call it a trial run if you wish. During that time I can do any minor tweaking to the equipment and iron out any bugs in the program before we go international. The small lecture room should be quite adequate for both purposes. However, if that place is too small for our foreign visitors we might have to convert the main auditorium for that purpose,' he replied and Jean-Claude nodded in agreement.

'How soon?'

'Shall we make it Friday, in two days? No point waiting any longer. We can go international after that.'

'That's truly incredible news!' Jean-Claude replied, realizing that finally some of their efforts were being paid off.

'And the special tests?'

'The first batch has been administered. Jeremy and his assistants are currently analysing the blood samples. We had to set aside a sterilised section in the hospital for that program. Too much is at stake, you know,' the professor replied, slightly stressed.

'Don't worry! Everything will work to plan, and we shall win the day,' Lumak replied with confidence.

'Ahhh! Michael Cockburn called and would like you to contact him urgently about your lecture.'

'I almost forgot about him. Did he decide to remain for the lecture?' Lumak inquired.

'Yes! He contacted his head office and they agreed.'

'I think he is a good contact for us to have in the States. He is a useful man with a thorough knowledge of legal matters and the publishing business. He also appears to be quite honest and hard-working. We shall need people like him in our future organization,' Lumak said.

'He gives me the impression he is overstretched with his present job and his boss must keep constant tabs on him... if he has to call his office every time he moves a foot.'

'In that case, I think we should keep our eyes on him for future head-hunting. He should join us on our first lecture to see what we are about. However, we should ensure he gives us good coverage in his magazine before he switches sides,' Lumak said and Jean-Claude smiled at Lumak's devious ways.

'And now I must leave you for home. Some more important work to do,' Lumak said and left the professor.

CHAPTER 33

Lumak and portals

Finally, the day of his first lecture had arrived so Lumak rose early to have a comfortable bath and composed himself for the experience. It was to be his first lecture on Earth so he was optimistic of a high turnout. Although his audience was mainly students, he could judge their reaction. They would be his guinea pigs to springboard the method for a more international audience.

Today he would wear his white gown and golden sandals. Many of his students would consider him eccentric to say the least, but they should equally have accepted him for what he was. He didn't like to hide anything from anyone, least of all his close friends. He represented The Greater Purpose in all things and would always wear his Special Attire of Office and Insignia on such occasions.

If only people wasn't so prejudiced and resistant to change. Most humans and even more advanced species felt threatened by such simple differences. They didn't like their concepts of realism threatened in any way. That factor was mainly due to environmental and cultural programming. It was usually difficult to modify unless tackled from birth. Yet, any attitude could be altered in time, and he had lots of that changing commodity to play with, or so he thought. Nevertheless he had to gradually expose Earth's people to his brand of technologies and in the process hard choices had to be made.

This time he decided on a hot relaxing bath instead of the usual shower. It was a new experience and most edifying to his senses.

His mind strayed as he remembered his first trip to the Library of Lud and his entry through a large rotating portal that could handle more than twenty students each time. That was after preparing for the first lecture on Stellar Sciences that was given by Siend Steinak.

The Siend was equivalent to one of Earth's professors and

considered one of the hottest in that branch of science. He later found that both local portals were over two kilometres apart. Lumak pondered the concepts behind their operation. The portal, although a doorway, acted like a type of inter-dimensional mirror. Such a spacial mirror reflected light, energy and matter through a second portal to which it was linked by a higher symmetry. Yet, that symmetry could be modified in a precise manner by simply altering its programming.

The corridor he saw in that building was over two kilometres away in another. He also remembered changing his destination code by manually pressing the buttons on the side panel and observed the corridors change to reflect that of his new destination several kilometres away in a third portal. However nothing happened until the rotation button was pressed. He was completely dumbfounded as to the nature of the technology. Later on that day he couldn't resist stopping the Siend to ask for an explanation.

'Siend Steinak! Could you please explain how the main hall portal works?'

The Siend immediately stopped in his tracks and stared at Lumak with keen interest, as if gearing up to face a new challenge. He started off by attempting to explain the symmetrical nature of the Cosmos. For despite utter randomness and chaos at the quantum levels, there were a few ordered sequences or invariance within the Sea of Chaos and of All Possibilities which were resistant to change.

Those particular tendencies and lines of invariance led to the creation of our orderly material universe in the first place. That was also the reason why our universe had similar characteristics to her parent. Very much like living trees, universes had something akin to a DNA that was handed down through the Sea of Chaos and of All Possibilities. Those qualities were transferred to sibling universes, thus limiting certain forms of chaos during their existence for better longevity.

'Lumak, order in the form of causal events is a type of symmetry,' he said, 'some forms of order are easily neutralised by chaos, while other forms are highly resistant, like sub-atomic particles and so on. Two absolutely similar objects can mutually enhance their causal reflections if they were not affected by Chaotic Nodes. Thus forming a specific causal bond in time and space. Like some identical twins, remotely feeling each others pain or even thinking each others thoughts.

'That very same principle is used by our universe to maintain stasis between its space-time boundaries. The same principle prevents the duplication of matter or nothingness appearing like little black holes everywhere. Given normal energy densities, visible and invisible matter cannot be created nor destroyed. However, certain forms of invisible matter can condense into visible ones and vice versa to control our universe's expansion and contraction given certain probabilities. Every particle and wave exist because of those principles. Nevertheless all matter and energy are forms of order that exist because of their resistance to chaos or they would soon have been corrupted and neutralised back into the Sea of Chaos and of All Possibilities, from where they had arose in the first place.

'How does a simple portal function, Siend,' an impatient Lumak inquired, in an attempt to shorten the professor's long-winded explanation.

'Well, if you could create two highly symmetrical forms that are also symmetrical to themselves and others of a similar nature, and you could somehow mislead the primal system into thinking - here I mean reacting in a specific manner through the homogeneity of the Cosmos - they were in the same space time, you would have the makings of a portal. This is because surpluses or deficiencies in energy would be instantly compensated for by the above principle, once it realizes a change had occurred to cause an imbalance. This is because matter and energy are one and the same and can only change from one state to another and vice-versa with no losses or excesses. In other words, many principle attributes like energy, charge, etc., are conserved. However, such a device would have to be designed in such a manner as to permit external objects within its fields to be affected as well.

'Put simply, if you suddenly disappeared from your present position, the universe would immediately re-create you with the same amount of matter, energy, momentum, etc., as when you disappeared. That is simply because energy in its many forms cannot be created nor destroyed because of conservation laws. So if during your disappearance you could somehow mislead the system into sensing you were elsewhere at the time of your disappearance, your body would be re-created there instead of at your present position, with virtually zero loss of energy to the universe.'

They entered the class of over fifty students and the Siend decided to answer questions on that very same topic. It was one that appeared to intrigue him.

'Siend, how is it possible to be in two separate places at once. Because the portal can link two places at once and at the same time!' Lumak shouted.

There was a chuckle and soon the class was in an uproar. Pincers began to drum their desks as each student began almost to laugh their heads off. It was not really a human laughter, but more like a loud hissing with pheromones everywhere. When the Siend banged his desk with his small mallo hammer the whole class became silent once again.

'I take it Lumak... you mean when travelling through the portal?'

'Yes, Siend, through the portal. At that very instant of time.' The class remained silent during his explanation.

'Have you learnt about the Uncertainty Principle and forces involved during atomic linkage,' the Siend said.

'Yes, Siend,' Lumak replied and the Siend outstretched both arms.

'Look! My pincers are about two mecrons (about two metres) apart, so they must be in two different places at once and at different times. What do you think of that?' he asked and the young class was once again in uproar.

'Yes, Siend, but they are joined together by your central portion.'

Siend Steinak smiled or at least that was the sensation felt by those airborne scents and pheromones.

'My son, although they may appear to be so, if you magnified any part of the whole to a high enough degree, you would find that no individual parts of my body touch directly. I am a whole in as much as certain energies and forces hold me together. Every different part is at a different time and space. However, if these very same energies and forces could be generated, albeit in an artificial manner, would it not be possible for me to be in two places at the same time, roughly speaking?

'There is another controlling factor called the Zero Entry Paradox. Portals are designed about that principle.' He retrieved a small box from his circular desk. Then he went towards the large screen and entered an image containing a large door.

'If this device was a time machine to the past and you entered the doorway from this end, being our present time, what do you think would happen?'

'I would find myself in the past, Siend,' Lumak replied with little doubt.

'No, Lumak! You would not, because you are a product of the past within your time-line. Everything that you have done and accomplished up to this juncture have depended on a complex mesh of causal interactions and relationships in the Sea of Chaos and of All Possibilities. From the current positions of atoms and cells within your body to your presence within this university. The very atoms that now exist within your body would depend on the food that you absorbed and some of those very same recycled atoms could well have been within other living creatures in previous times. Hence, if you went into our conceptual time machine two situations could occur, and I stress the word could, because it doesn't really happen that way.

'Firstly, as you disappeared from this space-time continuum into the past, our past universe would become unstable, because of the laws that "primal energy cannot be created nor destroyed". Your mass would be lost to our present continuum since you have gone to the past, and as you entered the past, surplus matter would be felt by the system and here again the laws would come into force. This is a natural process that occurs even now between universes to maintain stasis.

'However, there is one more situation to consider. As you entered the Time Displacement Unit (TDU), causal changes that you may have introduced because of your appearance in the past will act in such a manner as to cause you only to exist at our present space-time. Therefore, as you approached the machine's doorway and reduced the time difference between past and present to zero, you would still not be able to enter the machine's doorway and visit the past until the time difference between both continua was zero, and that can only occur at our present time. In other words, the greater the time difference between present and past, the greater would be the amount of negative temporal feedback trying to keep you at your present time, and this temporal feedback works in both directions of time.

'The truth of the matter is that as you reduced the time difference between present and past, the amount of feedback would weaken and you would be placed even closer to the doorway of the TDU. However, you could only enter through the doorway when both times were precisely the same and all relative causation became interlinked at zero time and with zero difference. In other words, you would face an invisible barrier or force, that would prevent your entry into the past, because there were no causal links between the different time periods. The causal events of your would-be presence in the past would also tend to keep you away from the doorway in the future because of that kind of Temporal Feedback.

'Matter that exist at zero time will have virtually zero temporal feedback, but may not necessarily be at zero difference causally and here lies the concept of transposition and vectorization. Any matter that does not share the same causal continuum with our own may be considered separate. Then to all intents and purpose, that matter will not exist in relation to us, causally. But yet, it can be sensed by our universe as being whole and a part of its space-time. That is how it works with invisible matter and energy.

'Now, getting back to the original question, and this is a big if. If you were able to enter the doorway of the TDU when both times were identical, and your mass suddenly disappeared from our primal universe, then your symmetrically causal form would have to be re-created, not necessary at your point of departure. With two TDUs, the tendency would be to place you at the doorway of the second TDU.

'This is because the system will have to retain its own stability within its space-time boundaries. That act would have taken zero energy to complete in almost zero time. A similar occurrence would have taken place even in the past, assuming such an act was possible.

'The portal uses these very same principles of causal symmetry to deceive the universe or Primal System into creating you at another place or space, in zero time. But never at another time. The method is quite clever as little technology is required in confusing the primal system, and will cause it to create your body or indeed any form of primal matter in its entirety. This includes your angular momentum and all other parameters you had acquired before, in order to displace a mass imbalance at an infinitesimal time difference. To accomplish that great feat, the portal uses specially generated G-wave technology and intense field generators. Since the body is not created by a machine there is always only one copy of the original and not several duplicates, as can be the case with other methods.

'Lumak, would it then be possible to visit the past?' he said, in jest.

'No, Siend. I don't think it's possible in material terms, because of what you just said. Also, there would be duplication of energy since the atoms in our bodies also exists in the past.'

'I said that primal matter based on electromagnetism, within our primal universe was affected. I said nothing about parallel universes or other types of matter, energy or forces. One could still enter the past of our space-time in some other form or essence, providing they could not affect its energies and the causal flow of events we call continuum, which is like a constantly flowing river. However, what if you stood on its banks to observe. That would be a different matter, wouldn't it? Albeit even though in spirit.'

'Yes, my Siend. I think I now understand the concepts,' Lumak replied, still utterly confused.

That evening a young Lumak spent several hours walking through the Safona orchards while attempting to fathom the concepts behind causation and spent the best part of the night in an attempt to work out the intricacies of portal science from the information he learnt. It had taken him several decades since that time to fully grasp those bizarre concepts and to have even used them in his more advanced portals.

'Darling! It's getting late,' Sarah shouted and he opened his eyes.
  Lumak suddenly realised he was dreaming of his past experience within the University of Goh as a youth and immediately got out of the bath to get ready for his big day. He had since used those very same concepts to build intergalactic portals similar to the Omegron one. He wondered when and where it would be installed for the mass evacuation of Shadite Plato's people, who were the last remaining human population of Caefon in Andromeda and hoped he would be ready to assist before the Javols' arrival to consume them all.

CHAPTER 34

The Robe, Cloak and Belt

Lumak put on the white robe and pressed the winged insignia with the centrally positioned blue circle unto the garment above his left breast and it automatically stuck to that area. Both symmetrical wings of the brilliant metallic insignia were spread out on either side of the deep blue inner circle. He knew that when he wore those items he felt a lot more secure within himself and his attitudes correspondingly changed to reflect the cosmic powers he represented.

He pondered many things, including his duties to The Greater Purpose, The Greater Ecology and his home galaxy, Osmaron. Yet, they were all one and the same thing. And there was the dreaded Javols to defeat. That particular problem had initiated his presence on Earth. The task of defeating them appeared insurmountable. Nevertheless he had about 200 years to change Earth's technologies to the standards required to defeat the Javols. Even so, there were numerous swarms of Javols and more than a single world would be involved in the final struggle.

Finally, he thought of his wife to be and their future wedding. He really loved her and her species and would try his hardest to assist humanity in their long term survival. He must also protect her fragile body from future accidents. There were so many deaths about due to disease and unwarranted violence, and humans were so short-lived.

During all his previous existence on his home-world which spanned many centuries, never had he witnessed a single death from any member of his kind from unnatural means. However on this world humans seemed to take pleasure in administering pain of every conceivable kind. It was something that had taken him much time to accept, and one he could not tolerate. However such an existence was mainly due to sociological programming and was inevitable for most warm-blooded predator-type species. Then there were the many wars against members of their own kind. Humans accepted those factors as a normal outcome of living. He soon realized the fragility of life on Earth and contemplated Sarah's safety from all those dangers, but there was little he could do at that moment in time.

'Perhaps I can recruit Sarah into the fellowship of the Shadites and get her one of the cloaks for protection. Yet, she is so stubborn and set in her ways,' he thought.

He would also be required to get her a ring as was customary for marriage, and arrange a date for the ceremony. Nevertheless it was a significant blessing he was able to involve her in his future projects, albeit of her own free will. If anything, those interests will begin the process of her learning and in time change her attitudes. She also liked his work, which was mainly to do with saving people and other life-forms, so that aspect would never be a problem for her. Perhaps he should begin to train her as his secretary with the help of the professor and Jeremy.

'I think I shall have our engagement ring engineered within the Mind. It will be the first of its kind and the Grand Lord should not mind if I used materials found on Earth. I must immediately sketch some ideas and communicate those concepts to the Mind. I shall give that design my best attempt,' he thought again.

He was now ready to leave, dressed in the almost ancient Greek attire. He took some papers from his briefcase, placed it on the table and went into the kitchen to make himself a cup of coffee. Then he returned to have a last scan of his notes and separated a few for photo-copying at the university. He had recently adjusted his White Gown to more fit his present environment, but it was still a strange attire. He was soon to be joined by Jeremy.

'I heard someone moving about and came to investigate. My God! What on Earth are you wearing?' he exclaimed, in utter amazement at Lumak's attire.

'My functional clothes, of course! I intend to wear these during the normal course of my lectures. Call it a form of uniform if you wish. It represents my spiritual organization and what I stand for. Why? don't you like it?' Lumak replied, sarcastically.

'I didn't say I didn't like it. It's just that it looks so... ancient Greek. Have you found it in one of those costume shops?'

'No!'

'Anyway, I don't think it's appropriate for your lecture today. You have all those students and VIP's to consider, and they may think you...' Jeremy said, stopping short of any further criticism, suddenly changing the topic.

'You meant eccentric?'

'If you don't mind, I would like to sit-in on your lecture today. The professor has given most of his senior classes leave during that period and senior lecturers and doctors are also expected from the neighbouring medical units. There are also some important officials and a mention of televising the complete program. You know, the professor and I have lots of faith in you and we wish you great success. I mean, today.'

'Yes, you have a remarkable professor and you are also extraordinary in your own ways. You must continue to develop those good qualities, even though you still do not appreciate my present attire,' Lumak replied, with more sarcasm.

Sarah was soon on her way downstairs to see Lumak off. Her eyebrows and eyelashes extended when she caught sight of him in his famous white robe and golden sandals, but she ignored any comments.

'My Darling, I wish you success on your first lecture at the university. Karen and I shall be along later to assist you with the pamphlets' distribution.' She gave him a prolonged kiss.

Then he collected his briefcase and decided to walk to the university while meditating on some relevant topics as he did. Jeremy offered him a lift but he declined. He wanted to be free from the seat of cars and traffic jams on this of all days.

THE WHITE CLOAK OR PLEATED ROBE

The White Robe or Gown was indeed a strange looking garment. It was pleated and coloured radiant white with a high vertical collar that formed a rigid section with its highest parts behind the wearer's head. That collar reduced to a V-shape at its front.

There were no visible signs of fasteners or clips. The garment simply bonded molecularly when worn by its authorised wearer. Just below the waistband the robe broke into an array of vertical pleats.

Hanging from two golden shoulder rings were an optional crimson cape that ran with more circular pleats. Similar pleats from the gown extended downwards toward the carves to cover the golden cris-cross bands that extended upwards from the flexible golden sandals. The complete footwear extended to just below the knee. That robe also contained many types of advance class 9 technologies including a powerful force field.

That garment was not of human design and perhaps the most advanced of its kind in Osmaron. Even so, it was made for him in his present human form on information received from the Mind, which was not always accurate for time and place. Nevertheless being of a Nano-bot microid design, it was truly self-cleaning, self-repairing and self-perpetuating.

As if a living organism, it could subtly alter its dimensions, colour and texture to reflect the mood or other basic requirements of its wearer to match the environment. It could also become invisible above normal clothes or make its wearer invisible. Its pockets were bottomless with no limits and could contain numerous items by shrinking them.

It was composed of many layers of microids that specialised in energy conversion, portal translation, gravity neutralisers and a host of other specialised tasks that were assisted by the Greater Mind. All of its many functions could be selected within the menus of Lumak's brain implants.

THE BLACK SHADITES CLOAK

That cloak was of a similar microid design to the White Robe, although more specific to survival in harsh and unfriendly environments. It communicated with its wearer through special brain implants. Those cloaks were in three grades, with Grade 3 being the least advanced. Grade 1 was for the most adept Shadites and contained incredible technologies. While making lumak indestructible, it could transform Lumak into the most adept ninja warrior with incredible speeds and superhuman response.

The hood and other less important parts could be absorbed within the body of the cloak. That garment was much thicker and heavier than the White Robe and a lot less flexible, yet it was designed to cover every part of its wearer's body with the exception of a small area about the face when worn by a human. That area fitted well the special oxygen face-mask used on dangerous inter-stellar missions. Because of the high levels of absorption by its surfaces, it always appeared completely dark, as if no light existed within its immediate vicinity; for it used such ambient energies for its own rejuvenation. Because of those reasons it cast deep shadows. However, it also had a hibernation mode that could be initiated when it was stored for long periods.

The black cloak had the unique ability of changing the appearance of its wearer to many different forms. That aspect was probably due to the strange way in which it could reflect, bend and focus light. However, that great feat could only be accomplished through its wearer's brain implants.

To all intents and purpose, the Hooded Shadite's Cloak of Goh was invincible and would lend those powers to its authorised wearer, mortal or otherwise. However, that particular cloak, unlike the robe, could only have been worn by Shadites. They were the special guardians of the universe, a type of priesthood.

THE BELT

That item was made of a strange flexible metallic alloy that could adjust its dimensions to that of the wearer's. It was indestructible and like his other Class 9 technological devices, could project itself within the Greater Mind. It was mainly used for manual control of some basic functions when its wearer were unable to use brain implants. It was also a utility device with a range of tools and gadgets and was handy for carrying small containers and such like.

Its main control was its large buckle that included an outer segmented ring with many buttons. Those and their inserts could be pressed in certain specific ways for many functions, including gaining the attention of superiors like Lord Vektron the Ploran. Other modes were for communication and entering the Greater Mind for doing his experiments or searching for information. He always wore the belt underneath his clothes and could make it invisible through his brain implants. Because of security reasons, that function was only available for relatively short periods of time.

On this occasion, only the White Robe was required and both the Black Shadites Cloak and belt would remain vectorized and invisible on his person.

Lumak soon arrived at the university and went directly to Professor Jean-Claude's office to discuss matters of importance.

'My day of trial is with us at last. I just hope my lecture is acceptable to our keen students.' Lumak said, and Jean-Claude could hardly believe his eyes.

'This attire of yours is truly... fascinating!' a surprised Jean-Claude commented, never having seen such a type of clothing before. Yet it made him authoritative and gave Lumak the appearance of an emperor of worlds or another Christ.

'Yes, I know! I had similar complements from Jeremy, earlier. Not to mention Sarah's millisecond gaze. I hope everyone sees it in a similar vane to my present company. Anyway, I think it adds to the flavour of the moment, don't you?' Lumak took a pile of printed paper from Jean-Claude's desk to Sarah's new office.

CHAPTER 35

The lecture

With the exception of the first row of chairs marked for special guests, the lecture room was filled with many of the university's doctors and students. A few other chairs at the front were reserved for the university seniors and some important visitors. Even so, there were many standing on either side of the main corridor and some still entered the room.

Lumak walked in amidst claps and cheers and stood between the large screen and his desk. He sent a thought through his brain implants and the large plasma screen lit up, displaying an image of Osmaron (our Milky Way galaxy) as seen from another part of the universe, with his parent satellite, the globular cluster of Kalboron. Just underneath was the winged crest of his organization. He spoke to his audience with a positive and welcoming voice.

'I sincerely thank you all for coming!' Then he bowed to the audience and they cheered.

'Today, you will be shown the basic concepts of a new type of bio-engineering. For reasons of simplicity, this main subject will be subdivided into two branches, Organic and Microid Engineering. However, both can be created by the same engineering processes within a suitable environment.

'The primal cells that were created by Mother Nature can also be created in the laboratory and DNA programming may be included to form larger organisms from these basic building blocks.

'In a not too dissimilar manner, Microids or Micro Robots may be linked and controlled to fulfill certain specific requirements to perform important functions. The byproduct of the latter is within the subject we shall call Micro Robotics or Microid Engineering. It is a small part of a branch of science better known to you as Nano-technology.

'However, from now on we may consider all naturally occurring cellular or microid structures to be within this field. When considering cellular structures I would rather relate them in light of Microid Engineering, since this methodology can be utilized elsewhere in other technologies of a similar nature. However, for our present lecture, we should consider the Organic branch for now.'

He gave another thought and the picture on the screen changed into a complex cellular structure with a helix slowly forming, branching and unfolding out into substructures. He thought again and the complex image began to expand outwards from the screen to rest in mid air above their heads, as if floating in free space while it slowly rotated in a myriad of colours.

'These are the complex protein chains common to most primal life and these are the genes and chromosomes of which all primal carbon-based organic life is formed. I call this the Universal Genome, since all carbon-based life within the universe may be created from this single structure, by the removal or inclusion of specific standard links to complete the programming. The different colours represent their differing levels of stability and functionality. Take note of the red bonds which represent the weakest and the blue that are the strongest.

'For now we shall consider the weaker bonds and their relationship with other substructures in the formation of cancers and tumours. The stronger are sometimes connected to certain metals to build complex Microids. These Microids can be designed to receive instructions through microwave or their own internal programming and are to be discussed later in this course. Furthermore, this method may be used to design a much stronger life-form.

'Now let us take a closer look at an important part relevant to today's lecture...' The molecule expanded outwardly, filling the room as it appeared to focus on a smaller part of the structure. Many of the audience in that room tended to move their heads as if to avoid collision with the large structure as it expanded above their heads, because it was so realistic and in full 3D. However, it was just a multicoloured hologram.

He continued his lecture on the biology of the human body and methods used to prevent and remove cancerous tissue, showing all the necessary technologies and methods, until he came to the end of the final part of his lecture dealing with cancer. The strange visual effect was so realistic that some stood aside just to check where they were. At other times they became fearful of collision with the floating object and would duck.

The students admired the man, despite his strange attire and liked his new and visual approach in his presentation. All the images were fully three dimensional and so lifelike. They asked many questions to which he always had precise answers, until the lecture was concluded.

Finally he gave another thought command and a large sphere appeared on the screen with a much smaller one close by. The smaller sphere began to grow while the large one became smaller. The growing ball was magnified a million fold to eventually reveal myriads of micro robots moving from the smaller to build the larger. They could be clearly seen as the image expanded under extreme magnification.

'Fantastic! Fantastic!,' cried the audience, but he stretched his hands forward to calm their excitement.

'This is Micro Robotics at its best. They, like cells, are the true engineers of the future. From linking neurons in the brain to building even planetary structures.'

The students were ecstatic, for never before had they seen anyone like him or had even heard of Micro Robotics. The foremost questions in their minds were how could anyone create and control such infinitesimal structures that were not even visible to the naked eye.

That preliminary lecture was a great success. By the end of that evening the news had spread throughout the campus. The complete university was alive with his concepts. Some were calling him, The Prophet, as a nickname because of his strange attire and rumour of his cures got around.

Several reports had been released to the scientific fraternities worldwide and most were astonished by the new concepts portrayed by a previously unknown British doctor living and gathering fame in such a relatively insignificant part of the globe. Many tried but couldn't unravel his multi-dimensional type of mathematics and strange matrices, yet they were excited enough to arrange a special committee to visit and speak with the previously unheard of genius.

The students were also aware of the recovering patients, all of whom were worst case cancer victims with a short time to live. There were also his many published papers on the new subject of Micro Robotics and Professor Jean-Claude Chairmowich found himself being dragged along by the currents of that time as other demands overtook his schedules.

The local and world media, including television broadcasters, were also getting interested in the so-called prophet scientist and doctor, with a lasting cure for cancer. Those types of stories appealed to the masses who at that time of recession couldn't have had enough. Almost everyone in that part of the world knew of Doctor Longhurst, although not in person. The news of his cure for cancer had propagated everywhere by now, even to the highest levels of government.

The international press was busy printing those incredible issues and that was not all, thousands of meteors had been sighted over the American continent. They had apparently descended and disappeared before hitting the ground. The air-force was airborne and military submarines placed on alert, but it was yet another false alarm.

Then a very bright starlike object was seen moving across the sky. It was so bright that it became daylight in some states during night time. The ball of light disappeared in thin air while people and scanners watched. Many associated those sightings with mass hysteria. There was general confusion everywhere which re-enforced their focus on Lumak.

After the success of that day, Lumak and his assistants, including Sarah, went into Jean-Claude's office for debriefing. They always used that method to find weaknesses in their methodology. Then with such feedback, they would find solutions and correct the program before his next lecture.

'I don't know much about you, but I think that went very well.

As a matter of fact, it went better than I had imagined. At our present levels of sophistication, this is more than satisfactory for our foreign visitors. However, I think we should get a few more confectionery and drink dispensers in the corridors,' Jean-Claude said.

'Perhaps we should also redo our canteen and get a few good chefs in to organize things on a more professional basis. After all, our new systems are here to stay,' Lumak said and Jean-Claude decided to take notes.

'By the response and reaction we had today from our home crowd, I think we must seriously consider using the main auditorium for our next lecture. And by the way your Greek costume works. It gives you a godlike look,' Jeremy said.

'That's good to know.' Lumak replied.

'Why don't we build a brand new wing, with its own canteen and auditorium for our purpose,' Sarah interjected and they glanced at her in amazement.

'Brilliant idea! I don't mind donating the bulk of our initial profits to such a necessary venture,' Lumak replied.

'I also think a new building to be necessary. That will take the pressure off some areas of our existing university,' Jeremy advised.

'In that case, I shall have to make a few calls,' Jean-Claude said.

'Ladies, I must thank you very much for your efforts on my behalf. I think we should have a party to celebrate my first lecture in this university, don't you? Anyway, did you have any problems with the brochures and their distribution?' Lumak inquired of Sarah and Karen.

'I like the party idea very much, but is there such a thing as a brochure dispenser?' Sarah replied and Lumak and the others smiled at her mental flexibility.

'Personally, I think this lecture was the most brilliant I've ever witnessed, and the equipment worked beyond our wildest dreams. We can always update and modify to suit our future needs,' a happy Jean-Claude said and they were all agreed that the format was also suitable for their international visitors.

After the success of that day, the women left on their own while Lumak stayed behind to complete some important paperwork. Then he decided to walk home.

CHAPTER 36

Assassins in black

In the weeks that followed Lumak saved the lives of many through his program of free assistance to all terminal patients in the city. He became quite popular and many got to know of his good deeds, including a few fanatic religious leaders.

During that time he would arrange for the seriously and incurably ill to visit clinics where tests were made by chosen nurses and suitable cures administered. Since Turkey was quite modern and main-stream European, many ignored his progress, thinking he was just another British good-doer. Nevertheless other more extreme leaders thought their ancient religious beliefs being eroded and were seriously threatened by his benevolent actions. They even thought he was depriving their god of souls by healing them and not allowing them to die naturally.

One particular leader who was extremist with terrorist connections, saw him as a threat that could change their whole way of life.

'This English good-doer is set on doing Allah's work for him. He heals the dying from the worst types of cancer. Soon they will have no need for us or our beloved, Allah. They have even began to lower themselves to him and call him Prophet, Lord, even Messiah. Such blasphemy is intolerable!' the Shiite cleric Nasidin Ahmadi complained.

'Yes, My Mullah. And he is a filthy foreigner! Yet, he appears to be a most noble one that will give his life to save the poor and dying,' Krekar Al Mud replied.

Although Nasidin was not a proper Mullah, he didn't mind being addressed as such by one of his junior clerics. As far as Nasidin was concerned Krekar was well out of line in praising the foreigner for so-called noble deeds. He thought Krekar was indeed very naive in thinking such deeds would be beneficial to their organization, which was presently gathering momentum in other parts of the country. Lumak took publicity away from their organization and that was bad for business.

'Have you heard yourself recently? Do you know what will happen if he continues, with his program of free medicine and miraculous cures. Let me tell you, our people will worship him instead and forsake Allah. That is exactly what will happen! Then our mosques would be empty and we shall starve. Do you want that to happen? Would you like to see our Mosque empty of all our worshippers and everyone turn away from Allah for this pretense English prophet? We must do something about this imposter and quickly, before his evil disease spreads throughout our country!' Nasidin shouted.

'Yes, My Mullah!' Krekar replied, humbly.

'Yes! And the people call him Lord and Prophet! That is blasphemy in the face of Allah. Didn't you know that! He is a false prophet of Satan and his presence here can destabilize our whole way of life and our firm beliefs in Islam. He must not remain to continue his treacherous efforts. Allah will not want him to continue to do his work for him. He is an English doctor and is not even a member of Islam!' another senior cleric advised. Their minds were made up. As far as they were concerned Doctor Jeffery Longhurst would soon be a dead prophet pushing up roses instead of helping terminal patients.

Nasidin left for a public place with his stolen mobile to make a call.

'Heh, Hag!'

'Hi, Naz! I could tell that voice anywhere.'

'That was a cool job you pulled in Istanbul recently. I heard you took out half a block including a pagan church.'

'And 50 souls for Allah. We try our best. How can I be of assistance?'

'I have a little job for you. Nothing too difficult. Just a harmless doctor.'

'I'll send three of my best. When do you need it done?'

'Now if you like!'

'I want this nuisance guy out of my way as soon as possible!'

'Ok, then! Consider it done!'

Then he cut the call. He wore gloves to conceal his DNA and fingerprints. As he left he threw the phone into the nearest thrash bin.

'Darling, do you think it's safe for you to be wearing your special robe today? A large bomb went off in Istanbul a few days ago and took out a Christian church with half its congregation. They reckon it's another of those extreme Islamic fundamentalist factions. There are many of those about these days, since we became more modern Europeans. They want us to return to the old ways of our ancestors, and the unrest is spreading,' Sarah advised.
'Don't worry about me, Love. You should know by now that I'm not a normal person. Whatever transpires, we still have to follow our way of life or we might as well be dead. Anyway, I'm not an easy one to kill,' he said and left for his lectures.

'That day lumak was later than usual and decided to walk home via his favourite temple. He had no idea he was being shadowed. Not that he ever cared.
As he turned a bend in the road he was stopped by several men dressed in black with their face hidden by what appeared to be striped scarves. They were from an unknown faction.
'Our leader reckons you are a false prophet and also a fake one in the eyes of Allah, so its time you met your evil master in hell,' the tall one said. Then he took the first shot at Lumak's head and nothing happened. The bullet went straight through and had no effect. It was then that the others recovered their machine guns from beneath their coats and began to fire hundreds of bullets at the saintly figure. The bullets rained in his direction, but simply passed through his body and pelted the near wall and distant tarmac with their full force. When they found he could not be killed by those means, they threw their weapons into the nearest waste bin and ran for their lives.
They had no idea that Lumak's body would automatically vectorize away from normally vectored matter at the slightest

sense of such dangers. The process was subconscious and built into his implants. Once vectorized he would have felt comfortable in the middle of an exploding hydrogen bomb or at the centre of our sun. Such were the powers of his type of technologies.

Despite the fact that most of the people in that area disappeared when they saw the masked gunmen shooting. They soon came running out of their hiding places and crowded around Lumak to see whether he could still be assisted. Some even touched his body while observing him closely for wounds, but there was not a single drop of blood anywhere.

'Come on friends, I'm quite ok, so please go about your business and let me go about mine,' he beckoned, but they still remained.

The only one that viewed the complete incident was a poor vagrant who had nowhere to go when the gunmen arrived. He was still bending over the pavement in prayer to Allah.

'Most gracious Allah, please let them go away. Let these vile people go away!' he prayed.

When he was finished praying he got up and found the assassins had ran away, except the saintly Lumak. Then he pointed an unsteady finger towards Lumak.

'He is the great prophet, himself! The one foretold! For no weapons can affect him. I tell you people. He is the true son of Allah!' he yelled, still pointing a finger at Lumak. Then Lumak went up to him and gave the poor man a wad of notes. He took the money and ran away limping as fast as he could. He was another one Lumak thought was in real need of medical care. His present circumstance was mainly due to his adopted way of life and Lumak knew he could do little about such people.

Since the police, reporters and others were on their way Lumak had to make a quick getaway. He seized the opportunity soon enough by disappearing from the scene when the crowds turned their attention to the arriving police cars. In a flash he had faded from their space-time only to reappear just outside his house.

'Thank goodness I've got the knack of transposing my body without the use of the Cloak,' he thought as he appeared in front of the door and rang the bell.

'Darling, you are just in time for dinner! Did you have a nice day?' and innocent Sarah greeted.

Sergeant Anil was soon on the scene with many people standing by.

'What happened here, people?'

'A guy just got shot, but we can't fine his body!' A woman shouted over the crowd.

He went over the area collecting spent bullets and shells while observing everything for blood, but there was not a single drop anywhere.

'A tramp saw the whole thing. I tell you, three guys blasted him at point blank with machine guns and he was still on his feet. I don't know what to believe anymore!' she said.

'And I suppose he just disappeared into thin air?' he inquired.

'Seems that way. Doesn't it?'

Although he realized something was amiss, no one made any sense and the scene showed little evidence of a wounded victim. To make sure he wasn't missing anything, he contacted the local hospitals for recent admissions with bullet wounds, but there were none. He bagged the little evidence he had and filed it in the Crimes Unknown section. He assumed the person involved was wearing a bullet proof vest and let it go at that.

The would-be assassins had left the area in haste and were soon back in the subherbs of Ankara for debriefing.

Later that day a call was made.

'Sorry, Naz. It can't be done. My guys reckon he is the true profit. They rained hundreds of bullets at him with no effect. They just went through him. I have decided to give this one a miss. That guy could be protected by Allah himself. I just cant take the chance,' Hag said.

'Or he could be wearing a bullet proof vest!'

'They also fired at his head!'

'You guys call yourself true Islamists! You call yourselves terrorists. If these are your best, I wouldn't like to see your worst. He is just an English doctor for heaven's sake. How difficult can that be?' Nasidin blared and hung up. He never liked failures or defeat and seldom retracted when he had someone in his sights.

That was an experience Lumak didn't want repeated too many times. Neither did he like the idea of becoming a noble prophet. That type of vocation seemed to serve little purpose other than the adoration gained from the multitudes. He was a doer and wanted to heal his people, not preach to them.

Despite everything that had occurred he feared no one and assumed his assailants were from one of those extreme factions that felt they were losing power. That could only be a weakness on their part and meant he was winning whatever game they were supposed to be playing together. Anyway his invulnerability will give them something to seriously consider in the future. Neither would they mention those special attributes to others in their organization. Not if there was the slightest chance they were going to believe Lumak was the true prophet with special powers.

It was another one of those situations Lumak was used to taking in his stride and would put it down to insecure people trying to lash out blindly at others.

Lumak hoped the complete incident would dissolve away like morning mist. The incident was too bizarre to be believed by the police and others in authority. Nevertheless that day there was mention of the incident on television. They referred to a holy man in a white robe being shot by vandals. However his body was still missing. Only a highly intuitive Sarah realized it was Lumak they were talking about.

'So Darling, I see you made the news again. This time you are even on TV.' she said in jest. Then she became a lot more serious.

'Darling! Was that really about you on Tele. Did those cowards really shoot at you?'

'They tried! Keep it a secret between us for now.'

'Good God, and you do not even have a scratch?'

'It's my special coat. It's also bullet proof.'

'This place is getting too dangerous for us. First the robbers on the coach and now extremists. It's like we cant please anyone these days.'

'Yes! Seems that way! Don't worry, we'll be off to America soon,' he replied

'I wonder what will be next on the news? ... America?' She commented.

'Que Sara, Sara, Love. The skies could be next for all I care,' was his reply, while he continued glancing through his evening newspaper.

The following day he took a different route and visited a different area. He stopped off at another temple to meditate on the successes and his recent unexpected ambush and realize both the good and the bad went side by side. He was once again thinking of his past, family, friends and other dangerous missions. Missions which involved the lives of billions and required his unique efforts in planning and implementation to save all those lives. All such problems with rebellious gunmen were quite petty by comparison.

He also thought of his beloved friend Gemmi, who was now a Grade 2 Shadite and on a new mission somewhere within the three galaxies. He prayed that they would all be kept safe from harm and that they would meet again in the not too distant future.

CHAPTER 37

The engagement ring

'While meditating he suddenly sensed he was on Earth and in a human body. With sadness, he realized he was dreaming of a past mission, his home-world and past friends and family.

He observed but ignored the poor elderly gentleman sitting next to him and continued with his prayer, but the man gently placed his hand on his, quelling his concentration.

'My son, things are now proceeding quicker than estimated. Your path appears to be clear, and I brought you a small gift for your future bride.

'I must now leave, but continue your present course of action,' he said. The elderly man in rags slowly got up and placed the small packet in Lumak's hand. Then he walked away and disappeared from view.

Lumak was then dressed in his beautiful white gown with the imperial crest and golden sandals. He opened the small box and viewed its contents.

'It's a ring! A most beautiful engagement ring!' He ran after the figure to thank him, but he had already gone. It was indeed a most spectacular ring by Earthly standards and emanated an essence of its own existence.

The large central gem glittered in many radiant colours that never remained at a fixed value and there were many equally strange diamonds. They formed a circle around the central gem, where the rays would be further reflected at different angles. It was truly a ring among rings and most enchanting to observe. He knew it was from the Grand Lord, but how could he have known of his own intentions in getting Sarah an engagement ring. It was just an idea he had this morning and he had not communicated those thoughts to the Mind since. This situation is truly remarkable, and so he thought.

He bravely took his usual route home on foot wearing his

unusual attire. It made him appear quite dignified but completely different to anyone on Earth. As he journeyed many of the people would get out of the shops to greet him or ask for his autograph and he would talk to each in turn. Some even called him prophet and lord, but he soon corrected those and told them his proper name, which he gave as Doctor Longhurst.

At that time he felt on top of the world and immune from all further assassins. However he soon realized they could get to him through Sarah. Further, Jeremy and Karen were being put at risk because of his program. What if someone decided to place a bomb near their house? All those factors worried him. Therefore he had to find a safer place to live without those religious extremists.

After his marriage he was sure those events would become public knowledge, including his current address which would be dangerous for all. It was then that he made the decision to move to the USA.

'My Lord, please sign this for my little girl?' an elderly woman asked and he obliged. This time he didn't correct her but accepted the title. He was tired correcting people when they called him "Lord" and "Prophet" and decided to remain silent, if only to save his voice.

'The students' nicknames must be getting around,' he thought. He held his head high as he walked with purple mantle flying in the cool breeze and looked quite dignified.

'Yes!' he thought. 'The Greater Purpose and I have accomplished much since my arrival on Earth and humans are not as alien as I first thought. They are unique and beautiful in their own ways and I wouldn't give up Sarah for anything in this universe. Not even for lovely Gemmi.'

When he arrived home, Sarah and Karen were patiently waiting outside the house with a crowd of reporters and others. He was disturbed when so many knew his address but signed a few more autographs and apologised to others before entering the house.

The moment they closed the door he was greeted by Doctor Emil, who appeared to be very tired from another long and bumpy trip from the country village. He had apparently heard the news of their urgent wedding from the professor and couldn't miss the excitement. Anyway, most of his very ill and cancerous patients had been cured by Lumak's serums and he had little surgery commitments over the few following days. Therefore his wife being a good nurse could take over during his absence.

Sarah's father, Ben, was also on his way and would arrive later that day.

Doctor Emil had offered Ben a lift to the city but he declined, saying he had to do some last minute work on the farm which included acquainting Marion and Simon with their duties.

Since Marion's cure from terminal cancer, she and her husband, Simon, had insisted on taking over Sarah's family home with its animals during their absence. Marion had made a full recovery within a few days and had an age reduction in the process. That particular feature was a necessary side effect of Lumak's cure. Therefore Marion would presently have done anything for the couple, who doubtlessly had saved her life.

Lumak took Sarah aside and handed her the incredible ring. She held the item for a moment while viewing its strange emanations. Then with extreme excitement she placed it on her finger and it pulsated and changed colour.

'I got it specially for you. It's a ring for a queen!'

'Darling, it's so beautiful! So delightful! Where did you find it? Anyway, thanks for this most precious engagement ring. Now all we need is a party to celebrate!'

Sarah realizing the strange powers of her husband to be, did not wish to enquire further. They embraced and kissed. Overexcited Sarah then went directly to Karen and the others to show off her special ring.

'It's the most beautiful thing I've ever seen! It's out of this world!' Karen exclaimed. If only she knew how close she was to the truth. At that time Jeremy was at the university hospital organizing more tests for a new batch of serum.

Ben soon arrived and greeted his daughter Sarah. Then he dropped his case and went over to greet Lumak, giving him a big hug in the process. Then they went to the lounge to have a soft drink and discuss wedding matters. Ben had also brought them an important gift.

'I would like you both to have this ring for your wedding. It belonged to my grandparents and theirs before them,' he said and Sarah took the item from him and began to observe its qualities of simplicity.

'It's solid gold and yet so simple in its design. I would like our relationship to be like that; very precious and not too complicated,' she said to Lumak.

'In that case, we already have our wedding ring.'

'And I shall get you something simple and precious to remember me by when you are away,' she said.

'My love, I shall ask Jemmy to be my best man and dad can take you to the altar in the traditional manner. However, we need someone of seniority to conduct the ceremony,' he replied.

'I have just the man for you,' a happy Ben interjected.

Then he left and soon returned with Doctor Emil. They didn't realize the doctor was also a magistrate.

'Why did you think I journeyed all this way from the village. I wouldn't miss this wedding for all the tea in China!' Doctor Emil exclaimed.

'In that case, why don't we set the date for Friday, with your permission of course? This gives us time to send out invitations,' Sarah said. He nodded in agreement, gave her another hug and they went out to meet their friends and gave them the good news.

Jeremy and Karen's home was getting fuller by the minute. It appeared that if the situation continued most of the men would be sleeping on the floor and in tents outside.

They had finally settled down to watch European cable television with subtitles in English when the phone rang.

'For you, Jeffery. It's the professor!' Jeremy yelled.

'Hello, John,' Lumak replied, wondering whether Professor Jean-Claude also wanted to join the merry group.

'I had a call from our president. He would like to meet you and your future bride. I told him I would have to clear it with you first. Sorry, but I also told him that you intended getting married soon, no date implied. I hope you don't mind? Anyway, we can make it for sometime next week. There is also a committee from Western Europe and another on their way from America, and letters are piling up in my office,' the professor said, somewhat dismayed.

'Can't it wait until tomorrow? If we get in early, we can work through them together. Sarah can also give a hand with the correspondence. I would also like to talk with you about the chemical plant.'

'Ok. I am sure they can wait for a day or so. However, I had to let you know, things being as hectic as they are,' the professor said.

'Why not come over now and party with us? We have finally set the date for our wedding. It's to be on Friday next, so we are celebrating our engagement tonight.'

'Yes, Jeff, I would like that very much. I need a break, anyway,' the professor said and hung up.

That night the television was alive with news of the new miraculous cures for cancer and everyone viewed intently.

The professor appeared later than expected and congratulated Sarah and Lumak. Then he joined them for an alcohol-free drink and left for his home shortly after his wife called.

'Darling, I would like you to be more involved in my work in the future. I am going to arrange a job for you at the university. From now, you are to become my personal secretary. We can arrange for the necessary training in one of the empty offices there. I am going to ask the professor tomorrow about some assistance in that area and I hope you don't mind?'

'I am already your full-time nurse and soon to be your secretary. I only hope I can live up to your expectations, Darling.' Sarah willingly accepted his demands.

The following morning Lumak went directly to the professor's office wearing his blue suit with briefcase in hand. Sarah was to follow later.

He greeted the professor and they made themselves comfortable. Lumak had become used to calling him John and the professor called him Jeff, thus doing away with time-consuming formalities.

Taking the initiative, Lumak opened his case to retrieve some papers.

'I have made some notes on urgent matters and foreseeable snags, so I shall go through them individually and we can discuss each in turn until we agree on their solution.'

'Ok. Lets here it!'

'Our first and main problem is that of communication. In my opinion, that problem can only be solved by a new and more modern switchboard with forty-eight new and faster lines with decoders. If necessary, we shall have to jump queues, because our current projects are of national importance and are also life-saving. Once the telephone company knows that our president has given us his blessings they will jump to it,' Lumak said and the professor nodded his approval.

'Yes, I agree!'

'Secondly, I would like a personal office for myself, so I can communicate freely with the outside world. It may however be necessary to monitor all calls on sensitive lines in case our receptionists and secretaries miss important information. Also, all information given to foreigners, including reporters and writers, should be recorded for legal reasons, but always with their knowledge.'

'Yea, that's important. Reporters lie and exaggerate.'

'Thirdly, I would like, with your permission, Sarah here to assist. Perhaps as my personal secretary. This will be good training for her and inevitably take some of the strain off your office. However, she'll require a few days training in basic secretarial skills, but she is a quick learner and can be quite useful,' Lumak added while quickly scanning through the pile of paperwork on the professors desk.

'May I then suggest the two vacant rooms close to the bio lecture room. They can be very quickly converted. One can be used as your own personal office, where you can hold private discussions with external visitors and the other by your future bride,' the professor replied.

'Finally, and most importantly is the chemical production plant. From the areas on our list. I have decided on the one closest to the city and here are my reasons and the list of materials and costs,' Lumak said while handing copies to the professor.

Jean-Claude quickly glanced through the information, but could not have assimilated it all there and then, so he held on to copies.

'And in the mean time we may continue to make reasonable quantities here in our own university labs,' Lumak said.

'I have arranged for a patent lawyer to draft the necessary documents and make relevant searches. This will protect us in the interim stages should there be a counter claim.'

'That's good thinking!'

'Leave it with me for now and I shall organize the necessary purchases and carpenters for the offices. Farouk has fully recovered from his illness and would be pleased to complete the rooms for you. My secretary can contact the phone company the moment she arrives.

'When can we make an appointment to see the president? It's nothing official,' Jean-Claude said.

'Anytime this weekend, if he is available. I would like to leave next week as free as possible for the wedding on Friday. We have only just begun to organize invitations and there is lots more to do... and all your paperwork has been sorted into three relevant piles. One for me and two for you,' Lumak said.

The professor couldn't believe that while they were talking Lumak had sorted his pile of hundreds of documents into several neat piles in relevant categories. Then Lumak took the largest pile with him to his temporary office.

'How on Earth does he do that?' Jean-Claude thought, realizing that all his letters and document had already been sorted and ready for filing.

Later that day Jean-Claude's secretary called to say that the appointment with the president was scheduled for the coming Sunday and that Lumak and Sarah's friends were also expected.

By that afternoon Farouk and his crew had already began work on the two rooms while the telephone company had sent engineers to assess their demands.

He later phoned Sarah and told her the good news about their meeting with the president on Sunday and of her own little office.

'My love, guess what!' he said.

'What, Darling?'

'The president has invited us to his palace for dinner. What do you think of that?' She was silent and in disbelief.

'What on Earth am I going to wear?' she exclaimed and put the phone down on him.

She couldn't really accept the bit about the president, but eventually believed his words in her usual manner. She was now looking forward to a major celebration and was concerned about her dress for the occasion. Therefore another shopping trip was planned for the following day.

Lumak always smiled at the feminine nature of his wife to be. He was also quite pleased with the way he had adapted to human life on Earth. He realized his future marriage with Sarah would in all probability have made his stay on Earth quite permanent. Nevertheless with the technologies of the Mind, anything was possible and he could always change into other forms when visiting other worlds, including his now almost alien family and friends.

On his way home that day he took the same route and once again entered the temple for prayer. As usual, his mind began to wonder as nostalgia of his home-world and past missions began to absorb his thoughts during his meditations.

CHAPTER 38

A meeting with the President

While in his favourite temple Lumak was awakened from his deep contemplations of past missions by Sarah giving him a gentle tap on his shoulder. However he could not retract the strong images of those past experiences immediately.

'Dear Gemmi, Zahkan and most beloved King Olav...' he uttered aloud.

'Darling, have you been dreaming, again?' an innocent Sarah inquired. Then he looked around to take his bearings.

'No Love, just thinking aloud. I was very tired. I suppose I could have dropped off during prayer.'

'Darling, don't forget! We are to visit the President's Palace this Sunday for dinner!' Sarah insisted.

'I know, Love. Don't worry, it's all been sorted.' Was his calm reply.

All things considered it was a great honour so they wore their best for the occasion.

That Sunday he was again dressed in the special white robe. He had toned it down through his implants. Sarah wore a suitable shade of grey which complemented his outfit. Karen and Jeremy were also invited and were well dressed in anticipation of their meeting with the president of their country. All considered it was a great honour and wore their best for the special occasion.

Professor Jean-Claude called early to take them to the palace with his new Mercedes. After clearance by security, they were escorted to the president's own private area of the palace.

President Amal and his wife sat with a few dignitaries. The moment Lumak entered the room he stood and introduced his new visitors. Then he asked Lumak and Sarah to take a seat on his left side with his wife on his right.

'Jean-Claude, I have heard that you are very busy these days recovering many of our dying patients from death's door?' Amal asked humorously, but with curiosity. Amal himself also had a ginormous workload from Lumak's endeavours. His appointments had increased many fold since Lumak's incredible cures for cancer.

'Yes, Sir, busier than I have ever been since I entered the profession. All thanks to our enthusiastic friend here, by the name of Doctor Jeffery Longhurst. He insists on healing the sick and doing other incredible miracles. The only thing we are unable to do at this time is resurrect the dead. My complete hospital is presently involved in his program. But I must say, I find the challenges quite exciting,' he replied with equal humour, while glancing in Lumak's direction.

'We are becoming quite active here as well. I even had a call from the president of the USA two days ago, offering us more financial aid. Many large European countries are also getting on the bandwagon. Suddenly, our noble country has become extremely popular. Many of our past enemies are asking for appeasement. Even our established religious organizations are worried,' Amal said, then he turned his attention to the one dressed in the strange robe.

'And Doctor Longhurst, what do you think of our present crisis of demand, due to your own incredible handiwork?'

'I think it's very encouraging. I am happy for everyone, even when they are extremely overworked, but we must let it work in our favour. We have an opportunity here to realize many benefits from numerous countries and companies, and should involve only the most reputable ones for the sake of our country and its people, even if we have to import new brains to handle such a crisis of demand,' Lumak replied.

'Said like a true politician. Gentlemen, we can take care of the political aspects. However, my main worry is whether you are suitably funded to handle your end as demand begins to build. Anyway, you have my full support and backing on this project, so should you require anything within my powers, please feel free to ask,' the president said.

By now his wife had taken Sarah and Karen away to show them

the palace, while the men continued their lively discussion.

'What would you like to see come out of all this, Jeffery?' Amal asked, now feeling more at ease with his present company.

'Mister President, I would sincerely like to see our country become one of the strongest, with all its subjects in work, enjoying good health with a reasonable standard of living. This gives us the opportunity to make those changes.'

'Yea, I fully agree!'

'I cannot imagine any political opposition standing in the way of such necessary progress so I shall try my utmost best towards achieving those goals. However, we should not exclude our neighbours from such ventures. They have always been with us and we know very little of those more distant so-called fair weather friends bearing gifts. Neither do we want them to feel completely left out of our successes,' Lumak said and the president listened carefully to his words.

'What a very interesting character? He may be a doctor, but he has already convinced me into following a new course of action. What he says make lots of sense and he never mince his words. I think I am getting to like this Doctor Longhurst,' Amal thought.

'Furthermore, we must ensure our secrets on the anti-cancer projects remain with us and retain royalties on all sales worldwide. Our products now being patented are unique to our country and should be licensed only to those stable countries with the necessary qualifications in manufacture.'

'Yea, yea!'

'All the key components of our products should be made and supplied by our own production plants here and elsewhere, thus returning to us large amounts of foreign currency. However, it is imperative that we cope with current and future demands. I must seriously stress that point.' Lumak replied.

The president realised the project was in capable hands with Jeffery at the helm. They were soon called to lunch.

Sarah, Karen and his wife soon returned to join them at the table.

'Sarah, what do you think of all this, including leaving your free and healthy way of life in the country,' the president inquired.

'Sir, I love my Jeffery dearly and will visit anywhere if it meant assisting him in his holy mission to save lives,' she replied.

They talked casually, mentioned about their wedding plans and were congratulated.

CHAPTER 39

The second lecture

Lumak's second lecture was arranged for Monday afternoon. Due to the great demand from overseas it was to be held in the main auditorium. Therefore all the special equipment had to be dismantled and moved to that area and then thoroughly tested and reassembled. Since they didn't expect present demands to wane, his lectures and equipment would be permanently sited within that area until the new building was ready. Such were the appeal that it was thought more than two thousand would be present, including many foreign doctors, reporters and dignitaries.

This time many television sets had been arranged throughout the university hospital and within the classrooms, so that everyone could view the televised version of his lectures. Because of the numerous foreign visitors, students and their seniors were not allowed within the auditorium as on previous occasions. They would watch the televised program instead.

Jean-Claude had sent out invitations far and wide and expected visits from many foreign delegates and VIPs over the ensuing weeks. Therefore Lumak expected to be very busy during that period preparing and performing many lectures on related topics.

Lumak's personal offices had already been fitted and the telephone company busy installing the new switchboard and lines. The university hospital was astir with human activity everywhere as they prepared production to feed current demands.

He had decided to take Sarah along that day and introduce her to her new office and future job, so they arrived early and went directly to his own office. Many students greeted and congratulated them as they travelled through the corridors.

She soon began to arrange things more to her liking by shifting her desk and chairs around until the place was more to her personal taste, then she began her official duties as personal secretary with Lumak's assistance.

It always made him feel more confident and self-assured when Sarah was around. It was a feeling for which he had no explanation. They had always worked together in the country and she always tended to bring out the best in him.

The original small lecture room was soon rearranged into a meeting place with a few tables and chairs set in rows for private meetings. Theirs were connected by a direct door and decorated more like comfortable lounges.

Sarah sat at her desk while opening the empty drawers one by one, then she closed them while looking at Lumak with a satisfied expression.

'Now, Love, you will need a word processor and a small telephone extension,' he said smiling. He was quite amused by her determination.

'But I don't know what a wordprocessor is and can't even type a word. You are the one to put me in the deep end and will have to get me out of it,' she replied, adamantly.

'Don't you worry about that problem, my dear? I have arranged for a professional typist to train you on a daily basis. She has a diploma in business studies, so she will be able to teach you at your own pace. There is also the voice recognition system. You may use that program if all else fails. However, I would prefer it if you attempted to learn using the most difficult ways first and progressed to the other more efficient methods, once you mastered the basics... But if you would prefer it done another way, please let me know,' he said with equal firmness.

'No, Darling. I am very pleased with everything the way they are, and I don't mind being at school again.'

She observed the tell tale signs in his eyes when he tried to get one over on her. Among other things she was also a keen mind reader and would not succumb to his arrogant superiority on this occasion. Therefore she was determined to become the best to prove her capabilities and wipe the smirk off his face.

'Karen should be along shortly to assist with the pamphlets distribution, so relax until then. I must now leave you to prepare for my second lecture. But if you need me I shall be next door,' he said and left.

When he visited the auditorium later that day it contained a full audience with many standing along the corridors. As he entered everyone stood to clap and he bowed his head.

He walked directly to his desk and thought into the equipment. Everything came alive as before, showing the Osmaron galaxy and its Globular clusters. That image of Osmaron (our Milky Way galaxy) could only have been recorded from another place within the universe and many wondered about it's authenticity. Finally the Solar System was highlighted, then Earth with its single Moon.

'Today we shall concentrate on longevity, with a view to its impact on society, due to overpopulation and technological change, partly to do with social evolution. We shall also discuss some important aspects of micro-robotics,' Lumak said. He thought into the system and the image abruptly changed to a large molecule with many coloured bands along its several helixes. Then the displayed image floated out of the screen and was suspended in mid air above their heads, while it slowly rotated.

This time he continued the lecture focussing on a group of sub-molecules that were coloured red.

'You may appreciate that most of these structures are the result of primal evolution. They have been formed in such a manner as to balance the sociological and physiological needs of the organism for optimum survival within its planetary environment. Even the human life-span is programmed within these helixes. Life-span relates to survival competition, resources, predation, optimum learning and other sociological factors within the social groups of this type of species.

'You should also realize that there are sociological pressures attempting to keep things the way they were. For instance, many would not wish to exist in a society of moderate longevity. One in which their grand children were of the same physical age as they. Furthermore, think of the repercussions today if all of humanity lived for a thousand years without the necessary changes in minds and attitudes?

'*Many long-lived species seldom bear offspring. In most cases they will choose artificial means for that purpose only when there is a specific requirement. In all naturally evolved cases, sibling spacing can be related to both death rate and longevity, depending on predation and detrimental factors within the environment. Most of these factors have been programmed into our genes. Those basic tendencies are reflected by our subconscious minds through our genes during the long process of evolution. Even death in some cases may be brought about by suggestion, which is itself a function of mind. So mind plays a significant controlling role in our evolution.*

'*Mother nature always has a hand to play in the long term survival of all naturally evolving species, but her efforts can sometimes be assisted or negated by the arrogant and uncaring within an advanced technological culture. Therefore, within any evolving primal system a natural balance should be met between longevity and population growth and such growth must be held within planetary constraints by strict rules and methods, and never by economical or political means or gains.*

'*Nevertheless, there is always a time lag between primal change, due to the natural order and the progression of intelligent species by the application of technology to enhance such change. In other words, technology is always faster then Mother Nature, when it comes to constructive and orderly changes within any given environment. With most technological species, one tends to offset the other, with the usual overshoot and over compensation, thus leading to chaos. What may be accomplished in a few years by technology can take several hundred thousand years, even millions of years through natural evolution, given the correct conditions.*

'*For instance, while Mother Nature is attempting to reduce an advanced population by the introduction of pandemic disease, the highly technological will try to offset nature by creating antidotes and cures, thus offsetting the natural order to the long term detriment of all.*

'*That is when system controls become less primal and more technological. When that happens there is usually a period of crisis, and only a few advanced species have been known to survive the upheaval.*

'That period can be associated with depletion of most energy resources, as technological advances due to social evolution progresses ever onwards to fuel our ever changing needs. At that time the dominant species may become quite self-indulgent and wasteful, squandering most of their non-renewable resources within but a few generations. Within their isolated bubbles of self-satisfaction they continue to ignore and neglect all others to their detriment.

'During this period the dwindling resources may be accompanied by more desertification with the resulting consequences of famine on a global scale, which in turn breathes more discontent, disease and pestilence, to thus sustain a detrimental spiral from which no short term recovery may be expected.

'During the turmoil that follows, the general public is unable to rationalise those unexpected changes, which deprive them of all their social comforts and freedom. Gross insecurity will make them jump to wrong conclusions, leading to strife and destructive riots when their demands are not met.

'During this period of change fear becomes predominant and neighbour will stand against neighbour. However, the worst elements of this period is the riots and unrest, which will further aid in the destruction of civilization as its main utilities and services are destroyed. Call it another dark age if you wish and the symptoms are already with us on this still beautiful planet. However, it is during such periods of crisis that new and stronger species evolve.

'If only technology could precisely control population growth. But who can tell the hormonal couple or newly wed that they will not be allowed to have children because of the long-term survival of the greater public. We are the byproduct of our genes and are driven by our initial genetic programming. We are also a byproduct of our past and of our hormones which are millions of years older than our present societies with their technological changes. Because of those reasons there will always be a pull in

the opposite direction that will always lead us along the path of mutual destruction. It will take Mother Nature another million or so years to remove those urges and desires from mind and body,' Lumak said.

Then he pointed closer to another group of molecules that were coloured brown.

'This is the group that represents the life cycle of the human cell before division and is triggered by these mechanisms here and here.' Then he pointed to another similar structure.

'This is almost an identical model to the one we have been studying. If you observe closely, you may identify a new molecular bond with a slightly different structure to control its adhesion. That extra is a neutral connective and will not impose any functional changes to the general structure of the whole.

'If we replaced the brown with the blue and its connectives, the cell will become slightly heavier, but in the process much stronger.' The large molecule began to transform into yet another structure and slowly rotated.

'By this simple addition the life cycle has been extended over twenty times, but in so doing we have also significantly increased molecular strength and adhesion between cells. Hence, life-forms composed of these non primal structures may suffer little from environmental damage. In most cases, it would be difficult to cut through such tissue with a scalpel. Yet, although exceedingly tough, it will be very flexible in its movements.

Furthermore, an estimated life cycle for such a human life-form would be in the region of several thousand years, given the correct genetic programming. Such a unique human life-form would never be plagued by the common cold or indeed any natural infections during its life cycle. Longevity may be further increased by taking finer steps during the design process and by replacing some groups with certain metallic types.

'You should also realise that the offspring of such life-forms will be almost identical to their parents.' The screen changed into a structure full of metallic bonds.

'*At this juncture, I shall introduce you to Micro Robotics with a view to neuronic communication. However, before I continue, this audience may feel free to ask me some relevant questions. After that time we may have a break.*'

'Sir, why would anyone wish to live forever?' One of the doctors in the front row inquired.

'*That's an interesting question that can only be answered by the individual concerned. How many here would like to live forever? Don't be too quick with your response. You must first consider several facts before you lift your hands. Firstly, all the people you see about you, including your loved ones, friends and family will be gone within the first hundred years or so. Then you would be left alone to find new relationships, hobbies, careers and such like, if you are to avoid perpetual boredom.*

'*I am sure if we were rulers of worlds we would always be too busy to ask such ridiculous questions. Furthermore, if one was completely selfless in their attitudes to assist others throughout the universe, then they might think ten thousand years not enough for such a mission which might pass too quickly. I'm sure a great scientist like Einstein wouldn't mind living forever.*

'*So it depends to a great extent on the individual and what he or she wants out of life or has set as their final goal. Furthermore, within such a long-lived society there would also be sociological pressures and a requirement for the reduction in boredom and other detrimental factors. There might also be the technology to transform those individuals requiring the occasional change in mind and form. Not many might want to continue to exist in their original bodies to eternity, when there are so many other options and alternatives for change.*

'*For instance, many may consider a change in career or physical form, including a change in sex, even to a completely different life-form, after every hundred years or so. All such changes could become acceptable if everyone within the system had those choices, always cared and loved each other and were educated to cope with such an incredible way of life,*' Lumak replied and they were amused and cheered.

CHAPTER 40

Micro Robotics

After answering more questions and refreshments, Lumak continued with his lecture, changing its tone more to audience participation.

'I know many of you have come from afar. It is not easy to compact all aspects of such complex subjects into a single session, so a range of such lectures have been planned for the next few days. Therefore I think this is the right time to take some of your probing questions. Many papers are now available from our information section, so please help yourselves on your way out, after this session is ended,' Lumak said.

A hand went up from one of the rear seats.

'Sir, my name is Doctor McKenzie from the United Kingdom. I represent a well-known anti-cancer organisation and would like to ask a question if I may.

'I am doubtful whether it's really possible to engineer cells to such a high degree of complexity. In particular, the process of adding such small fractions virtually to any section of the DNA during replication. During our experiments we found that as we got down to comparable scales of bio-engineering, a large proportion of the samples either became contaminated or formed incorrect links, even with the necessary bio-assistant chemicals and enzymes. So far the best we were able to achieve by such methods was a 30 percent change in the sample mass. Yet by implication you seem to have everything under perfect control, as with a Lego or a Meccano Set.'

'Yes, Doctor, I realize your problems. I am sorry, but I was slowly getting to that part of cellular engineering. That area is covered in detail and can be accomplished by Micro Robotics. This is part of a field of science better known to you as Nano-Technology.

'Visualise, if you may, a beehive or ants' nest. Now if an

individual decided to repair a damaged part it would take a finite time to complete that operation. That task however may be accomplished much quicker if all bees or ants were involved in their own specialised tasks. A Microid Robot may be as small as one millionth the size of an ant, but once given specific instructions can complete specific tasks within a cell to virtually any levels of miniaturization and complexity. Call it a micro operation if you wish,' Lumak said, leaving the doctor even more confused than before.

'Let me show you an example, if I may.'

Lumak removed a small rectangular block from a drawer and placed it on his desk. Then he retrieved a hammer and saw from another drawer and began to abuse the block with both tools, but no damage was apparent. The block was shown to many in the audience, but they could not find a single scratch or dent on the block.

'Doctor McKenzie, perhaps you would like to join me and attempt this experiment, yourself.'

The doctor got up and followed close to Lumak's position on the stage. He was handed the saw and attempted to cut through the block but there was not even the faintest mark.

'Please hold the block in the palm of your hand, Doctor.' To which the doctor obliged. However the moment he placed the block in his hand, it began to change from rectangular to a perfect sphere and then to a cylindrical form. Yet it was still a solid block. The petrified doctor was amazed by the strange occurrence. He promptly handed the item back to Lumak and returned to his seat.

The cameras and video displayed the process in detail to the audience who were equally astonished.

'Gentlemen and ladies, this block is composed of several billion Micro Robots or microids. Some of you might even use the more familiar term of nano-bots or nanites. They are mainly composed of heavy metals and can take the form of any item of a comparable volume. However, unlike cells, these particular ones are held together by physical bonds and can be controlled externally by multi-phased micro-waves,' he said, while removing a small blinking block from underneath his robe.

'Microids can be controlled by external programming or by their own internal mechanisms, in a similar manner to our own biological cells and antibodies. Since they are composed of atoms and exceedingly small molecules, a human body made from such structures can be the size of a tiny flee and still contain all his body and brain cells. These microscopic robots can enter the body and repair specific areas within cells, repair or add neurons within the brain, link suitable connectives in the brain for telepathic communication, and may be used for a host of other functions and applications. Doctor, I trust I have answered your question.

'Yes, Sir!' McKenzie replied, still confused by the whole affair.

'Would anyone like to partake in a simple experiment? I can assure you it's perfectly safe and will only involve about one hundred microids per individual. Can I have some volunteers, please?'

Five brave hands went up and he called them unto the stage. He offered them five small capsules.

'You may remove the top and inhale their harmless contents, and try not to sneeze.'

They followed his instructions.

It was however not long before they began to behave strangely.

'I can hear you speak even without the movements of your lips, Doctor,' one said.

'The special microids that you inhaled have made temporary connection to certain areas of your brain and are now able to directly relay visual and other information to those similarly connected to mine. However, your thoughts, as with speech, can only be transferred with your direct intervention and approval. You may feel free to converse with each other through your new implants.'

What transpired was unbelievable. They could each communicate directly without moving their lips. Several blind checks were carried out to disprove their mode of communication, but the checks proved his experiment each time.

'It will now be possible for any of you to absorb detailed information by such modes of communication. This microid system

can also be used by the deaf and blind to overcome their disabilities. Furthermore it is now possible for you to complete your entire post graduate course in several days instead of the usual three years, with the exception of the practical areas and even those may be completed by using Virtual Environments. However, since all our perceptions and senses are a product of our minds, virtually any feeling or movement may be experienced within a Virtual World in your mind. Virtual Worlds can be programmed within such implants for training and will appear to the individual to be as real as any other external environment within the so-called real world. Even pain and all our other sensations like taste and suchlike may be simulated by such methods. By so doing, all connections to muscle groups can be updated in similar manner as with any real world experience.

'The fantastic thing about such methods is their ability to extend our perceived life-span. If we could exist within a Virtual World where every event moved a thousand times faster, then we could do shopping, meet our friends, even go on long holidays for several weeks and when we returned to the real world only a few seconds or minutes would have passed by. This is yet another method for longevity.

'Therefore, with such methods even the practical areas can be carried out within your mind in a Virtual World, where everything can be made identical to this one, and any movement portrayed; for what is reality? Such methods may be utilized in certain types of brain implants that can extend ones brain power and memory by at least a factor of ten.

'With such advanced technological methods, there will be little need for people to spend their childhood years in schools and colleges. Why not have a brain implant with several doctors already included within its original programming, to be used as and when the need arose. Then all that would be required by its user was to locate the relevant menus within their mind and follow into the help or training areas.

'Once within such training areas or rooms in our Virtual Worlds, Virtual Human Assistants or Trainers could be made available to guide us and by so doing update our real memories by those

Virtual Experiences.

'*Since such implants are transparent to the normal workings of the brain, and interwoven into our nervous system, even the experience part can be included within the learning process. By such methods, a Virtual cup of coffee could taste and smell exactly like a real cup, even the temperature sensed will be as real to the user.*

'*Therefore, microid based implants may be used to give new layers of functionality to the brain without significantly increasing brain size in the process. Furthermore, such implants can do calculations and other complex processes in a fraction of the time taken by even the best mathematicians with calculators. Many such tasks may be completed while the user is asleep and even without his or her knowledge, while functioning in the background. Even the number of hours slept may be programmed, including the addition of important reminders.*

'*I must also stress that many of such tasks may be completed within virtual space and time, which can be hundreds of times faster than real time. Think of their uses with pilots or controllers of fast moving vehicles, where quick decisions are required.*

'*Once linked to such a Virtual Mind, it could be made to encompass our complete world, including the Internet. Then our brains become peripherals of an infinitely greater mind. We would then have the ability to use all that information as if it were the extent of our own minds. Thus giving us almost infinite potentials to accomplish our destinies.*

'*The microids that you inhaled were specifically programmed for this demonstration and will dissolve naturally within the hour, leaving behind not a single trace or side effect..*

' His audience were truly astonished.

'*You may now return to your seats,*' he said. He continued the lecture for another half hour then he mingled with the audience for a while answering more of their searching questions.

The audience were truly amazed by the technology that could transform every bit of human consciousness and concepts. Even what was considered humanity itself, could become a much freer creature functioning at a much higher level of consciousness. One that could create virtually any environment within their minds in their own privacy. One that could take them anywhere and make them experience virtually anything. Even ancient historical events like great battles could be re-lived through such 3D simulations, where anyone of us could be placed within the scene and seamlessly merge with it through our senses and emotions. By so doing, we could become great king Nebuchadnezzars or indeed one of his slaves and be greeted and treated in like manner.

When he closed his lecture that day everyone stood and applauded continuously. The place was in an uproar.

The senior doctors were insistent that he held a further meeting with them and the foreign diplomats wanted him to visit their respective countries for further lectures.

CHAPTER 41

Lord of science

Sarah was in the auditorium that day, sitting on the side in her beautiful white cream suit while assisting with the handing out of brochures. She had become friendly with many of the senior students and treated with respect and admiration by all.

Professor Jean-Claude had decided to arrange a meeting with the English doctors for the following morning and they left in a state of utter excitement in the direction of their respective hotels. They were still overwhelmed by the lecture and in particular, the new concepts of Micro Robotics and the use of brain implants for paraplegics, the deaf and blind. To them it was the greatest technological breakthrough since splitting the atom.

'The man, Lumak, was completely unheard of before. He had appeared out of the blue, as if from nowhere. And yet, such a genius with novel ideas in medicine and robotics could easily change the whole structure of life on Earth. Those microids could solve problems in every conceivable field of science, including the communication problem,' McKenzie said.

'He is something, Man! I cant imagine any of it yet!' a colleague replied.

'Those breakthroughs will completely change the status of humankind within the universe. He had come up with those novel ideas all by himself and in this hitherto technological backwater. I say again, the man is a bloody genius!' doctor McKenzie said to his colleagues on their way out of the building.

They had to quickly return to their hotels and contact their superiors to give them the news of those incredible scientific breakthroughs.

'I need a line to England!' Doctor John McKenzie shouted to the beautiful female receptionist.

'Take this one, Sir!' she replied in almost perfect English, while handing him a small mobile phone. He dialled a code and the image of the recipient was displayed crisp and clear on the small hand-held screen.

'Hi George!' Professor Strongman replied.

'Hello John. How did the lecture go? Was it as incredible as you thought it would be?'

'Sir, it was much better than we were led to believe. It was truly incredible and beyond anything I've ever seen or could ever have imagined. Have you heard of Micro Robotics?'

'Yea... some organization in the States did some studies on the subject some years ago. I think I read it was to be a future important branch of Nano-tech or some such, but they did not come up with any substantial breakthroughs. I thing NASA was also involved, but I haven't read anything on the topic since. They could have stopped because of limited funding. I might still have an old copy of an original report filed away somewhere. I can fax you a copy if you wish.'

'Don't bother, George. This is a million years beyond anything you have seen or heard. He can make micro robots one thousandth the size of a human cell do almost anything to order. They can even build a bloody house. But the bit I like, is being able to inhale them into the system to make general repairs to cells and tissue. By such methods even neurons in the brain can be connected to order. They can also be linked with other neurons for total telepathic communication and a lot more besides, including making the cripple walk, the blind see and the deaf hear. That guy is even better than Jesus.

'Bloody hell!'

'He also has ideas on tiny brain implants that can extend the human brain some ten times and give them several doctors in the process. Pal, I think the whole of our structure of education has now become completely obsolete. With those implants, children will not require schooling in the normal way. All they will do is visit a special centre after they become a teenager and have an implant fitted. Thereafter they automatically become a bloody genius. Can you imagine that, George?' John McKenzie exclaimed with utter excitement. George Strongman remained silent as if stunned by John's words. He always trusted John, for he was one of his most promising research doctors and never of a frivolous nature.

'Should I come, John?' he asked calmly as if anticipating a request.

'Yes Sir. Please! We have a meeting set with the doctor tomorrow morning. Please try to be here by then. I also heard lots of Yanks are on their way with major bucks, and you know what that means... very soon this whole place will be a little part of America with McDonald's everywhere,' John replied.

'In that case, I am already on my way. What's he like? I mean, the doctor.'

'A bit eccentric, I thought. He is supposed to be English but was dressed in a white robe. Like an ancient prophet, I suppose.'

'Or another Doctor Lawrence of Arabia, perhaps more like the great Omar Khayyam.' George replied, sarcastically.

The receptionist girl who was listening intently to John's side of the conversation, suddenly interrupted.

'Sir, you have met with our... Lord?' she asked while going over to kiss him.

'Yes, we have!' he replied, breaking from his current telephone conversation.

'He saved my mother from cancer. Look, I have his autograph here in my bag,' she added while retrieving the card.

'I am sorry about the interruption, George. The local receptionist reckoned he, her lord, saved her mother's life. Most of the locals here seem to call him Lord, but you can understand why. There is a lot going on here and I can't explain half of it.'

'You and your team should try to put something together before my visit. That way it will save time when we have our meeting after my arrival.'

'We are already doing it!'

'I will try to catch this evening's flight, but I can't promise anything,' George said. John glanced for a moment at the young receptionist and walked towards her desk.

'I would like to talk with you about your mother's recovery. My colleagues and I are from England and we are doctors. If you like, perhaps we could have a drink after you finish your shift. You speak very good English,' John said.

'I am sorry, Sir, I don't drink alcohol, but I will speak with you about my mother. I can't stay too long though,' she replied.

'They were surprised when they learnt that her mother was completely cured of the cancer within 3 days and that was not all. After the cure she appeared to be more than ten years younger.

Doctor George Strongman arranged his flight with a little luck and arrived early the following morning. He booked into their hotel soon afterwards, having woken John to collect him from the airport at 4 a.m.

They had a lengthy discussion and then decided to catch up on some sleep.

That evening Lumak took his usual route home with Sarah, greeting friends and entered the temple to say a prayer.

Sarah was very excited with her new career which involved meeting so many people and took it all in her stride. She realized it was quite a change from that of a poor simple shepherdess in the now remote hills, but missed the animals all the same. They discussed the wedding and realised that Jeremy's house was much too small for that event.

Lumak wanted to station some guards close to Jeremy's home, but realized their presence could lead to more complications, so he ignored those security issues for now. Anyway, the house was usually vacant during the day and he was at home with them most evenings.

An excited Michael Cockburn had again arrived for some more first-hand information on yet another of his scientific articles for the Times, and Jean-Claude decided to hold another one of his grand parties in his country manor. Lumak decided to foot the bill for that one and insisted he would only accept yes for an answer, so everyone of importance was invited.

It was arranged for Wednesday evening. That was because much preparation was needed. Sarah and Karen decided to give the professor's wife some assistance in the kitchen. Nevertheless most of the food for that function was imported from a respected local restaurant.

The party started at 8 p.m. and Lumak invited all his family and friends including President Amal, but he was unavailable.

This time Lumak was dressed in a grey suit and Sarah in her usual cream. By eight-thirty the place was almost full. Even the English doctors and their professor had been invited and were present.

It was not long before the Minister of Finance arrived with two enthusiastic security officers who were keen to search the house and its surroundings, but the minister held them back and pointed them to the outside.

Jean-Claude walked towards the entrance to greet him and his wife and then began introducing him to Lumak and Sarah. Apparently the minister and Jean-Claude were old friends and knew each other since their college days in France.

By nine, the ladies and men had separated and were discussing their future wedding, while Lumak was discussing more complex matters and answering more technical questions. That was the nature of the party and many wanted to acquire as much information as they could about his projects before they returned to their respective countries.

'I say, Jeff, if you don't mind me calling you on first name terms,' the minister said.

'Not at all.'

'How shall I call you?'

'Please call me, Ben, short for Benjamin. The president asked me to convey his apologies and sent me in his place. He has a few urgent matters to attend. You know how it is in his position, and most of it is due to your important work.'

'No problem!'

'You know, Jeff, I must sincerely thank you for placing our country on the international stage once more. You know, we are now being considered by all the major companies and countries. They are all trying to force money down our throats.'

'That's good news, Ben!'

'Most importantly, the larger countries in Europe want to give us a personal hand ahead of the Americans and I need your advice in this matter. I don't know if I should take what they offer now and suffer the consequences later or hold off for a while and lose precious time. A period in which we could improve our conditions in the short-term with the extra funding.

'I see!'

'Anyway, the president asked me to mention those considerations to you. He seems to hold you in high esteem.'

'Ben, our once great country is now exceedingly weak and poor. Many of our young people leave for Europe after learning to read and write. We have many poor and suffering that require our urgent assistance. There is also the area of encouraging outside industries to assist in forming a more solid infrastructure, while employing our large and virtually unused labour force... not to mention their welcomed investments.

'We require a broad range of facilities including new universities, schools, hospitals and clinics. There is also the public transport problems that require a new fast railway system and more adequate roads for our coaches and busses. The list is endless and all these changes require substantial funding.

'What little crude oil we have is imported at exorbitant prices from many of our neighbours, and friend... as they say, blood is thicker than water. We must always give to our people first before giving to others.

'Another thing: we can always make changes in the future if we leave those agreements open ended. By then we shall be in a much better position of hindsight with greater financial powers. So my friend, take what they offer, but use it wisely and let them have something in return by way of medical and other assistance for a reasonable price, but do not sell out our country in the process.

'Let us become the richest, but also let us assist the poorest countries so that we are always remembered, appreciated and respected by all. And those countries also include our poorer neighbours,' Lumak said. The phone rang and was answered by Jean-Claude's wife.

'The President is on the phone for Doctor Longhurst,' she yelled and the room was suddenly silent. Lumak excused himself and went to answer the president's call.

'Hello, Jeff. I wanted to personally apologise for missing your party, but I had some prearranged meetings with important foreign delegates. Anyway, what would you say if I asked you to hold your post nuptial celebrations at my palace. Obviously, at no expense to you, and including all those you and your future bride have already invited.

'The wedding ceremony itself can be conducted at my palace or elsewhere at your discretion. Then we can have a full house here at the palace for the celebrations and make it a great affair. That is, if you and Sarah don't mind. Just tell her that the palace will handle everything. All you have to do is be present. Please talk to Sarah about it and let me know as soon as possible. This is my personal number and please keep it confidential,' he said, while rendering the eleven digit codes.

'Yes, Sir. Thank you very, very much. I shall mention it to her right away and call you back today,' Lumak replied, with excitement.

'By the way, did my finance minister ask you for some advice?' the president asked.

'I said a big yes to financial and other assistance and explained the reasons why. He seems to have accepted my arguments.'

'Thank you for that, and see you soon,' the president said and hung up. Lumak immediately contacted Sarah.

'Darling, guess what?'

'What!' she replied, innocently.

'Our president is arranging the post nuptial celebrations for us at the palace and all our friends and family are invited. What do you think about that?'

Sarah embraced and kissed him there and then and in public. This time she was not worried about clothes to wear. She had now got herself a full wardrobe to suit almost every occasion.

'That is incredible news, Darling, and will make my life a lot simpler. Like lifting a ton of wood off my shoulders. I didn't know where to begin while arranging such a major deal and didn't wish to get Karen involved again. She is always there to assist and I don't want to stretch our friendship to the point of breaking. Darling, we must show the president our appreciation and gratitude, and take them a beautiful present,' she replied.

'In that case, you and Karen can do some more shopping to find something beautiful for the president's lovely wife. You know how useless I am at such tasks,' he said.

The party at Jean-Claude's house ended just after midnight and they went their separate ways.

CHAPTER 42

More foreign delegates

A more intense meeting was subsequently arranged. It was to be held in the small lecture room for the benefit of Michael Cockburn, Professor Strongman and his other English associates. That meeting was planned for the following morning. The security of the complete university campus had been significantly increased and the small lecture room made private with a security officer standing close to the door. Lumak stood at the head of the large conference table with Jean-Claude at the other end.

'Doctor Longhurst and present company, I would like to take this opportunity, on behalf of my colleagues and myself, in sincerely thanking you and your country for allowing us to visit at such short notice. We have also found your lectures to be the most enlightening.' Strongman said.

'We are very happy to have you guys.' Lumak replied.

'I shall however get directly to the point. We are here simply because you have something that we would like to use for the benefit of our cancer patients. Perhaps you could furnish us with test reports on cured terminal patients and any other documentation that we may require to implement a cure. We would also like to know more about Micro Robotics and Brain Implants, but those topics can be discussed more thoroughly at a later date,' Strongman continued and sat down.

'Well, Professor Strongman, you can have it and as much as you want. I am not in a position to supply our lifesaving drugs only to our so-called higher bidders. I have set a fixed price, to be reduced only by our customer's involvement and assistance within the broader picture,' Lumak replied. The professor was extremely surprised and thought he would have had to seriously compete with the Americans and others.

'Thank you, very, very much!' he replied, surprised.

'But you will no doubt appreciate the present condition of our growing country. So I will be equally direct with you when I say that the serum has been patented. However, your signing a simple agreement will guarantee your deliveries of the key powder and other relevant components at a most reasonable price.'

'That's fine with us, providing there are no strings attached.'

'No strings, Professor. We have prepared a folder which includes a brochure and other necessary forms. Please ask Sarah for one on your way out. And don't worry about test results and such like. We have prepared a thorough document on all aspects of this cure. This information you will receive in due course.' Noting what Lumak mentioned about "a broader picture", Strongman realized perhaps he could gain more perquisites by getting in with the man while the iron was hot.

'Perhaps we could also assist with some of our own equipment and trained doctors. We are currently involved in many fields of research.'

'Perhaps, Professor. It's my intention to visit Western Europe soon, including England, so perhaps you could show me around your laboratories during that visit. Then we can take it from there. We have lots of projects in the near future and I am sure you will soon be involved.'

To an excited Professor Strongman the matter of their involvement had more or less been settled. Having read some of Lumak's reports he now wanted to observe several of the recovered patients personally, before committing himself, and that visit was planned for the afternoon.

As the meeting continued most of their questions on the serum was answered and still more questions were being posed.

'Doctor Longhurst, I am also an astrophysicist. I am very interested in the use of Micro Robotics for space exploration. Presently there are a few companies in England involved in many aspects of space research. Do you have knowledge of such things?' John McKenzie inquired.

'I have knowledge of many things. Some however more than others. A matter of personal choice I suppose. For instance, I am now considering the development of an LPD drive system that can propel ships across our galaxy in under a month. The problem is how to manufacture the necessary components with present planetary technologies.'

'What system is that, Sir?' John McKenzie inquired.

'It is a Linear Progressive Drive system. An inertial converter if you wish. LPD for short. It utilises a new concept in sub nuclear fusion and contains its own inbuilt fusion generator, with zero pollution generated as a result, but quite complex to assemble. Once initiated, it will convert hydrogen and transform the energy produced into a type of forward inertia. You should realize, Professor, that such changes of inertia may be accomplished at the sub-atomic level by altering certain aspects of symmetry. Since the propelling items weigh very little and are highly efficient, very small fuel payload is needed. However, there are other additional items for neutralizing acceleration and gravitational effects within the environment of the ship. Furthermore, at speeds beyond light, the ship can be made to travel within its own inertial frame in what you call hyper-space.'

'Really?'

'Yes! Given the availability of necessary equipment and raw materials, this particular item should be completed within approximately two years,' Lumak replied.

Professor Strongman looked intensely at Lumak, wondering whether the man was serious or insane. Lumak also realising their expressions of doubt began to draw some sketches on the board, explaining the ideas as best he could about the concepts behind an inertial diode.

'There goes Einstein's theory of relativity,' muttered Michael Cockburn, who was recording everything for his future scientific articles in the Times.

'Would you like my people to assist you in such an incredible project?' the professor inquired, excitedly.

'If you wish, Professor, but when I begin such projects I would rather handle them outside of government interests. That way they can be kept well away from the military until the time is right.'

'No problems there! We are a private organization!'

'In that case, consider yourselves part of our LPD project. I shall send you a file in due course to get you started. You know the problems faced in the future, with Global warming and other detrimental factors to humanity and other planetary life. Well, I intend to form my own global organization for the benefit of our planet. Those dedicated scientists like yourselves, who are interested in such ideals may feel free to join with me for those altruistic reasons,' Lumak replied.

The meeting was concluded and they returned to their respective hotels feeling on top of the world.

After interviewing a few more recovering terminal patients, Professor Strongman signed the necessary forms then he and his group were soon on their way back to England to await Lumak's future visit.

CHAPTER 43

A strange report

Professor Harry Lennox was in his late thirties, very tall at six foot eight inches, well built and brilliant. He had spent several years in NASA on the space program while training future astronauts. However his main interest was in the behaviour of human biological systems during long space flights. Particularly during prolonged conditions of weightlessness and extreme acceleration. He had also designed and constructed a complete portable integrated recycling station for processing body waste at reusable standards and at high transfer efficiencies. That system was currently on display at NASA's museum. Harry had written many reports and papers on those topics, thus becoming one of the main authorities on the subject of human survival in space.

Due to general cutbacks in the space program at NASA and elsewhere, he had become disenchanted with their change in direction and other unwelcomed pressures of office. The last straw that broke the camel's back was probably when several important interplanetary projects were cancelled by new management. There was also his constant struggle with his new boss and the finance department for the necessary funding for his projects. He was soon offered a post in Washington DC as chief science adviser in a special presidential committee in areas of "the after effects of biological warfare". He soon accepted the important post, although not too excited by his more senior role, which included the lack of real hands-on research.

Although the large countries were presently at peace, the more extreme elements were always at war with everyone and their savagery was increasing. They had included the use of biological weapons in their armoury and at their chosen time would willingly use them on the unsuspecting public. There were many such extremist factions and cells in the USA. The planet was going through a new period of recession, as most of its oil reserves had reduced to a fraction of previous decades. Thus, fuel costs soared. Further, many became displaced because of intolerable weather and rising seas and oceans. This made it difficult for the poorer countries in general and many fought back in subtle ways. The larger criminal syndicates always took advantage of those situations to gain ground.

Many sought immediate change and some went over to the most revolutionary side, who usually were the extremists. That course fraught with destruction and violence usually led to a dead end, with everyone much worse off after the dust had settled. Their brutal measures further weakened those with the knowledge to assist, since they tended to pick on the wrong establishments and the most knowledgeable. Only the clever scientists could find answers and ways out of our planet's dilemmas. Those problems were usually man made and required technological means in their solution.

Harry Lennox had only recently started his job, without even a suitable team or premises and had not prepared anything on his current projects. Therefore he was surprised when the current president of the USA called him into his office at the White House for a private chat.

'Professor Lennox, I am very pleased to meet you at long last. Since your recent appointment, I hadn't any time to greet you properly. Anyway, please take a seat while I pour us a drink. This conversation is meant to be private between us, so it must go no further,' The President said while firmly shaking his hand.

'Likewise, Mister President,' Lennox greeted.

'What do you think of our current sightings of UFO's and those strange meteors that showered the sky over our city yesterday?' The president was attempting to invoke a particular response from Lennox.

'I don't know, Sir. I saw the objects myself. The large one appeared to travel under its own steam. I subsequently called a colleague at our local early warning station. They monitored the objects visually and used some sensitive measuring equipment at different wavelengths to monitor its progress. I think they had enough time to complete a full and most thorough spectral analysis of all objects in question.'

'Wow..! They did? With all the knowledge you have, I want your honest opinion on that strange occurrence. Do you think it could in any way be attributed to weather balloons, clouds or just random meteorites? Because I do not believe those sightings were due to mass hysteria or hallucinations, as our defence office have led us to believe.'

'I don't think so, Sir.'

'No? I suppose they could be....perhaps due to a combination, or all together could contribute in giving those bizarre effects?' the president asked. Lennox opened his case and retrieved several pictures, which he spread out on the nearest table and the president was impressed by his thoroughness.

'Although our propaganda department is quite good at their job, if you want my honest opinion, Sir, it could not have been weather balloons, a combination of natural phenomena or man-made objects. Nor could it have been anything of a psychological nature for the following reasons: first of all, our astronomical friends took a spectral analysis of the object and here are the pictures, Sir. You see here, the internal temperature of that ball was more than three hundred million degrees Celsius and it was mainly composed of gases. If you like, it had more or less the same structure as a small star and was composed mainly of ionized nuclei. Further, I don't know if you considered anything about the behaviour of such hot plasma within our relatively dense atmosphere. Well, both should make a highly explosive combination unless thoroughly screened from each other.'

'Wow!' The President was aghast by the implications.

'It was subsequently calculated that there had to have been an incredible force holding that sphere together and concealing its proper mass. From the information received, that apparently small sphere could have had an equivalent mass of our planet or even greater. And there are other aspects of the data that still confuses us completely,' Lennox said.

'Go on! Go on!'

'Well, Sir, the distribution of its radiation is not what we expected. It's almost as if the object was shielding all of its most dangerous radiation from us, plants and animals. Finally it disappeared in mid air after travelling at speeds in excess of fifteen thousand kilometres per hour. As it did, so did the others, including the supposed flying meteorites, without even leaving a trace.' The president was quite worried by this time.

'Do you think it's some kind of invasion?'

'From where, Sir? Do you mean extraterrestrial in origin?' Lennox replied, cautiously.

'Perhaps? But keep it to yourself. As I said before, this is a free discussion but our conversation must go no further. You know, I think it's only a matter of time before someone or something appears from outside our solar system and they can't be all good and benevolent. But I was hoping in this case it was only a fluke,' the president said, somewhat disturbed.

'Mister President, I honestly do not know the answer to your questions. If they are that advanced what would they need from us, anyway?'

'Perhaps just curiosity or loneliness. Life is not just survival and technology you know, my friend,' the President replied.

'Sir, I am still studying the current data, but whatever it was, it sure scared the bloody ... out of me and that's putting it mildly. I apologise for swearing, but it's the way I feel about this thing.'

'I needed this chat with you because I had similar worries, so please don't apologise and keep me apprised on your future findings.'

'Yes, Sir.'

'Now I am going to change the topic.

'Have you heard of a Doctor Longhurst?'

'No Sir, never!' Lennox replied in a most positive manner.

'Harry, he found a permanent cure for cancer. All forms of cancer. He can modify genetic groupings to specification, and that's not all. He can design tiny robots a thousand times smaller then the size of human cells and control them with microwave transmissions to perform virtually any task.' The president pointed to a red folder on his desk.

'It's Bio-engineering using Nano-bots, Sir, but at a very

advanced level. I completed some studies on the subject a year ago, when I was with NASA, but we didn't get very far; financial resources not permitting. It was then within the field of Nano-technology.'

'This contains a report that was sent to us by one Professor Jean-Claude Chairmowich, who is in charge of a university hospital where the doctor works. I want you to read its contents thoroughly. I would like a report on your findings and comments at a committee meeting to be held at ten a.m. tomorrow. I shall be presiding, so you will be called to the rostrum.'

'Oh...!'

'Leave whatever you are doing and get on with this report! It's very important! Now I must bid you good day!' the president said. Lennox promptly took the folder and left.

'Wow! What a meeting? I have never seen our president so rattled. Like he is scared of his own shadow. I wonder what this is all about?' Lennox muttered, while planning his quickest route to his office.

Harry Lennox arrived at his temporary office soon afterwards, told his secretary to cancel all personal calls for that day and left for his new Washington apartment to carefully study the report in quiet.

Lennox got through about 30 percent of the document and could go no further. He had read several technical reports in his time. After all, it was one of his main tasks - sifting through such reports for the security services, including those collected by the CIA - but this one was unlike any that he had ever seen. It was so advanced, so cleverly constructed and the mathematics was so darn complex, as he would put it. Like pealing an onion a thousand times with each peal representing a complex dimensional matrix that represented bonding energies, rotational angles and another he called primal entropy. He paused and went to the fridge to get a glass of orange juice before lifting the phone to make a local call.

'Can I speak to Professor Laroche? It's urgent,' he said to the secretary.

'Who is calling?'

'Professor Harry Lennox. I am on a special committee to The President.' Lennox thought his last words would carry some weight.

'I am very sorry, Sir, but he is in a special meeting which is about to be concluded. Shall I call and ask him to contact you immediately?'

'Yes, and tell him it's very urgent. A matter of life and death. This is my number.' He gave her his home number before hanging up.

It was not long before the phone rang and Lennox left what he was preparing in the kitchen to answer.

'Hello, Harry. What's up? My girl tells me that you are in trouble or something. A matter of life and death?'

'I am sorry about that exaggeration, John, but I had to get hold of you in a hurry. I have been given a report by our President on Bio-engineering and can't make heads or tails of the math. I have to report to one of our presidential committees tomorrow and thought perhaps you could assist. Its very important.' Professor Laroche was silent for a moment, but never gave up on a challenge.

'In that case I am on my way. I suppose you can provide supper?'

'Don't worry. I am already cooking.'

The professor arrived one hour later and was given a tall drink. Then they discussed old times and the strange sightings before sifting through the report.

'Harry, get me some paper and a cup of coffee. Help me to move all these things off the table,' LaRoche said, impatiently dragging them across by hand. Then he made himself comfortable and began to read the report while taking notes. It was not long before Laroche became stuck. He cried out in anguish as if in a painful state of juvenile insanity.

'Bloody genius! Bloody genius! Bloody genius! I have never seen anything like it in all my sordid life. I can go down to about ten levels of the analysis, but the eleventh depends on my memorising and converging the previous functions. Here he has created a dimensional matrix to link these odd groupings which branch into these evens and odds to give a result that in turn links with... like complex functions acting within and without other functions.'

'I couldn't even get that far!'

'Perhaps the computer might help?' Professor Laroche was completely stumped by the new and strange mathematics.

'I am sorry, but this type of super-complex mathematics is beyond even me. And I think for any human brain that I have ever met. And I have met most of the best minds on the planet. This has been prepared and calculated by a genetic freak. Someone that is born every ten thousand years or so. With such a mind, assuming it isn't alien, he wouldn't need to go to any of our schools or universities, as they would just waste his bloody time,' Laroche said in disgust, while throwing his pencil across the room and taking a large sip from the glass of whisky that was recently placed where the cup of coffee once stood. The poor man was completely dumbfounded, frustrated and disappointed by his more than modest effort, with little gain.

The following morning a disappointed Lennox entered the meeting and was abruptly called to speak.

'Mister President and fellow colleagues. My purpose here is to explain the nature of the special report sent to us by Professor Chairmowich, regarding a lasting and general cure for cancer. May I also thank the eminent mathematician, Professor John Laroche for his kind assistance in unravelling some of the extremely difficult mathematics involved? Hitherto unknown to our sciences. Nevertheless, most of the more complex multidimensional functions we still find to be beyond our grasp.

'What do you mean exactly?' shouted one of his senators.

'I mean exactly what I said. I would also add, that there are some expressions within the report that are not familiar to our sciences. Perhaps yet invisible unknowns that we have not yet discovered. However, I shall continue with the substance of the report.' Lennox went on to explain the information relevant to the action of the serum on the basic and cancerous cell structures and mechanisms.

'You may further observe that as we get beyond this point in the analysis things suddenly become extremely complex as Professor Laroche explained to me last night, and I shall repeat what he said word for word.'

'Please go on!' the president said.

"Beyond this point in the analysis the human brain shrinks to that of a mouse by comparison. For it can only be done by calculating perhaps a thousand different equations simultaneously and by adding their resultant answers into other equations. Thus formulating new equations based on previous results, and while you are equating those results other answers are converging to form arguments of other equations that may or may not have been connected to the original equations, but necessary for the final solution."

They sat quietly in their seats and patiently listened to Lennox's strange story.

'Professor Laroche then went on to say that the scientist involved could not have been a present day human, because there was a huge alien content in the report. I am not suggesting for a moment that he is extraterrestrial, but he thinks that due to the laws of probability, it is possible for such a human to exist within ten thousand years or so, given our present population, or within a shorter period given a higher human population.'

'At least he is human!' shouted another member sarcastically. Lennox continued his deliverance.

'Taking the report in its entirety, the results are simple and conclusive; a total cure for cancer has been found. There is however one more astonishing implication to this report, and that relates to the area which contains cell structures and cell life. From what we have deduced, Doctor Longhurst has also found a way to increase our lifespan by more than twenty times. I must however stress the seriousness of these conclusions in light of population control. The staggering implications are that we now have a technology that can make us immortal and cure virtual any illness or disease on the planet.'

'Oh My God!' The president shouted and there was an uproar.

The whole thing was unbelievable.

'Even at this moment, we are not quite sure of the full extent of the doctor's knowledge. For his knowledge of mathematics could also imply an equivalent knowledge in other sciences, including sociology and ecology. A complete knowledge of planetary dynamics and perhaps even stellar dynamics,' Lennox said. Then he collected his papers and sat down. The senators and others began to talk among themselves.

The bewildered president straightened up and went to the rostrum.

'Please be Quiet! Fellow members, we have all heard the conclusions of Professor Lennox. I am sure we would like to receive more precise information on this incredible topic before we are completely certain, one way or the other. So I have decided to send Professor Lennox along with a chosen team to observe this Doctor Longhurst and assess to what extend this report is valid. I shall therefore call this meeting to a close until we have more positive evidence,' the president said and left.

Soon after, Lennox organised a team of best scientists in all relevant fields backed by the president. Those included a few security officers under false credentials. All were on their way to Eastern Europe. They were to use whatever methods available to assess the knowledge and powers of this Doctor Jeffery Longhurst.

CHAPTER 44

Lumak and the Americans

Lumak was well briefed on current events, but also wanted to make contact with the most technological species on the planet, which at that time were the North Americans. That was his long term goal and one of the primary elements of his mission. How else could he have wittingly introduced his own brand of Class 5 technologies within the allotted time of 200 years before the Javols' invasion of our galaxy. Everyone within the local galaxies depended on those endeavours in changing Earth before the arrival of the evil, blood sucking and rapacious Javols. Therefore he intended to give the North Americans a show they would never forget. He had his lectures completely revamped for their benefit and more modifications made to his display equipment to improve image quality and intensity.

That day the main auditorium was full of visitors. This time a well dressed Professor Jean-Claude Chairmowich introduced Lumak to the main stage.

Lumak walked towards the rostrum with power and confidence in his stride and was cheered by all.

As usual on such occasions he wore the White Robe. This time the mantle was a deeper purple that contrasted well with the creamy white. Most of the pleats had shrunk. The insignia was boldly displayed on his left shoulder.

As he approached the screen sprang to life and into a myriad of colours that coalesced to form our galaxy and many of its globular clusters. All were displayed in incredible detail. At the bottom of the screen were his famous insignia which stood for The Greater Purpose that represented all life throughout the Cosmos.

Lumak focussed his attention on the American group.

'It is a very great pleasure to have you and your group with us Professor Lennox. I trust your president is not too dismayed by current events. Anyway, all your pressing questions will be

resolved in due course,' he said. Lennox was quite astonished by his words and wondered whether he also had the ability to read minds. Yet, he bowed his head to Lumak and he continued.

'Ladies and gentlemen, I shall quickly scan through the basic biological program for the benefit of those of you with little knowledge of those concepts. However, I would like to cover more of the relevant applied mathematics with a little on Micro Robotics, Mind Control, and other topics I consider relevant to the aging process.'

Then the screen suddenly changed to display part of a magnified cell which unravelled and spiralled out of the screen in a myriad of colours. Once again the image remained suspended in mid air above their heads, still slowly rotating so they could clearly view each part of the complex structure in three dimensions while he explained its modus operandi.

'We, primal creatures attempt to model the real world by symbolism. Yet, these symbols can only represent basic concepts. One can never find the real truth while groping about in the semi darkness of partial blindness. We must first remove the blinkers of self-prejudice and bias before we can ever dream of seeing the complete light of universal truth. Whatever we observe through our senses will always be a mere function of brain. Most of what we have learnt is biassed in ways necessary for our survival causation. Furthermore, not everything we feel or observe is true to the external universe and those aspects may be further accentuated by our other senses and needs at the time.

'As humans, our main limitations are to do with our perception of the real world. Although we are able to perceive and store such data, it is acquired mainly in a two dimensional format. We require the additional temporal elements to improve the validity of those observations and sensations. Comparisons are constantly made by the brain to substantiate those observations, with its own fabrication and filtering. Additions and subtractions are combined with relevant feedback to aid, by controlling muscles and suchlike. This process can lead to further errors, exaggerations or enrichment of the truth as the brain attempts to make sense of sensations and observations. No two people can ever supply

identical accident reports. Even when they were standing next to each other and witnessed the same events.

'Take as an example this projected image. You can only observe a small part of its surface or layer at any given time. In order to increase your perception of the image we rotate the object. Hence, time has added a new dimension, so to speak. The eye also takes a finite time to transfer those images to the brain which also includes its own delays and translations in the process. Finally, we have to rely on what the brain tells us as being true. Most of which is based on prior knowledge and evolution of the species, which in turn relates to how our brain was wired from the beginning.

'There is little doubt that each of us, including the so-called lower life-forms, exists within our own universes of the mind. Virtual Universes that are shared and transparently linked to form the perceived real universe. It seems that during the course of evolution we have been made prisoners to certain concepts. Call it a mind set if you wish, that promotes our survival causation. Whether what we observe is real or otherwise are irrelevant in those circumstances. For all we know, we could well exist in a Virtual World within the mind of a universal computer.

'All those factors limit our perception of the real world, which in turn limits our deeper understanding and concepts in mathematics, for instance, and the manner in which we perceive the true universe about us. However, it would be a much better situation if we could eliminate those primal senses all together and link all received information directly to the memory pathways, lobes and layers of the brain. Such may be accomplished by the use of Brain Implants,' Lumak said. Then he turned his attention to the American group sat in the front row.

'Perhaps Professor Lennox wouldn't mind assisting me with my first experiment.'

The nervous professor stood up amidst cheers and made his way towards the stage. Lumak had a high regard for Lennox and observed in him a pure and searching mind.

'Now, Professor Lennox, here is a seemingly solid block of metal. I would like you to distort this object as best you can with *these tools.'* Then Lumak handed him a hammer and saw.

Lennox first hit the rectangular block several times with the steel hammer then he attempted to saw it, but to no avail. He could not observe a single dent or scratch on its shiny surfaces. He took the item around to his colleagues, but they could not observe any indentations or scratches.

'Now place the block on my desk.'

He carefully placed the block on the centre of the desk. Suddenly and as if by magic the block began to transform into a small male statue that proceeded to walk across the table. Then it picked up an envelope. One of its hands transformed into a paper knife. The envelope was opened and a letter withdrawn. The little statue handed the note to Lumak and bowed.

'Thank you!' he said while bowing to the little figure in jest. The audience clapped and cheered. Lennox and the audience were dumbfounded by the occurrence.

'This block is composed of billions of individual microids that are each under computer control. They receive instructions from a microwave transmitter which is capable of transmitting precisely polarised and phase-modulated information.

'As you have seen, such macro bodies can transform almost instantaneously into any shape or form and complete any set tasks twenty times faster than the most capable person.'

The audience were roaring with excitement.

'Would you like to assist me with one more experiment?' Lumak asked Lennox and he again agreed, nervously.

'This experiment relates to memory expansion and thought control, using microids to make the necessary connections.' Then he handed Lennox a small capsule.

'You may now remove the top of the container and inhale its contents. Try not to sneeze during this operation.'

Lennox took the small capsule from him, but displayed a most worried look and hesitated for a brief moment.

'Don't worry, Professor, it's absolutely harmless. Just inhale its contents, please. There are only one hundred microids and they have been instructed to make temporary connection to certain areas of your brain. I shall also inhale a similar amount so that

we together may hold a telepathic conversation.' Lumak inhaled a similar quantity of the brown powder. Then he took the note which contained a list of instructions and handed it to a neutral member of the audience for safe keeping.

'These instructions are unknown to the professor, so if he follows them to the letter it is conclusive proof that the method employed is one of telepathy.

'Now, Professor, I would like you to follow my thought instructions to the letter.

'Remember, audience, he is not under my control and can terminate these sequences of events if he so chose at any time.'

Then he transmitted a thought to Lennox who immediately walked out of the lecture room, to soon return carrying a chair from the neighbouring room. He sat momentarily on the chair, then lifted it above his head. Finally he returned the chair to its proper place.

The instructions were displayed on the screen in view of the whole audience. The one with the note was asked to read the instructions, to verify that they were identical to what was on the screen. The instructions matched word for word his movements, precisely.

'To those of you unable to cope with the mathematics in my report, I have several microid capsules that have been programmed to assist you in that effort, so please ask for one before you leave. The microids that we have inhaled will dissolve in our systems within one hour, but the information we have received will remain as if learned through our own senses.'

Having discussed a broad range of subjects, Lumak changed the topic to Brain Implants and explained the processes involved and the efficiencies gained by utilizing a Virtual 3D World for communications and other forms of entertainment.

'By using such advanced methods within brain implants, in the near future we shall be able to create virtually any world, even ancient Rome or ancient Babylon and partake as a player within the complex story. Anyone of you, whether male or female, could become king Nebuchadnezzars himself at battle, with an arrow

wound in his shoulder and witness the same amount of pain and other problems necessary to make the experience as realistic as possible. Even the scents and noises on the battlefield would be as real as within the perceived real world.

'Scientific experiments could be conducted on virtual guinea pigs and virtual patients within a virtual laboratory hundreds of times faster. To all intents and purpose, all such experiments could be made identical to those within the perceived real world laboratory, thus removing the cost of constructing and stocking such places, but most importantly, eliminating the suffering of those innocent life-forms used in such experiments. All such Virtual Worlds can be constructed by large Macron Computers and all such programming may be fed directly into your brain through your implants.

'When we call our friends in North America from here, we could suddenly find ourselves within their homes and when they offer us a virtual cup of coffee it would taste exactly like the real thing, even to the point of satisfying our thirst, for all these are functions of the brain and can all be modified by our brain implants.'

They were amazed. Everyone in the audience began to cheer once more.

Lumak sent a thought, the floating image vanished and the screen went off. The class stood up and began to clap and cheer and he smiled and left.

The Americans were utterly impressed. Lennox still couldn't believe what had occurred including the technological implications of other parts of his lecture.

'Come on guys, we have work to do,' he said to his group as they left the conference room in a mad hurry.

Soon after Lennox got his group together in one of the hotel conference rooms to discuss that morning's lecture in detail, while his security men were out gathering more information on Lumak.

'Guys, make yourselves comfortable in this place because we are staying for a while. We have also been invited to the doctor's wedding. You guys must keep your heads up and show a little respect for the natives. I want us to leave a good impression behind. They admire the doctor and we need him on our side.'

Don't worry, we'll behave like virgin saints!' Paul replied.

'Now, guys, let's discuss business. What did you think of the doctor and his lecture?' Lennox inquired.

'It was like out of this world, literally. And he is definitely out of this world with those clothes,' remarked the shortest and stoutest of the group. Lennox nodded in full agreement.

They went through their notes and discussed the topic for an hour.

'You know, I wish Professor Laroche was here instead of me. This whole darn thing including the math is so incredibly difficult for me. I feel like a five-year-old trying to learn calculus. Inhaling the capsules should increase our abilities, but having taken one I don't feel any different. Perhaps it will be flushed out when I decide to solve a very difficult problem. Anyway, the telepathy did work, didn't it?' Lennox said. They nodded in agreement.

'And he made you look like an ace jerk doing it. I couldn't help laughing at the whole situation,' Paul said.

'Now I know exactly how you must feel when you try to play the fool with me,' Lennox replied and Paul, his second in command, remained silent.

'You know, guys, I have seen an awful lot in my short life, particularly when I was at NASA, but never in my wildest dreams could I ever have imagined it possible to make robots the size of microscopic cells.

'Can you imagine a robot that size, that can walk and even fly? You know, with his type of Nano-bots, which are close to atomic size, one could create a complete human body with all its cells and brains the size of a tiny flea. Such a tiny device with its own inbuilt energy sources can be very complex.'

'Yea! They make the perfect quantum fly on the wall,' Paul said in jest.

'Yea? These are things the human eye could never see because it is so darn small and yet may be used to collect all kinds of information from our enemies? Even to plant new information within their unsuspecting minds. Yea! Such a device could make the ideal spy. How could anyone design anything that small?'

Then there was a knock on the door and one of the receptionist walked in.

'Professor Lennox, I have a special delivery for you.' He took it from her.

'Hello, Professor Lennox, I am having a little celebration this evening and would like you and your group to join us and meet my future bride. Please don't bother with formal dress.
Jeffery Longhurst.'

Lennox read the note to himself. He thanked the girl and handed her a ten-dollar bill, then he returned to his group.

'Guys, we are invited to a party in four hours, so get a little shut-eye and be ready by eight. Wear something casual and don't over do the drinking. This is just the break I've been waiting for, so don't you blow it for me. It's at Doctor Longhurst place.'

Lennox was concerned about what Lumak had mentioned about unresolved problems and wondered whether it was anything to do with the strange appearances of the bright objects recently experienced over Washington DC a few days ago. He also realized that his president had become seriously disturbed by those occurrences and wanted the matter resolved. He had never seen his president so worried and stressed for the sake of his country and its people, and would like to get to the bottom of those strange occurrences. Nevertheless if anyone could assist his president that person would be Doctor Jeffery Longhurst, so his invitation was fortuitous.

If Lumak knew about those matters what else could he have known about and could he have been an alien in disguise while passing himself off as a human being. All those questions had filtered through Lennox's mind and he wanted answers. If only to satisfy his worried president and make him feel more secure since the recent sightings.

CHAPTER 45

Lords of the universe

Professor Lennox and his company arrived at Lumak's address and were greeted by Sarah at the door. Then they were introduced to Jeremy, Karen, Ben and others and finally Lumak, as Professor Jeffery Longhurst. This time Lumak was wearing casual ware which surprised them.

'It's nice to see you and your company again. Come, let me get you all a drink,' Lumak said and they followed him into the sitting room with its makeshift bar. Lumak preferred a small amount of vodka and lots of tonic, but the others had a varied choice. He began to chat with them about life in general in the USA.

'Professor Lennox,' Lumak said. 'I have heard a lot about your beautiful country and would like to visit sometime soon for a brief holiday, if at all possible.'

'You are welcomed there at any time, Sir, even to stay permanently, and please feel free to remain at my apartment in DC for as long as you wish,' Lennox replied, also showing keen interest.

'Thank you very much for the invitation, Harry. My future wife and I might take you up on that offer quite soon, after our marriage. However, I would like to speak to you about a more serious matter. Something that concerns us all.'

'What matter is that?'

'By the way, have you made any headway regarding the mathematical contents of my lecture?' Lumak said, diverting slightly from the main topic of their conversation. Yet, Lumak had planted a thought in Lennox's mind that would constantly nag him until he asked again what it was about. He would learn the answer to that question several years later, when the time was right.

'Yes, I have done a little, but I am still confused by some of the math. Perhaps my good friend Professor Laroche will assist me on my return. I suppose you don't mind, but I've taken an extra Microid Capsule for him, just in case.'

'I shouldn't worry too much about that, if I were you. The information is most probably in your head waiting to be flushed out by a more intensive application of your mind. You and your president obviously realises the importance and implications of the new technologies involved,' Lumak said with a sarcastic smile.

'How do you know my president is involved, Doctor?'

'I assumed it was to do with his curious nature. I have sometimes thought your president could have made a grade-one scientist, if only he had taken it up earlier and pursued it further. He has that extra intuitive quality. Nevertheless, he is a great president and it's never too late for anyone. Did you know that?' Lumak said jovially while sipping his drink.

'Until he gets too old or dies,' Lennox replied, waiting patiently for Lumak's response.

'What if he could never grow old, or die? What if he wasn't composed of normal electromagnetic based matter. Elements that could not be affected by such types of normally vectored matter, not even within the centre of our sun.'

'I would say that...it was impossible, Sir!,' an amazed Lennox replied.

'Harry, in as much as you would consider it impossible for a hot ball of plasma to exist within the Earth's atmosphere above Washington DC - a ball with a presumed mass of our complete solar system - yet, the situation still existed in space and in time. Can you put forward another plausible explanation?' Lumak said, while they collected drinks from Sarah.

'How do you know of such things? This information is held at the highest security level. No one has been told about the technicalities. Is this ball of energy in any way linked with your program here?' the startled Lennox replied.

'In answer to your first question, there are no spies or bugs involved, just intelligent deduction. All of my information comes by legitimate means.'

'How is that?'

'In answer to your second question, I will give an unequivocal yes, but I can assure you that it is not what you think,' Lumak said, looking straight through Lennox.

'Please continue, Doctor?' Lennox said with growing interest.

'How many different life-forms do you think exists on Earth?'

'I suppose several million, including plants,' Lennox replied.

'And how many do you think exists within our galaxy?'

'Millions times millions, I suppose? But nothing has yet been found to substantiate the latter.'

'And why do you think that is the case?'

'Well, I suppose we are either too insignificant or perhaps our world is situated in an inaccessible part of the galaxy, well away from the trodden paths of the more advanced species.'

'Or both. But what would you say if I told you that we have recently been discovered and have been entered into the greater galactic computers. Furthermore, what if I told you that this whole universe was conquered billions of years ago, even before Earth itself existed and has since that time been ruled by super beings like gods?'

'I would say that I needed some darn convincing evidence to support your claims.'

'Evidence like the super-heated plasmic ball flying over Washington DC?'

Lennox was by now a little confused and could not accept Lumak's claims, but wanted to hear more of what he had to say.

'Perhaps, Doctor. But let's hear some more of your argument.'

'The Grand Lords are roughly the age of the universe itself and some say, were formed from its original plasmic clouds during an earlier period of existence. No one really knows exactly when, as time itself was young. Causality was in its infancy and just getting into its act. The Grand Lords, as they are usually called, sometimes use their original forms when visiting new worlds, but can take on virtually any shape or form. They can affect matter in any conceivable manner, cannot be affected in a detrimental way by any material means and are truly omnipotent and omniscient. Furthermore, they have always been the prime movers of order within the seven universes.'

'You mean to say that the ball of light over Washington DC was due to the visit of a supreme being; a deity in his own indigenous form?' Lennox replied, fully amazed by Lumak's words.

'Yes, and in answer to one of your original questions, as to how I was able to know of his flight over Washington DC. The Grand Lord entered those experiences and observations within the universal computer known to many as The Greater Mind. Call it the collective consciousness of all intelligence if you will. Anyway, I am able to access that computer and scan its many libraries and data banks.' Lumak was convincing.

'You mean to say, there is some large galactic computer that you and others are able to tap into at will? A computer that stores information on all life and technologies within the galaxy?' Lennox replied with excitement.

'Not just the galaxy, my friend. More like the complete universe. Because all minds are interlinked, universally. However, some information is a lot more important than others to a searcher, and some are hidden.'

'If that is the case, and I am not yet convinced, do they intend to take us over and impose some new order of their own upon us?'

'The Grand Lords are super-ecologists. They do not like to interfere with the natural order or the development of any primal species. They only become directly involved if an advanced or primary species face unintended extinction, as in the case of novae, supernovae, interplanetary wars or whenever destruction of worlds are imminent. In our case, it is because Earth has gained significance in the scheme of things. But also......'
'But also what?'

'I'll come to that later. They do not interest themselves with local or planetary governments and their politics, in fear of those bodies having too much power over their subordinates. They will however encourage individuals like myself to flourish and develop to their full potentials within the much greater universal order, called The Greater Purpose.'

'That's fantastic!'

'The Grand Lord has selected us, humans, to form one of the main branches of thrust within The Greater Purpose in the foreseeable future. I made the choice of joining many years ago. Some of the things I invent will be available to all. In the future I shall always try my best to assist my fellow creature in his or her quests for good health and advanced technologies, providing those technologies are not used to implement or sustain suffering, destruction or wars.'

'You know, Doctor, I have a feeling you and my president will get on like a house on fire. He has very similar views to yours. As a matter of fact, he even believes in extraterrestrial life and reckons it's just a matter of time before we get a visit. It seems from what you have just said that he was right, but I am still not convinced. Anyway, how do you form such an altruistic organization. I mean, pulling all good and unselfish scientists together for the benefit of humankind and other life-forms?' Lennox said, doubtfully.

'With enthusiastic and dedicated people like yourself, Professor. People that really desire interstellar adventure or perhaps just scientific fulfilment in areas beyond basic planetary existence. Once money becomes irrelevant, then we can work diligently towards the greater goal. Anyway, all the technologies already exists, even to take you across the galaxy in a couple of weeks. It's just a matter of getting a few good teams together and there are no strings attached.'

'Yea, but space exploration needs lots of bucks. Bucks we don't have at this time.'

'Our main problems on this planet at this time is overpopulation and climatic change, leading to global crises. I just hope we are able to take Earth out of this unstable situation before she becomes too critical and begins to compensate. Then we shall all be in big trouble.'

'Yea. We'll also need major bucks for that one which is more important than space exploration.'

'You know Professor, very soon everyone within our organization will be equal partners and multi-millionaires, with the ability to possess whatever they wish, so freedom will never be a problem for us. Are you interested, Professor Lennox? Think carefully about what I've said and remember, this conversation is in confidence between us two, Professor John Laroche and your president.'

'This is all too much for a little guy like me to absorb in a single session. I need some time to consider what you have said but I shall keep our conversation confidential,' Lennox said and left to rejoin his group.

Having had a most enjoyable and enlightened evening, Lennox and his group returned to their hotel.

There was so much new technologies and ideas floating about Lennox's head that he felt completely inadequate. Then there was the idea of an all powerful super being who had arrived on Earth. He had never been a very religious person and now realized supreme beings really existed, but not in the religious sense. They were just very advanced super beings that had evolved with incredible powers and most likely were not all good. However, thank goodness there was only one such benevolent super being in charge of our part of the universe. They must be like universal anti-bodies. If he nurtured the first seeds of life and was so caring, why would he want to destroy his creation. That evening Lennox pondered those incredible thoughts until he fell asleep.

CHAPTER 46

Grand Lord Gerra and the President

President, Arnold J. Turner, of the USA had a very stressful day in congress. He was on special medication for his high blood pressure which his doctor had recently prescribed. On top of all those problems, one of his favourite horses had broken a leg and had to be put down, so he was feeling miserable.

He decided to cancel all calls and meetings for the rest of that afternoon and went directly to his study to sign some urgent documents. As he entered he was surprised to find a visitor sat there waiting patiently for his return.

'Who are you? Who let you into my private study without first warning me?' he snapped showing utter annoyance.

'I am your lord and I entered through the wall. Let me show you,' the figure said, then disappeared through the nearest wall only to reappear a moment later.

'Now do you believe me?' the Grand Lord said. The president froze in his steps.

'Ple... ase sit, my... my Lord,' the president stuttered and the figure casually sat on the near settee.

'I have come to hold a private and friendly chat with you, and by the way, that bright ball you saw moving across the sky recently was myself. It's my first visit to your world in person and I had to create a memorable impression. I trust it didn't initiate too many problems? Anyway, enough said about myself.

'No, My...My Lord! No prob...lem!' The president stuttered again.

'I have observed you to be not a very well man. I have detected a heart problem and a few clogging arteries, which will soon cause you great distress. You need to take your work less seriously and have more rest.'

'Yes, My Lord! Heart problems!'

'While here may I repair your organ deficiencies... with your permission of course. Don't worry, you wont feel a thing and the process will be completed within a few seconds.' He floated towards Arnold and touched him over the area concerned. There was a bright glow and the job was done.

'Shall I also make you ten years younger? I might as well do a proper job of work while I am here,' the Grand Lord said in a mild and sympathetic voice, but his soothing words were felt directly in the president's mind.

'If you please, my Lord,' he replied and the visitor placed his hand over his forehead. There was a brief reddish glow that encircled his complete body.

'That's better, now we can have a serious chat.'

The president felt a lot better and began to recover from the shock of recent experiences. It was as if a massive weight had been lifted off his shoulders.

'My... my Lord, would... you like some refreshments?' he asked, nervously. Little believing in his recent experience and the presence of the supreme being standing before him in radiant white.

'Yes, thank you! Please make it a vodka with some tonic.' The president pressed a button and a young maid soon entered.

'Please, Liz, get us two vodkas and a bottle of tonic water. Hurry!' he said and she was soon back with the drinks on a tray.

'To be honest, I am just passing through, on my way to another distant system within the galaxy. Nevertheless, I greatly enjoyed this visit to your world, with its many peoples and their incredible cities. Never before have I seen so many cities on a single world.

'We are like that, my Lord. We like building things.'

'Anyway, your planet Earth has recently been listed and is now on record within The Greater Mind. Your species have been chosen to assist in the restructuring of this galaxy. Although they will not become involved immediately, the doors have been opened, so they may enter when ready.

'That's incredible news, My Lord!'

'In other words, your race have now come of age, so I've decided to give Earth the keys to the door, so to speak. However, it may take many centuries before you gain rewards from future ventures regarding your new status. As always, I am unable to partake in interplanetary politics or take sides one way or the other. I would however appreciate your cooperation in the future in relevant scientific matters; for they will take you out of your present planetary crises. Nevertheless, before you are able to do great things as a race, you must become one people and one race with a single global structure of government. When all borders have been removed, that is when you will be ready to enter the door of which I speak. I'm afraid, those changes are in the future for another president to fulfill so you should play your own important role for now.'

'You have it, My Lord!'

'In that case, I must thank you in advance and leave you now,' he said in the most pleasant and tranquil voice and vanished in full view of the president, leaving him completely perplexed.

Arnold could not believe his recent encounter with the Grand Lord and had to check himself in the local mirror. There he stood for a while eyeing himself with curiosity; for he was now a much younger and fitter man. He suddenly felt he could take on the world and win. His only immediate problem was his trousers and shirt. They no longer fitted his near perfect body. He quickly retreated to his bedroom to get an old pair of pants to wear. Then he got on the phone to his local tailor for a new fitting and he was on his way.

'My God. I see myself but I don't believe what I see. My wife, senators and other colleagues will think the same about my mysterious changes? But what do I care!' he thought rebelliously, while closely observing himself in the mirror again while whistling a merry tune.

Lennox and his team were still away and about to visit the last of Lumak's lectures when his hotel phone rang.

'Lennox, is that you?'

'Yes, Mister President!'

'I want you back here immediately! Your company can remain for the wedding. You can rejoin them in a day or so, but I want you back here right now! It's very important!'

'Yes, Sir! I am on my way!' Lennox realized there could be some serious problems brewing in his home country.

Professor Lennox arrived at midday and went directly to the White House. To his surprise, Professor John Laroche was also there awaiting his arrival. Both men appeared more serious and bleak than ever he had seen bad weather.

'Sorry I couldn't make it any sooner, Sir. The usual in-flight delays,' Lennox apologised, while both serious men listened patiently as if their very lives depended on what he had to say. Lennox then went on to explain Lumak's conversation and briefly described the lectures. During all this time Professor Laroche found the conversation unbelievable. There he remained as if in a daze, nervously tapping the table with his fingers while Lennox viewed the much younger and more active president with utter curiosity.

'It's all truly incredible and all in one day. I never knew any of it would happen in this way and including a supreme being. The GRAND LORD of our universe. The one with many names!' the president interrupted. Then the disturbed man walked towards the window as if to gather his fragmented thoughts.

'The man, Doctor Jeffery Longhurst, seems to be the key in all this. Yes, I think he is the real key that we have been given to open the universal door for the whole of humanity! It is for our survival... Our planet's survival, you know!' The president shouted!' The others listened patiently to his words. He acted as if he was possessed.

'We shall have to give this doctor Longhurst all of our assistance in the future. Better yet, we shall entice him to come and live in our country. He must hold the key to this strange situation!' the president said, even to the point of repeating himself many times.

'Lennox, my friend, you heard our boss, we must have the doctor over here at all cost. He is now the most important person on the planet and we must have him before any other country gets their filthy hands on him. It's as simple as that, so please take note of our president's decision in this matter and follow his wishes,' Professor Laroche stressed.

'Lennox, are you getting all this. You are to get the doctor over here at all costs. This is your main assignment from now, and keep me informed of progress on a daily basis. Use whatever means and facilities you require, even the CIA if you need their more clandestine services, but get him here!'

'Ok, Sir. I will do it!'

'I have appointed Professor Laroche to head our science committee in your absence, so he can take over your present scientific duties, aided by some of your senior biologists. Anyway, with what's coming, I don't even think we'll need your department anymore, so John can remain as one of my personal advisers in relevant topics. Your future job will be to assist the Doctor.' John LaRoche was chuffed with his new position.

'Gentlemen, this is very important to us and our waning country. Anyway, I would like a report on this project within two days so keep me up to date on every bit of progress. You may now leave us, Lennox, and return to negociate with our good doctor. Now I must bid you good day, Gentlemen,' the much younger president said and they left.

After briefing Professor John Laroche, Harry Lennox caught an evening flight and was back in Turkey. He immediately called his group together to discuss new developments.

'Guys, we have a new job to do. This change in emphasis comes direct from our President. During this project you will be briefed as and when necessary, and purely on a need to know basis. So I would like you to cooperate as best you can in the circumstances. For this to work, we need very strong security, so don't worry too much about details. Just do what I say by the numbers and follow the book on this one. Anyway, I'll make it up to you guys later, when this one is all behind us.'

'Ok, Go on!' said the shortest guy, Gil.

'Now, you know that you were selected by me because you are all tops in your fields. I know your capabilities, so from now on I don't even want you to discuss your individual programs with your friends and colleagues and that includes everyone. You will each receive your programs directly from me and follow them individually or in preselected small closed groups, who will discuss their findings with me privately. That way, if there are any leaks I can quickly trace the culprit and locate the contacts. Understood?' Lennox said and they nodded in agreement.

'Yes, understood! I also read the book!' his second, Paul said.

'I must now arrange a meeting with the doctor for tomorrow. The earlier, the better. The results of that meeting will indicate to us what our next plan will be. I suggest you have an early night after having received your individual folders. That's all for now.' They collected the pile of information which he began to hand out. Then Lennox phoned Lumak's home.

'Hello, Professor Lennox,' Sarah replied,' Please hold for a moment while I connect you.'

'That urgent eh... In that case, make it for ten a.m. tomorrow,' Lumak replied and Lennox was once again happily on course.

Sarah followed Lumak to the university that day. The meeting was held in Lumak's private office.

'Doctor, on behalf of my people and myself, I would like to thank you again for seeing us at such short notice. However, this meeting could not wait. I was recently recalled by my president. During that meeting he told me of a strange visit. The details of which I am not at liberty to divulge, but I think you know what it's about. Anyway, the long and short of it is that we would like you to join us in the States. The President says that you will be given all necessary resources to develop your own programs and you can operate independently if you wish, while assisted by large government grants, of course. Form your own organization there if you like, but we must have you, and your family, of course,' Lennox said.

'Sarah, Darling, what do you think?'

'It will have to be in a nice and peaceful area in the hills somewhere, with some animals. We must also be free to visit our country here whenever we wish?'

'You heard my fiancee. Can you arrange all that for starters?' Lumak said.

'Consider it done, Sir! I know of such a place in North Dakota. It also has a small river and a forest. It is all yours for the taking,' Lennox replied, almost crying with excitement and the knowledge that Lumak had accepted the president's invitation with such little fuss. He realized there was no need to get the dogs out to coerce him into making the move. It was almost as if Lumak had known about the move even before he was asked.

'You heard that, guys. Doctor Longhurst is coming home with us. In that case, we can remain for the wedding and organize the move for him and his family afterwards. That is if the good doctor agrees.'

'It may take a month before I can leave. I have to inform a few people and set certain wheels in motion, but I've agreed in principle. I trust this little discussion of ours is only going to stay between us until I have discussed it with others?' Lumak stressed.

'Yes, Doctor, and thank God, later on today there will be a very happy president,' Lennox replied, enthusiastically.

CHAPTER 47

Back to the hills

Somehow the excitement of their future visit to America had tended to overshadow everything. Even so, they had to keep their future intentions a secret for now.

Lumak realised that Sarah was not her usual happy self and soon took her aside to assess what was wrong. He wondered whether it was anything to do with their future move to the USA.

'What is the matter, Love? I can detect a glimmer of sadness in your eyes, and I am wondering why?'

'To tell the truth, I am feeling a little home sick. The thought of going to America has brought back sad memories of our country home, animals and people up there. I only wish I could visit the house and say a prayer for my mother... even to see the animals again... before we leave.'

'We are not going right away, you know. Anyway, I understand how you must feel. If it's any consolation to you, I sometimes get those nostalgic flashbacks myself. What would you say if we had one week's holiday up there in the hills and made the most of our visit?'

'I would so love to, if you don't mind, Darling?' She hugged and kissed him. At that moment she could have been the happiest woman in the world.

'Do you really want to live in the States?' Lumak asked, trying to tap directly into the source of her worries.

'I think it will be a lot better for you over there. I can always find something of interest for myself. We have to move with the times and its changes, you know. Anyway, it's not the end of the world and we can always visit our place here in time.'

'You know, deep down I don't really want to leave our friends behind, but I think we'll have a much better life over there and more opportunities to aid the poorer countries and other life-forms after we get established. Furthermore, my job here is now almost at an end. I have taken things as far as I can. The serum is finally being produced in quantity and the large chemical plant is being constructed. It leaves me free to develop other advanced projects that can only be done cost-effectively in North America.'

'Yes, Darling. I know!'

'I just hope Jean-Claude and Jeremy don't take the idea of my leaving too badly. I don't want them to know until I tell them myself after our honeymoon. Anyway, let me see Jean-Claude now about some transport to the hills.' Then Lumak kissed her on the cheek and strolled away. He didn't tell her that one of his main reasons for leaving Turkey at that time was because he constantly worried for her safety.

Later that day Lumak visited the university hospital and went directly to Jean-Claude's office to assist with their usual pile of correspondence from the four corners of the globe. Those he cleared almost immediately to Jean-Claude's utter astonishment.

'How does he do that?' Jean-Claude would comment each time, but he was never bold enough to ask Lumak about his super efficient secrets.

'We would like to have part of our honeymoon at Sarah's home in the hills, but the country trip is so exhaustive. I wondered whether it was possible to arrange flight to that place as soon as possible?' Lumak inquired of Jean-Claude knowing he had many contacts.

'Why not hire a small helicopter? I have a few military friends with little to do at present. Would you like me to make a few calls on your behalf?'

'If you don't mind. They can just drop us there and collect us after a week or so. It will save us a long and bumpy trip.'

Later Lumak decided to discuss the matter with Ben.

'Sarah and I have decided to take part of our honeymoon at our house in the hills and wondered whether you would join us by helicopter?'

'Never in a helicopter, my son. I can't stand anything to do with flying. Suffer from bad vertigo and sickness by just looking at the ground from those heights. As far as I am concerned, the air was created solely for the birds and only for us to breathe. You must have this holiday together. Marion and Simon will be there to assist, so go and enjoy yourselves,' Ben said. Lumak knew that Ben was always against travelling by air, but had never realized the extents of his future father-in-law's phobias.

The wedding was held at Jeremy's house and in the traditional manner. A single marquee was placed at the rear with enough hired tables and chairs. Only family and close friends were present during the ceremony. Since Doctor Jeffery Longhurst was thousands of kilometres away from his supposed home in England, none of his relatives could be present. At least that was a good enough excuse for those present. Doctor Emil read the necessary passages after binding the couple in the traditional manner.

As planned, the wedding reception was held at the president's palace a day after the wedding. It was one of those occasions when everyone was informally dressed. Many foreign dignitaries were present including Lennox and his team. Gerald Fraser, the current American Ambassador, had arrived later than the others, but hadn't been given any information about Lumak's future visit to the States. Anyway, Lennox and his team knew the score and less said on that matter was better for all concerned in the circumstances. Michael Cockburn was also there, having delayed his flight back to America until after the celebrations. He also knew nothing of their intentions to visit and live in the USA.

Jean-Claude played the part of master of ceremonies for the grand occasion and read several telegrams from well-wishers to the married couple. During the banquet President Amal gave a speech, thanking Lumak and wishing both the best for the future. Lumak replied with a small speech of his own. It was a happy occasion that was enjoyed by all, without any further security problems. Sarah got Amal and his wife a beautiful antique vase, painted in large flowers.

Jean-Claude had arranged a helicopter, so Lumak and Sarah were soon on their way to the hills. Sarah's father, Ben, remained behind with Jeremy and Karen.

When they arrived there was some turmoil which prevented the helicopter from landing. Marion thought she was being invaded by the enemy and had a pitchfork in hand to chase them away. That was until they landed and Lumak began to wave to her. Spotty the dog was barking furiously and ran towards them the moment the helicopter had left and so did Marion.

'You lot almost scared me to death. Simon went to the village to get me some groceries and left me here all alone. Anyway, it's a pleasant surprise to see you guys, and you look great! If only we knew you were coming.'

'Marion, we got married yesterday. Sorry we couldn't invite you, but it was a simple wedding. I brought you a little gift and decided to spend part of our honeymoon up here with you guys. How are you and everything else in this place?' Sarah asked, before giving her a big hug. Spotty couldn't control his emotions and constantly interrupted for more attention.

'I am now fully recovered. Thanks to your lovely husband and you shouldn't have bothered to get me a present. Do you want the whole house to yourselves, now?'

'We are only here for a week. So we can use my room. Then, between you and I, we are off to America for an extensive vacation. Stay on as long as you wish and don't worry about money. You will both be taken care of, and please hire some responsible young people from the village to do the hard work.'

'That's fantastic news!'

'You know, Marion, you do look much younger and fitter! Anyway, we have made arrangements with Doctor Emil to give you a monthly allowance, so please inform him if there are any new workers or changes in the finances.'

'I don't know what to say, Sarah? I must thank you so much for all that. And don't you worry about this place in the future! I am so happy for you and the doctor. You seem to have both achieved your ambitions. It must be Allah's will. I think you will be going away for a long time?' a perceptive Marion asked.

'We are not going away forever, you know. We'll try to be back at least once a year and we are in the process of instructing a company to build a larger house in this area. We are not really leaving, just building a new business over there in addition to what we have over here. We seem to be in great demand these days,' Sarah said, trying to dissipate Marion's worries. Lumak couldn't stop playing with Spotty. He got him a multicoloured ball which he enjoyed trowing around and catching.

The following day they took Spotty with them and decided to view the farm in its entirety. For once in what appeared to them to have been a lifetime, they had never felt such happiness and freedom. They soon realised how beautiful the green hills were when compared with the city and viewed by estranged eyes.

They had become like city tourists on their first outing to the country. Before that, they had taken it all so much for granted. Being always a part of it and labouring every hour of the day with every aggravation in order to survive.

'I can't think that I have lived here all my life only to just realise the natural beauty of this place,' Sarah said while taking a deep breath.

'As they say, Love, beauty is in the eye of the beholder and one must really want to see it before it can be revealed,' a philosophical Lumak replied.

'Do you remember that first day, when we found you in the bushes over there?' She said, holding his hand, tightly.

'Yes, Love. How could I ever forget. I was cold and scared, wondering whether I would be shot by your father or eaten by Spotty. It's incredible how things have turned out. Now we are man and wife and everything has changed for the better.'

'And now, we are going to the States and don't even have to buy the tickets for the trip. You are a prophet after all, but whatever you are I dearly love that person,' she said, snugging up closer to him.

'I still can't believe how beautiful and green this place really is. Perhaps we can take some of the animals to the states after we are settled. That might make you feel more at home over there.'

Lumak still couldn't believe that he had gained so much territory in such a short time, even with the assistance of his Grand Lord.

'That would be very difficult, Darling. Governments are very strict when it comes to transporting animals. Anyway, we can always get some from over there. Don't worry about our animals here, they will be well-taken care of until our next visit and they have grown used to the surroundings.'

'As you wish!'

'You must visit the temple with me tonight and tomorrow we can take the sheep to the hills for the last time,' she said, calmly.

'Yes, Love,' he replied, patiently.

'I can't believe how well Marion has recovered. She is like a new woman and at least ten years younger. You are a miracle maker after all.'

'Yes. I'm afraid the serum has that effect on terminal patients. It saturates the system and that process also causes slight rejuvenation. It also extends their lifetime, but the amount of reduction depends on the genetic type.'

'That is truly incredible, my Darling. It means you can also extend precious life. If only Mum was hear now to see such great wonders?' She kissed him on the cheek to show her affection.

They entered the old temple at sunset and began to pray for the departed, their family and friends, and for life in all its varying habitats on Earth and elsewhere. This time Sarah followed Lumak almost as his disciple; for she now realized he was really a prophet from God.

For a moment Lumak thought of the beautiful field way up in the hills and began to contrast it with the harshest living planet that he had ever visited. It was Tarran the planet of cats and he remembered the young and noble female warrior by the name of Bawaki.

'What a race of superb hunters. They must be the most ferocious hunters in the whole of our galaxy,' he thought.

CHAPTER 48

Village celebrations

The following day Sarah and Lumak got up early and had a haughty breakfast before travelling towards the stream to observe the fish, flora and fauna. That stream flowed at the bottom end of the temple and its banks were always full of flowers.

'I got most of my first laboratory samples from this place and your kitchen,' Lumak said with a happy grin.

'I know. I could never find potatoes when I needed them. It's a good thing you and Dad didn't mind going to the village at short notice, or you wouldn't have had supper on most evenings,' Sarah replied and they both giggled.

'And thanks for being so loving and patient with me at that time. Oh how I've grown to love the atmosphere of this place, including its great people like Marion and Simon,' he said.

'Good morning, Mister and Missis Longhurst!' a voice came from behind. As they looked around they could see Doctor Emil plucking some daffodils.

'Oh! Hello, Doctor! When did you arrived back?' Sarah inquired.

'Only three hours ago. After your ceremony and having met so many distinguished guests and important people, I couldn't help feeling the mood for an extended vacation. I haven't had one for ages, and thanks to your husband most of my worst patients have been cured,' Emil replied.

'I am so pleased to see you! We wanted to treat you to a helicopter ride, but you had already left,' Lumak said.

'Yes. Thank you for the belated offer, but I also had my vehicular transport to consider.'

'We decided to visit this area of the farm today and once more avail ourselves of its beauty. This place makes me feel so good in early summer and it's not only the pure air!' Sarah said, smiling.

'I followed you here from the house. May I apologise in advance for stealing some of your wild flowers, but I find them irresistible at this time of year. They appear to spring up everywhere in this place. It must be the fresh air at this altitude.'

'They are even more beautiful in the hills where we take our sheep to graze,' Sarah replied.

'Do you intend to sell your lands here about's when you move to the city?' Doctor Emil asked as if intending to make an immediate offer.

'No, never! We intend to build a larger house over there, just beyond the trees. That house will be a country retreat for Karen, Jeremy, Jean-Claude and others, including present company. When we travel abroad we can always return here from time to time. This is our permanent spiritual home, you know. When we are not here, part of it can be used by our friends and guests in transit. We shall also let you have a key to the main house when we are away. Then you will be free to use its facilities.'

'Wow! That is great!'

'We would also like the village to benefit from our success, so we are in the process of creating a trust fund, but we don't yet know how it should be used. Jeffery thinks a modern school and I think a small hospital. What do you think, Doctor?' Sarah said.

'I can't really decide and I shall be professionally biassed in saying that I prefer a small hospital, but a school is equally important,' Doctor Emil replied.

'What do you think, Darling?' Sarah asked Lumak.

'I think both will be a fine thing. Perhaps the good doctor might like to complete a cost estimate of both requirements, including the necessary buildings, staffing and equipment. Then we can decide on which to build first?'

'Leave it with me, Jeffery. I shall put a small honest team together to assess the situation,' Doctor Emil replied.

'You must join us for tea after you have collected your flowers,' Sarah said and they strolled towards the house.

Marion was busy baking something that resembled pancakes and was also attempting her first vegetarian dish. She realised that the couple were fully fledged vegetarians and couldn't prepare her usual supply of mutton while they were around. Therefore she decided to experiment with a few vegetarian dishes from the recipe book that Sarah had given her as a present. In her mind, if one couldn't beat them, they should join them and the couple seemed to be quite healthy from their present diet. Anyway, she needed to lose some more weight.

She hadn't realised that there were so many vegetarian recipes. Even items that looked like meat but was made from soya beans. They were not as tasteless and drab as she had originally thought when seasoned properly. At least, flower, potatoes and rice were used by all alike and those formed the bulk of most meals.

When she was finished, she laid the table and they sat down for an early lunch.

'Very delicious. What is it?' Doctor Emil inquired.

'A simple meal from the recipe book Sarah gave me... with horse meat and a few other special ingredients,' Marion replied. Doctor Emil almost choked on that mouthful.

'You must be kidding me? And what are the special ingredients?' he exclaimed, still holding his mouthful.

'You don't want to know!' Sarah interjected, smiling.

'Obviously, I am kidding, Doctor. There is not a single bit of horse in the complete meal. I couldn't find any in the village butchers. It's all vegetarian with soya beans for meat. It's the way you prepare it and it can be done to taste like horse meat if you prefer. I couldn't believe the taste myself!' Marion replied, while taking a mouthful to convince doctor Emil that she was speaking the truth, the whole truth and nothing but the truth..

Emil still couldn't believe that Marion was on his cancer death list, with just a few weeks to go. Now she was looking ten years younger and even healthier than himself.

When it was time for Emil to leave he called Marion to one side for a few private words.

'We in the village have decided to hold a little celebration on Wednesday for the happy couple. Keep our intentions from them for now, because we want it to be a surprise. Make sure they can visit the village first thing on Wednesday morning before the procession starts at 10 a.m. I shall mention the ideas on the new school and hospital to the mayor. That should make him even more enthusiastic.'

Once again they visited the upper hills with Spotty, to check on the sheep and viewed the distant hills and vales. The fragrance from the flowers were overwhelming and the scene romantic. While there they felt exalted and on top of the world. They realized they had a greater purpose to fulfill. But destiny worked against such freedom. Once again they observed the small waterfall in the distance and had a yearning for travelling to far away places, but also relished the closeness of home.

Sarah remembered all those yearning moments on that lonely rock, when she thought she would never find anyone to take her away from her lonely shepherdess existence. How wrong she was and how strange and unpredictable were the hands of faith in moulding one's future. Since the arrival of Lumak all that had changed and all her wandering wishes had finally come true.

'You will never leave me?' Sarah asked while placing her arms around his waist.

'What made you say that? No! Never, my love. I will never leave you. Wherever you go, I shall always follow,' he replied.

'And the same for me,' she said, full of happiness and contentment.

After an early breakfast on Wednesday morning, Marion suddenly developed a severe backache. Her husband Simon had already taken the sheep to the hills, and had disappeared soon after his return, leaving her in a dilemma. She required some urgent groceries from the village that couldn't wait. Not realising it was a ploy to get them in the village, the couple soon volunteered to collect the items for her.

They harnessed the horse Saracen to the cart, remembering the times they drove together on that bumpy village route and found the nostalgia irresistible. This time the seat on the cart had thicker cushions that were more comfortable. Despite that fact the dust-road was more pitted, with bumps and potholes everywhere.

As they approached the main street, they could observe banners waving and flags flying. Many rows of school children were dressed in their beautiful uniforms. Further down the street were a makeshift platform with many people standing and cheering. The couple wondered what special occasion was commemorated by that event and in whose honour the celebrations were held.

Suddenly a well-dressed gentleman came towards the couple, held the bridle of their horse Saracen and began to guide them through the crowd amidst cheers. They felt a little bewildered as cameras began to flash, taking pictures of them sitting on the cart, with Saracen getting more irritated by the second. Then several reporters began to ask them about their honeymoon. The camera flashes began to disturb Saracen, who moved his head a few times in annoyance, slightly upset by the turmoil, but the stranger held firmly to his harness.

They were soon guided to the platform and the proceedings began. The main group was led by none other than Doctor Emil himself who had begun to give an introductory speech. Then he stopped and focussed his gaze on the couple

'... and now a few words from the eminent Doctor Jeffery Longhurst,' Doctor Emil said and the crowd chaired as he jumped off the cart and walked towards the platform.

'Mister Mayor, Doctor Emil, my wife and friends. I must say, this is one enormous surprise and well planned by the look of things. I thought something was amiss when Marion insisted that we got her some groceries from the village at short notice. And how convenient Simon had gone missing just at a time when he was needed.

'However, on behalf of my wife and myself, may I say it's a great pleasure to be here with you all. And what an honour that you think so highly of us. We shall try to return your gratitude by building a school and hospital within this village as soon as possible.

'Because the good Doctor Emil has had a hand to play in this clandestine operation, perhaps he wouldn't mind being in charge of your new hospital. Furthermore, this is now our home, so even if we travel throughout the world, we shall always return to our home in the hills which we consider to be the most beautiful and restful place on Earth, and when we are away you will always be

in our hearts.

'*I must thank you again for this great honour and wish each of you well in your future endeavours,*' Lumak said and the crowd chanted, clapped and cheered as he went towards Sarah, while they both frantically waved back.

They were taken along with the crowd as the band began to play and the children followed towards the small village hall. There the children were served drinks, cakes and biscuits while Lumak gave several people his autograph. The mayor approached them both and placed two golden chains about their necks. The chains held large golden medallions with their names and the name of the village inscribed at the rear.

'Doctor Longhurst and Sarah Longhurst, I hereby nominate you free persons and life councillors of my village. May your future endeavours be pure, honourable and successful,' the mayor said.

'I accept your nomination, but you must realise that we will not always be here to play an active role in this community. However, we shall try our best to serve you in whatever ways possible,' Lumak said and the crowd cheered again with happiness. Sarah was surprised that they had gone to so much trouble just to celebrate their honeymoon homecoming and thought of ways in which she could show her gratitude.

Marion and Simon had been collected by car and was also there to aid in the celebrations.

Finally Lumak and Sarah visited Olaf the chemist to thank him for all his assistance during the laboratory experiments; for it was his equipment that was used in preparing and testing the last batch of serum samples.

'Olaf! Where are you!' Lumak shouted.

'Only over here!' he exclaimed, while he drew back the beaded curtain that separated the front of the shop from the rear.

'We got married yesterday. Sorry about the invitation, but it was all the way in the city,' Sarah said and he was utterly surprised by that knowledge.

'Congratulations to you both!'

'Pal, I will always be indebted to you for your kind assistance during my experiments. Should you require anything in the future, even from Europe or the States, just let me know. If you need to get hold of me when I am away, please contact Doctor Emil,' Lumak said.

'You really did it! Even now I can't believe you really created a permanent cure for cancer and with such old and used equipment. I never thought it was possible. Can I use that fact in my adds and brochures in future?' Olaf said.

'Whatever you wish, Pal. Mention my name if you like, but only in a nice way.' he said jokingly.

'Of course, I will. You two are the greatest! I will always remember you!' he said, with great admiration for both.

'Anyway, we must leave you before it gets too dark. Always keep in touch,' Lumak said and they left.

They departed during late afternoon for home and all four squeezed into the cart for the uphill journey. A slow and happy one that Saracen took calmly in his stride.

'Darling, I am in the mood for celebrations! It's a pity we do not have electricity and other facilities in the house, or we could have had a party and invited everyone,' Lumak said.

'What are you saying? That has never stopped us before. You developed a cure for all types of cancer in a filthy little room with very little facilities, so why should we let those deficiencies hinder us now!' Sarah replied. Lumak couldn't help but smile at his wife's devious and long-suffering nature.

'Whatever you say, my love!' he replied, realizing they could move the world if they had the desire.

CHAPTER 49

Goodbye Home

On Thursday morning Sarah called Marion aside for a few private words.

'Marion, we must have a little party before we leave. I know this place is not very suitable for anything big, but perhaps we could borrow a few large tables and have them placed in front of the house. The sitting room can be organised to increase capacity and everything can be prepared in the kitchen and taken outside to a marquee or large tent. Or perhaps we could hire some equipment and have a barbeque. We haven't had rain for a while, so the marquee is not strictly necessary. And there shouldn't be too much of a problem with flies and other insects this time of year. What do you think?'

'I think it's a marvellous idea. But I don't think a barbeque is necessary. I can make a shopping list if you like. We can serve a variety of those small vegetarian patties and hors-d'oeuvres... but the shopping will have to be done soon. When do you think is the best day?' Marion asked.

'We leave on Saturday morning, so Friday evening is a best time for the party. Shall we say Friday evening, then?'

'I know where we can get some tables. The town hall has several and I don't think the mayor will mind,' Marion said.

'Why didn't I think of that, and the mayor is also invited,' Sarah replied.

'I can also get us a musical band and a magician. Their parents are good friends of mine.'

'In that case, I shall tell the men of our intentions and they can collect the tables and chairs while we get on with the invitations and shopping. It's a pity Dad isn't here to partake, but I shall invite some of his friends, anyway,' Sarah said.

The two women told their husbands of their intentions and the place was astir with activity. It took them the best part of the day to clean and decorate the small four-bedroom house. It was without mains driven electricity or indeed any modern conveniences. The only available electrical power was the small petrol driven generator that Lumak had used for his laboratory equipments and that one only supplied one kilowatt of power. Nevertheless the place was homely and they always had several powerful gas lamps and cylindrical gas cookers with a good supply of logs. The generator could then be used for lighting and other electrical devices as needed.

Early Friday morning both women left for the village to do their shopping and arrange the delivery of the furniture.

Four tables were placed close to the hand driven grinding stone. That grinding stone was the iconic essence of the place and represented their hard efforts in the face of diversity. It was about 1 metre in diameter and mounted on a wooden frame with metallic spindle and handle. There was another well worn and cracked one lying on the ground nearby. Those large grinding stones were used by Ben and Sarah over the years to sharpen their axes and other agricultural tools.

Five gas lamps were hung on wooden poles about the area along with many LED bulbs of different colours. Then the place was adequately lit throughout.

The cars began to arrive from seven p.m. onwards. There were many more visitors than invited, but Sarah was pleased with the high turnout.

The outdoor party went without a hitch and the band and magician well appreciated by all. Marion and Sarah was not sure of their guests' dietary requirements, so another of Marion's special vegetarian dishes were served, to be enjoyed by all.

They spent most of Friday sorting themselves out for their new life ahead. Lumak saw it his duty to return all his borrowed apparatus, including laboratory equipment to their rightful owners. He had also to return some equipment to, Olaf, the village pharmacist, with more thanks and a promise to supply him with new drugs at a special rate. Then Doctor Emil's patients could get all their prescriptions through him.

Sarah decided to take with her some of her special clothes, jewellery and other items she had accumulated over the years. Although many were not of significant value they would constantly remind her of home while on her travels.

She had also bought a brand new collar for Spotty and a lovely bridle for Saracen as a going away present and personally fitted them to the animals with tender loving care.

As previously arranged, the helicopter arrived to collect the couple on Saturday morning. That was after they said farewell to their sheep, the horse, Saracen, and dog, Spotty. Then Sarah hugged Marion and Simon, and thanked them for their precious time. Having decided to rent their village house, Marion and Simon would remain as caretakers indefinitely. A significant allowance was arranged for them through Doctor Emil and the local bank.

Soon the couple was collected and their helicopter hovering above. Each waving to the other with Spotty darting hither and thither on the ground below. Tears of sadness filled Sarah's eyes and Lumak equally saddened by their leaving.

'Will I ever see my little Spotty and Saracen again?' she cried, as the helicopter darted off in the opposite direction while Marion and the others stood watching and waving.

'Yes, my love. In about one year. So this is not the end. It's just the beginning of our lives together,' Lumak replied, while she wiped the tears from her eyes.

CHAPTER 50

Return to the city

Just before lunch they arrived at Jeremy's home by car from the local airport. Lumak and Sarah were carrying two small suitcases each and hand bags.

'We are back!' cried Sarah as they lugged their cases and bags into the house.

'Hi! Did you both have an enjoyable honeymoon?' Karen asked.

'Yes, thank you. It was most delightful and peaceful, with a few moments of excitement. I didn't realise how enchanting our country home was until I could see it with the eyes of someone from the city. Why don't you and Jeremy take the occasional break? The clean air up there will do you the world of good and you can stay as long as you wish, anytime you like,' Sarah said.

'I might take you up on that offer quite soon. After you dump your cases, you can both join me for lunch. It's almost ready, and you can tell me all about your holidays and Jeremy father's village. I have never been there, you know. Jeremy had to go and interview some chemical engineers for the production plant, but he'll be home soon,' Karen said.

After lunch, Lumak had retired to the drawing room to do some sketches of their future country house and also make a mental note of some suitable builders. Out of a list of five construction companies, one came to mind. That company was well known and owned by a man whose mother he recently saved from a most painful death of cancer.

'That one will build my country house, the school and hospital,' Lumak muttered to himself before lifting the handset to call the man's office for an appointment. He also phoned Jean-Claude to say that he was back from holidays and would be at the university late on Monday morning. Then he told the women of his intentions. Lumak never left anything to chance and always hit while the iron was hot.

Jeremy returned just after lunch and was very pleased to see his beloved friends had returned.

'You guys look so good together! You must have had a most pleasant time,' he commented.

'Your dad was also with us for a while. Anyway, how are you progressing with the serum plant?' Lumak asked.

'Everything is moving to schedule, but I sometimes have to kick a few butts. I believe the whole world is changing in this respect for the worse. There is far too much slackness and too many people nowadays take their salaries and jobs for granted. The government and unions also tend to assist the decay by allowing by far too many workers' rights,' Jeremy said in an adamant mood.

'Pal, don't take it all so seriously. People are always free to choose the mode of their existence. If one method fails try another, until you get it right. And remember, there are many ways to peal a banana,' Lumak replied in another of his funny moods.

'Including cutting it in half, eh!' Jeremy replied, equally philosophical.

'Jeremy, I am going to the USA very soon, so anything you need can be sent directly from there. You can join us later if you wish. But unfortunately, I wont be able to supply you with reliable workers from that location,' Lumak said.

'You are going to live there, permanently?' Jeremy inquired as sadness befell his features.

'No, not permanently. Just to complete my microid and space drive research. The Americans have all the necessary equipment and technologies that I need. However, I shall also be involved in ecology with some powerful organizations that can affect the whole of humanity and our planet's future. Nevertheless, you will see me back here at least once each year.

'We shall let you know each time we visit, so you can join us at our country residence and also have yourselves a break in the process. We can always have frequent conferences via satellite, if you like and there is always the phone. Since I now consider you and Karen a major part of my family, the country house is also for your use. Your father is now responsible for its upkeep, so please collect a key from him. And please feel free to use it whenever the need arise. It's now yours as much as it's ours. You are also to keep an eye on all my projects in these parts. I have therefore decided to make you and Jean-Claude senior directors of all our joint undertakings in this part of the world. I will arrange all the legal paperwork before I leave, including share certificates and such like. I shall also arranged for you to have all other relevant papers and keys. My friend, our organization is like a family business that is to be shared by all,' Lumak said, and Jeremy was astounded by his generosity.

'That is incredible and so very kind of you. I mean, for all that trust and the position of director... not to mention a partnership. I shall also accept your offer about the occasional country holiday. I can spend time with my parents when I visit,' Jeremy said. His features suddenly lit up and he became a changed man. For some reason, the thought of being a powerful person within a large organization with no future financial problems had caused all his lingering and nagging worries to dissipate.

'Jeremy, you earned it and I meant what I said about you being a major player in our ventures over here. From now on, my friend, you will become one of the richest people in the world and a major player in my plans, so chin up and take it all in your stride, with pride in the realization that we have gone this far by ourselves together. And there is no need for you to do all the donkey work in future. Hire a few organizations to assist.

'When you are a bit tired of things here, you are welcomed to join me in the States on microid development, but first, you must get this place up and running and put someone responsible in your position before you can leave. Anyway, Jean-Claude can always take over on his own in your absence. He thinks he is getting close to retirement, but he doesn't realize that we will shortly have a cure for his aging, so retirement for him has flown out the window,' Lumak said, in jest.

'Yes, I have to make sure the serum plant is in full production before I can hand it over to a new manager and at our current rate of progress that process can take anything up to a year,' Jeremy replied.

'In that case, I shall leave it in your very capable hands and you can keep me informed of progress on a regular basis. Anyway, our university with its new installations is coping well with serum production so we can review everything when I next return from America, including adding the new wing to our famous university hospital,' Lumak said.

Lumak arrived at the builder's office first thing on Monday morning. He was dressed in his white robe as usual and looked dignified and princely.

'Sir, The Lord is here to see you,' the receptionist said over the intercom and very soon the place was in turmoil, as the word quickly got around that Doctor Longhurst was on the premises. The staff stopped whatever they were doing and crowded around him for autographs and handshakes. The proprietor had to fight his way through his workers to rescue Lumak. Then he took him to his office after severely reprimanding his staff.

'Thank you for gracing our humble establishment with a personal visit. How can we be of assistance to you?' Faizal asked.

'I would like your company to do some work for me. Most of it is for charity, so I would like your best rates. If they are good, you will have a lot more work from my organization in the future, both here and abroad. However, your first project will be in the country. Here are a few sketches I made recently.

'First of all, I would like a large house built in this area. The other two items are a school and hospital. They are to be constructed in the local village. I have donated these buildings to the people of that village, so I would like them built to last and earthquake proofed as much as possible. There are many skilled craftsmen in the village, perhaps you could employ a few of them,' Lumak said. Faizal briefly glanced through the sketches.

'Very well done! But these structures are truly enormous, the house alone has over one hundred rooms. Do we have enough land for these buildings?' Faizal inquired.

'As much as we need. The hospital land is about 60 acres and the school about 20. Most of it is relatively flat and on solid limestone, so there shouldn't be any problems with foundations and such like. All I would like you to do is build them to last for my people.'

'I shall give these to my architects and fax you an estimate tomorrow, including surveyor's costs. For you Doctor Longhurst, everything will be done close to cost and I shall try to use local labour whenever I can,' Faizal said.

'In that case, I shall leave it in your very capable hands and await your quotations,' Lumak said as he firmly shook his hand in the normal way.

Lumak went directly to the university hospital to catch up on some of his work. There had been several recent calls from Professor Lennox, who had already made most of their travelling arrangements, including tickets. All that was needed from the couple was their departure date.

'I needed to see you urgently about a few things and Lennox has been on the line several times,' Jean-Claude said, as he entered Lumak's office, feeling slightly uneasy with his increased workload.

'What's all this about! I heard you were going off to America for an indefinite stay?' a bewildered Jean-Claude asked.

'When did you here that. I wanted to explain those matters to you myself ... Since the rabbit's out of the bag, I suppose it doesn't matter anymore. I am not leaving our business here, just expanding globally.'

'Really?'

'I have decided to form my own organization for developing advanced technologies like micro robotics and stellar drives. I would also like to assist endangered species and improve human existence on our dying world. We have too much to lose as a species if we continue blindly in the direction we are going. The cancer research and serum production will be handed over to Jeremy. You can be my deputy here, if you like, to ensure everything runs smoothly in my absence.'

'Ok?'

'I have also decided to build a new home in the hills and have donated a school and hospital to the local village there. Here is some information relating to these future projects including our new hospital wing.'

'That's incredible!'

'The Americans offered me a lot and have no objections to forming my own organization for developing those scientific projects, so I have accepted their terms. However, I shall return here at least once a year. I do this for the good of all and Sarah understands. Anyway, I shall always be available to you and Jeremy. If you need my urgent assistance, we can hold a satellite conference. Other less important information you can E-mail, phone or fax.'

'It's all so fast!'

'I say we should hit while the iron's hot. Now we move internationally, my friend. My special students can always follow me to the States, if they so choose. You and Jeremy can follow when things become more automated over here.'

'I understand, but as far as following you to the States is concerned, I am getting older and shall be retiring soon. How can I be of assistance to you after my retirement?' Jean-Claude said.

'When you work for the organization, my friend, you need never retire. Very soon we shall have the necessary serums to rejuvenate the human body. You have observed what our anti-cancer serum can do on terminal patients regarding an age reduction. So you should never think of your retirement from this position as the end of your working life. Think more of it as a change in career and the start of a new beginning. You should also realize that in future you will have a much easier life and be able to have whatever holiday breaks you require, so why retire and lead a more boring existence, when you can be your normal creative self and have the choice to do as you please. Since you will soon be made a senior director of our projects here, you need never work again if you so wish. The choice is up to you.'

'Are you serious? I mean, about being a senior director?' an appreciative Jean-Claude uttered.

'Of course I'm serious! I've never been more serious in my life!

And not just a senior director. You will also become a full partner in all our undertakings in this part of the world. So I would like you to arrange the necessary paperwork for you, Jeremy and myself as directors and partners in this new venture,' Lumak replied, handing him a list of relevant changes and Jean-Claude swallowed hard.

'In that case, I shall call my solicitor in the morning to arrange the necessary paperwork. How soon do you leave us?' Jean-Claude asked.

'Within the month. I have decided to give Lennox a date today. However, I have to ensure that everything here is left in good hands before my departure. I also want to speak with a few of my promising students. You should realize that because of the great demand for our products, very soon we shall become a very large organization globally, and that is just to manufacture and supply the serum and other relevant medical products. The wheel is now in motion and cannot be stopped, so at this stage it is important for us to give it as much impetus as possible. Please keep all talk about my departure under your hat for now, until I have spoken to others. I don't wish for anyone to feel in any way left out of my plans.'

'I fully understand!' Jean-Claude nodded.

'Don't look so worried, my friend. I shall never forget my friends and people here, and plans will be made to build many more schools and hospitals when the royalties come rolling in, so if anything, you will be a lot more active from now on as my deputy. I have not left, it's just that you have taken my place and don't worry about money. You will be on a nice retainer from now on. So do you accept?'

'Do I have a choice?' Jean-Claude replied, sarcastically.

'No!' said Lumak, with similar attitude.

'In that case, I have no choice but to accept. I can always make the usual excuses to the president and his politicians if their curiosity is unduly aroused. Anyway, they will soon have a thriving economy from your products, which does not require your presence, so why should they complain. Nevertheless, I have never been able to understand those jumped-up politicians that always harbour ill fortune by ignorance. Such ignorant individuals can get very rough when they think their future is in any way threatened, and you happen to be their goose that lays the golden egg,' Jean-Claude said.

'In that case, it's time this goose flew off to another perch,' Lumak replied.

'Can I speak to Professor Lennox, please? This is an important call!' Lumak said to the secretary and he was soon transferred.

'Hello, Doctor Longhurst. Are you still visiting for your honeymoon? As I mentioned before, you are welcomed to remain at my Washington flat for the duration of your stay,' he replied, pretending in case someone was eavesdropping on their conversation.

'I have decided on a date for our visit. It will be in three weeks time, on the twenty third. We shall be carrying four large suitcases, so please get things organized for me at your end. Your guys here can return to the States with us at the same time,' Lumak said.

'I shall leave two of my security men behind to keep an eye on you during transit and guide you through our strict customs. They have special clearance, so don't worry about anything. They will not get in your way. I will feel a lot better if I knew you and your wife were always absolutely safe.'

'I understand. Anyway, see you soon,' Lumak said and hung up.

They held their farewell party at Jeremy's house. All local friends were invited, including a very happy Jean-Claude and his wife. Their going away was kept very low-keyed. As far as their friends were concerned, they were off to America for their real honeymoon. Only Jeremy and Jean-Claude had been told the real story and Lumak knew that they would not reveal any details to anyone.

Once again Sarah and Karen went shopping for more clothes and presents. Sarah also wanted to get Lumak a special present, which soon turned out to be a golden ring with an engraved winged insignia on its oval face. The small insignia resembled his own large one, but in miniature. In the centre of the wings were inserted a small stone of lapis lazuli that resembled the planet Earth.

Having discussed their intentions with her father, Ben, he decided to follow later, after they had settled in their new American home.

'You know, my daughter, how I feel about flying. I prefer to manage rough seas instead,' Ben replied.

Sarah realized how stubborn her dad was regarding any form of flying. Because of that phobia it would be several weeks before her father was able to join them in the states.

CHAPTER 51

Lumak's worst day

After his missed opportunity to kill Lumak, Nasidin was enraged, but not deterred. Although he realized something was amiss with his recent attempts, he put it down to a bullet proof vest worn by the target and gross incompetence on the part of the chosen hit-men. They were contracted for that job and were an unknown quantity. However he was not a person easily deterred and would always try and try until the job was done to his satisfaction. He only had to succeed once. He also realized that the university hospital was a prime target with all those foreign visitors, medics and patients.

It was also used for serum production. Once the serum production stopped, so also would the healing of cancer patients. There was also Lumak's family and friends. If he tried to take them all out at once, he could not miss them all and the pain of their demise would slow the false profit, Doctor Longhurst, in his steps.

To prevent further mistakes he called on the assistance of outside professionals. He wanted this job to be clean and efficient and the police seldom considered foreign terrorists. This time he was going to make his point and get a lot of media coverage in the process, thus killing two birds with one stone. An important hospital full of dead doctors and patients from such activities always made the news.

'So you are the mad bomber?' he said eyeing the European mercenary. He was tall, blonde, well built and kept spinning a small blade between his fingers. He spoke with a German accent.

'One million US dollars, and the job will be done to your satisfaction in one week. But first, I have to check the places before I bring my guys in. Is there a local building we can use?' Manfred inquired.

'Yea, we have a small mosque in the area. You can use the basement, but be careful. You will have fifty percent to start and the balance on completion. Krekar, get him the file on the targets,' Nasidin said. Manfred nodded approval, took the folder from Krekar and decided to leave.

'I don't want to see your face again, as long as I live!' Nasidin shouted as he left.

'Suits me fine! I'll be out of your hair before the job is done!' he shouted back.

'And don't you forget my balance...!'

Manfred was well known by many in that underworld as an efficient free-lancer and had a reputation for completing his contracts on time and to the satisfaction of his clients. But there were no guarantees with timed explosives.

He took great pride in his chosen profession and never had a failure from the device not going off at the set time with the predicted blast, but could never guarantee the kills. Being European, he could always pass himself off as a lost tourist and wander into most places. He was a specialist in such designs and knew exactly where to plant his devices for greatest effect.

As far as he was concerned the planet was already too populated with filthy defective humans who were not of pure genes, so the more he could dispatch from this life, the better. He was not Moslem, but belonged to a radical European terrorist group with strong Nazi baring. In the year 2041 the planet's human population was over 9 billion and many wanted a reduction, but not by extreme means like violent culling.

Once he had found the locations of the places involved, he called his engineering team together and they began their precision handiwork.

It was just before six in the evening when both bombs exploded. Lumak was in a local Mosque at the time when he heard the blasts and knew what had happened. He immediately transposed to Jeremy's house. That place was in shambles. Karen had been blown many metres away and had lost most of one arm, along with numerous wounds throughout her body. Sarah was still stood in the house close to where the bomb had exploded without a single scratch. Luckily for Ben, he was at his brother's place. Jeremy was at the new factory setting up more production equipment with his new manager. Therefore both were unscathed.

At that time of day everyone was usually at home, but thank goodness their plans had changed due to the couple's visit to the USA. The only casualties were the helper Faizal, along with a few reporters who were stationed outside the house at the time.

Lumak observed that Sarah was ok and immediately went to Karen's assistance. He would have liked to take Karen to a special place where he could heal her complete body, but that was too risky at the time, so he tied her arm and called the ambulance. Her arm would be repaired at a later date when he had created the necessary technologies.

'Quiet, my girl. Don't worry, everything will be ok. The ambulance is on its way,' he said in a low soothing voice and Karen, although in shock, felt more relaxed.

Sarah was still standing in the same spot as when he first arrived, completely dazed. Lets take Karen to the Hospital, the ambulance is almost here!' he shouted and she moved from her spot, still dazed but unscathed. The ambulance soon arrived and they boarded.

'What happened?' Lumak asked, quietly.

'Must have been a bomb. I could see most of the bits from the house hitting me with full force, but nothing happened. I was enveloped in a field of some kind. They just bounced off me, like I was superwoman. How is that possible?' she asked.

'It's your engagement ring. It has those powers.... to protect you,' he said and she was aghast.

'All that power in such a small ring?'

'It has to be recharged. Let me borrow it for a while,' he said and she handed the object to him.

The ambulance men had administered morphine and Karen had

stopped moaning from pain. She was also placed on a drip and oxygen as the ambulance made its way through traffic.

Although seriously wounded, Karen was stable and would eventually recover from her wounds.

The military were out in full force, but as usual the culprits had long since left the area. Those bombs were well hidden and on timers. Nevertheless the police knew most of the likely agitators in the city and several arrests were made, excluding Nasidin and his close group, who had alibis and a large following. The government didn't want to stir things up too much on the religious front and have more bombs explode in their faces. Anyway, they couldn't prove Nasidin was behind any of the recent fiascos.

Jeremy had gone to see the new factory site and quickly made his way back to the hospital after a call from Lumak.

'God, They also took out our hospital, with John and the others. You stay here with the women and I'll go and see if I can help,' Lumak said.

CHAPTER 52

Hospital in pieces

Jean-Claude was in his office at the time when the place blue up about him. That bomb was much larger than the one at the house and placed in a van at the rear of the auditorium. It could have been over 1000 kilograms of explosives. The wall may have shielded some areas like the canteen from the full force of the blast.

Many students and patients had died, along with Jean-Claud's secretary, but he and Farouk survived with a few cuts and bruises. Farouk was in the canteen at the time, which was the least affected.

The complete hospital was in shambles. Jean-Claude found himself trapped under a pile of rubble with half his part of the building blown away. He was soon rescued by the Fire Brigade. He dusted himself as best he could and ignored his bloody face from a cut he received on his forehead.

He looked and beheld all his life's work in utter ruin and shambles.

'What have I done to deserve this!' he murmured to himself, while climbing out of more debris while assisted by the fireman.

'Sir, are you ok!' the fireman asked.

'I think so. Have you found my secretary?'

'Sorry, Sir. She didn't make it.'

'Dam these extremist! She was such a loving individual. What have anyone of us done to deserve this?' he said as tears trickled down his pallid and dusty cheeks.

Lumak transposed to the place in an instant and was near the source of the explosion. He observed the scene of devastation for a while until he found the source of the blast.

Then he observed a bloodied Jean-Claude being escorted by a

fireman to a nearby ambulance. Lumak was relieved and ran up to him.

'I'm so sorry, John!'

'Yea, these demons are everywhere these days! Now I know the real reason why you are moving to the States!' he said.

'I'm sick to the stomach of all this. I feel completely helpless in the face of such barbarity and carnage. Pal, we needed a brand new building, anyway. They will hit us but they will never win. Now we'll buy this whole place for next to nothing. Next time this hospital will be much larger and better, with all the latest gadgets and equipment. They will never... never... win. We in the organization always take care of our own and we shall never be defeated!' Lumak said, somewhat enraged, and Jean-Claude took courage from his words. But the shock of the place and the loss of Brenda, his secretary, made him less responsive. Even so, he had never seen Lumak in such a state before. Then he calmed a little.

'So much misery and suffering... my poor students and patients. I hope most of them are ok,' Lumak said, wishing he could turn the clock back or do more to assist.

'I think they were lucky this time. Many of them left early today,' Jean-Claude said.

'Thank God for that! The cowards also blew up Jeremy's house, you know. Karen lost part of her left arm, but will be ok. Thank God, most of them are ok!' Then Lumak surveyed the debris and picked up a small piece of the equipment used on his 3D projection system. Then he kicked it away with full force, as if it would bring him closure to an important episode in his life. He would do a much better job next time.

After the dust had settled, the loss of life at the hospital was not as much as previously thought. Only 9 had died in the hospital, including 5 patients. But most were wounded from flying debris. At Jeremy's home there was the helper Faizal and one reporter. All things considered many were extremely lucky that day.

The destruction was everywhere on the news. Very soon the President and other politicians were in contact to offer commiserations. However they realized the extremists knew nothing of the new factory that was being equipped or their plans to build a most modern hospital in place of the damaged one. If anything, they had done Lumak a favour in levelling the place for him to buy at a cut-down price.

They soon moved into Jean-Claude's home while repairs were made to Jeremy's house. Jean-Claude insisted, but was now alert to the dangers and soon had several soldiers guarding his premisses.

Two weeks later Karen was ready to leave hospital and they turned up in a black Limousin to take her home. She was always a most cheerful soul, but could never recover from such an experience without Lumak's help.

Once they were settled he called them into the dining room for a pep talk.

'It's nice to see we have survived the worst things that can be thrown at us. From now on I do not want any of you to worry about a thing. I have recently isolated a gene that can be used to regrow limbs. So Karen's arm will be regrown in due course after we have acquired the necessary technology.

'This crisis marks a major turning point in our lives here. We'll never be the same people again.

'They were after me and the organization, you know. They think we were depriving Allah of dying souls by curing them. They also think I'm a false profit or Anti Christ, come to destroy their religion and distort their beliefs, by being kind and generous to others. What a warped sense of right and wrong. By their own religion, isn't it wrong to take lives and not assist the dying. Isn't it also wrong to allow poor people to die from cancer without lending a hand. I thought all such good deeds were directly from the hands of Allah.

'Anyway, they are mainly after me and soon I shall be in the States, so you will be safe from their hands in future. The cancer program will now work through distributors and other organizations, so you will not be directly involved in public lectures and such like. The new hospital being built in the city will

be another University Hospital, but a thousand times better than before. It will not be targeted in future, because I will not be there to give anymore of my lectures.

'Since we now go global with our organization, everyone of you in this room will be an officer and draw a substantial salary from our efforts.

'Our factory is on continuous production from today, and we have numerous orders from all over the world, so be happy and help each other so that we may succeed in our ambitions. We are already a successful organization and that cannot be changed.

'We have a great future ahead of us, so let us please place this turmoil as a small setback on our way to greater accomplishments. You know;

On every living thing a little rain must fall,
And even the smallest drop can help the little tree grow tall.
For even on the darkest night,
The stars above will still shine bright.

'Soon, we'll even have the technologies to bring an individual back from the very doors of death, so we are not going to be stopped by such extremists, who do not know the difference between right and wrong,' he said.

'Will we really be able to grow complete limbs,' Jeremy asked, while hugging Karen.

'We can do it now, but I would prefer if you guys waited a little while for us to build and assemble the necessary equipment,' he said and they were astounded. Karen couldn't hold back a smile and was ready to start that part of her new life in the organization. She was determined to get her own back in whatever ways possible.

Then they celebrated their survival with a glass of champagne.

'To our glorious mission, the organization, family, friends and those lost during the struggle for a better future!' Jean-Claude shouted and they responded by linking glasses.

Meanwhile the Shiite Nasidin was not amused.

'Dam it, we missed our false prophet again.' He scanned through one of the evening newspapers in utter disappointment. He had to try all over again.

'I told you he could be the true profit. Then he will have Allah on his side,' Krekar replied.

'How can an English doctor be a true profit of Islam. Now you are blaspheming!' he shouted and there was silence.

'Do we pay the full amount?' Krekar asked, but was ignored by Nasidin. He was afraid of what Manfred would do if he was short changed in any way. You didn't mess with such people.

'Anyway, we had some success in stopping his operations for a while. Also, many of his foreign friends will think twice before visiting our country and corrupting our people. We also had some good publicity. Next time he will not be so lucky!' he said. Then he went and wired the half million dollars to Manfred's untraceable offshore account. After that he went for prayer.

CHAPTER 53

Lumak in America

Lumak and Sarah arrived at the airport in the black Limousin and were seen off by all their friends. Karen shed a few tears but Sarah gave her a big hug. The others waved as they departed to the checkout area under strict security. Since the explosions the airport was under strict security.

They caught the six a.m. to New York. It was their first intercontinental flight and Sarah was quite nervous in anticipation. With the exception of the helicopter flight from her home in the hills, she had never been on an aircraft before and found the process of checks and waiting to be quite nerve-racking. Once on the plane she held Lumak's hand for reassurance but soon got used to the idea while persistently chewing bubblegum. The whole idea of being over eight kilometres up in the stratosphere made her quite queasy, even with her recently charged ring of invulnerability. Their two security escorts were never far away.

Professor Lennox and two of his most senior colleagues were waiting for them at the main airport at their destination. Lennox had left word with the chief of customs security, so they were speedily moved through customs aided by their two security companions. On arrival they were greeted by Lennox and guided through a local exit.

'We are to catch a flight from here to DC on an air-force jet from a local airport. You are to meet The President tomorrow. Therefore, I think you should spend a few days in DC and acquaint yourselves with some of our American ways before you catch your later flight to Minneapolis. That is if you don't mind. Anyway, I shall discuss it all with you during the flight,' Lennox said.

Lumak had been on many LPD flights in his time, but had never travelled by jet or helicopter until just recently.

'These crude aircraft are so noisy but remarkably stable,' he thought, as he looked beyond the terminal buildings unto several rows of parked jet planes in the distance.

Everything tended to overwhelm Lumak when they travelled through the expansive city of New York, with its many skyscrapers, over crowdedness and extreme traffic. There were numerous reckless taxi drivers that had to break rules to get anywhere on time. Large areas of New York had been walled to hold back the rising ocean, but that process could not go on indefinitely. Global Warming was taking its toll.

They were only able to spend two hours in that city before their next scheduled flight.

They arrived at Washington DC late that night and were immediately taken to their apartment by a waiting limousine.

'I've found a nice little place for you. If you want to stay longer than a week, just mention it to reception and don't worry about money. It's all taken care of,' Lennox said.

They soon entered the foyer, checked in at the desk and were taken towards the nearby elevator. Lennox handed Lumak the key and he opened the door while the two security officers nosed around. The room was one of the largest bridal sweets on the topmost floor of the building.

'It's a standard furnished apartment, in a medium size hotel. We use this place frequently because the security is good. I hope you like it. Buzz reception if you need anything. Now you can get some well deserved rest and when you have settled in tomorrow, please call me.'

'Will do!' Lumak replied.

'Your meeting with the president is set for three-ten p.m. tomorrow, so someone will be here before then,' Lennox said, being always over zealous, careful and concerned.

'Thank you for everything, Harry,' Lumak said and shook Lennox's hand. Then he handed Lumak his card and left.

'I must say, Darling, this is a most spacious and delightful room,'

Sarah said, as she observed its many features and facets. Then she sat on the side of the bed to test the water movements of the mattress.

'Everything about this country is big, but I prefer this city to New York,' she said.

'It's a beautiful city and not with many skyscrapers as New York. The people are also much fewer, but I'm not too sure about the mad cabbies,' Lumak said. Then he drew aside the net curtain to view the area more thoroughly from that floor. In the distance he could observe the tall needle shaped Washington Monument bathing in artificial light, giving him the urge to go strolling, but it was late and his eyelids had already begun to close. Even so, the most recent part of their journey had given them hungry appetites and they buzzed room service.

They quickly unpacked their belongings and retired soon after they had consumed a light meal.

Lumak had little sleep and was up early from excitement. Sarah soon followed him out of bed.

'Darling, why don't we have breakfast now and afterwards get a car to take us to some of the most famous places until lunch? Then we can get ready to meet the president,' Sarah said.

'Yes, Love. I would like to visit some of those historical buildings to get a feel of this country, its people and its past as Lennox advised.' However one of Lumak's main intentions was to locate a suitable building for meditation and prayer.

They hired a car from the hotel and were soon travelling through the streets of Washington DC. The first building to be visited was the Washington National Cathedral. Lumak could not quite take in the enormity of the place when compared to some of the temples he had visited in Turkey. That building, including its ambience was truly overwhelming. As far as Lumak was concerned all religions were one so he sat for a little prayer as he had in the other temples. He soon realized the famous cathedral was a place for non prejudicial worship. It was strictly nondenominational and that concept of free worship pleased him.

'My glorious One, please let my important mission on this

beautiful world be successful and may all our major problems disappear with the passing of the winds of change,' he prayed.

He observed the tremendous Rose Window with the many banners and wondered what past historical events they signified. After having observed most of the building's interior, their driver and guide decided to take them to the Lincoln Memorial.

Finally they visited The Capitol building and viewed its many statues of past great people. By that time it was already noon, so they decided to postpone their visit to the museums for another day.

They returned to the hotel and had a haughty meal. Then showered and dressed for their special occasion with the President.

CHAPTER 54

Lumak meets the President of the USA

The limousine had arrived and the well dressed couple were finally on their way to the White House.

Lumak looked radiant in his white robe, now a mild cream to match Sarah's suit. He always included the blue circled and winged insignia on his left shoulder, which highlighted that area. Sarah was dressed in her stylish cream suit with a large silver broach studded in diamonds pinned unto her left lapel. It belonged to her mother and had been handed down through the generations.

Many of the hotel staff thought he was a foreign prince and rumours flew wildly.

President Arnold J. Turner was about 25 percent Sioux Indian, plus Caucasian and a republican. He had attained his position by meritorious hard work and was probably the only scientific president the USA had seen for generations.

As a doctor of physics, he had spent most of his earlier life doing cryogenic research and teaching some areas of physics at major level, but had never taken that field as his only career. There were too many problems that needed political clout and he made sure they were always highlighted. He used to be one of the main contributors in many of Washington's most boisterous demonstrations in his youthful past and had gained most of his popularity by so doing.

When he was not fighting for his good causes, he was a keen amateur astronomer, with a moderate interest in the arts and affiliated sciences. Currently his main interests lay in rising seas and oceans, industrial pollution, global warming and numerous other topics that needed his undivided attention. There was also Earth's dwindling sources of fossil fuels for petroleum, which placed a great burden on his country's industries.

President Turner, now looking ten years younger, was just past his fifty-sixth birthday, a little over two metres tall and with a tanned complexion. He was aggressive looking with a damaged nose since football days, but very honest and with a most pleasant attitude once one got to know him.

He had moved into politics when he saw the devastation done to the planet by opportunists. He wanted to be a force for good in stopping the rot and impeding further movements in the wrong direction. Luckily for him, the tide had turned in his favour. Most Americans were presently aware of the devastation caused by global warming and worried for their future. He considered the major problems facing a damaged world that would remain with humans thousands of years in the future:

To begin, there were the great expanding ozone holes hovering above both poles with the resultant increase in skin cancer globally, Although it had dwindled during the previous decades, it was expanding once more.

There were also the substantial increase in sea levels. That was now his greatest problem. It was presently more extreme than previously predicted. All coastal cities were presently at risk from flooding. Many islands in the Indian and Pacific oceans had simply disappeared and their populations relocated elsewhere.

The increasing global temperature also caused major problems. Those effects were felt by many people within northern and southern regions as the ground beneath them began to contract due to the reduced levels in permafrost, thus causing large cracks in roads and buildings.

Low-lying coastal regions had begun to be flooded by a combination of increasing sea levels and a more unpredictable and turbulent climate with higher rainfall. Everyone worried to what levels the south polar ice would melt, for there was enough to lift the worlds oceans by over sixty metres. Greenland glaciers had melted significantly.

Hurricanes constantly bombarded the Carribean islands and the

Southern States, putting a great strain on his disaster fund and the frequency, size and strength of tornados had increased significantly and were on an upward trend. And that was not all, many were concerned that the Great Conveyor or Gulf Stream that fed warmth to the northern latitudes would come to an abrupt stop, and in so doing trigger another lengthy ice age. If that occurred most of the planet could undergo extreme climatic change while the ice accumulated in higher latitudes. Such extreme climatic change could make a large part of the planet unsuitable for human habitation. With over nine billion humans on Earth in the year 2041, to where would people in those latitudes have gone.

The number of all such disasters had increased and the trend was set to continue. Countries were spending a large part of their gross national product in aiding those natural victims from so-called acts of God. Since insurance was not always available because of impossible premiums, large government sums were spent on damage due to such unnatural disasters instead on more useful ventures. The problem was worsening each year globally. It was a period of ecological and financial crisis and the President of all people needed answers.

Everyone realised that the ecologists had been right all along. If only governments had taken their warnings more seriously instead of focussing on financial gains and capitalism. If only they had taken the necessary corrective actions sooner?

Like a cigarette smoker, they observed the warnings on the packet but were too addicted to their capitalistic way of life, until the cancer grew. Then it was too late.

Therefore all blame was layed squarely at the doors of government. Nevertheless it was the type of problem that could not be solved by any single government. The population problem was due mainly to procreation wherein everyone could be blamed.

Despite the many conventions held worldwide, most of the large developing countries were only interested in industrial growth and were more than willing to worry about negative consequences at a later date or leave their mistakes for the next generation to put right. They had linked population growth with financial gains, not realizing that those were just human considerations and did not take into consideration the dire problems caused by such self-indulgent processes of supply and demand. Further, all such draconian methods of economies ran contrary to planetary evolution, which included numerous other species in a complex food chain and not just greedy and short-sighted humankind.

President Arnold had spent tens of billions of his taxpayer's money giving grants to renovate many of the nation's most important buildings and monuments, not to mention protection of coastal cities from flooding. He had also given substantial sums to aid in relocation and others due to so called acts of God. More recently he fought and won the north western forests for the conservationist at the expense of the local commercial loggers and their communities. Despite his success in that great battle with the unions, he had to compensate them financially. The tax burden was high on his country's people and economy.

Since the visit of the Grand Lord, the President had become a changed man. New technologies occupied his every waking hour. He was convinced that humanity was presently on the verge of a great breakthrough, a renaissance, and felt it was to be in several sciences at once. He was also convinced that Lumak was the chosen one and key to all those changes. The chosen Christ, through whom those changes would flow.

This strange, and yet unknown person had a gift, call it a psychic gift if you will, with an intellect that excelled any living human. Just one man with such intelligence could have irreversibly change the course of humankind within one's lifetime.

He had become extremely worried for the future of humanity and his world, realising that the non-renewable resources like fossil fuels, mainly petroleum were dwindling and very soon other forms of cleaner fuels would have to be found. Fifty percent of Africa had already been decimated by man and was slowly joining the Greater Sahara. No one could stop the slow crawl of the deserts and seas. The cost in lives was much too high.

The continent of Africa had become the proverbial hell's hole, with numerous wars, famines, pestilence and strife, further reducing the human life expectancy to barely twenty-five years in those regions. Japan, China, Russia, Eastern Europe, areas of Asia and South America all had similar problems. It was just a matter of time before they followed a similar faith to Africa. Then there were the problems of an ever mounting number of refugees from so many countries trying to resettle in unwilling countries. The main cause was all to do with human population growth. He reasoned that half the present human population would cause one quarter the problems, as detrimental circumstances fed on themselves further aggravating the situation.

The relationship between a sustainable environment and the same with a 10 percent increase in population was sometimes exponential. Since humans could always defeat the natural order by technology or medicine, their thoughtless short-term actions prevented nature from using her own brutal methods of population control. There could be little give or slack in such a system. This would eventually lead to complete ecological failure with little chance of recovery. Any small change in a critically balanced system could easily upset the balance and most systems had already become over critical. Although Mother Nature would try to maintain a balance by introducing pandemic disease, scientist would soon device cures and antidotes. Thus nullifying her long term plans in maintaining a stable world.

Earth's humans were not like most other known life-forms. They were highly self-indulgent and fun-loving, with extreme territorial needs. Such a predatory life-form could only be truly concerned with the selfish day to day needs of itself and its immediate family. Short term humans behaved more like a virus that didn't care whether their host was sucked dry.

The once wealthiest country in the world was now a net importer of fossil fuels and other raw materials. Luckily, they had learned to harness wind, wave and solar energy, which now accounted for just over 30 percent of the country's energy requirements. A further 20 percent was due to hydroelectric and ten to nuclear power, leaving 40 percent for coal and oil. Nevertheless transportation took the bulk of all fuel imports with the resulting high levels of air pollution.

If only there was a less polluting form of energy for that purpose? Scientists had tried since the last century to find a method of fusion power, but that technology had eluded them and was still well beyond their reach. Hybrid electro-petrol or Elepet cars were getting more and more numerous but still quite expensive. Hydrogen fuel could also be cleanly extracted and combined with other materials in a more solid and less explosive cellular format for such purposes. However those vehicles were quite expensive and such methods never carried the same amount of power or speed with a zero carbon footprint. As petrol dwindled, many began to convert to alcohol, mainly ethanol and methane gas, which could be produced from sugarcane and other easily acquired crops and materials. Some even returned to the ancient horse and cart.

The most efficient compromise was Elepet cars that utilized their front or rear wheels for an electric drive through induction motors. Those included a combustion engine in front or rear for driving wheels in an emergency. Many such cars contained retractable panels of solar cells on their roofs for charging powerful batteries while parked.

Others were driven by hydrogen, which gave off non-polluting steam as exhaust, but expensive petrol was still used as a standby emergency source. Hydrogen separation could only be achieved through a process akin to electrolysis. It required a higher amount of electricity in its processes, thus placing an increasing strain on the national grid with a finite carbon footprint. Although the hydrogen fuel could be supplied in fuel cells, the cost of hydrogen separation was still significant. Alcohol (Ethanol) and bio-gas still remained the least expensive of all methods with a near zero carbon footprint. Therefore the time was ripe for some new form of kinetic drive that was fully self-contained. One that functioned at the sub-atomic level, with zero carbon footprint and gave off no toxic exhaust fumes.

President Arnold Turner had given serious consideration to all those questions and realised the one man on the planet that had *the answers and could assist him in attaining those goals was none other than the strange character called Doctor Jeffery Longhurst(Lumak).*

They arrived at the White House and were guided to a comfortable reception room. The president's secretary soon escorted them to another private room.

'Ah, Lennox, and I presume you are the most eminent Doctor Longhurst and his beautiful wife, Sarah,' Arnold greeted, while firmly shaking their hands, then he took them into his private study. There sat several of his key senators and advisors. The President introduced him to each in turn.

'I am sorry about the problems you recently encountered back in your country with those evil terrorist. I hope your relatives and friends are now ok. We have had our share of such terror activities in the past.'

'Thank you, Mister President,' Lumak replied.

'Let me introduce you to Professor John Laroche. He is our chief mathematician and scientific advisor.' Then he called a helper and asked her to bring in some cool drinks.

'Have you been able to view any parts of our beautiful city since your arrival? I am very proud of this place, particularly Capitol Hill. One way or another, we have fought and won many great battles from this place. Whatever anyone says, it's still the heart of our great nation and holds most of our history,' Arnold said, proudly.

'Yes, Sir, we visited the National Cathedral and The Capitol building, but hadn't any time left to visit other places,' Sarah replied in reasonable English.

'I have been told by Lennox that you have great powers. The ability to communicate with a Greater Mind. Truly an incredible revelation. I have also scanned some of your scientific papers. They make very interesting reading, and those are the small parts I am able to comprehend. I do believe you to be a scientific genius and Professor Laroche and Lennox will back me on that observation,' an excited Arnold said and sat down.

Sudden Lumak stood up to say his bit.

'I don't quite know where to begin in thanking you for having us here. But I already feel at home in your most pleasant country and will endeavour to assist in any way that I can. I have analysed the problems of our planet in detail and have found ways in which they may be resolved, in time. However, they are exceedingly long term and there are several other more important dangers approaching the horizon which also require attention. In light of those and our immediate needs - within the next ten years or so - I have put forward a plan of action. The initial phase of that plan will include two projects.

'Gentlemen and ladies, both projects will take approximately two years to develop. I shall require your full cooperation and guarantees that they will not be transferred to the military during a period of time, that includes the development period and one year thereafter.

'From henceforth, I am committed to the good of our world, which includes all life and the environment. Therefore I will not partake in the destruction of others or be seen to do so either directly or indirectly. Having said those words, I would like all funding to be released to Solarian International. It's a name I have decided to call our organization. It can only operate within the private sector, so I would like your full agreement in this matter.

'After each project has been fully tested, it will be released unto the public sector for further testing. The USA shall have first privileges to all projects developed within its jurisdiction. They can be used militarily only after they have been fully exposed to the world markets through exhibitions and trade fares. However, the major profits will come to the USA through royalties and such like. The larger companies here will have the extra privilege of becoming agents and distributors for others here and abroad. In actual fact, Solarian International will be like any other American business with a government grant to develop projects for the American people, and later through marketing, to the other people of our planet.

'Mister President, those are my stipulations,' Lumak said, in as

firm a stance as could be taken. His charisma was overpowering and the president was also in an agreeable mood.

'All that can be easily arranged and we have already decided to keep your projects in the private sector. As far as we are concerned, you and your organization will be just another government-approved company, carrying out the occasional development for us.'

'Thank you!' Lumak said and nodded.

'Professor Harry Lennox has found the ideal spot for you in North Dakota. It used to be his uncle's ranch, but he has since departed. So the place is yours once you sign the relevant documents. Further, there are several abandoned military bases and bunkers in that area and five within a distance of fifty kilometres from the house. Several of those can be immediately released to you from the Air Force authorities. They give perfect isolation and are secure.'

'Thank you!'

'I have decided to send Lennox along with you to assist in those choices and to finalize the necessary paperwork.'

'In that case, Mister President, here are two reports I prepared earlier,' Lumak said, while handing the folders to the president. He then handed one of the folders to Professor Laroche to unravel any of those tight mathematical knots and glanced through the other himself.

Laroche had since taken one of Lumak's strange mind-bending capsules and could now understand most of his work. However his new problem was explaining what he knew to others. Because of his new powers he tended to rattle on in his explanations and had become very boisterous in his attitude when asked to repeat himself.

'My first project will be related to automatons. We shall develop intelligent microids that can build anything more than twenty times faster than any human. That way, our future infrastructures may be constructed in a fraction of the time, without the usual delays, long breaks and strikes.'

'Those will be ideal for building our sea walls. These days the water levels move almost at the same rate as our builders,' Arnold said.

The second project is related to automation and is an inertial drive called LPD for short. LPD stands for Linear Progressive Drive technology. A suitable basic system with such devices can take us to the nearest star within a month or so. However, since it utilizes pure hydrogen for fusion, it's non-polluting and is based on a completely sealed and modular design. It is the most basic form of an inertial drive and can be further improved in time. Such devices can also be used for any type of vehicular transport on the surface as well. During this time I shall assemble a separate team of scientists to continue my work in genetics and medicine.

'Those are my immediate intentions and here are my cost projections for the next two years. By then, many large companies will be willing to pay for a small slice of the cake and any existing loans can be repaid forthwith,' Lumak said and handed some more sheets of paper to the president. During all this time his senators remained perfectly silent as if stunned by the strange figure in the cream gown with violet cape looking like the Messiah himself.

'Doctor, let no one say we are not a generous people. I shall double your financial requirement to five-hundred and sixty million dollars with another two-hundred million kept aside in case you need some extra funding. You never know what might happen,' President Arnold said and Lumak smiled and nodded in appreciation. He could have gone up to the president and hugged him.

'So it's all to do with complex symmetry. I mean the universe. Certain symmetries act on others, giving resultants like gravity and magnetism, and some pseudo symmetries can be created to mislead the primal system and others to neutralize inertia in any given direction, causing a kind of inertial diode that will allow motion in only a singular direction. But it can only be done by making use of sub-nucleic forces and they have even found a way of doing that with other symmetries.'

'Yes, Doctor.'

'Portals can transmit us to anywhere in the known universe and twins can really feel each others pains. Telepathy is really a fact, but in a different way than we thought. All taken from the so-called Sea of Chaos. So much for Einstein's universe. God, bless his soul! Is there also such a thing as life after death, Doctor?' Professor Laroche inquired, completely overwhelmed by the implications of the technical report in his hand.

'Of course, Professor. Please study them carefully. Then you can advise our president on those projects when we communicate in future. Should you require any further detailed information don't hesitate to contact us,' Lumak replied, always trying to uplift and improve his fellow person.

'I think I shall invite you all for lunch tomorrow. I shall cancel my lunch with the Iralian Ambassador for another time. This is far too important for me to miss,' Arnold said, completely overcome by the excitement of the moment.

They had a lengthy afternoon tea and discussed many things with Arnold and John Laroche. Then Lennox escorted the couple to their hotel in one of the special White House limousines.

'You guys are bloody great, you know. And you have really impressed our President. So much in fact, that he cancelled most of his appointments for tomorrow and I think you will love it over here,' Lennox said, being pleased with himself for all his successes of the past weeks in trying to get Lumak over to his country.

'I also think your president to be a great person with incredible vision. I can also speak for my wife, when I say we have already grown to love this country of yours. So from now on, please think of us as fellow Americans,' Lumak said, trying to relieve some of Lennox's stresses for his country and president.

'Do you really mean that, Doctor?' Lennox inquired, feeling more at ease with the supposed strangers.

'I always mean what I say and think that very soon you will enjoy being a part of our projects.' Lennox realized he might soon be getting back into the type of work he preferred. At present he felt he was in no-man's-land since his original job had somehow dissipated.

While in the hotel the word soon got around that they had been to see the President and many, staff included, were asking them for their autographs. Soon there was an article in the local newspaper about the arrival of a brilliant and eccentric English scientist, who was the one responsible for a permanent cure for all types of cancer and the press and their reporters descended on them like vultures.

They went to lunch with the president once more and Lumak answered many of their searching questions, except of course those relating to life on other worlds or space travel to other systems. He only answered questions relevant to his current projects.

After they parted company that day, the president was a much happier man. For he could finally see a distant light in the darkest tunnel of Earth's survival.

CHAPTER 55

Home in North Dakota

They had taken the midday flight from the main airport in Washington DC and landed at Minneapolis in the late afternoon. From there they entered a helicopter for their journey to the large ranch near Jamestown. That place was just twenty-five kilometres from their future residence. A military helicopter and pilot had been assigned to them for an unspecified time, so they were free to observe the expansive ranch in greater detail from the air.

The medium-size helicopter landed on an existing pad at the rear of the building and Sarah couldn't contain her excitement.

'Do you like what you see, Love?' Lumak inquired.

'Darling, its so truly massive! How am I ever going to clean all those rooms?' Sarah exclaimed.

'Don't worry about that. There's a family of helpers and several farm workers are based on the ranch. They have been with my uncle since I was a little boy. I'm sure you will be able to organize them to your liking. Since my uncle's death, they had to become more self-reliant and had to take work where they could find it. I'm afraid, farming is highly competitive and not very economical these days,' Lennox said.

The house included 30 bedrooms, three large sitting rooms, two studies including a large library, drawing rooms and many utility rooms. There were also several stables, a granary and storehouses, workshops and a large barn. It was truly a mansion by any standard. The ranch had been used extensively in past for raring cattle and growing a variety of vegetables and grain.

The house and its surrounding buildings were in disrepair, having been neglected and left vacant for many months. The place had potential and Sarah liked the environment she observed from the air. Some of it reminded her of her own home in the hills of Turkey, including the small stream and large pond close to the house. But her place was a drop in the ocean compared to this ranch. The house was set in 1400 acres of land.

When the helicopter landed not a single soul could be observed anywhere and the garden could not have been in a worst state. They wandered into the large house with circular polished wooden staircase that led to a central veranda.

'This place does need a little work. Despite its size, it's position reminds me of our place in the hills,' Sarah commented.

'Don't you worry, Love. You will be surprised what this place will look like in 6 months,' Lumak replied.

They chose the largest bedroom on the first floor which was not the cleanest and assigned Lennox to one of the tidier guests rooms on the same floor. The helicopter pilot had a smaller room further down the corridor.

Soon after their arrival Lennox made a local phone call and a new Mercedes was on its way. Lumak liked that make of car, having used it extensively at the university with Jean-Claude's permission. However he never drove himself and had always employed a chauffeur. So the helicopter driver doubled as their chauffeur for more financial benefit.

The following day Lennox took them to James Town by car to complete some well needed shopping and at the same time introduced them to his uncle's friends and a few distant members of his own family. His parents had left for California at the turn of the twenty-first century and had later retired there. Nevertheless he had always loved that area and the ranch for its tranquillity and fishing.

'My friend, you must feel free to come and stay with us as long as you like and whenever you feel the need for some company and a nice meal. Our home is always open to you,' Lumak said to Lennox.

'Thanks a million, Pal. I appreciate that offer very much. During holidays I spent many youthful days in this place with my uncle and won't like to give up on it all together.' He had grown to admire and appreciate the couple who were also very generous.

Although advanced, Lumak reflected simplicity itself and he felt in a similar vane when close to nature as he was at that time.

The farm was still being maintained by a local family of eleven, comprising three generations. No one ever liked the idea of a new landlord, so after the house was cleaned and the main rooms partially refurnished Lumak decided to hold a small house warming party. During that time local friends, tenants and employees would be invited.

They were as curious in meeting him as he was in them. Many were dissatisfied country folk that had been living on the breadline for many years. As they entered the great house one of the young family members recognised him from the New York Times and another from Scientific American and they began to talk among themselves and mention about his importance to their other family members. From that moment on they were as humble as lambs. As the woman of the house, Sarah knew her responsibilities and soon came forward to greet and introduce them to Lumak and her other guests.

'Darling, this is the McCririck family and here are their parents, Ann and Joseph McCririck. Joseph is our current estate manager,' she said while asking them for their names. She soon introduced them to Lumak until their numbers were exhausted.

'Do you all work on the farm... I mean, ranch?' Lumak asked, getting slightly muddled by the terms as he couldn't yet tell the difference between them. Nevertheless he later learnt from Lennox that a ranch was a large farm that was mainly used for breeding livestock like cattle.

'No, Sir, only the men are involved on the ranch. Elaine works in Jamestown during the week and the younger girls are still at school,' their mother said.

'Well, if anyone needs more work we can do with some extra help about the house. Furthermore, I have decided to give all the working people on my ranch a 50 percent raise in salary from the beginning of next week. Mister McCririck, please tell your people about their change in salaries and I would like to discuss this ranch, its resources and ways of improving its livestock and the environment with you on Monday morning. It has been going downhill far too long. As things improve here, so also will all our lives,' Lumak said.

They soon realised there were changes in the wind and had already benefited from those changes, so they were eternally grateful to him and eager for any more beneficial gains.

The house warming party went well and the tenants very happy and pleased with the new owners.

The following day Lumak decided to check the local missile bases by helicopter and Harry Lennox went along to review those areas. Some of the roads were rugged and overgrown since their abandonment several decades before, so travelling that way by wheels was out of the question. After viewing the five bases he decided on one about 20 kilometres and another about 40 kilometres from the house.

Sarah remained home that day and after preparing lunch had decided to view the local area on foot. She followed the path towards the little stream with its small forest and large fishing pool. She sat for a while on a large log near the expansive pond admiring the place, thinking of ways to improve the house and its immediate surroundings. Most of all she would have liked a small temple for her evening prayers.

It was then that a large beaver came up to her and introduced himself.

'So what's your name?' she said playfully. The creature made a playful welcoming screech and dived into the pond.

'You guys over here are quite friendly,' she thought.

When they returned, they sat together for a light lunch.

'I would like so much to improve this house, but I don't quite know where to begin. The place is so massive and so much needs doing. How can I turn it into a more delightful place, when I am not very good at interior decoration,' Sarah said, disappointingly.

'Don't you worry, my lady? I know of a great interior designer. She used to be my girlfriend when I first moved to DC. I am sure she wouldn't mind taking this place on. She likes a challenge and will do a beautiful job for a reasonable price. As a matter of fact,

I don't think you will be able to recognize the place after she is finished, or be able to tell the difference between it and the White House,' Lennox said and they were all amused by his choice of words.

'Well, why don't we get this good person to do a complete job before we get too settled?' Lumak said.

'If you don't mind, Darling? I am just worried about the costs,' Sarah replied, still unsure about money matters and always counting the pennies.

'That's no problem! Let it be done!' Lumak said.

Despite everything, Sarah was still a little homesick. There were also the kickbacks from the traumatic experience of the explosion. She still didn't believe she survived that ginormous blast unscathed. Then there was poor Karen with her lengthy recovery. The activities of the past few days had taken her mind away from home until she visited the stream, then it would all come flooding back.

'I wish Spotty and Saracen were here with us, and we have to make plans to get dad over here as soon as possible. He'll never come by air, so we'll have to arrange his journey by sea. If we could get his papers arranged now, he should be with us in a few weeks,' she said, disappointingly.

'Yes, Love, perhaps our good friend Harry can assist us with your father's situation. He has a few powerful friends in immigration and he is also well known in the State Department,' Lumak said.

After explaining the situation to Harry Lennox he was immediately on the phone while decisions were being made. Relevant forms were sent to be filled in and her father Ben was called to the American Embassy and further advised.

Lumak soon knuckled down to his own projects and began to compile a list of requirements, including technical, scientific and other vacancies.

'All we have to do now is re-surface the roads and carry out the necessary renovations to those barracks and bunkers. Then we can transport the required scientific and other equipment to their relevant locations. I only wish my best students were here with me now. Their presence would save us a few months in training new people and there isn't even a proper university locally. It seems we shall have to use a room in this house for our temporary training. Anyway, I now have enough to consider and there are no restrictions to my importing students from abroad on a special license,' Lumak said to Sarah.

'I realize your problems, Darling. It's like starting all over again from scratch, but this time it will be much bigger and better, and Harry is good with such things.'

Lumak got on the line to Jean-Claude and explained his situation to him. Jean-Claude couldn't hold back his excitement.

'Jeff, I wish I was there with you now. You can have all your old students if you wish, even the complete university. They have no where to go anywhere, with the place a smoldering pile of rubble. Thank goodness I can still access their records via the Internet. I shall have words with each of them later today,' Jean-Claude said, laughing and happy.

'Tell them they are not to worry about their tickets, money or anything. They will get lots of it here and their parents should not object, knowing I am responsible for them. Just get me their names so I can get their tickets arranged.'

Over the following few weeks the renovation and construction had begun at the two bases. Then government documents were signed and witnessed by Harry Lennox. Ben had signed all relevant papers and were on his way by ship.

Heavy construction equipment and cranes were at the bases while their house had been completely taken over by the interior designer and decorators. The large barn was cleared and partitioned for the fourteen students soon to arrive. More would come later. Lumak had become their guardian and their training had continued in the large adjacent workshop. The students were excited but amused by their new way of life and loved the fresh and clean mountain air.

Slowly, the house was being transformed into a most beautiful country manor and the other outbuildings similarly renovated. Lumak always considered the students a continuation of his own family, so very soon the girls moved into the manor on a more permanent basis.

Within the month Ben had arrived looking slimmer and highly stressed from his long sea voyage. It seemed that he was also prone to sea-sickness and perhaps even more so than air-sickness. Sarah made sure he had a very healthy diet to aid his recovery.

Their second home and other buildings in the hills of Turkey were being constructed and Sarah would call Karen and Marion almost daily to hear the local gossip. Although their initial thoughts were of complete isolation from their friends and family in Turkey, the complete opposite was true. With modern video, web-cams and mobile phones they were able to observe the construction process in Turkey and even communicate with the animals.

While in Turkey, telephone lines and electricity was soon routed to the new country guest house near their small home in the hills. Their original home was also renovated and wired for electricity. They were then able to contact Marion and Simon and also shout over the phone to their dog Spotty, who replied to their voices by over excitement and constant barking.

The Future

At that time many couldn't realized that the hospital built in the country village would have one day become one of the largest centres on Earth for longevity and other forms of human biological research. Professor Jean-Claude Chairmowich became a director in control of all such operations in that part of the world, with free access to all areas of their global operations.

Jeremy and his father Doctor Emil were also directors. Jeremy being responsible for all their chemical production facilities. As Lumak had promised, Jeremy would become one of the wealthiest people in that country and acquire many of his own Nobel Prizes in the intervening years. They now had the powers to reduce their years and would take those options in the future to become eternal living entities. That benefit of eternal life also included their favourite pets.

As promised by Lumak, once the special equipment had been installed in the main hospital, Karen was taken to a machine and given the necessary medication to regrow her arm. The process was uncanny, as microids quickly regrew every part of that arm, including fingers from a biological template. However fingernails took a little longer.

Lumak and Sarah's new country manor in Turkey was built north of the temple and east of their little house. That massive building was on four levels and mainly used by members of Lumak's organization in that part of the world. It contained every facility imaginable for recreation, rest and entertainment. There was also a helicopter and several vehicles freely available to its many residents and guests. The whole place was run by a team of well trained and competent assistants.

Gone were the bumpy old pitted road to the village. It was extended and properly engineered with a bridge over the small stream. The noble horse Saracen could now take a leisurely pace to the village with the many visiting children. The sheep still roamed and wandered the local hills while tended by Spotty and a more youthful shepherdess by the name of Marion. That was when she was not needed for more important work.

Their original house was redecorated and updated, but kept in its original form. It now had historical significance and would be visited by many tourists in future years.

TO BE CONTINUED WITH

The Power of One

Epilogue

Earth-time... 2041 CE (Lumak arrives on Earth).

The Shadite Lumak discovers a Class 1 civilization in a hitherto uncharted part of Osmaron (our Milky Way Galaxy) and dispatches interstellar probes to investigate. Lumak, previously a Semonite (a giant bee-like creature), is subsequently transformed into a human and transposed to the world they call Pleron. That previously unknown world is called Earth by its human inhabitants.

Lumak is to advance Earth's technologies to Class 5, from its present, Class 1. This classification represents advancement on a scale to the power of 10. By this method Class 5 would be taken as 100,000 years more advanced than Class 0. A Class 1 civilization would have discovered, understood and developed nuclear devices. This was considered a critical period for most civilizations and only a few survived that testing period without mutual annihilation.

That classification scale included all intelligent technological species throughout the Cosmos and represented technological levels of 1 billion years of technological growth in the past to 1 billion years of technological growth in the future.

During Lumak's visit to Earth he lands in the hills of Turkey and meets the hillbilly shepherdess Sarah and her father Bengizara Khan. Sarah later becomes his wife.

Lumak falls in love with Sarah and soon finds a general cure for cancer, introduces Micro-Robotics, Stellar Drives and a Longevity Serum.

However the almost indestructible Javols are presently on their way to our Milky Way galaxy and will arrive in about 200 years. The Javols intentions are to use all primal life for food and sacrifice.

The few survivors remaining on Planet Caefon in Andromeda are soon to be transferred to the Solar System. They must be evacuated within a period of two years before the arrival of the rapacious Javols in their part of the galaxy Andromeda..

Lumak must now develop a range of advanced technologies including super weapons and prepare all life within our galaxy before the arrival of the first swarms of the enemy. They will stop at nothing to decimate all significant life from our galaxy and cannot be easily stopped.

Earth's humans are not easily tamed and continue their self-indulgent ways. With major changes due to Global Warming, Lumak soon realizes that the only way to save Earth is to introduce a Terminal virus that will prevent human reproduction for 100 years. Only 500 million humans will be given the Antidote and allowed to procreate. The others, which are over 9 billion, must live out their natural lives without any children. This situation leads to many crises, including the separation of humanity into two races, the Fertilates and Infilates, with more resulting turmoil.